In Walked
Some Money

David Peckham

ISBN: 9798865209652

For Jillian

This book is dedicated to my wife Jillian, who encouraged me to embark on this new found literary journey during the early days of the first COVID-19 pandemic lockdown in 2020 and to whom, I extend my sincere thanks.

My thanks are also offered to my dear friends Winifred and Simon Harwood, who so painstakingly proofread my story and corrected the mistakes, grammar and punctuation.

The author was brought up in the village of Templecombe, South Somerset, England and lived there throughout the Second World War. Consequently he was familiar with life in the surrounding area during the time in which part of this book is set and when American military servicemen were present prior to D-Day 1944.

Table Of Contents

In Walked Some Money

1.   The Big Red Car

One Monday morning during early June 1968 in the small north Dorset village of Thimble Hardy, close to the Somerset border, 42 year old Linda Smart stood behind the bar of the Dog & Whistle public house. She gently tapped her fingers against an empty glass in rhythm to some 1940's music playing on the radio. There were only a few people in that lunchtime and as the wife of the landlord, Linda wondered how the pub was going to cover its costs that day. Husband Bob, who had been made redundant from the railway when Dr. Beeching wielded his axe in 1966, was busy in the cellar changing the barrels around before the brewery dray was expected to arrive.

The two old ladies sitting just inside the door, were daily regulars who took up that position specifically in order to watch the comings and goings. Village gossip was their staple diet and what Winnie Brown did not know, her companion Madge Wilson would make up. Linda tolerated them as the bottle of stout that they both bought each lunch time, did at least contribute something to the takings.

Onetime farmhand George Pullman and retired council worker Billy Watkins, were quietly playing crib whilst enjoying their second pint of the morning. Both had been doing this twice a week since they had entered their 75th year. They had taken to playing crib in order to avoid getting into conversation with Winnie and Madge, for they both knew that they would otherwise be questioned about what was going on in their lives since they had become widowers.

The only other person in that morning was 24 year old Tony Button, a strong, good-looking lad who had been laid-off from an engineering works in Sherborne, when the company had been taken over by a bigger concern in the London area. Tony was willing and had become a friend to Linda and Bob through helping out in the pub on the odd occasion during busy times. His financial input to the takings did not contribute much, as Linda would often slip him an extra half pint in return for a favour that he had done for them.

A cigarette drooping from his mouth, Tony threw one dart after another at the board that hung on the wall at the far end of the bar.

He had come to the pub after doing some repair work to the bicycle of Connie Burt, the postmistress. Tony also had a job to do for the vicar later in the afternoon, who had asked him to fix the churchyard gate as it had come off its hinges when some kids had swung on it.

"Tony," Linda called over to him, "be a love and wedge the main door open for me and perhaps it will entice someone else to come in." "Certainly, anything for you Linda," Tony quipped back with an alluring glance. A remark that Linda appreciated would have led to something more promising if she were only 20 years younger.

Thimble Hardy was a very quiet village at the best of times, disturbed only by occasional farm vehicles travelling along the narrow High Street to collect, or deliver items to the various fields around the scattered farms. Sometimes there was an additional raucous cawing from rooks in the old elm trees along the side of the church.

Bob emerged from the cellar and passed the time of the day to Winnie and Madge, knowing that if he didn't then he would become the subject of their conversation for the rest of the day. "How are you both today?" He immediately knew that he had made a mistake, for they both responded with a blast about their rheumatism and how it was the government's fault that their pension did not allow them to buy a second drink. He had heard it all before, but acted as if he was hearing it for the first time, as he could not afford to lose their custom.

Moving on from the two ladies, Bob suggested to Linda that he could take over behind the counter if she so wished. Linda appreciated that, as she was bored with doing nothing and would certainly like to make herself a nice mug of coffee in the kitchen.

Bob rearranged the few sandwiches that sat within a glass cabinet on the counter and then opened the till. He grimaced when he saw only a few coins staring back at him, so he fiddled with the cash, as though that would make it look more than it actually was.

Then, suddenly a sound of squealing animals could be heard coming along the High Street, coupled with the noise of a tractor. As the commotion pulled up right outside the pub door, the noise was established to be coming from some pigs that were being towed in a covered trailer behind the tractor.

Clearly the animals did not like the journey and it was as if they knew that they were on the way to the bacon factory in Gillingham. From the tractor slid farmer Jim Pearson, who then walked with a true farmer's limp into the pub.

"Morning Jim, - usual?" enquired landlord Bob, as he lifted a pint glass to fill with cider as soon as Jim would give him the nod.

"Yer, ave ee seen the'ck posh red car that's running round the village?" enquired Jim. "Looks like a feller who's got a bit of money, if you ask me."

"Can't say as I have Jim, what sort of car is it?" Bob asked while pulling Jim's pint.

"Oh I don't know, but he certainly ain't from around yer."

Immediately two pairs of ears sitting by the door latched onto the conversation and two minds swung into action. Winnie opened up with, "where's ee from then, if he ain't from around yer?" Both Bob and Jim ignored the remark and acted as though they had not heard it. Madge though, replied with the comment, "must be ee's a stranger." Winnie came back with, "could be ee's visiting the Big House," referring to the manor house at the bottom of the drive on the Billington country estate nearby.

"That's it", said Madge, sitting back with pride and taking a sip of her stout. "Ee's probably after one of those girls down there, them's always having strange blokes come for parties and the like."

From the kitchen, came Linda who had heard part of the revealing conversation. "So what sort of a car was it then Jim - a Rolls Royce?" Leaning back from the counter and swallowing a mouthful of cider, Jim spluttered out, "no, nothin as fancy as that, but it were a big un."

Tony Button, taking a break from the dart board, then offered his opinion. "Maybe he's looking to buy a couple of your pigs Jim." That remark brought a variation of laughter from all within the pub. "Well, ee'd certainly looked as ee could afford a couple," said Jim in his raw West Country accent.

Although he had not seen the car himself, Bob, being a cautious person, weighed up the evidence and thought that if the owner of the car had been through the village a couple of times that morning, then probably he would be looking for something, or maybe somebody. He kept his thoughts to himself in case his assessment was incorrect. But Bob wondered, why else would he be trawling through the village - maybe he just wants to buy a house in the area, he thought.

Bob, who was 10 years older than Linda, had married her soon after he had come out of the army in 1946, when she was a single mother with a two year old son. Bob had never enquired of the circumstances that had brought Linda to that position in life and she did not volunteer the information. He was just pleased that they had met and was happy to bring up young Malcolm as if he was his own son.

It had been a very happy and successful relationship, with all three enjoying whatever came their way. Malcolm, or 'Mac' as Linda preferred to call him, had had a good education that took him onto the Grammar School, where he excelled at maths, geography and all things sporty. Like Bob, he had found employment on the railway, but three years ago when he was twenty, wanderlust had caused him to leave the village for more rewarding times in the USA.

"Afore I go landlord, I'll have one of they sandwiches, what sort are they?" Jim enquired of Bob. "Well, we have cheese and pickle and we have pickle and cheese," Bob replied, holding back a playful grin.

"OK, I'll 'ave one of each," Jim answered.

Linda, needing the money, was quick to serve him before Jim could work it out and change his mind.

After a while, Jim, coming to the end of his last sandwich said, "Funny that red car going around like that."

George looked up from the crib game, saying something along the lines that the driver had every right to do it, as the road is a public highway. That was a bit too much for Jim, as he did not want to get into an argument about what people can and cannot do in the village. So, brushing the crumbs off the front of his shirt and draining the last drop from his glass, he prepared to leave.

"Afore I go landlord," Jim again said to Bob. "The'ck second type of sandwich, pickle and cheese, tasted much better than the cheese and pickle one. You'd do well to make em all like that in future."

Bob was not sure if Jim was being serious, or whether he was just playing the same game as himself. Anyway, Bob took his money and Jim set off back to his tractor and squealing pigs.

Winnie and Madge were quick to pull Jim to pieces when he was out of the way. "He's a rough diamond," Winnie said, looking at Madge but hoping that everyone else would hear the remark. "Yes he is and his boots are dirty," Madge muttered without really understanding what she was agreeing to.

Still hoping that some others would come in for a drink, Linda walked over to the open door and looked out just as the big red car in question pulled up alongside her. "Say Mam, do you do meals in your establishment?" enquired the driver of the Mercedes with a distinct American accent. Although the pub did not offer meals at lunchtime on weekdays, Linda did not want to lose the opportunity of adding some more cash to their meagre takings, so she answered in a positive way and beckoned the driver to come in.

Out jumped a tall, slender, well dressed man, a little older than Linda. She escorted him into the pub and offered him a seat away from the locals who were all staring at him in an inquisitive way. She asked the stranger if he would like a drink while he waited. "I'll have a lovely glass of your very cool beer and could you bring me the menu?" the stranger replied.

Menu, what menu? Linda muttered to herself, we don't have one, but she could not let this well-to-do gent know that. So she hurried into the kitchen and beckoned Bob to come too. After telling him to organise the drink, she informed Bob of the food request and said that she had better make up a menu from what she could find in the larder. Then, in order to give her some time to think, she suggested to Bob that he should keep the stranger talking for a while.

Back went Bob to behind the bar and as he was about to pull off a pint of the local brew, he noticed that Winnie and Madge had beaten him to the conversation that he had expected to have with the visitor.

He could hear Winnie saying, "so you'm a visitor round yer then?" A remark that Madge repeated in a confident manner, as though Winnie had pinched the line from her before she could get it out. "Yes and No", he replied. "I was once around here with the US army during the second world war."

Bob was not happy that the two old busybodies should be the first to quiz his customer in such a direct way and interrupted politely by saying, "your beer is ready, Sir" and took it over to him without asking for payment. Linda also added to the interruption by coming out of the kitchen with a neat sheet of cardboard on which she had written the menu.

Tomato soup
Sausage and Chips
Egg, Bacon and Chips
Fish Fingers and Beans
Extras if available.

Not really a menu to impress such a man of his bearing.

"What no steak?" the visitor asked.

But Linda was quick to answer, "yes we do have steak on the menu, but only in the evenings."

"Oh I understand, that's fine, then I'll just have one of your sandwiches for now and I'll come back this evening for a wonderful steak then."

Linda was caught in two minds, she wanted him to come back, but she had no steak and the butcher's shop was probably closed by now.

She quickly disappeared back into the kitchen leaving Bob to sort out the sandwich and guessed that she had better run quickly to Charlie Burt, the local butcher, and beg for the best steak that he could offer before he closed at two o'clock.

When Linda arrived at the butcher's shop, Charlie was in the process of putting his meat back into the cold room. "Charlie," Linda called out to him, "have you any beefsteak, I need the best for a client who has turned up unexpectedly." Charlie mopped his brow and thought for a moment. "Yes, but being the best it costs the best you know."

Eagerly wanting to make sure that the handsome visitor would return that evening she gave no thought to the cost, she only wanted the best. "Sure I know that, can you cut me a decent sized one - no, make it two just in case something goes wrong during the cooking."

Charlie disappeared back into the cold room and returned with a large joint, from which he cut a well proportioned steak. "Will that be what you'm after my dear?" asked Charlie. "Fine," said Linda, "make the other one a little larger." Both seemed to be happy with the exchange and Charlie carried on closing his shop for the day, well happy with the last minute sale.

When Linda got back to the pub, she found Bob had fixed the visitor up with an overnight stay in their guest room and immediately thought that this was all going too well. After all, the pub had commenced the day financially with a shaky start and now one person was beginning to improve the situation.

After putting the precious steaks into a deep pan, she put the pan into the larder and listened to the conversation that Bob was having with the visitor. It was something about the quaint name of the village.

"Well I'm not sure about the Thimble bit Sir," Linda heard Bob say, who was now sitting at the table with the man. "But the Hardy bit must have come from our famous author Thomas Hardy." But with little knowledge of Hardy the writer, the American was about to seek more information, when suddenly he saw the return of Linda passing from the kitchen to the bar.

"That's quite a cute barmaid you have there landlord, what's her name?" Bob, not wanting anything to upset the promise of his repeated custom later in the day, did not let on that Linda was his wife. "Certainly Sir, her name is Linda," Bob replied.

"That's a nice name and by the way my name is Hank, drop the Sir and just call me Hank." "OK Sir, - sorry Hank, then my name is Bob."

After the visitor had finished his sandwich and downed another half, he thought that it was time to go. "What time do you serve dinner this evening?" enquired Hank.

"We open at five-thirty," said an eager voice back in the kitchen.

Linda emerged and asked, "what time would you like to eat Sir?"

"Say about 6.30 Linda? - by the way I'm Hank, please call me Hank."

Linda was taken aback with the way that the visitor had become so familiar in such a short time - but who cares when money is at stake.

The two doorkeepers were well satisfied with information that they had learned about the visitor way in advance of anyone else in the village, except of course the crib players and Tony.

The owner of the posh red car was an American who's name is Hank and he had previously been around these parts when he was in the American army during the war. The three of them were now on first name terms and the chap was going to stay the night in the pub.

Winnie and Madge were going to have a field day spreading that information around the village - with no doubt a little extra added from their own imaginations.

Just as Hank was saying farewell to his hosts, Tony came across and informed him that he thought that his car looked a beauty and that he must be very proud to own such a vehicle.

"Oh, that's not my car," said Hank. "I normally drive a Ford whenever I come to England, but this time it was the only one that the hire company had available when I arrived at Gatwick Airport yesterday. Although it is a bit over the top for what I want on your small winding lanes, I accepted it for the same price as a Ford." Linda was somewhat disappointed to learn that the car did not belong to Hank, but she did not show it.

Still talking to Tony, Hank asked him if he had ever ridden in this model of Mercedes, to which Tony replied in a negative manner, adding that one day he might though.

"Well, why not right now?" said the ever pleasing Hank. "Come with me and I'll take you for a spin." Tony's eyes lit up and he nodded to Bob and Linda in a very confident and pleasing way as he accepted the gesture being offered to him. As the two walked briskly out of the main door, it was clear that the two gossips now had a further bit of knowledge to add to that already gleaned from within the bar. *The car did not belong to the Yank!*

"He had only hired it, so maybe he's not as rich as he is making out," remarked Winnie to Madge. "But he still looks very smart," added Madge rising to her feet and ready to leave the pub.

With the two old ladies out of the pub and Tony away with the visitor, both George and Billy packed in their game of cards, replaced the crib board back on the shelf where it belonged and left the premises. Bob then closed the door and locked it whilst Linda cleared away the empty glasses. At last they could both relax and weigh up the mornings proceedings.

"Who do you think he is?" asked Bob of Linda. "I'm not sure," she replied. "First I thought that he was some rich tycoon, as he isn't concerned about spending money, posh clothes, happy to pay to stay here overnight. Then again he has only hired that car as any one else could and paying to stay here is not quite like the Ritz, is it?"

Cautious Bob offered his own theory, "I think that maybe he's just looking at the area before deciding to buy a house. Or it could be that Hank just likes the countryside around here and is taking a bit of a holiday." Linda brought the subject to a close by saying, "anyway, it's not any of our business and as long as he pays us for what he gets here, he can drive around as many times as he likes."

"So have you got fixed up with a steak for this evening Linda?" Bob enquired. "Yes I caught Charlie just as he was about to close for the day and he cut me two beauties." "Two, why two?" Bob asked in a disapproving manner. "Belt and braces my handsome, in case something was to go wrong with the first one during the cooking," Linda mumbled back at him.

Unlike Bob, who had been born locally, Linda started life in Dorchester hospital and had only come to North Dorset in 1940 when her father was conscripted to work at a factory close to Sherborne, that made parts for the Westland Aircraft company in Yeovil.

As a 15 year old girl and well trained in cooking by her mother, Linda soon picked up what was needed to feed the employees at the factory and with further advice from others, she progressed into being an excellent cook. Bob knew that two steaks would be unnecessary, as nothing would go wrong with Linda's cooking.

He had learnt that by the time Linda was 18 she had become head cook at the factory and was catering for some 200 workers each day. So now at 42 years of age, she was more than capable of cooking a decent steak for their visitor that evening.

Sitting with their feet up in the private quarters of the pub, their thoughts were on the fact that there was to be a skittles match in the back room of the pub at 7.30 that evening. Then came a banging on their back door and when Bob went to investigate, he found Tony in a high state of excitement. "I must come and tell you Bob," Tony poured out. "I have had a fantastic hour with Hank in that Mercedes and I have learnt a lot about him too." "Come on in," said Bob, "would you like a drink?" "Yes please I would love a mug of coffee."

Before Bob could finish making the coffee, Tony was pouring out his enthusiasm about the big red car and how Hank was such a good driver, bearing in mind that he was driving on the wrong side of the road to that which he is used to. He went on about the luxury of the interior, the smoothness of the road holding and the powerful acceleration. Bob chipped in with a few questions about the car, but Linda was having enough about the vehicle and said in an irritable manner, "That's fine, but what about Hank himself?"

"Well, as I said, he's a fantastic driver." "No, not his driving, what about him as a person. What did you find out?" Tony had not really found out anything in that direction, except for the fact that he had been in the military and lived in a tent somewhere around here before being shipped off to France on D-Day. "Didn't he tell you about his private life, like is he married and what he does for a living?"

"Nope," replied Tony, "we didn't talk about that - oh, hang on, yes he did say something about he was looking for the field where his tent had been in 1944. But he could only remember that his whole regiment was in several fields near a place with a name like a *Bottle of Port*. "Bottle of Port?" laughed Linda, "he was kidding you."

Bob was busy thinking about the evening skittles match and hoped that the visiting team would bring a few extra people to boost the takings, while Linda started to make a few sandwiches for the same reason.

"Tony, can you come in this evening, just in case we get a crowd that would fill Wembley Stadium?" Bob jokingly enquired. "Yep, OK I'll be here Bob, but I must get on and fix the church gate, or the vicar will be after me," replied the the ever willing Tony. He enjoyed the thought that Linda would probably fix him up with a free pint in exchange and in any case he enjoyed being in her company.

When Winnie and Madge had left the pub they did not have to wait long to spill out their newly obtained gossip. For they saw the postmistress Connie Burt, pushing her bicycle along the High Street. "Connie," called out Winnie, "ave ee got a minute, cause we got something to tell ee?"

A Big Red Car being driven by an American.
He had been here before - in the army.
He's going to stay the night in the pub.
What's more he's on first names terms with the Smarts.
And by the way the Yank does not own that car.

The information was all there for the postmistress to hold and distribute to others as she thought fit.

As Connie passed the butcher's shop, Charlie, her brother-in-law, was outside putting some rubbish into a bin. "Ave ee heard the story about the driver of the big red car?" Connie enquired.

"Well I guess that he's Linda's client who has turned up unexpectedly earlier today," Charlie innocently replied. "How do you know that?" Connie asked. "She told me when she rushed in asking for some steak to feed him this evening. Didn't spare the pennies either." So now Connie had more of the story to pass on as she pleased.

Just as the brewer's dray was leaving the pub car park, the pieman arrived to fill the spot. It was a regular visit, from whose van Linda usually purchased a few meat pies to keep in her old fridge.

The pieman was a jolly fellow and always had a joke to offer when trying to offload items that he had a surplus of. Today's 'Best Deal' would be meat slices at half price.

Linda saw the pieman arrive and went to the carpark with her restricted order clearly fixed in her mind.

None of that 'Best Deal' nonsense today for me she thought, for the cost of those two steaks had more than overspent her budget.

"Hello my dear, how are you today?" The usual opening gambit rolled off his tongue. "I'm fine and I'll only have six steak and ale, and six steak and kidney." "Fine," said the pieman and what about todays "Best Deal?" Linda knew that it would come from him as usual. "No not today, I have already spent out more than I should."

"How can you say that my lovely, you don't know what it is and it's the best 'Best Deal' that I've been able to offer for a long time," replied the jolly pieman.

"OK, what is it then?" asked Linda in a disinteresting manner. "Beef Slices - the best Beef Slices for many a mile around here and you won't get them cheaper anywhere else," the pieman retorted in a very convincing manner. "Tell ee what my dear - to you as you're a good customer - HALF PRICE!"

Linda's business mind quickly brought her to the thought that if they are half price and she could charge full price, plus her own mark up, then maybe this could be a good business opportunity. But was he telling the truth she wondered. "Can I have a look at them?" was her reply. Sure enough, the pastry looked fine on the one she could see through the cellophane package and the price marked on the packet was twice that which he was asking for them. "OK, I'll have just four for now," Linda begrudgingly answered. Delighted that his sales patter had worked, he gathered Linda's purchase and placed them into a greaseproof bag that he pulled from a bunch hanging inside the roof of his van and happily put the cash into a leather bag around his waist.

Back inside her kitchen, Linda laid out the pies and looked at one of the packets of the meat slices. It felt thicker than just one meat slice and so she opened it and out fell three individual slices. Two more than she thought that she had bought. So she actually had twelve in all. Far too many than she really wanted, but if the evening's skittles match were to bring in the right customers, then perhaps she could get rid of them. If not, then maybe they would go to someone's dog, as they would soon go off after sitting in the bar all day.

After telling Bob what she had bought, she quickly set about preparing a meal for the two of them as opening time at 5.30pm was fast approaching. "An omelette, fried tomatoes, peas and some chips, will that be OK Bob?" "Fine by me," answered the landlord, who was in the bar looking at the skittles fixture list.

Running his finger down the list, he found that the visiting team was called 'The Dunkers', a team that he had not heard of before. Could be that they are a factory team from Sherborne, which would not be good news for selling food, as most of them would have had a good dinner in the factory canteen that day. The home team, made up of a bunch of 'All-sorts' from around the village would be captained by 'The Major', a name given to Terry Smith by the rest of the team because he was a serious person and frequently told people about his time in the army during the war.

Although 'The Major' was a good time keeper and would always arrive well in time to prepare himself for the match, most of the others usually turned up just in time to grab a pint before the start without wanting food from the bar. This left Bob contemplating about how the evening would go financially.

"Stop worrying my lover," Linda said to Bob as they finished their meal. "We have managed through the two years since we took on this pub and we are still alive to enjoy life together." He gave her a loving kiss on the cheek and rose from the table with the empty plates. Linda thanked him with a smile and told him to leave the plates in the sink as she would be doing other cooking for the American when he returned later.

Bob had forgotten about Hank, as he had not come in when Tony had returned earlier in the afternoon and wondered if he was serious about coming back and staying overnight. After all, he did not ask to see his room when it was offered and he has not left any luggage. Also, Bob had let him put the cost of his lunchtime food and drink on 'The Check' as Hank had called it. Was he a trickster? Bob thought. Linda, on the other hand, was excited about the expected return of Hank as she could put one of the expensive steaks to good use before the skittles match would start.

She put two of each pie and three of the meat slices aside to warm up and offer in the bar later. She then put the rest of her purchase into the larder and brought out the two steaks. Looking at each as she laid them out in front of her, she mentally valued one as 'Very large' and the other as 'Enormous'.

Which one shall I cook for Hank this evening, she contemplated.

She arrived at the thought that she would use the very large one and keep the enormous one as a replacement if something were to go wrong in the cooking of the first one. In other words, it could be served as a 'sorry' if Hank did not like the original.

Right on 5.30pm, Bob unlocked the pub door and took a step outside as he always did, just to see if anything unusual was happening in the High Street. A boy on a bike whizzed by and a young girl, still dressed in school uniform, came the other way. Could be that she was involved in something at school after normal lessons, or maybe she has been to someone else's house before going home. Anyway, neither involved Bob, so back inside he went, rearranging some chairs. As he did, he could hear Linda handling pots and pans in the kitchen but did not disturb her as he knew that she liked to be left alone when cooking.

Into the pub came Tom Williams - 'Old Tom', as he was known. He was a thatcher of about 60 years, who had a son known as 'Young Tom' who worked with him. Young Tom was a member of the pub skittles team and would be along later, but in the meantime his Dad called for his usual pint of mild & bitter before journeying home for his dinner. "Hello Bob," said Old Tom, "have ee seen that red car?"

Before Bob could answer, the very same red car pulled into the pub carpark and out stretched the long legs of Hank.

What a relief, thought Bob as he excused himself from Old Tom's conversation and went to inform Linda, but she had already noticed the return of the handsome American. Suddenly the steak became very important in Linda's life.

"Hi Bob," Hank called out as he came through the open doorway.

"Good evening Hank," Bob replied, "have you had a nice day?"

A very affirmative response came from Hank, with the added statement that it had been tiring from driving a lot of miles.

"Would you like to go to your room?" Bob asked. "Sure would Buddy" Hank replied. "I need a good shower to bring me back into this world." Bob then called out to Linda and asked her to show Hank to his room as he could not leave the bar unattended.

As she straightened her hair and came into the bar, she was met with a flattering remark from Hank, "Hello lovely Linda, you look wonderful this evening." Linda's body quivered with delight, while Bob thought that was not the thing to say to someone's wife in front of her husband. Then, with a jolt, he realised that he had not told Hank that Linda was his wife. Shall I tell him now, thought Bob? No don't do anything to upset the applecart at this time he decided.

Taking a key from off the rack, Linda asked Hank to follow her up to his room at the top of a winding staircase leading off from the side of the kitchen. Hank found pleasure within him that a woman of Linda's attractiveness should be taking him to 'a room above'.

She unlocked the door and let him in.

"It's not a very posh room Hank. Because this is an old pub and the brewery will not spend money on its refurbishment," she said apologetically. " Don't worry Linda dear, I have laid my head in some pretty awful places throughout my time and this is fine by me." Linda opened the door to the en-suite and showed him how the shower worked. "Would you still like dinner at 6.30?" Linda asked. "Sure would," came the reply. So off she went back to the kitchen to prepare what she wanted to be a success.

Later on, she served a well cooked steak, mushrooms, tomato, fried onions, beans and some all-important chips, or would he call them French Fries. It was all there neatly arranged on a nice warm plate that Linda placed in front of the handsome gent sitting upright at the table in the part of the bar reserved for eating.

"Can I get you anything else?"

Hank thought for a second and stated that as Bob had already served him with a drink, he had no other request for the time being.

As Linda turned to go back to the kitchen, she noticed that there were more people in the pub tonight than usual and Bob was working hard to serve them all. She wondered what was happening as the skittles match did not start for another hour. Even Winnie and Madge were there and they hardly ever ventured out in the evenings.

As she went behind the bar to see if Bob needed help, Linda heard someone say, "That's him over there." Several others were also glancing in the direction of Hank with enquiring looks. Then she heard Winnie say, "someone must have put it about that a stranger was in town." There was a laugh from a few who stood near to her and a voice said, "I wonder who that could have been Winnie?"

As more people came into the bar, Bob could see Jim the farmer and his wife Betty approaching him. "Evening Landlord," Jim said, leaning his arm on the bar. "Hello Jim - evening Betty," Bob replied. "What brings you two out in your best bib and tuckers this evening?" Jim, with an eager grin said, "got a good price for them pigs at market today, so thought I'd give the missus a treat." Then came the real reason, "came to see who was driving the'ck big red car - the Yank, like Connie told me when she brought the post." He ordered drinks for the both of them, stood back and took an interesting glance in the direction of Hank, who was enjoying his food.

"Tell ee what Betty, what if we ave a meal over there ourselves?" Bob thought that was a master stroke of Jim to get closer to Hank, but why complain and he called to Linda that she had another sit-down food order to take. "OK Jim take a seat over there and Linda will be with you a minute," Bob smiled at Betty.

Jim took a table as close as he could to Hank, got Betty seated and plonked himself down with a face-to-face view of the American.

"Evening guvner," Jim said to Hank, who replied with a more polite greeting, while adding a 'Sir' on the end.

"Looks like you'm enjoying that grub," the farmer poured out. "Yes Sir, it's the best steak that I have had for a long time - Linda's a very good cook," Hank lovingly advised Jim and Betty. Jim replied with, "Looks good to me too," as he took a good look at the uneaten bit on Hank's plate.

Linda came to enquire what the two of them would like from the kitchen and smiled at Hank as she did. "Seems like we are wanting a couple of those fine steaks that this gentleman is recommending to us, ain't that right Betty?" Jim said, making up Betty's mind for her.

Linda was about to say that she did not have any steak left, then into her quick mind came the thought that she could slice that enormous one into two normal sized ones. "OK Jim, how would you like them done?" "Oh, any old 'ow, I don't mind, we ain't fussy, are we Bet my love." "With all the trimmings?" Linda enquired. "Just as this Gentleman 'ad." Linda then disappeared back into the kitchen, while Bob was busy keeping up with the demand behind the bar.

Luckily, Tony had arrived and was giving Bob a hand, when through the door came the mad rush of the visiting skittles team, together with many supporters. From the front of the bunch a large red faced chap of about 35 years, announced to Bob that they were the 'Dunkers' - a team of young farmers from Stalbridge way, who had been in the fields all day and were in need of some cider and solid grub before they set about the Dog & Whistle lot at skittles.

Bob looked after their cider requirements while Tony sold them hot pies and meat slices. "What about chips?" asked several of the hungry lads. So Tony went into the kitchen to ask the same question of Linda, who was busy cooking the order for her two sit-down customers. "Linda, several customers in the bar are asking for chips, do you have any?" he enquired.

Linda could not believe what she was hearing. Chips yes! And they could have eggs with them as well - that would bring in some extra profit, she thought. "Yes Tony, but you will have to take orders, perhaps for the half way break in the match if they like. In the meantime, I'll bring some portions of chips to eat now."

Tony went back behind the bar and gave Bob the information about the availability of eggs and chips at half time. Tony then told the lads in the 'Dunkers' group, who immediately started to call out their orders. Bob also explained the situation to The Major as he knew that Terry would not like to be left out of anything that could upset his normal routine.

"OK" said The Major, "We'll arrange a break of twenty minutes at 8.30." Then, as both teams had been served with their pre-match requirements, they all moved into the back room to start the match.

One-by-one, others in the bar started to leave, satisfied that they had now seen the Yank who drove the big red car around the village today. However, they were none the wiser as to why he had come all the way from America to the small village of Thimble Hardy.

Bob pulled Tony a pint in gratitude for the help that he had given him and excitedly remarked, "That was an unexpected extra sale of cider." Looking at the empty glass cabinet on the bar, Tony replied, "Yes, and of food too Bob."

Linda, in a more controlled manner continued to serve Hank, Jim and Betty at their tables, even though she had the same thoughts as Bob and Tony. Now she must look at the bar snacks orders that had been taken and get herself into gear for 8.30.

Jim continued to try to draw Hank into conversation about his need to be in Thimble Hardy, but Hank preferred to talk to Betty as she had less of an accent than Jim. "How did you two meet then?" Hank enquired. Betty was pleased to tell him that she came to Dorset from the London area as a Land-army girl in 1940 and was placed on Jim's father's farm. Hank was aware of the Land-army scheme as he once had a couple of buddies in his regiment who had 'Walked-out' with such girls in 1943. "So you took a shine to young Jim here?" Hank said as he laughingly looked at Jim grimacing in his seat." "Yep, we worked well together, didn't we Jim?" Betty said, as she touched Jim on the arm.

Jim thought to himself that they were now on quite good terms and that the time was right to ask the direct question about why the American had come to the village that day.

"So, why'm you yer then? - they say you'm looking for a field and there's plenty for you to pick from," Jim blurted out with a chuckle loud enough for Bob to hear at the bar.

"Well, that is one reason," Hank replied uneasily.

Bob rescued him by calling across, "So you have sold your pigs Jim and now you want to sell our visitor a field?" That brought laughter from them all and served the purpose of breaking up the inquisitive conversation that Jim was trying to have.

Just then the door opened from the back room and the skittles people began to poor into the bar again, looking for more cider and their half time pre-ordered eggs and chips.

Linda was well on top of the situation as she had recruited the help of Tony in the kitchen. Out they both came with the food, while Bob pulled one pint after another that made the till ring with the sound of falling coins. This is a blinking good night all round, both Bob and Linda thought.

As the skittles lads had downed their mid session feast and were returning to the skittle alley, Hank excused himself from the company of Jim and Betty and asked Bob if he could go and watch the skittles being played. Bob was all for that and waved him through.

"Well best we be off", Jim said as he eased himself up from his seat. I'll go and pay the bill." Betty followed and agreed with Jim when he said, "Landlord, that were a lovely meal and I enjoyed the conversation with that there Yank." "Thanks Jim'" Bob replied, "Hope to see you again soon and drive safely."

At the end of the evening, Tony helped Bob collect up the glasses and he took the empty plates through to the kitchen, where Linda gave him a hug and said, "thanks Tony, I don't know how we would have managed without you." Tony reluctantly stepped back as Linda released him from her clutch and he wondered which he enjoyed most today - Linda's loving hug, or the spin in the big red Mercedes. Then he thought, what's wrong with enjoying them both.

With all the customers departed and Hank gone up to his room, Bob turned out the lights in the bar, said a farewell to Tony as he left by the back door and sat down with Linda in the kitchen.

"Well my love, that was an eventful evening," said the landlord to his 'Barmaid'. "But well worth it financially," she replied.

To which Bob stated "You could say - **In Walked Some Money!**"

2   Who Could This American Be?

As Tony, Linda, Bob and Hank lay in their respective beds that evening, each contemplated situations that they could not release from their minds.

Tony, with the constant thought of Linda and how much he liked her company, even though she was old enough to be his mother.

Linda, with the delight of how the day had gone and how in the morning she would have to quickly replenish the depleted stocks from her larder and fridge.

Bob, on the other hand, was troubled by the thought of just who Hank was and why he was here at all.

Then Hank, who had three things on his mind.

Where is the field that he spent the last few days in England before being marshalled across the English Channel in 1944.

What's going on between Linda and Bob as they seem to be very close, even though she is only his Barmaid - or so he thought.

And then there is the real reason, for which he had come to England.

The next morning, after he had finished his breakfast, Hank paid his bill and bade farewell to his hosts, saying ,

"Thanks for everything, I'll be back again one day."

Then the big red car disappeared down the High Street and out of sight.

Linda set about making breakfast for Bob and herself, with the two eggs that she had held back from the hungry 'Dunkers' the evening before. It was to be a 'Full English' for them both as she thought that they had earned it and could now well afford it.

Still troubled in his own mind about who Hank really was and why he should have been in Thimble Hardy yesterday, Bob turned to Linda and said, "I wonder what Hank will be doing today."

"Forget him Bob and think about where the next bit of good fortune for us is likely to come from." A statement that Bob realised was right, but he was still full of intrigue about the American.

On the phone to the Co-op in Sherborne, Linda was asking if they could add a couple of dozen eggs and some more cheese to her order that she had placed two days ago. With an affirmative reply from the lady on the other end, Linda informed her that she would collect the items later in the day. Bob, also wanting to replace his depleted stock of beer and cider, was eager to use the phone and call the brewery for an emergency delivery as soon as possible.

With the administrative work out of the way, landlord and 'Barmaid' both set about cleaning the bar area in time for the morning opening time, even though they both knew that the day would not produce a repeat performance of yesterday.

Bob opened some windows to release the traces of smoke still lingering in the room and then went to the cellar to make sure that all was well down there. Linda cleaned the glass sandwich cabinet and put a few cheese and pickle sandwiches on the two shelves - or, were they pickle and cheese? as Bob and Jim had called them.

With the pub door wide open for business again, the first person to arrive was Tony's father, Henry Button.

"Hello Mr Button, how's things with you today and what will you have?' asked happy Linda. "I'm fine Linda and I'll just have half of mild thanks."

She pulled his drink and handed it across to him.

"So what brings you out so early on this bright sunny morning?" Linda asked again, loosely starting a conversation.

"Just passing on my way to the library and I thought that I would let you know that Tony was very happy for you last evening. He could not stop talking about the big surprises that you had yesterday and is full of praise, particularly for you Linda." "Well that's nice of him to say that Mr Button and I am well pleased to have Tony around to support us from time to time."

"Trouble is though, he's a well qualified mechanical engineer out of a job at the moment and he isn't doing anything to find employment. The only thing he really likes, is to come to the pub and help out," said Tony's father.

Linda looked a little puzzled at that remark and wondered if Mr Button was leading up to asking if Tony could be employed in the pub full time - something that the pub takings would not stand.

"What I would really like to ask of you Linda is, could you have a word of encouragement with him about getting back to his real work. His mother and I have tried but he won't listen to us. I know that he takes a lot of notice of what you say and coming from someone outside the family may have a better result."

Tony had served a 5 year engineering apprenticeship, studied by part-time/day release at the local technical college and had obtained a National Certificate in Mechanical Engineering. What is more, his company, that manufactured dairy machinery, had paid for him to take a further endorsement in Stainless Steel Welding, because it needed more trained engineers with that skill.

Linda was taken aback by the flattering request from Mr Button and did not quite know what to say. Bob, on the other hand, who had heard the conversation from the other end of the bar, agreed with Tony's father. "He does seem to do anything that you ask of him Linda and if it does work out it would be a good way of us repaying him for what he has done here in the past." With more than a little concern, Linda agreed to at least try to do something in that direction and Mr Button thanked them both in return.

Bob went back down the cellar, leaving Linda to handle the bar alone, when all of a sudden a loud mouthed chap arrived. It was Tommy Chant a 43 year old dumper truck driver who worked in the local quarry. He did not usually come to the Dog and Whistle as he was a member of the darts team at the Five Bells pub in the next village.

"Well, hello Linda," he bellowed out. "I hear that you are still attracting the Yanks!" Obviously he had heard about the visit of Hank and how he had stayed overnight in the pub.

Years before, Linda and Tommy had been very close friends, but she stood him up in 1944, when she had met a GI at a dance in the village hall one Saturday evening during the time that American troops started to arrive in the area, and while Tommy was away doing his military service in the British army.

Americans in smart uniforms, showing the girls new dances and dishing out gifts, became too much for the local lads and Tommy had carried a grudge against Linda ever since for doing so.

Linda went cold and tried to ignore the remark, for she was scared of what he would come out with next. Attack was the best form of defence she thought, and threw out a question of her own.

"So how are you Tommy and your second wife? And your five youngsters must be growing up fast." It was the politest way of shutting him up that she could think of without being rude to a customer. Tommy reluctantly accepted that as a 'put down' as he did not want Linda to enquire further into his own sexual life, otherwise revelations may emerge about a recent illicit affair that he was having in the village.

"So what really brings you here today Tommy, the beer or the company?" Linda asked as she noticed Winnie and Madge come through the door and make for the bar.

"A beer and a favour you may say, but certainly not the company," he remarked as he took a glance at the two old gasbags.

"It's like this, the darts team at the Five Bells needs a few more players and seeing as you don't have a darts team here I wondered if you could as much help by asking some of your regulars to come and join us."

What, thought Linda. Pass some of our few precious customers to another pub - not likely, she firmly believed to herself. Then thinking deeper, Linda wondered if this was yet another of his rotten schemes to get back at her for the way she stood him up for an American GI back in the 1940's.

"I'll have to ask my husband and to see what he thinks," was her reply just as Bob re-entered the bar.

Not wanting to get into a conversation with Bob, who he knew was more intelligent than himself, Tommy finished his half of cider and hurriedly left the pub. "What did that bounder want when he doesn't usually drink here?" asked Bob of Linda. "I have heard something recently about his affair with a married woman in the village."

Linda told Bob about Tommy's request for dart players and added her own thoughts about how that could lead to them losing some regulars if they did announce it in the bar. She did of course keep the other bit of her thoughts to herself, as she did not want to bring the delicate subject into the open with Bob.

Having agreed with Linda's summing up of the situation, he praised her for her quick view on the matter and said that he would handle it direct with the landlord of the Five Bells later on.

As it was a quiet lunchtime, Bob suggested to Linda that she could leave and go to collect her shopping from the Co-op. "OK Bob," Linda replied. "Is there anything that you need while I am in town?"

Bob thought for a moment and then suggested to Linda that it would be a good idea to get a couple of packets of cigarettes to give to Tony as a small token of their appreciation for the work that he did last evening. "Good idea, I know what he likes," replied Linda and off she went.

A couple of people came and went into the pub, the two old ladies left without much to add to their locker of knowledge and with half an hour still to go before the morning session closing time, 'The Major' appeared. "Hello Terry," the landlord greeted him with a smile. "What can I get you, so early in the day?" "Oh just a half of bitter for now, but I have something to propose to you."

Bob, serving up the half, was all ears and invited 'The Major' to come out with it. "Well it's like this, we got a good hammering by the Dunkers at skittles last evening and it hurt. So I've been thinking that we ought to get our lot to improve somehow."

The Major went on to suggest that he thought that it would be a good idea if he could get the team to come to the pub on another evening for some 'Practice and Improvement' - PAI, he said, using an old army term. "Also, I believe that we should draft in some others so that the team can see that their place is not always guaranteed."

"What a good idea Terry, I'll go along with that. Will you arrange it?" Bob answered, thinking of how that would no doubt sell some more beer and the odd sandwich beyond what the pub usually sold. Thanking Bob for his positive answer to his suggestion, 'The Major' drank up and went on his way saying, "I'll come back to you Bob when I have more details."

Time had arrived to close up for the afternoon and as Bob took his usual glance up the Hight Street before locking the door, he saw Tommy Chant coming along on his bike. He pulled up alongside Bob in the doorway and blurted out, "Hello Mate! So have ee made up yer mind of which people you'm going let us have for our darts team then. What about that bloke Tony?"

That riled Bob, who told the mouthy Tommy, that he would talk it over with the landlord of the Five Bells later. "No need for that Mate," said Tommy, in a worrying manner. "I'm the one dealing with it, just give me the names."

Bob could detect that all was not on the level with this conversation and just as he was about to tell Tommy so, the phone rang back in the bar. "Sorry old chap, that's my phone, so I'll have to be off," said Bob thankful for the interruption.

With the door firmly shut, Bob picked up the receiver and announced "Dog and Whistle public house." A voice at the other end asked politely, "Is that you Bob - my Buddy?"

Bob immediately recognised it as Hank and with a pleasing reply said, "Hank, nice to hear you, what brings you on?" Hank then asked if his room was still available for this evening. "Sure," said Bob. "But it's still in the same state as you left it." "That's great," answered Hank. "I need to stay in the area for another day as 'The Major' has put me onto a very good lead. I must go, I'll be back at the pub sometime just after five."

That was good news to Bob, as it would bring in some extra money again. He knew that Linda would be happy also. Then the intrigue set in again in his mind. He knew that 'The Major' had been in the army from when he was a young boy aged 17 and that he had completed 15 years service, for it was something that he had told people over and over again. So, could the lead that he had given Hank have something to do with the military?

Then again, Bob also knew that Terry Smith joined the police force when he had left the army and that he rose to the rank of Inspector before he retired on his 53rd birthday. So, was the 'lead' to do with some international police investigation and was Hank a member of Interpol, MI5, MI6, 7, 8, or 9, whatever they all did.

Terry's last employment was as an Estate Agent, so perhaps Bob's first thought about Hank looking for a house was correct and 'The Major' had put the American onto a decent property to purchase. No doubt Hank would tell him when he returned later - so Bob thought!

Alone in the bar with his thoughts, Bob cleared away glasses and dumped the unsold sandwiches, mumbling to himself about the loss of profit as nobody wanted pickle and cheese this lunchtime.

Then he heard their car pull up at the back door and the sound of Linda bringing in some of her shopping.

He was eager to inform Linda of the unexpected return of Hank for another overnight stay, but Linda called him to give her a hand to bring the rest of the shopping into the kitchen.

When it was all in and the car put away in the garage, Linda came back into the kitchen with a surprise of her own, before Bob could inform her of the repeat occupancy of the guest room for this night.

"Guess who I met in the Co-op?" she eagerly poured out, and before Bob could even hazard a guess she said, "Margaret Bond!"

Bob, with a puzzled frown racked his brain to try to identify who this Margaret Bond was.

"You know, Maggie, who worked under me at the factory in 1940."

Bob had heard Linda talk about Maggie in the past and about how they became good friends and went to the village dances together, but he had not actually met her.

"Yes she is still cooking and has recently taken on the job as head cook to Lord Billington at the Big House."

Linda then happily informed Bob that they had arranged to meet later in the week for a good old chat about times gone by.

"So, how have you done while I have been away then?" A remark which Linda did not really expect an exciting reply.

"Didn't do much trade, but I had a few interesting conversations," he replied. Then he set about telling Linda about the suggestion that 'The Major' had made about the skittles training evening and how he thought that it would bring in some additional sales. "That's a good idea," Linda replied, wondering why that had never been done before.

"Then that bounder Tommy Chant pulled up just as I was locking up and demanded to know the names of those who we were going to offer for the Five Bells darts team." "You know Linda," he said, "I just don't trust that bloke, I reckon that he is trying to do something underhanded."

That made Linda go cold, as she thought that Tommy may well have told Bob about some of the times that they had experienced together down in the old Thatcher's Barn around the time before Mac was born.

"But, the best bit of news is that Hank phoned and is coming back to stay another night because, in his own words, 'The Major' has put him onto a good lead."

Linda was delighted to hear that news. "So what is the 'good lead' then, did he tell you that?" she excitedly enquired. Bob replied that Hank did not have time to explain anything on the phone, but he would be back around five o'clock.

"Crikey, that means that I have to prepare a meal for him and Charlie Burt has closed the butcher's shop for the day." Then with no more worry, she said, "I know, I cooked some stewing steak earlier and I'll make it into a large steak and ale pie with lots of gravy. So if Hank asks for steak again this evening, I can tell him that it's in the pie!" she laughingly stated. Bob was happy with that, as he loved Linda's steak and ale pies and if it was going to be a big one, then there would surely be some left over for himself.

Bob left Linda in the kitchen to get on with whatever she needed to do and went through to their sitting room and quietly dozed off for a nap in the large armchair.

When he came round, Bob realised that he had a lot of things going on in his mind and tried to summarise them.

He needed to get more supplies from the brewery, who so far, had not responded to his emergency call.

What will 'The Major' come up with about the skittles practice evening and who would he draft in?

How would Linda handle the talk of encouragement that she had agreed to have with Tony?

What is that bounder Tommy Chant really up to?

Who is Hank and what is the 'Very Good Lead' that Terry has put him onto. Is it Police, Military, or Property related?

Then, of course, he had to start thinking about opening the pub for yet another evening session.

He went into the small closet next to the kitchen and doused his face with water to bring himself back into the land of the living, just in time to hear the big red car pull into the pub carpark. Hank was back as promised, so hopefully some explaining would now come to light.

In through the back door, Hank arrived carrying his usual overnight bag, a briefcase and an armful of paperwork. "Bob, my Buddy. I'm so thankful that you could put me up for another night as I have not had time to look elsewhere."

Then turning to Linda, he said, "Hello lovely Linda, how are you today?" To which she spontaneously replied, "Hello handsome Hank - I'm all the better for seeing you." A remark that she regretted saying in front of her loving husband.

"So, we're all Fine and Dandy then - I'm pleased to hear that," Hank replied with a puff of his cheeks and lingering on his glance at Linda.

"Are you going to serve me with another of your wonderful steaks again this evening Linda?" Hank enquired, after taking a good whiff of the meat cooking in the kitchen.

"Yes Hank, steak is on the menu again this evening, but not as you would normally have it - just wait and see."

Hank could not wait to find out what Linda had on offer for him later that evening and he climbed the stairs to settle in the room that he had vacated earlier in the day.

3   What is he after?

After taking a shower, Hank thumbed through the bundle of paperwork that he had brought with him and had left on the bed.

He sorted it into smaller piles according to their interest.
Trash.   Possible.   Very Good.

However, nothing came up to the 'Lead' given to him by The Major and as he was about to dig deeper into the facts, Linda called up to him from the bottom of the stairs, that his meal was about to be served. So he put all the papers away into his briefcase and wondered what delights Linda would have waiting for him down below.

Hank sat in the same chair that he had occupied on the previous evening, with a good view across the bar area. Bob asked him if he wanted a drink and Hank, catching on to local traditions, asked for a glass of cider. 'Sweet or Rough?" asked Bob.

"Sweet or Rough, what does that mean Bob?" came the reply.

After explaining the difference and adding the word 'Scrumpy' to the description of the rough cider, Hank said that 'Scrumpy' sounded an enticing type of drink and so he would try half a pint.

From the oven in the kitchen, Linda extracted the large Steak & Ale pie that she had made in an eight inch square dish. It was steaming hot and smelt delicious. In her mind, she divided it into four equal portions, each with a crusty corner. Onto a large warm plate she laid one portion for Hank, together with freshly cooked new potatoes and vegetables that Bob had grown in their walled garden at the back of the pub carpark. She added a good helping of beef gravy, thick enough that one could almost stand a fork up in it.

Bob could smell the pie from his position in the bar and went to the kitchen to take a closer look, eagerly hoping that there would be a portion left over for him later on. Linda nudged him to one side and took the plate, together with its deliciously smelling contents, through to Hank who she found grimacing from the taste of the cider called Scrumpy.

"Here you are Sir", she politely offered, "I am sorry to have kept you waiting."

With a loving look back at Bob's so called 'Barmaid', he thanked her, whilst at the same time stating that he could not take too much of that Scrumpy.

Having returned to his place behind the counter with his nostrils full of the smell from the pie, Bob served a couple of lads who had come in for a quick half prior to going off to have a knock-about at cricket in the recreational ground before it got dark.

The next to arrive, was The Major and his wife Joan. "Hello Terry - hello Mrs Smith - good to see you both," Bob said in a slightly puzzled tone.

Mrs Smith replied with a "Nice also to see you Bob, how is Linda?"

Niceties out of the way and with drinks in their hands, The Major said to Bob, "I was hoping that I could catch the American this evening before he departs - is he around?"

Hank had seen them arrive and had heard the question. "Hello Terry, come and join me." An invitation that Terry and Joan were reluctant to accept whilst Hank was eating his dinner, but as he insisted, they ambled over and took seats at the table next to Hank. "So what brings you looking for me this evening Terry?" Before answering that question, Terry introduced Hank to Joan.

Hank thought that The Major had picked a good looking 'Babe' here, even though she was getting on a bit these days.

"What about joining me at this table and have some of Linda's delicious steak and ale pie. Come now, let me buy you a meal in return for the wonderful lead that you have given me."

As they had only had a light snack earlier and the smell of the delicious pie tempted them, they thankfully agreed. Hank then called out to Bob that he had two more for dinner this evening.

When Bob gave Linda the good news about the additional custom for her pie, he became concerned that there would only be one portion left - the portion he hoped was to be his. He was therefore left in two minds, additional pub takings, or his personal desire. So, he half hoped anxiously that no-one else would come in to eat this evening.

When they had finished eating, Terry gave Hank some more important information about the lead, which Hank was delighted to receive before he was due to leave the locality in the morning.

"Terry, that is wonderful news, it means that I could conclude my search earlier than expected. Thanks so much for coming."

All three were talking over some pleasantries and laughing about how the big red car had caused so much interest the previous evening, when in walked the Vicar with another man.

The Reverend Theodore Smythe-Brown, 'Timmy' to his friends, was thirty-something-plus, rotund and a happy person. People in the village liked him as he always had a good word to say about them all. He loved the village, even though he had only been in Thimble Hardy for two years, since leaving a parish in the East End of London. He had come to the pub this evening, along with the Verger, Bert Mant, by invitation from The Major who had informed him that the skittles team needed some new blood.

After serving the two with drinks, Bob informed Timmy that The Major was sitting over the other side of the room having a meeting with an American guest. "That's fine Bob," said the vicar, "we won't disturb him - can we go and have a roll-up on the skittle alley?" Bob was delighted that two people who were not regulars to the pub had ventured out specifically in response to Terry's 'Call to Arms' earlier in the day. He showed them through to the back room and put the lights on over the alley and left them to return to his work at the bar.

Linda was still busy in the kitchen clearing away pots and pans when she took a lingering look at the remaining portion of her steak and ale pie, wondering what to do with it. Then, came the thought that she would serve it up right now for Bob and she would relieve him from behind the bar.

Seeing Terry and Joan saying their goodbyes to Hank, Bob took the opportunity to tell Terry of the arrival of the vicar and verger in response to his request. Happy with that news, Terry decided to pay his respects to both of the two willing new skittle players and into the back room he dragged Joan.

Hank, having been left alone at the table, watched and listened as he saw Linda and Bob exchanging happy conversation about the last portion of pie. "I don't want to be rude," said Hank, "But why don't you come and sit with me Bob and then we can have a chat about the world together." The landlord was not in the habit of eating with the guests, but somehow this seemed to be acceptable with Hank, as he had become his Buddy. Linda agreed and thought that Bob had earned this little treat and in any case he may find out a little more about the friendly American's reason for being here.

Taking a drink for them both, Bob walked over to the table and sat down opposite Hank. In no time came a plate with that remaining portion of steak and ale pie, which Bob quickly stuck his fork into, believing that in doing so no-one else could claim it.

Hank looked at him enjoying the food and in pleasant conversation, casually asked him a couple of questions about the village, its people and Bob himself. He was interested in the skittles and likened it to ten pin bowling, a game that he had played many times, both in and out of the military.

He said that he also liked The Major and how impressed he was with the efficient way that he organised things. Bob agreed and said that it was probably because of his military training, followed by the years that he had spent in the police force.

Whilst Hank was interested in Bob's replies, he could not keep his eyes off Linda, who he thought could well have fitted into his life sometime in the past. He admired her efficient handling of the bar work, he loved her cooking, but most of all he had become besotted with her looks, however one thing puzzled him about the 'Barmaid'.

She seemed to be in the pub all the time, early morning, late at night and he guessed that she was also there throughout the day. So did she not have a family, or a home of her own and what about Tony, could he be her son, as he was always showing affection towards her?

Bob, having finished his meal pushed his plate to one side, licked a piece of the pie from his lips and raised his glass towards his customer, to which Hank made a similar gesture in return.

4   Revelations

"So, how long have you owned this pub?" enquired Hank of Bob. "Own, I don't own it, the brewery have that privilege," the landlord answered. "We are only tenants." Hank was rocked back in his seat at that revelation and doubly surprised at the use of the word WE!

Is there a sleeping partner somewhere, or does his barmaid have a cut in the business, he wondered. Not wanting to be left with unanswered questions, Hank politely pushed the questioning along. "So how does that system work, do you just take a salary from the brewery - you and your partner?"

Bob explained that he lived rent free in the building and was allowed a small percentage of the alcohol sales after all the running costs had been covered. He went on to add, "But we are allowed to keep all the takings from my wife's cooking."

It was like a bomb had exploded in Hank's head, as it was now revealed that Linda was Bob's wife! On the one hand, he was somewhat pleased to know that the couple who seem to have such a happy working relationship, were also bound together by marriage. But he was shattered to now understand that the door was closed to him making anymore amorous remarks to the 'Lovely Linda'.

Hank was lost for words, but did not want to show surprise at the devastating news that Linda was married. He continued the conversation along the business lines, "Can you make a good living from the percentage that you receive from the alcohol sales?"

Bob gave him a reply along the lines that he could make more if he was not tied to selling only the brewery's brand of products. "Some other pubs do alright if they are a 'Free House' as they can offer a wider range of beers to suit the preferences of their clients."

Hank was surprised to learn of such restricted practices and thought that it was a non-win situation all round, as neither side was budgeting to expand their fortunes.

The brewery was being very negative in accepting a run-of the mill situation and the publican was putting up with the stranglehold put upon him, just to keep a roof over his head.

After the Reverend Timmy and his verger packed up their pleasurable game of skittles, they left the pub with the other drinkers. Linda then arrived to clear away Bob's empty plate and Hank gave her the the same affectionate smile that he had done all along, but this time it did not have the same conviction in his own mind.

"Time that we should be closing, do you want me to lock up?" Linda asked Bob, as she knew that the landlord may still have questions of his own that he wanted to ask of his client. "OK love, will you do it, as we're having a nice chat here?"

Bob thought, there's no time like the present - strike while the iron is hot, - there may not be another chance - several clichés ran through his mind.

"Well, so what's your background Hank?" Bob asked in a pleasant manner.

"Me? Oh when I finished at Harvard Business School, America had joined in the second world war and I was immediately drafted into the army and sent on a strategy course. In no time I was given the lowly rank of Lieutenant and together with another guy from the same course, we were shipped over to England and attached to an artillery brigade as Intelligence Officers".

"After we arrived in Plymouth, we were then put on a train to a place with a small railroad station that had a name something like *Bottle of Port*." Bob laughed, as this was the second time that he had heard Hank come out with that description. "I think that you may mean Milborne Port. It's a village not far from here that used to have a small railway station until the powers-to-be closed it a few years back."

"Milborne Port, that's it." Hank was pleased to hear Bob confirm that, as the time that he spent in that locality flooded back into his memory. He recalled the weeks spent under canvas in fields nearby, the muddy conditions when it rained, the village dances, the crummy musicians and the local girls. However, above all, he recalled to Bob how the mighty military moved from their muddy fields and massed across the English Channel on D-Day and were met by heavy German opposition.

Bob sympathised with Hank when he heard of the many traumas that happened to the young Lieutenant's regiment after they had advanced from the French beaches. None-the-less, Bob had yet to find out the reason for this ex-GI being in the area of Thistle Hardy right now, so he approached the subject by asking Hank what he did for a living since then.

"Well Bob, it's difficult to put a handle on it these days as various opportunities have reshaped my career while I have trodden the business path." Bob thought that Hank was hesitating and maybe trying to put him off the real reason for being here. His mind returned to his previous thought, Interpol! Why else the secrecy?

Bob was disappointed with that answer and felt the need to pursue the topic, after-all if things were that secret then Hank had only to say so. So back in he went with a question that he thought would narrow the matter to a particular field of activity.

"So, what is this business path, still military?"

"Oh no, I left all that behind me years ago, when I took up employment as a trainee real estate negotiator."

"OK, I've got it Hank - you are now a property tycoon looking for a nice holiday home in Dorset," he chuckled out directly to Hank in a playful manner.

That was greeted with a remark that narrowed the subject even more, when Hank stated that it was not a holiday home, but that he was looking for a business on behalf of a client back in the US.

"You see Bob, I own a company, employing 30 people that searches out run-down businesses that have potential to be regenerated into profit, or have the potential to be divided into resalable packages for other purposes." "We do this for clients who wish to be anonymous, or do not have the time or facilities to do this for themselves. It is a very lucrative business for me, but in recent years it has become very competitive, with people trumping and over-trumping on deals that have the potential for success. I try to keep my activities under wraps and travel in a very simple manner so that competitors do not become aware of where I am operating."

Whilst Bob was now grateful for the explanation, he thought to himself that travelling in a big red Mercedes around small villages was hardly a way of keeping 'under cover', but then he remembered Hank's explanation about the hire company only having that one vehicle available when he arrived at Gatwick Airport three days ago.

Hank continued with more detail when he told Bob that his US client specifically wanted such a business around the North Dorset/South Somerset area as the client's company had connections with the Westland Aircraft Company in Yeovil. He went on to say how lucky he was to have received help from The Major who had helped him narrow down his search, following a chance remark while he was watching the skittles last evening.

"So, you have now found such a business?" Bob asked. "Yes, but please accept it when I tell you that I can not release any further information until it is a done deal. I ask if you will be good enough not to tell anyone about this and also respect The Major's position in this by not letting him know that I have given you this information."

As Hank had at last come clean, Bob gave him his word about secrecy and added that he would not even tell Linda. That pleased Hank and he shook Bob's hand with a firm grasp, adding that he expected to be back again soon with his client to conclude the deal, if all went well following a meeting that he was to have in London tomorrow.

Bob was now happy that his mind had been cleared of this mystery and asked Hank to join Linda and himself for a nightcap.

"What will you have Buddy?' Bob enquired using a reverse offering of the US affectionate phrase. "Scotch on the Rocks," came the bold reply. "Well I'm not sure that we have ice at the moment," Linda chirped in from the bar. "That's all right Linda, I'll take it as it comes when you are offering it." Linda thought that remark was a 'Bit-near-the-bone', but inwardly accepted it with pleasure.

Next morning, Linda cooked the departing guest a huge 'Full English', a real West Country farmer's portion. Hank marvelled again at how Linda was such a good cook and thought that on Linda's reputation alone, the pub ought to be doing much better than he had detected it was.

After breakfast, Hank collected his belongings from the bedroom, paid his bill and told them both that he would be back in the area together with his client in about three weeks time. However, at the request of his client, he pointed out that they would both be staying at an hotel in Yeovil, but assured them that he would make time within his stay to visit the two of them.

"Good news then?" Bob remarked as he warmly shook Hank by the hand, adding "It has been a pleasure to have met with you - Sir."

Turning to Linda, Hank thought that a hand shake was not enough to be leaving this lovely lady with, so on impulse he wrapped his arms around her and gave her a big hug, leaving her with a memory that, unbeknown to Bob, she would secretly treasure.

Then just as he was about to go out of the door, Linda called, "Don't go without signing the visitor's book." Hank dropped his baggage and willingly placed a very complimentary review of his stay and signed it - **Harold Burnett, Junior. (Hank)**

He then closed the book, replaced it on the hall stand and bade his final farewell, for the second time of leaving.

Seeing the big red car turn out of the pub car park, they both thought that an unusual phase had just passed through their lives and were now left to pick up the pieces and return to normal pub life again.

Bob readied himself in the bar with the normal tasks before morning opening time and Linda cleared the kitchen of the breakfast dishes before setting about making some sandwiches for the glass case on the bar counter.

Cheese and pickle as usual, or, as she chuckled to herself, pickle and cheese again. Then, with a new spring in her heals, she thought, what about something else for a change - what about some luncheon meat sandwiches, yes luncheon meat. So from the larder, she came back with a medium sized tin of Co-op luncheon meat and opened it onto a wooden board and made several rounds with mustard for the bar

"This will make the locals sit up and take notice," she firmly said to Bob, as she placed them into a prominent position within the cabinet. "Blimey love, they will think that you have won the pools," referring to the weekly football betting competition.

Then remembering the dodgy request that he had received from the dumper truck driver about the darts team, Bob thought that while things were quiet, he would ring the landlord of the Five Bells and learn of the request direct from him.

"Five Bells public house," a voice answered. "Hello Sam, - Bob, from the Dog and Whistle." Sam was pleased to hear from Bob, even though they were somewhat competitors and after complaining to each other about the poor state of business, Bob came out with the reason for his call.

"Short of darts players? News to me, we're not short of players, if fact a few customers are disgruntled because they are not being picked for our team and I have a problem stopping them from wanting to come over to you and to play skittles instead," Sam replied. Bob then went on to explain that he thought that Tommy Chant seemed to have some sort of ulterior motive for saying such a thing and wondered if Sam could throw any further light on it.

"Well Bob, it could be to do with the fact that he is banned from your pub." Bob was surprised to hear that, as he had not banned anybody from drinking at the Dog and Whistle. "Yes, before you took over the licence, there was a fight in the bar one lunchtime that resulted in the police being called."

Sam went on to tell Bob what he knew of the incident, which came about when Tommy Chant passed a remark about Madge Wilson's intelligence. "Seems he was not happy when he heard Madge pass a comment about him having so many children and Tommy replied by saying that Madge could get her brains in a matchbox and still have room for the matches. That caused Winnie to stick up for Madge and she hit Tommy in the mouth with her handbag."

Sam went on to say that Len Scott from the paper shop tried to calm things down, but Tommy punched him in the face and broke his nose. Some others got involved and it was then that the landlord slung Tommy out into the street and called the police. "Tommy was let off with a caution, but was told never to return to your pub again."

"So he now holds a grudge against me and is trying to get one back?" enquired Bob.

"No, I don't think it's particularly you, but the pub in general, as he can't let sleeping dogs lie."

Bob was astounded to hear about that and wondered why he had not heard of it before. Maybe the two old ladies did not want to talk about it as they realised that Tommy's original remark was somewhat true. Then what about Len Scott? - I guess that maybe he is too embarrassed to admit that he came off worse.

Sam brought the conversation to an end by saying, "Don't worry Bob I won't be pinching any of your customers for our darts team and I'll have a word with Tommy when he next comes in." Bob was relieved to hear that and even more so that he had a good explanation to tell Linda. So he ended by thanking Sam and put the receiver down.

Linda was surprised to learn from Bob about the fight in their pub some time before they had both arrived. However, she willingly accepted Sam's reasoning for Tommy holding a grudge against the pub, but inwardly she knew that Tommy had another reason, one that she could not reveal to Bob or anyone else come to that.

Anyway, another day was waiting to present itself to the landlord and landlady of the Dog and Whistle and so both got on with their well rehearsed routine that needed to be done before morning opening time. Tables cleaned, chairs properly arranged, beer pumps checked and a window opened, that was Bob done, before he unlocked the pub door and waited for customers to come in.

The first person through the door was Tony, cheerful as ever and with a happy greeting to Bob, followed by a large affectionate smile for Linda. "Anything you need me for today Bob?" enquired the willing lad. "No, I don't think so Tony," Bob replied - then suddenly he remembered the promise that he and Linda had made to Tony's father about how he ought to be looking for a proper job.

Bob looked at Linda and gave her a wink, for which she accepted that as it was a quiet time, this could be an opportune moment for her to have a few words with Tony.

"Well there is one thing that I would like to talk to you about Tony, if you can spare a couple of minutes," Linda nervously replied. "Can you come through to the kitchen so that we can talk in private?" Tony was surprised, but excited, to have such an invitation from the one person that he had ever wished to be alone with and so quickly followed her into the kitchen.

Linda did not find it easy to open the subject and even more difficult standing in amongst the pots and pans of the kitchen. "No, this is not the place to talk Tony, let's go through to our sitting room." Then, taking him by the hand, she led him through the narrow passageway into the private part of the pub. He had not had the privilege of entering this room before and his thoughts filled him with immense desire for Linda, even though she was the wife of his friend Bob.

Linda invited him to take a seat wherever he liked and he chose to sit at one end of their comfortable settee, all ears waiting to know what Linda would want him to do for her. Linda, on the other hand, stood with her back to him, a pose that delighted Tony as he could see her shapely silhouette in the sunlight shining through the window.

Having gathered her thoughts, Linda turned and took a seat on the settee close enough to set Tony's pulse racing. She opened up with. "Tony, I know this is not really any of my business, but I am worried for your future."

"Worried - why?" asked Tony, "I can look after myself." "Yes I know you can and that is why I believe that what I am about to say, you will take in good faith and hopefully act on it." Linda went on to say, "You are always willing to help us, without a lot of reward and you have been a God-send at times of pressure, but this is not what you have been so highly trained to do." She went on to say that although he may for the time being, be able to live on the redundancy money that he received when he left the factory, the time would come when he needed to again work for money.

Tony was suddenly disappointed to learn that Linda's request was not what he had anticipated and he took on a disinterested frown that Linda immediately noticed. Furthermore, he began to see Linda in the same light as his parents - telling him what to do with his life.

"Tony, you know that I have feelings for you and I would not like to see you ending up on the wrong side of the street, so to speak," Linda said with real feeling.

She reminded him again of how well trained he was at the job he had studied so hard to achieve and just because he was out of work, it was not through any fault of his own. "One day you will get married and have a family of your own to support and that will be difficult if you are not in a position to earn a decent salary," Linda pointed out.

"I'm not bothered Linda, I get along okay for now," he said blowing an uncontrollable puff of air from the side of his mouth. He no longer saw her as an object of desire and all his thoughts in that direction disappeared from his mind and his body.

Realising that there was no point in continuing with this conversation, Tony stood up and began to make his way back to the bar. Linda, now feeling that Tony was hurt from what she had said, stood up right in front of him, took him by the hand and gave him a hug, followed by a warm kiss on the cheek. "Tony, please do not think the worst of me for what I have said, you will always be one of my closest friends," Linda said, trying to console him. "I only want what is best for you."

This last action of Linda's did at least bring some desire for her back into Tony's mind and he returned her kiss with one of his own before they both walked hand-in-hand back through the passageway, with Linda going into the kitchen and Tony into the bar.

Bob looked at him and could see that Tony was not at all pleased and so acted as though nothing had happened. Then suddenly he remembered the cigarettes that Linda had bought to give to Tony.

Picking up the two packets from behind the bar, Bob went across and with a "Thanks for your help the other evening," slid the cigarettes into Tony's hand. Tony looked at them and at first did not want them as he thought that it was all part of the plot to get him back to work, but common sense prevailed and he thanked Bob with, "any time Governor - you only have to ask." He now accepted the situation as it was and told Bob that he had a job to do for the postmistress and left the pub.

Linda came through into the bar and when Bob asked her how she had got on with the discussion, she replied that she thought the talk had done more harm than good.

"Well that is a shame," Bob stated, "I only hope that we have not lost a willing hand." To which Linda replied with a certain amount of emotion, "and a very good friend as well."

They both solemnly leaned on the counter with their thoughts, when in came George and Billy looking for their first pint of the day and ready to play yet another game of crib.

"Cheer up you two," said George, "You look as though you have lost a quid and found sixpence," quoting an old saying and hopefully wanting to spur the pair of them into action.

Linda faintly smiled at the two of them and left for the kitchen, while Bob greeted them with a warm smile and "What will you have lads?" to which Billy answered, "Usual Bob - can't afford anything else on our pensions."

Pulling the pints, the landlord thought to himself, "Why are these daytime customers always bleating on about their pensions?" Then right on time, in came Winnie and Madge, who would no doubt have added to Billy's comment had they arrived just a few minutes earlier. Then, each having got their routine bottle of stout, smiled at the crib players as they passed and took up their usual well polished seats.

No sooner had the four of them settled in, when in came a well dressed young man carrying a rectangular object and asking to speak to the landlord. "That's me," called out Bob, "Can I help you?" Looking the chap up and down Bob quickly identified that the fellow was here to try and sell him something.

"Oh, fine," he said with a rather posh accent. "I'm James Farthing from the Clear & Strong Display Cabinet Company and If you will allow me, I would like to show you a product that could help to increase your business." Bob had heard many a salesman come out with that yarn before and thought here's another one - I wonder what it is this time. The salesman placed the object on the counter, looked Bob straight in the face and said, "A fantastic glass display cabinet."

There then followed a very slick presentation of a different style of an old product that Bob did not want. After-all, he still had plenty of room for more sandwiches in the glass cabinet that had been left in the bar by the previous landlord two years ago.

So, not wishing to be rude and accepting that the chap had to make a living just like himself, Bob declined the offer but suggested that the landlord of the Five Bells may like to have a look at this wonderful new product.

Deflated at yet another non-sale, James rewrapped his sample cabinet and thanked Bob for the lead onto Sam at the Five Bells. Then before he left he politely said to Bob, "I would like to buy half of your local brew, but I don't want the drink, give it to the next needy person who you feel would like it." Bob, thought that James was a real gentleman and it was a pity that he was not in a position to purchase from him, but he took his money and tossed it into the till.

As James was on his way out, he smiled at the two women at the door and Winnie said to him, "You should try the paper shop down the road, he's called Len Scott and he could put it on his counter wee a few fags in it - and by the way, if he buys one, tell him that Winnie and Madge recommended it. Then again, if eh don't and he wants to know how you got his name, tell him that it were Gert & Daisy." The salesman was pleased to have got the information without asking and was quite amused by the way Winnie had offered the advice.

"Gert and Daisy?" Madge enquired. "We ain't Gert and Daisy are we?" Winnie as usual took a sideways glance and said, "no we Ain't Gert and Daisy, they'm the two on the radio who's quite funny. "Oh yes that's em I know, do they come in yer for a drink then?" she asked. Winnie took a deep breath and replied, "Yes - occasionally!" Both George and Billy chuckled out loud at that remark and Bob could not hold back his amusement either.

Then, while pulling second pints for George and Billy, a very smart twenty-something lady came into the pub and asked for Bob. "That's me," replied the landlord, what can I do for you?"

Feeling that the crib players were listening and the eyes of the two old ladies were piercing into her, she moved closer to Bob at the bar and lowered her voice saying, "Jim has sent me."

"Jim? - May I ask Jim who?" enquired Bob.

"Jim Pearson - farmer Jim, who keeps pigs down at Long Bottom Farm."

Bob was right on to that as there was only one Farmer Jim around here, he thought. "So what is he up to in sending you to me today then?" Bob said with an inquisitive chuckle.

"I'm Mary Pearson and he's my uncle Jim - my Dad's brother." The smart young girl said. To which Bob replied, "Well, I would never have thought it - how can I help."

Mary went on to say that one of her friends would be having a birthday over the coming weekend and that she and others would like to treat the birthday girl to a surprise meal. "Well that's a nice thought, what have you got in mind?" asked Bob, hoping that some unexpected business may be heading his way.

"Uncle Jim has told me that he and an American business friend of his had a most enjoyable steak and ale pie here earlier in the week and has recommended it as something that we would all enjoy."

Bob had to laugh inwardly when he heard that Jim was boasting about Hank being his business friend, but controlled himself when he could see a future sale of more portions of Linda's steak and ale pie.

"Well that's nice of Old Jim - sorry, your uncle Jim, to say that, and to pass on a recommendation. I think that you should talk to Linda, my wife about it as she handles all the affairs of the kitchen."

Bob then called Mary over to a table just outside the kitchen doorway and invited her to take a seat while he fetched Linda.

Linda appeared and welcomed Mary, while Bob asked her if she would like a drink. "Oh, just a lemonade thanks," came the reply. "So, you are Mary, Jim's niece and he has told you about our famous Dog & Whistle steak and ale pie then?" Linda politely enquired.

Mary repeated what she had told Bob about her birthday friend and asked if Linda could accommodate them. "Certainly Mary, how many people are there likely to be and which evening are you thinking of planning this for?"

Linda was more than surprised, but hugely happy to hear the answer. "About 18 of us for this Saturday evening."

Linda thought blimey 18 at such short notice, while all the logistical problems of handling a meal for 18 people at the same time went through the turmoil in her mind. She had not had to do that in the whole two years since taking on the pub. However, she could not let this golden opportunity pass and would work out the answers later.

They agreed a price between them and then Linda suddenly thought of the financial outlay that she would have to make beforehand - and what if they did not turn up on the night. So, in a businesslike manner, Linda said, "Yes that is fine, what time would you want to eat and of course I would need to take a deposit with the booking."

Mary was pleased that Linda could accommodate them all at such short notice and accepted the request for forward payment. "If you like, I could pay you the full amount now because the others have each given me money up front so that I could settle a deal without complications about payment." Linda explained that that would be unnecessary as who knows what the final bill would be, but if it was OK with her, then she would accept £150 now and the balance after they finished their meal. So from an inside pocket of her jacket, Mary pulled out a huge wad of notes and counted out the amount that they had both agreed on. The two of them then got up from the table, shook hands on the deal and Mary asked to pay for the lemonade, but Linda told her that it was on the house this time.

With Mary gone, Bob followed Linda into the kitchen and rejoiced in the fact that they had received this unexpected order recommended by Jim their pig farmer customer. Then Bob fell about laughing at the thought of how Linda would be able to handle the logistics of the situation. "Don't worry my handsome, I'll find a way," Linda replied, while tucking the handful of notes into her handbag.

Then they both heard someone call from the bar and so from the kitchen Bob left Linda to go and find out who was calling. It was Winnie, to say that Connie had been and left the morning post on the counter adding, "There's one from America."

Bob thought, nosey old woman, but thought better of it and thanked Winnie for her call as both she and Madge drank up and left the pub.

Bob thumbed through the post, leaving the one marked 'US Postal Service' to one side and discarded what he knew to be junk mail or begging letters. He then opened the two remaining letters, which also turned out to be of little interest, as they were both bills for some work that he had done to the skittle alley some days earlier. He recognised that the American letter was from Mac as it was addressed to Linda and so he took it through to her immediately as he knew that she always cherished letters from her son and would down tools straight away to read it. So entering the kitchen, Bob called out, "Letter from America darling." He handed it over and returned to the bar to serve a couple of lads who had come in from doing some road works for the local council.

Mac had gone to the US three years ago in answer to a recruitment drive made by a large hotel chain, who were looking for young Englishmen to train as future hotel managers. Fares were paid and a six months intensive course on all aspects of hotel management were given free. At the end of the course, Mac had excelled on all subjects and had been quickly promoted through many positions at several different hotels within the group over the past two years and was now Deputy House Manager at a prestigious hotel in New York.

Quickly opening the letter and reading the opening pleasantries, Linda came to a most exciting part that told her that Mac was entitled to a couple of weeks leave and that he was coming home for part of it. This was exciting news for Linda and she knew that Bob would be just as excited, as they had both got on so well together, even though Mac knew that Bob was not his real father.

However, the booking for Saturday evening soon returned to her mind and she thought that she had better go and see Charlie Burt the butcher and make some arrangements to get the meat part of the order underway. Bob agreed and told her to go now before Charlie closed for the day.

Charlie was just as surprised and happy as Linda had been to hear of the party that Jim's niece and her friends were going to have at the Dog and Whistle on Saturday evening. "Certainly I can," he told Linda when he heard what she wanted. "Tomorrow OK?" "Fine."

In the bar, without Linda, Bob was approached by yet another surprise. "Are you Bob," asked a woman of about the same age as Linda.

"Yes I'm Bob - and who may I ask are you?"

"My name is Maggie - a friend of Linda - is she about?"

For a moment, Bob's mind went blank as he tried to recall who this friend actually was. Then it clicked. "Are you the Maggie who is a cook at the Big House?" With a nod of her head, Maggie said, "Right first time Bob."

Bob explained that Linda was not here at the moment, but that she would not be long and asked if she could hang on for a while. Maggie agreed and explained that both she and Linda had agreed to meet up and have a chat about old times.

"That's fine, will you have a drink while you wait?" Maggie declined, saying, "I have just had my lunch and slipped out before having to prepare things for afternoon tea at the Big House."

Bob could hear that Linda had returned through the backdoor and so he called out to her saying, "I've got a surprise for you in the bar." Linda was about to say that she could not stomach any more surprises today, when after walking through into the bar she was delightfully surprised to see Maggie smiling back at her.

"Oh how pleased am I to see you Maggie, you have obviously now met my Bob." Maggie gave a firm nod towards Linda as she was invited to go back through into the kitchen with Linda.

Maggie explained to Linda that she had only popped in to renew their acquaintance as promised and had to get back to the Big House as the Lord and his family were preparing to leave tomorrow for a two weeks stay at their villa in Spain. "So, does that mean that you have time off while they are away?" Linda asked. "Yes and No" came the reply, "I still have to cook for the staff who will not be travelling with the family, but that only involves breakfast and lunch. I do have the rest of the day off, so I could come and see you later in the day while they are away." Wham! In to Linda's head came the thought that here could be the answer to her logistics problem on Saturday evening.

"Maggie, will you be free on Saturday evening to come and help me cook for a party of 18 people - I'll willingly pay you for it?"

Linda went on to explain the predicament that she had landed for herself in taking such a large booking without the staff to handle it, but also how much it meant to the survival of the pub. After talking over what was needed and how it could be handled by two cooks, Maggie willingly agreed to come and help her long standing friend with the problem.

"Look Linda, I do not want any payment as I have a well paid job at the Big House, but I do have a young girl working for me who is an experienced waitress and is saving to get married. If you have no objections I could bring her along to do the serving and clearing up afterwards, if you would be willing to pay her a few bob in return."

"Maggie, what an excellent idea, please bring her as it will mean that you and I would not have to chase around on the serving side of things. It will then allow us both to concentrate on the cooking."

Maggie agreed and told Linda that she would have to go now, but would return on Saturday at about 4.00pm with young Jill. "Jill Wilson that is, you will like her Linda," Maggie said, as she left the kitchen and blew a kiss to Bob as she passed through the bar and out into the street.

"Blimey," said Bob to Linda, "She's a bit of a whirlwind." Linda nodded and said "That's the type of person one needs when there is work to be done."

Bob then went to close the door on the lunchtime session, when The Major popped his head in and told Bob that he had managed to round up a few new-ones to come for a skittles roll-up this evening. "Well thanks Terry, that's very kind of you - I hope that it will prove to be successful for your skittles team."

Having locked the door, Bob turned to Linda and said, "That has been quite a good morning love." To which she replied, "sure was and no doubt, **In Walked Some Money**."

5.   A Lead into a Deal

Hank left the village of Thimble Hardy and weaved his way up to the A30 road. He then headed in the direction of Salisbury, on his way to Guildford to attend a meeting with the owners of the business premises that he had identified as being of interest to his US client.

It was the remnants of an engineering company that had been stripped of its main products, when the new owners decided to relocate the manufacturing part of the company. The remaining facility, located on the outskirts of Sherbourne, consisted of several buildings that had been used as a machine shop and a very clean assembly area. It also had a large office block on two floors, a decent sized car park and extra land at the rear which had been granted planning permission for more light engineering use.

Hank thought to himself that it was a stroke of luck that he had made the acquaintance of The Major, who had inside information about the place. He knew that the new owners had tried to sell it off at the time of the original deal, but had no takers. The Major also knew that the premises was now being temporarily used as warehousing for a couple of local hauliers, in other words, the facility was now underused. All good information that would strengthen Hank's hand during negotiations with the owners later that day. Good old Terry Smith, he thought, I will see that he gets something out of this if the deal goes through OK.

Hank believed that he was in a very good negotiating position for his client, Ivan Framburg, CEO of the Boston based, **Aviation Pipework Company inc.** The owners appeared to be wanting to get rid of the premises, it was in a locality that did not stack up with the other parts of the new owner's business and it was surely not making a reasonable return from those two local hauliers. In other words, it was probably a burden on their other business.

So, Hank was feeling very pleased with himself as he drove into the car park of the owners in Guildford, but his experience in these matters told him to be careful about what information he should reveal, as once before in the past it had worked against him.

Back in Thimble Hardy, Bob was pleased to tell Linda that The Major had told him that several new skittle players would be coming in this evening. "Better fill up that sandwich cabinet then," Linda laughed. "Well, you never know," he answered. "What about those meat slices, have you any of those left in the larder?" To which Linda pointed out that they had all been sold when the Dunkers came earlier in the week and the pieman was not due again until next week.

"Well you could make some of your own," Bob suggested. "After all they are only like your meat pie, but a different shape and a lot smaller." Linda thought to herself, clever Bob, that's a good idea, why am I buying pies off someone else when the events of this week indicated that people just loved my steak and ale larger version.

"OK, you asked for it, but don't blame me if you still have them in your cabinet at the end of the evening," Linda quipped back at him, laying any blame that may come out of it firmly in Bob's court.

Then, as the bar was closed for the afternoon, Linda set about making a few of her own meat slices and told Bob to go into their living room and read the letter from Mac, as it was all good news.

Bob was pleased to read how well Mac had got on since he went to America. The hotel chain that sponsored him in the first place had seen his potential and aptly rewarded him for the studying and dedication that he had put into it. And now he was coming home to see them both. Sheer joy for his parents. As usual, Bob then sat in the big armchair and after dozing off for a while, he awoke to the smell of freshly baked meat slices.

Walking into the kitchen, he saw a dozen of them sitting on an oven tray and Linda asked if he would transfer them onto a couple of large plates, while she cleared up the kitchen. Bob was pleased to help and did as he was asked, then went through to the bar.

Linda then went to move the plates to the other side of the kitchen and took up a worried look when she saw that there were only eleven meat slices looking back at her. "I could swear that I made twelve," she uttered to herself. "Then, maybe not - or has a thief walked off with one?" Looking into the bar, she had a clear view of a contented looking thief licking his lips and wiping crumbs from his shirt front.

The first person to arrive into the pub on this Wednesday evening was Terry Smith - The Major, who announced to Bob that he would like to get the practice games started as soon as possible so that everyone who turned up would get an opportunity to show their worth.

He did not have to wait long for the Reverend Timmy and the verger arrived early with another young man. Bob and Terry greeted them and they all settled in with a drink each.

"So who's your colleague then vicar?" asked The Major, just as Linda came into the bar from the kitchen with a tray of warm meat slices to put on the counter hot plate.

Timmy replied, "This is my younger brother Gerald, or Gerry as we all call him. He's also a man of the cloth and about to take up his first appointment." Terry and Bob greeted Gerry with a handshake and a "Nice to see you."

Linda asked him if had he come far. To which Gerry replied, "Bristol - if you call that far." Linda considered that to be far and asked him had he eaten this evening. "No, not since lunchtime," came the reply. "Then what about a lovely meat slice to stop the worms from biting?" Linda said, seizing the opportunity to introduce her new products to somebody whilst they were still very hot. "Well that would be fine," Gerry replied and duly purchased one.

Not to be outdone by his younger brother, Timmy also bought one and the two of them looked very contented with a drink in one hand and a meat slice in the other. With the smell of beef wafting under their noses, both the verger and The Major also decide to join in with a purchase of their own.

Bob, thinking four from eleven only left seven to sell later on and jokingly said to Linda with a look that suggested butter would not melt in his mouth, "There you are love, I thought that eleven would not be enough, you should have cooked a round dozen."

Knowing the game that Bob was playing, she gave him a loving kick up the backside and said, "You're not as smart as you may look young man, as I did have another dozen in the oven that were out of sight when the thief came earlier."

More people began to arrive and Bob became very busy pulling pints of this and that. Linda came to help with the drinks and also drew people's attention to the range of sandwiches and meat slices that were available for this special occasion, as she put it. The Major then called that it was time to get started and suggested that they all should move into the backroom and get on with the evening of practice.

Clearing the glasses and plates from the various parts of the bar, following the disappearance of the bulk of the people to the skittle alley, Bob suddenly asked of Linda. "Did you see Tony among the crowd?" Linda did not have to think too long for her answer, for she had already noticed that he had not turned up this evening and guessed that it was because of her talk with him earlier. Putting on a slightly unconcerned manner, she answered Bob in the negative. "Funny, he has not been here at all today and that's unusual for him," Bob said with concern.

Their conversation was soon put to one side when in walked P C Willis, the local policeman. "Evening constable," Bob said wondering why he had arrived. "Hello landlord, just popped in to see what is going on, as there are more cars than usual parked outside and all along the High Street - a couple of tractors too."

Bob explained the reason and asked if the vehicles were causing a problem. "No they are not blocking anybody's driveway, so all's OK. But, how come I was not invited to take part in this skittles then?" Bob was relieved to learn that he was not in trouble with the law and even more happy knowing that the constable's question could be passed over to The Major. "Better that you have a word with Terry Smith about that, as I am not involved with the organising," Bob said smiling to himself. "Oh, OK I'll speak to him when we next meet." Then with a sniff of his nose, P C Will said, "What's that nice meaty smell?" Bob explained that it had come from Linda's meat slices that had all been gobbled up by the folks in the skittle alley. "That's a pity, it has made me feel quite hungry."

Bob, with a thought that he may need the Bobby's help one day, said "I am sure that I could find one just for you."

As Hank left the car park in Guildford, happy that all had gone exceptionally well in the negotiations and that he had a 'Letter of Intent' duly signed by a representative of the owners and also by himself, he decided to head straight to his client's solicitors in London. At the first sign of a convenient place to make a telephone call, Hank stopped and asked to speak to the senior partner of Lincoln, Jones & Lewis.

Having previously been made aware that Hank would contact him later in the day, David Lincoln was pleased to hear that negotiations had gone so well and that Hank was on his way to meet with him.

"I'll wait until you arrive Mr Burnett and as your client will be in his Boston office we can have a three-way conversation to decide on the next course of action," David Lincoln advised. "That's fine, but in the meantime, can you give Ivan Framburg a call to update him with the facts so far?" David Lincoln agreed and Hank returned to the big red car and made his way through the heavy traffic to Brook Street, W1.

David Lincoln had acted for Ivan Framburg on a previous cross-Atlantic deal and was no stranger to the property laws involving both countries. However, he needed to acquaint himself with details of the company that now owned the remains of the Dorset engineering works before Hank would arrive.

He found that the vendors were a major player in the mechanical engineering world and that the property arm of their solicitors was run by Arnold Goldberg, 'Goldie', a long time friend from university days, where he and David were members of the same jazz band. David thought that this was a stroke of luck, as it would cut out any of the usual nonsense when two parties spent time and money weighing each other up. He then made the call to Boston as Hank had requested and found Ivan Framburg absolutely delighted with the initial news that Hank had briefly given to David on the phone.

"I knew that I could trust Hank to come up trumps," said Ivan. "You will like him David, he has a lot of experience in these matters and worth every cent of his fee." The two then agreed to speak again later after Hank had arrived with more details.

When The Major called a halt on the evening practice session, the three church men and a few others left the pub immediately, all happily waving goodbye to Bob and Linda. Others, most of whom had been happy with their performance, hung around in the bar for more drinks and whatever food that remained in the glass cabinet and on the hot plate.

Bob enquired of The Major as whether or not he thought that the evening had been successful.

"Absolutely," came the reply from a very happy Terry Smith. "I am sure that we have sparked some better competitiveness among the regulars and I have found some others who will challenge them for their place before very long, assuming that I can retain their interest in the game."

Bob, drawing Terry a free pint, thanked him for his dedicated interest in the skittles team and for how his efforts had brought some more business into the pub.

Terry replied with the comment, "It just shows what talent there is in the village, when you dig around."

As the last customer drifted out of the pub, Bob followed him to the door and locked up at the end of a very interesting day.

6.   What has happened to Tony

Next morning, Linda, standing in the kitchen, took Mac's letter from her apron pocket and re-read it. She loved every word that he had written, then realised that it would be less than a week before Mac would arrive. She drew Bob's attention to that fact and told him that the spare bedroom would need to be cleared of the odds and ends that had been dumped in there over the past few months. Bob agreed to do that when he could find time, but the more important thing on his mind at the moment was opening the pub, for yet another challenging Thursday morning session.

Soon through the door came 84 year old Sarah Blunt from the cottage adjoining the pub, which was also owned by the brewery. She explained that she had not come to drink, but had some news to tell him and Linda. Bob invited Sarah to take a seat near the kitchen while he fetched his wife.

Sarah's husband had been a long serving beer salesman for the brewery and following his death, the brewery had agreed to let Sarah continue to live in the cottage for a nominal rent, fixed as part of her husband's pension. The rent contributed very little and in consequence the brewery did little to the upkeep of the cottage.

Seeing an impression of a bricked-up door on the adjoining wall between the pub and the cottage, Bob had always thought that the cottage may well have been part of the pub in years gone-bye.

"Hello Sarah, nice to see you so early in the day - how are you?" enquired Linda in a very loving way. "I'm OK for the time being Linda, but I'm not getting any younger and I find even the simplest of tasks harder to do these days." Bob quipped in with an offer to help if she ever needed it. "Yes, I know Bob, but my family are always on to me about moving to a more manageable place and I have accepted that the time has come when I should make that move." Sarah went on to explain to her neighbours that she had decided to move into a bed sitting-room with her eldest daughter who lives in Bournemouth. "As she is also a widow, we will be company for each other and besides, the sea air should do me good."

Both Bob and Linda expressed their surprise and asked when this was to take place. "Oh, I have given the brewery a month's notice, but I expect to be out sometime next week." Again Bob asked if there was anything that he could do for her, but Sarah informed him that her other daughter and son-in-law were coming to stay over the weekend and that they would be helping to sort out the items that she would be taking with her. "However Bob, there will be many bits of furniture that I will no longer need and you can have first choice, after the family have had their pick." Bob chuckled at that remark, but did not want to appear rude, so he thanked Sarah for her generous offer and left the rest of the conversation to Linda.

Into the pub came Georgie Bailey, son of Benny and grandson of old Stanley Bailey, who had started a small engineering works in Quarry Lane back in 1930. Stanley was originally a Blacksmith forging parts for gates and railings, but had ventured into repairing machinery for the many farmers located around Dorset and Somerset. His skills brought him more business success during the second world war, when iron work was needed for the army at Blandford Camp and other military establishments about the area.

Georgie's father, Benny, had entered the business from the day he left school and carried on the work when Stanley died. Georgie was now also well established in the business of working iron under the company name of Stanley Bailey & Son Iron Works Ltd.

However now in 1968, the work undertaken by 'The Iron Works', as everyone referred to it as, had changed due to the fact that most farm machinery manufacturers were offering longer warranties and providing their own service teams to carry out such work.

Benny, and now Georgie, were doing less farm work and had expanded into doing pipework and support framework as sub-contractors for the many factories that had sprung up around the area. Georgie had learnt welding at technical college to add to his skills, which had opened up the scope of service that the small company could offer. However, he could not master the specialised skill of welding stainless steel and so always had to turn that sort of work away.

"Hello Georgie, what brings you into a pub when you should be working?" Bob joked with him. "I'm looking for Tony Button and I know that I can always find him loafing around your pub," Georgie said, knowing Tony well, as he was married to his sister, Lucy Ann.

"You know Georgie, I haven't seen Tony for at least forty-eight hours, I hope that there's nothing wrong with him," Bob said in a slightly concerned manner. "If there is, I'll have to get my missus to have a look at him," laughed the iron man, who's wife was the District Nurse. "Guess he wouldn't want his sister looking inside his shirt," came the reply from Bob.

"Anyway, if he ain't here then he must be somewhere else - if you see him, tell him I need a word, will you?" Georgie said, as he made his way back out of the pub door. Bob agreed to pass on the message when he next saw Tony and then went over to pass the same request to Linda as he saw her helping Sarah get up from the table.

Next to pop in was the Reverend Timmy and his young brother Gerry. "Just wanted to say Bob, how much we both enjoyed last evening and I think that I have a good chance of getting into that team, with a bit more practice. Bob was delighted to hear that and was about to ask them what they wanted to drink, but before he could get the words out, Timmy said, "Sorry we can't stay, must be off and get on with the job, otherwise people will think that we vicars only work one day a week."

The rest of the day was vey quiet in the pub and when Bob and Linda retired for the evening, they both remarked about the fact that Tony had not been in the pub for over two days now.

Linda said, "It is obviously the result of my talk with him about getting back to work. "You are probably right love," Bob agreed. "It's amazing how when you think that you are doing someone a good turn, it ends up backfiring on you," Linda added.

Both were troubled by that fact as they struggled to sleep.

Bob's thought was still on the absence of Tony and also that he must remember to pass on Georgie Bailey's request.

Bright and early on Friday morning, Linda had but one thought in her mind, which was to get to the butcher for the meat that she needed for the large party on Saturday evening.

Hank, in a London hotel, was also up early in order to get to Gatwick Airport and return the big red car before catching the mid-day flight to New York.

Linda's situation was solved by Charlie showing her some prime stewing steak that he had sorted from his cold store only half an hour beforehand. That made her happy by the fact that now she had the ingredients to hand, she could get on with the planning of the meal.

Bob, having finished his breakfast, got the bar ready and unlocked the door in time for his first customer. As he stood in the doorway, taking his usual glance along the High Street, he saw nurse Lucy Bailey pull up in her car on the opposite side of the street, about to enter a house to check on a patient.

"Hello Bob," she called across to him. "Georgie asked me to check if you had seen Tony yet?" Bob thought that it was an odd question, when all she had to do was speak to her parents on the matter.

"No, I was believing that you could give me some news on that," Bob called back to her, hoping that some other bit of news may emerge about her brother.

"Sorry, can't help, must get on as I have a patient waiting to see me," she replied.

Bob turned and went back into the pub, none the wiser on the subject of why Tony was missing.

7.   Hank Recollects on his Visit

As Hank settled into his first class seat on the plane, he got out the brief that Ivan Framburg had given to him.

The facility should be close to the Westland Aircraft Company.

It should be of a particular size, with room for expansion.

It must have permission for medium type engineering work.

It must have adequate lock-up security to protect government work.

Easy access for large vehicles and a good sized carpark for staff cars.

The site is to be cleared of all rubbish at point of purchase.

Any remaining engineering machinery should be included in the deal.

It should be clear of any sub-letting arrangements.

The list went on with further minor clauses, but Hank knew that he had got all the major requirements covered, thanks to the help that he had received from The Major.

Although he had extracted a price from the vendor that was higher than that which Ivan had hoped to pay, it was in his own opinion, a fair price for what was on offer. Anyway, it would be up to his client to settle that when he would accompany Hank back to England in a few weeks time.

Hank recalled how incredibly lucky he was to have had the professional knowledge and assistance of Terry on an assignment that he knew would be generally acceptable to his client and, if all went well, be very financially rewarding to him.

Now well above the clouds and heading west off Southern Ireland, Hank put his paperwork away and settled back with a 'scotch on the rocks'. He allowed his mind to shut down on his business activities and drifted back to his previous few days around north Dorset.

The first person to reappear in his recollection was, of course, Linda.

Without doubt, he had fallen in love with her, or maybe he had fallen in love with the idea of being in love with the lovely Linda. That way, it was less of a crime than trying to steal another man's wife.

The flirting that went on between the two of them was very enjoyable and for Hank, it had a semblance of times when he and his pal had been camped around the same area back in 1944.

Then suddenly he gasped aloud. **"Yes that's it!"**

"Linda Tanner from the dances at Milborne Port during the few weeks before my buddy and I were shipped off to France." He spoke aloud, causing other passengers to curiously look at him

Two American Lieutenants and two local girls, what fun we had together - all spoilt by the death of my buddy on the second day that we arrived in France.

Hank frowned, chuckled and frowned again, then he thought, no, this would be too much of a coincidence if today's Linda turned out to be the same Linda from 1944. He searched his mind for any clues that would make the assumption to be correct, but as time had passed his detailed knowledge of those days had faded.

The face was not as he remembered, the hair was not of the style from those days, but the height and build gradually came back to him and could well fit, then there were the eyes and the smile.

Yes, the eyes and smile are the link, I'm sure of that, he thought.

Then Hank suddenly felt a change of gear in his mind; that guy Tony!

Could Tony be her son? They had a very happy affection for each other. If so, then this could be the end of the search that he had always harboured since leaving the British shores back in 1944.

Deep in thought, he was still trying to fathom things out when a hostess appeared in front of him asking what he would like for lunch.

"Meat, Fish, hot or cold?" he half-heard her say, but his mind was still dwelling on his previous thoughts of Linda and Tony.

"Oh, I'll have some cold fish and salad please. Do you have roll-mop hearing?"

"Certainly Sir," replied the glamorous and efficient stewardess. "Would you like another drink?"

Jokingly Hank said, "Sure, do you have Scrumpy?"

"Scrumpy? sorry Sir I'm not familiar with that drink. Is it a brand of American whisky?" the girl enquired.

Hank was amazed at that remark and asked if she was English.

"Yes Sir, I come from Manchester."

Hank then told her that in that case she was forgiven for not knowing the West Country's most famous drink.

"It's made from fabulous cider apples, grown on the best soil in England," he spoke with great authority.

"Varieties of apples such as, Lady's Finger, Pig's Nose, Yellow Willy, or Tremlett's Bitter," repeating verbatim what Bob had told him just a few days earlier.

The girl was quick to pick up on the word 'Apples' and linked it straight away with cider.

"Certainly Sir, we do have cider, but unfortunately not of the Scrumpy brand."

Hank let the matter drop and settled for a glass of orange juice with his lunch, but still puzzled about the existence of Linda and Tony.

He also recalled the terrible death of his Buddy after they had landed on Omaha beach on the 6th June 1944. Hank then thought how pleased his Buddy would have been to know that a girl from those days that they had spent in England had possibly reappeared in 1968.

The memories came flooding back.

8.   A Quiet Day

Friday mornings at the Dog & Whistle pub were traditionally quiet, due to the fact that the locals usually did their weekend shopping away from the village. Some of the towns in north Dorset had *Market Days,* that attracted people away from places like Thimble Hardy.

A few customers came to the pub, but did not hang around beyond the half glass of whatever they wanted. The two door minders, did arrive and Bob was again grateful for their purchase of two bottles of stout.

To avoid getting into conversation with the two ladies and their enquiring questions that they would no doubt throw at him on any subject that they needed information, Bob went through to the kitchen to see if Linda needed any help.

After a few minutes, he heard Winnie call out that someone had entered the pub, so Bob quickly returned to the bar and to his surprise found Tony waiting for him.

"Hello stranger," Bob greeted him. "So where have you been hiding yourself lately?"

Tony explained that he was at first unhappy that Linda should have tried to push him back to work and he needed time away to think things over. He went on to explain that he had also been approached by Tommy Chant to go to the Five Bells pub, as the landlord needed darts players of his capability.

"So, how did you get on there then?" Bob enquired, knowing that the invitation would have been a complete lie.

"Absolute rubbish, they don't need any more players and the Landlord denied all knowledge of such a request," Tony told Bob, whilst accepting that he had been the subject of a prank.

"However Bob, my time away has taught me how much I appreciate your friendship and that Linda was only trying to help me as a friend." Bob was sorry to hear of the prank, but pleased to think that Tony had spent time thinking about his future and offered him a drink as a form of consolation.

When Linda came through into the bar and saw Tony standing talking to Bob, she was so pleased that she greeted him with a very warm grasp of his hands. Stopping short of actually giving him a kiss, she hung onto him and asked where he had been and if he was all right.

Before he could answer Linda whispered to him, "come through to the kitchen and then we will both be out of earshot of certain people."

Standing up close to each other, Tony repeated what he had already told Bob and expressed his thanks for her advice earlier in the week. This thrilled Linda that he had actually thought more about it than he had shown at the time, and now she actually gave him a hug and a loving kiss on his cheek.

Linda's mind then suddenly turned to the rotten prank that Tommy Chant had played on Tony and thinking deeper, she knew that the nasty person had used it purposely to get one back on herself. But she could not let the real reason be known to Tony, or to Bob.

Having remembered the request that his sister's husband had made, Bob went through to the kitchen and told Tony that Georgie Bailey was looking for him.

"Thanks Bob," was his reply. "I have already spoken to Georgie and I have agreed to do some stainless steel welding for him on a large job that he has taken on from a cheese factory in Somerset."

Both Bob's and Linda's eyes lit up with delight, on hearing the news that Tony had at last brought himself round to getting back to doing what he had been so good at, before he was laid off from the factory.

"So, when do you start on this?" Bob enquired.

"Straight away - and that's another thing that I have come to tell you. I won't be able to help out in the pub during the daytime for a while."

Bob was not worried about that as the demand for beer during the daytime could easily be handled by himself, but Linda found herself in two minds. Pleased to hear about the work, but fretful at the thought that she would not be seeing Tony around so much.

Tony drank up and left by the backdoor so that the two doorkeepers would not have their gossip bank increased by more than they had already obtained.

Bob went back to busy himself behind the counter, when in came pig farmer Jim, who was treated to a warm greeting from the landlord.

"Hello Jim, so you've come without your pigs today?"

"Hello landlord, can't afford to buy em a drink everyday, can I," Jim laughingly quipped back. "But I need a drink myself, cos I've bin shovelling dung all morning."

Bob pulled him a pint of Scrumpy, while Winnie and Madge quickly latched onto the farmer's comment, with Madge saying, "Smells like it too - look at the state of his boots." To which Winnie replied, "Yes, the smell's enough to tell ee what ee's bin dooin a mile away."

Leaning on the counter, Jim turned his back on the two ladies and asked Bob what happened to the man in the big red car.

"What do you mean, what happened to him?"

"Well has he gone back to America, or has Linda got him locked up in a cupboard out the back?" The farmer went on to continue the banter.

"Well Jim, as you have been saying that he's a friend of yours, I would have thought that you could have filled me in with a bit more information on that score."

Holding the back of his hand up to his mouth, Jim tried to provoke Bob even more when he said, "my friend Hank did tell me quite a bit, but I'm sworn to secrecy in case them Ruskies get to know about it."

Thinking to himself, Bob wondered just what the 'Old Devil' did know about Hank's visit to the locality earlier in the week - after all he did spend some time with Hank over the meal the other evening. Then he dismissed the thought, knowing that Hank would not trust Jim with a secret that the Russians would like to know about.

Winnie and Madge could not keep up with the frivolous banter and no doubt bits from each subject would become incorrectly intertwined, when repeated in the village later.

9.   The Party Meal

Bang on 4.00pm, Maggie and Jill the waitress, arrived on Saturday to help Linda with the preparation for the extra work that would be required for the group meal later in the evening.

After introduction to Jill, Linda suggested that the three of them should take a seat in the bar area and talk over what needed to be done, in what order, and who was going to handle each part.

Linda outlined the three course menu that Mary had selected within the agreed price.

An Initial free glass of wine for each person to be served at the table.

> *Duck Pâté with toast*
> *Steak & Ale Pie*
> *Fruit Salad*
> *Coffee, or tea.*

Additional drinks to be bought and paid for at the bar.

Both Maggie and Jill understood the menu and Bob was called in to ensure that he also understood what was to happen.

Without further delay, Linda and Maggie went into the kitchen to get on with the preparation and cooking of the food, whilst Bob and Jill stayed seated to talk about the table layout and the serving of the wine. Bob was immediately impressed with Jill's knowledge of what was needed to be done in that department and told her so.

"Oh, thanks Mr Smart, it is something that I do every day for His Lordship at the Big House," Jill softly, but confidently explained.

"Of course, I was forgetting that you have been trained at such a high level - and by the way, I'm Bob," the landlord said.

Then Bob manhandled the tables and chairs into position and Jill set out the cutlery and glasses in a manner that would be fit for royalty.

When Bob looked at the finished layout, he could not help remarking that he only hoped that the customers would appreciate her work.

In the kitchen, it was agreed that Linda would be totally in charge of the preparation and the cooking of the pie, while Maggie would handle the starters and the deserts. That way it would be clear as to what actions each had to take and then they would not get in each others way.

Linda had first thought that she would cook three large pies, each capable of producing six portions to cater for the eighteen people that Mary had said would be attending. Then she decided that she would cook four pies just in case the party had anyone extra turn up, and anyway that would allow the surplus to be sold over the counter in the bar if not needed.

Maggie asked her if she had enough room in her oven to produce that amount of pie to be served all at the same time. To which Linda replied, "My main oven will take two of them and my old second oven will take another one. Then, if I have the fourth pie ready, it can be quickly put in the main oven when the first one comes out. It might mean that someone may have to wait a little longer to be served, but Maggie I'll take that chance."

Maggie was impressed with the way that Linda had thought things out, but then remembered just how Linda had always satisfied the large number of people wanting food at the same time in the factory all those years ago.

Bob and Jill were still busy in the bar area arranging where the wine would be situated, away from the general area that his normal customers would be using. Both could hear the noise of pots and pans being put to work in the kitchen and were glad that they were not part of it.

"So, where are you from Jill?" Bob asked her when he could see that she had almost come to the end of her layout work.

"I was born in Newhaven, East Sussex, but my parents moved to Templecombe when I was very young, because of my father's work on the railway. After leaving school, I was trained in hotel work at Bournemouth College of Further Education, before taking up full-time employment at the Big House."

As 5.30 was approaching and time to open up for the start of another Saturday evening at the pub, Bob asked Jill if she would like a drink and maybe a sandwich before the start of the evening proceedings.

Thinking that it may be some time before she would get the chance to eat, she accepted Bob's offer with an orange juice and a packet of crisps.

Bob then excused himself from her company and opened up the main door and saw a lovely sunset glimmering over the rooftop of the church, interspersed only by a few noisy rooks flying high before settling in the old elms for the night.

He did not have to wait long to see his first customers - farmer Jim and his wife Betty all dressed up for a night out.

"Hello Landlord," Jim said in his usual chirpy fashion. "Just popping in to see that all is OK for the meal being arranged for my brother's daughter and her friends, before we do go on to a show at the theatre in Yeovil."

Bob explained that all was fine and thanked him for the introduction of Mary to himself. "That's alright landlord, t'was that steak and ale pie that what done it for me. So if you'm going to give em the same, then they won't be disappointed, will um?"

Bob then showed the two of them how Jill had laid out the table for the very special occasion. Betty, in particular was very impressed and said to Jill, "I've not seen you here before, you're not from around here are you?"

Jill repeated what she had told Bob a little earlier about her past, to which Jim interjected by saying, "Well'm you be a Templecombe girl then, always thought that they were a bit more posh than us from around yer."

Bob could see that Jill was a little embarrassed at that statement and laughed it off by saying, "that's a real compliment Jill, coming from such a good judge of personalities as Mr Pearson here."

After that, both Jim and Betty wished the landlord and his new waitress a good evening and took off for the theatre.

Several other regulars started to arrive at the pub. 'Young Tom' Williams and his wife had arranged to meet Georgie and Lucy Bailey for a drink, before all four would be going on to a dance in Sherborne later in the evening.

Len Scott from the paper shop popped in for a pint and a game of darts with anyone who cared to play. Then in came Terry Smith, The Major, and his wife Joan. Terry explained to Bob that he thought that his presence would be wise in case any other potential new skittles players could be recruited.

Then, as the time approached 7.00pm, the birthday party began to arrive in several groups led by Mary Pearson, who waved to Bob in a very happy way. Bob greeted her and showed her the table layout for the dinner party. He also introduced her to Jill, who would be their host for the evening. Mary was pleased to hear that the evening appeared to be well planned and thanked Bob and Jill for their efforts so far.

Bob excused himself from the conversation, leaving Jill to continue welcoming the guests as they arrived, and he went through to the kitchen to let Linda and Maggie know that the party was beginning to assemble.

On his return, Bob started to satisfy the drinks orders that Jill had already taken and Jill invited those with drinks to take their seats at the table, so that the bar area would not be too congested.

Maggie was pleased to know that the guests had arrived on time and uncovered the duck pâté starters from the covering that she had put over them earlier, ready for when Jill would give her the nod that they would be needed.

"So, are you all here?" Jill asked Mary. "Yes we are eighteen as originally stated, but there is also a chance that two more may arrive later." Mary went on to say that the two in question were married and have a small child that needed to be seen safely to sleep before they could leave the babysitter to take charge.

Jill conveyed that information to the kitchen, then poured the wine along the row of seated guests to get the dinner party started.

The group consisted of twelve girls and six boys and from the excited and somewhat noisy chatter going on across the table, both Jill and Bob came to the conclusion that they were a gathering of ex-college pupils. Their subject matter centred around musical instruments, so the guess therefore, was that they had been together as budding musicians.

Emerging from the kitchen, Maggie quickly delivered the starters to Jill, who served them along the line. The excited chatter diminished rapidly for a while as they all began to eat.

As the chatter started up again, it was clear that some had finished their starters and so Jill and Maggie started to clear away the empty plates. Then all of a sudden the two late arrivals turned up to the cheers of those already seated.

After a welcome, Bob arranged a table with a glass of wine for each of them, whilst Jill informed the kitchen. Linda was delighted to hear the news as she had already removed one pie from the oven and replaced it with the fourth.

Jill introduced herself to the two newcomers and went back into the kitchen to collect their starters, only to hear Linda say, "Slow it down a bit Jill as I need time for that extra pie to cook through properly."

Jill was no stranger to that sort of request, as she had heard it many times from various kitchens when chefs were running late. So she continued to clear the plates from the main table before eventually serving the starters for the two sitting alone.

Linda, in the meantime, looking at the large steaming hot steak and ale pie fresh from the oven, scribed the top crust into six portions before scooping each out onto large dinner plates.

Maggie, in turn helped with the vegetables and the thick gravy that Linda had asked her to make by the jugful.

Jill then swung into action and delivered each plate to the six girls seated at the furthest end of the table from the kitchen. Then followed it up with the next six servings for the remaining girls and finally the last six for the boys.

Bob, who had also been recruited into the slowing down process, engaged the two late comers into conversation when he saw that they had finished their starters. "Have you come far?" he asked. Although not really interested to know how far, he followed it with, "would you like a drink from the bar?"

The compliments about the pie that came from those who had got stuck into it, caused even those who had not come into eat, to become very interested in what was going on at the table.

The Major and Joan, who had previously enjoyed the same experience when they were invited to join Hank earlier in the week, also extolled the virtues of the pie to others in the pub. This encouraged two lads who had joined Len Scott at the darts board, to ask if there was any available for them. So Bob went to ask the question of Linda, who happily agreed and the two lads were more than satisfied.

Bob, having applied his mathematical mind to the logistics of the fourth pie, worked out that two portions were for the the two late comers, two for the lads in the bar, leaving two more. One of which would certainly be available for himself later on. So he happily helped out with whatever Jill wanted him to do for the birthday party group.

Linda served up the two meals for Jill to deliver to the latecomers and set about clearing the pots and dishes, while Maggie prepared the third course for Jill to serve to all of the party group.

Spontaneously, a couple of the girls started to sing 'Happy Birthday' to the birthday girl, which encouraged all the others within the pub to enthusiastically join in.

Then, one of the lads, seeing an old piano at the far end of the bar, went over and started to play other slightly romantic songs for the birthday girl.

With the meal now finished and more drinks having been purchased from the bar, the piano player got into full swing with many old favourites such as *Nelly Dean, We'll be coming round the mountains, and Show me the way to home*. The latter ending what was agreed by all as a wonderful evening.

With all the customers gone from the pub and the singing continuing down the High Street, the wonderful smell of the Steak & Ale pie continued to linger in the bar. Bob knew that his portion of pie would be waiting for him as soon as he could bring the pub back to normality. So he locked the pub door and set about collecting the glasses and moving the the tables that Jill had so quickly cleared.

All was quiet in the kitchen following the exhausting time that the three had experienced in catering for 20 people all at the same time. Linda was pleased that she had met Maggie quite by chance in the Co-op at Sherborne and even more pleased that Maggie had brought the experienced Jill along to help. Linda knew how to reward Jill with cash, for Maggie had told her that Jill was saving to get married. However she thought that there needed to be something more that she could do for the two of them.

Bob continued to tidy the bar area and could not wait to get at his share of the pie in the kitchen when he had finished. He also wondered what was going to happen to the one remaining portion, better to eat it than to throw it away, he thought, licking his lips at the thought.

So with the final glass put back into position, he hung the various tea towels over the handles of the beer pumps, as was his regular routine, and turned out the lights before making his way to the kitchen and his late night meal.

As he turned into the kitchen, he was hit full in the face with the sight of both Maggie and Jill seated at the kitchen table and tucking into the last two remaining portions of Linda's wonderful pie!

Bob was so disappointed at seeing what he thought was his by rights, being enjoyed by the two women. He was lost for words and his eyes hunted around the kitchen looking to see if by chance, there was another portion available to him.

Linda broke the silence saying, "Bob what a wonderful job these two have done for us this evening and I am sure that you will be more than happy that they also should be enjoying the two remaining portions of pie - after all they would have only been thrown away."

10.   Preparing for Mac

By long standing tradition, the Dog and Whistle public house in the North Dorset village of Thimble Hardy had always remained closed on Sundays. The Landlord, Bob Smart and his wife Linda considered that Sunday was their day-off and they had always tried to do things together away from the pub.

This Sunday was no different, but Linda reminded Bob that her son Malcolm, Mac to everyone, would be arriving home from the USA later in the week and that together they should take the opportunity to get his room ready for his stay. He agreed and after breakfast they set about clearing the room of the many seldom used items that had accumulated in there.

Bob had always considered that most of the items would be of use one day, but Linda thought that it was a load of junk and should have been discarded ages ago - empty bottles, several mirrors, chairs with broken legs, part of a bicycle, an old standard lamp, damaged toilet signs. In less than an hour, Bob had removed all that he considered he was responsible for and left the final clearing up to his wife.

Linda was pleased to see that the room had at last returned to a habitable state, to which she would put the finishing touches over the next few days. So, feeling pleased with the outcome and as it was a nice day, they both decided to take a 'Run down to the coast', where Linda bought them a nice lobster lunch.

In church that Sunday morning, Terry and Joan Smith were amazed to hear the Rev Timmy announce during his village notices that the pub was looking to recruit more skittles players and that experience was not necessary. He went on to say that he was hoping to muster a church team, perhaps to challenge the pub first team in due course.

This brought a muffled snigger from some members of the congregation, but The Major thought that it was a good suggestion and if captained by Rev Timmy, it would dampen some of the strong language that often prevailed in the skittle alley. Although the Vicar had once been heard to utter a strong word himself, when he fired at a single pin and missed it by a whisker.

Postmistress Connie arrived early with the post on Monday morning and in true village style, pointed out that there was one from America. "Yes Connie, it's from Mac and he's coming home later this week," Linda replied, letting her know that she was clearly in charge of her own post. With that, Connie bid farewell and rode off.

As usual, Linda ripped open the envelope to eagerly read what Mac had to say about his expected arrival.

I will be flying overnight on Friday, landing Heathrow Saturday morning and will catch the train to Sherborne. Will phone from Waterloo to tell you the time of the train. Can you collect me from the rail station?

That was all that Linda was interested in, the rest was irrelevant.

Mac was registered at birth as Malcolm Arnold Tanner and the space for his father's name had been left blank. He was given Linda's family surname and her father's first name as his middle name. He had never had reason to change it, even though some people often called him Malcolm Smart after his mother married Bob Smart.

When it was known that Linda was expecting, her father went berserk and demanded to know who the father was, but Linda stood her ground and firmly refused to let it be known.

Her mother on the other hand, consoled her and had never attempted to enquire, believing that Linda would eventually disclose the information in her own time.

Both parents suspected that it was Tommy Chant, as Linda had been seeing him on a regular basis before he went away to do his National Service in the army. However, he did come home on leave occasionally, her father angrily told his wife. A couple of other boy's names had been mentioned at the time, but both parents dismissed them as being too respectable.

There were, of course, the American GI's stationed all around the area and who frequently attended the village dances.

Then, what about someone at the factory where Linda worked? This was another theory that Linda's father held for several years prior to his death.

He often said to Linda's mother, it could have been a married man, maybe her boss who could have threatened her with the sack if she ever told. Perhaps that would explain why Linda had never given Mac the true surname that he was entitled to.

Linda's father retained his anger over the situation for years and in consequence had never really taken to Mac. Her mother though, had the highest affection for him and helped Linda through the painful years when people in the village gossiped with false impressions of what actually happened when Mac was conceived.

With her father now 'Gone On' and her mother in a care home, the unhappy problem surrounding Mac's birth had calmed down and Linda believed that she was now in complete control of the situation.

Monday morning was quiet in the pub with only the two regulars by the door and the two council workers taking a break from the road works that they had been working on for the past week.

Then into the bar came Fred Bennett a dairy farmer from the small hamlet of Lower Thimble situated on the outskirts of Thimble Hardy.

"Well hello Fred, nice to see you again. What brings you to this part of woods?" Bob welcomed him as an occasional customer.

"Well as it's time for a break, I thought that I would see if old Jim Pearson was telling the truth about your hot Steak & Ale pie," Fred explained.

So Jim was spreading the word beyond the village and it was a pity that the item was not available on a Monday lunchtime to satisfy this new client.

Bob explained that the real thing was only available on Friday and Saturday evenings. "But I do have a smaller tasting version you can try as a sample," pointing to the four meat slices sitting on the hot plate." Fred accepted the explanation and bought two and washed them down with a pint of farmer's Scrumpy.

Happy with what he had tasted, Fred bid farewell and said that he would be back on Friday evening. "With the Missus," he said, within earshot of the two sitting by the door.

Early in the evening the eight men from the skittles team assembled before going off together to play an away match. They were soon replaced by Timmy and a bunch of people whom he announced were the response to his announcement in church the day before. Bob was unaware of the announcement, but was thrilled with Timmy's enthusiasm for the game.

"I am sure Bob, that we can get a good team together made up entirely of church members and perhaps next season we can enter a league that plays on a different evening to your pub team."

Bob could not believe what he was hearing and thought how good that would be for his trade. Then, surveying the group of people with the vicar and the verger, he saw two women. The verger's daughter Elizabeth Chant, who was a gardener at the Big House and married to Tommy Chant's elder brother. The other was unknown to Bob, but Timmy introduced her as Esme Roberts, accountant to His Lordship, also at the Big House.

Bob looked at Timmy and asked if they had come to support the team, to which Timmy replied, "No, they are going to be part of my team." Bob hesitated for a couple of seconds and said, "women in your team?" To which Timmy replied, "why not? they've got two arms and legs just like the men and they are all God's Children."

Bob had no reply to that and listened to Timmy telling them about the rules of the game.

"Skittles is a game played between 2 teams, each consists of 8 players, one of which is nominated as captain.
The team captain chooses the players bowling order, which must be retained throughout the game.
The game is split into an agreed number of 'LEGS' and each player has one turn per LEG."
And so he went on, having spent time learning the rules from scratch, within a week of playing his first game.

With the satisfaction that he had educated his team on the basic art of skittles, the enthusiastic Reverend put his hand in his pocket and bought them all a drink. "Don't expect this generosity every time," he laughingly announced to his followers.

Bob had informed Linda that farmer Fred Bennett had been recommended by 'Old Jim' to come to the pub to sample her Steak & Ale pie and that he was coming back on Friday evening with his wife for a meal.

"So did you take a booking then?" Linda asked. Whereupon Bob realised that he was asking Linda to do something that may backfire if Fred and his wife did not turn up.

Then the landlord, although feeling a bit foolish, saw an opportunity and replied with, "Well if they don't arrive, I'll eat the lot myself."

So as the week went by, Bob concentrated on trying to get others to also book for Friday evening and put up a notice saying -

Friday Evening is Steak & Ale Pie Night
Book now to avoid disappointment.

That did it, for several people booked and Bob added places for Fred and his wife and to be sure he added his own name to the list.

So, by the time Friday morning arrived, Linda had a list of 15 bookings and had ensured that Charlie the butcher could again supply the required meat. She had also contacted Maggie and Jill, who were willing to repeat the work of the previous Saturday.

As people came into the bar during the early part of the evening, Bob acknowledged those on his bookings list and after satisfying their drinks request, introduced Jill, who asked them to take a seat at one of the prepared tables. True to his word, Fred and his wife turned up and were pleased that places had been reserved for them.

Linda had made three pies, giving her 18 portions, leaving three that could be offered to anyone who had not booked. These were quickly sold when PC Willis turned up with his wife and daughter.

"So you got to know about our special night then Constable?" Bob asked. "Certainly landlord, there's not much that goes on around here that someone doesn't want to tell me about," came the reply.

When Jill had finished serving those seated, she informed Bob that it looks like one person had not turned up.

"Don't worry," Bob replied. - "He'll be here later!"

11.   Mac Arrives Home

Next morning, Linda, all excited, could not wait for the expected phone call from Mac telling her the time to meet him at Sherborne railway station. Bob would hold the fort in the pub and luckily Tony turned up. "Tony, can you come in this evening, as we are expecting Mac and I would like to let Linda have the evening alone with him?"

"Certainly Bob, it will be nice to see Mac again and I'll have a change from all that welding work that I have been doing for Georgie."

As Bob and Linda were getting ready to close the pub after the morning session, the phone rang with Mac informing the excited Linda that he would be arriving at Sherborne at 4.32pm. That would be perfect timing as he would be back home before the pub was due to open at 5.30pm for the Saturday evening.

Linda arrived in good time to meet the London train arriving at 4.32pm and as it stopped in the station she anxiously surveyed the small bunch of people alighting. Sure enough, she picked out Mac carrying a large suitcase and who looked so debonair.

Linda ran to him and flung her arms around him saying aloud, "Mac, my boy, welcome home." Mac hugged her and whispered "MOM."

Walking hand in hand to her car, Linda's first impression was of how her little boy had grown into a man during the three years that he had been away. Tall and elegant - and with a slight accent that clearly was no longer North Dorset.

Driving back to the pub, they both threw questions at each other that ranged through subjects from each other's health, to Mac enquiring about Bob and the pub business venture that they had both embarked on whilst he had been away. So much ground was covered over such a short journey.

Bob was eagerly waiting for them at the backdoor of the pub and, like Linda, he was amazed at how much Mac had matured in his presence. "Hi Dad - Bob." Mac was not sure how he should address him now that they had spent three years apart.

"Come on in and make yourself at home lad, we are so pleased to see you at last," Bob greeted him, whilst taking his large suitcase.

All three went through the narrow passage and into the pub sitting room, where in a typical English habit, Linda asked Mac if he would like a cup of tea. "Sure - I guess that it is what one should have when arriving in the land of tea-drinkers," Mac smiled at his mother.

Bob went through to the kitchen to put the kettle on and Linda enquired as to how long Mac would be staying at the pub.

"Well I'm in the UK for three weeks, but I would like to have some time sightseeing in London before I go back, so let's say about two weeks - is that OK?" Linda was delighted, as she had thought that he would probably only be in England for two weeks at the most.

Mac went on to say that his employers had been wonderful to him and now that he held a senior position in the company, he had certain privileges that he did not have in his early days with them.

"I have a beautiful apartment in the hotel with free room service whenever I want it. I have a nice new car, replaced every year. Also I have a very generous clothing allowance, which allows me to invest most of my salary each month."

Bob had heard most of the conversation and bringing the tea through jokingly said to Mac, "So I can't tempt you to come and work for me then?" to which Mac replied, "No, not until you make me a director of your brewery."

Over tea, Mac asked them both if they were happy that they had taken on the pub. To which Bob pointed out that it gave them a roof over their heads and they meet some very interesting people during the course of a week. Then suddenly he remembered that he should be opening up for yet another Saturday evening and left the two of them to enjoy the rest of the evening together.

Linda and Bob had both agreed that if anyone came in asking for hot food this evening, then he would have to politely inform them that due to other commitments hot food was unavailable, and hope that it did not turn anyone away.

Tony turned up on time and asked if Mac had arrived. "Yes he's in the sitting room with Linda, go and have a word with your old school mate before it gets busy."

The evening trade was slow to start with, but as it progressed several locals arrived asking if Mac had arrived. It seems that the postmistress, aided by two of her good friends, had made it known that another Yank was to be in the pub that evening.

One-by-one they all began to appear, Winnie and Madge, Jim and his wife, Georgie Bailey with Nurse Lucy, Charlie Burt the butcher, several from the skittles team and then Maggie and Jill from the Big House. "Blimey mate," Tony said to Bob. "You need to get a Yank in here every Saturday."

Bob could not believe that they had all come to see the homecoming of Mac, who they were calling 'A Yank'. He tried to explain to Winnie that Mac was the same Mac that left the village three years ago and that he is still English.

"Yeh, but he don't live yer anymore do ee, so that makes im a foreigner dun it?" Madge then added her two-pennyworth by saying, "I bet ee don't ave dirty boots like some others do round yer."

Both Bob and Tony were happy to see The Major appear, along with the Rev Timmy, for not only did it confirm their new friendship, but it served to break up the stupid conversation that the two old ladies were trying to prolong.

"Hello you two," Bob cheerily greeted them. "Skittles again?"

"No." Replied Terry Smith. "I've brought Timmy along to treat him to a good helping of Linda's Steak & Ale Pie as a thank-you for his valiant service in helping to round up so many new possibilities.

Bob and Tony looked at each other in a manner that portrayed immediately to The Major that something may not be to their liking and Tony stepped back to allow the senior man to explain that the pie was not available. Bob fumbled in his mind to remember what Linda had told him to say without turning them away. "Er, sorry gents, but due to other commitments we are unable to offer the pie today."

Terry and Timmy both expressed their disappointment, but took it all in good heart, saying that they would still have a glass of Scrumpy.

After cooking a light snack for the two of them, Linda and Mac continued their conversation in the sitting room, where Linda asked Mac if he had a girlfriend. "Oh no, I've been far too busy to get involved with girls," Mac answered confidently.

"Busy doing what?" asked Linda.

Mac explained that during the first six months that he was in America he was on a very demanding business course and when he passed out with his diploma, he spent the next six months learning the accounts side of the business. That was followed by working periods in every department for the next eighteen months, within several different hotels of the group.

"Finally, through more study, I have achieved the position of Assistant General Manager." Eager to learn more about his job, Linda asked, "So what does an Assistant General Manager do in this hotel?"

Mac explained that he had complete authority for the working of the hotel when the General Manager is off duty, which was mostly in the evenings, through the night, every other weekend and when his boss was away at company meetings. "You could say that I have to keep the managers of each department on their toes and ensure a smooth and profitable running to the satisfaction of our customers.

Linda was so proud to think that her little boy was now a 'Big Boss' and came out with more questions. "Did you learn about catering and buying the food?" "Yes, that was all part of my training, but the main concentration is always about the numbers."

"Numbers - what numbers.?" Linda innocently asked.

"Mom you should know what your numbers are if you are in any sort of business."

Mac went on to inform his mother that one should always know what ratios certain factors of the business are to each other and to be aware of whether they are changing up, or down - for the good or the bad.

Linda felt that she would need some training on that subject, but not today.

As the conversation in the bar appeared to be mainly on the subject of Mac being at home after three years away in America, Bob thought that it might be a good idea if Mac would put in an appearance and say hello to a few interested old friends. So, asking Tony to hold the fort, he went through to put his idea to the two of them.

Mac was immediately in agreement, but Linda thought that he was being put on show just to satisfy a few busybodies and in any case he would be wanting to get to bed after such a tiring day. However she did not want to disagree with Mac so soon after his arrival and so the two of them followed Bob back into the bar.

Well, the welcome that he got was if one of the Royal Family had suddenly appeared. Hand shakes all round, followed with a barrage of questions about his life in America, showed Mac the affection that the people of the village held for him.

Winnie said, "Ee's not like that other Yank that was here last week, ee's more friendly."

To which Madge added, "Yes and look at his nice clean shoes."

After sipping his way through a glass of warm beer, Mac accepted Linda's offer of her wanting to show him to his room and to get away from the milling mob in the bar.

With Mac gone from the bar and no Steak and Ale pie on offer this evening, most of the customers began to leave and the pub settled down to some form of normality. Tony collected the empty glasses and Bob took a pleasing look into the till.

"So, how did you get on with working for Georgie Bailey this week?" Bob asked Tony.

"Fine," came the answer. "I enjoyed working with Georgie, even though he's my brother-in-law, it's his old man, Benny, that I don't really care for. He's always on about how they did it when he was younger. Seems that he can't accept that repairing farm machinery is a thing of the past for his small company," Tony replied, having summed up the situation. "Working in the clean atmosphere of that Somerset cheese factory was a real eye-opener and a far cry to what Benny had been used to."

Having seen Mac safely to his room, Linda went back down to the sitting room to have another look at the lovely large brooch that Mac had bought as a present for her in New York.

On the way through the narrow passage, she turned to see Bob locking up the pub door for the night and in doing so she accidentally knocked the visitor's book from the hall table.

Picking it up she saw the last entry, **Harold Burnett, Junior (Hank)**

When seeing that, Linda's legs went weak, as she uttered aloud, "Junior Burnett - Junior Burnett, could it be the same Junior Burnett?"

She replaced the book when Bob came through and the two of them flopped into armchairs in the sitting room, to reflect on what was a very happy day for the landlord and his wife before retiring to bed.

Bob was soon asleep, but the name that Linda had seen in the visitor's book kept her awake. Harold Burnett, Junior (Hank), from which she had now shortened to Junior Burnett, a name from the wild and happy days when she and Maggie went dancing with the GI's back in 1944.

The military term 'G I' originally referred to 'Galvanised Iron' as used by the logistics services of the United States Armed Forces. It was then taken to mean 'Ground Infantry' and later was more frequently used as 'Government Issue', meaning anything belonging to the military.

Junior Burnett was just one of the group of Americans that had been camped out in the fields at the back of Milborne Port railway station when the American army had arrived in England in preparation for the D-Day attack on Hitler's army in 1944.

The names of several other GI's ran through her active mind, each in turn had a very happy memory, but the two young Lieutenants in their very smart uniforms remained uppermost for several reasons.

Over and over again, her mind continued to dwell on the names of Junior Burnett and his good looking, well mannered Buddy and she remembered how well they had danced together.

12.   Three Happy People

Next morning, as it was Sunday and also because she thought that Mac may be suffering from tiredness, she let him sleep on while she cooked breakfast for Bob and herself. "So what shall we do with Mac today then, my love?" enquired Bob.

Linda thought that it would be best to leave it to Mac to decide what he would like to do, if anything at all. But Bob did not want to waste the day and suggested that it would be wise for the three of them to do something together, as they may not get another chance, bearing in mind that one or the other would always have to be in the pub.

"OK" said Linda, "you choose - trains, boats, beach, country show, or some other interesting subject matter?"

Before Bob could choose from her suggested list, Mac appeared at the kitchen door fully dressed. "Come on in my handsome boy and take a seat while I cook you a good old English breakfast," said Linda eagerly looking him over with pride.

Mac did as he was told and Bob asked him what he would like to do, offering up the proposed list that Linda had suggested moments before. It was as if he had thought up the list, one that the English Tourist Board would be proud to offer to any visitor from overseas.

"Well I don't really mind, but as you have the pub to run six days a week, it would be nice to do something together. So, let's have a drive out into the country and find a nice restaurant where I can treat you both to a good English roast beef and Yorkshire pudding Sunday lunch." Then he laughingly added, "it will get you away from your pub and you can watch someone else working their socks off."

Linda was delighted that Mac had made such a firm suggestion and asked Bob to come up with somewhere situated in an area of outstanding natural beauty. Then, for a bit of fun, Bob comically suggested *A Highland Castle in Scotland, or a place on Dartmoor,* but finally he came up with the suggestion of the Golden Hind on the way to Wells, where they could go on to visit the cathedral.

"Yes that's fine by me, I like a bit of culture," said Mac.

After a lovely drive through the Somerset countryside, a wonderful roast lunch and a walk around Wells Cathedral, the three of them lounged in the sitting room of the Dog & Whistle with a large pot of tea and chocolate 'cookies', as Mac chose to call them since his adoption of the American-English language.

"So, what's all this numbers business that you started to tell me about yesterday?" Linda asked to Bob's amazement.

Mac, although not wanting to push his business knowledge down either of their throats on a Sunday evening, replied with, "Do you really want to know right now?" A question to which, both parents asked him to explain further.

"Well in America, the whole business ethos is based on what your numbers are telling you, good or bad, and if you do not act accordingly your business may suffer before you really realise it," came Mac's lead into his more detailed explanation.

"For instance, do you know what amount of your profit comes from the sale of beer against that of cider, or from the sale of food products - ie, what makes you the most money?"

Bob was quick to answer that he sold more cider than beer, but Linda added that the food brought in a reasonable amount of sales on a good day.

"Fine, but do you keep records of the amount of sales of each product group and their respective costs to bring them to the point of sale?" "For instance Bob, how much of your best seller is sweet cider and how much is rough?"

Although they had receipts for all the items that they purchased, they admitted that they did nothing with them, except keep them on file in case a tax man ever came to visit.

"So you don't really know if cider, beer, or food brings you the best result for your labours - I don't mean cash sales, I mean real profit?" He added, that if they did obtain that information, then they would be in a better position to concentrate on the product that gives the best return and also to apply some cost reduction to the others to make them more profitable.

Both had to admit that, although they thought that they had a good idea based on the sales, they did not know which gave them the best return according to their son's analysis. Mac explained that his example was only a simple version of what 'numbers' could do for any business and stated that there was more to be gained from it as one gets more involved. For example, you will probably find that only 20% of items sold will bring in about 80% of your real profit.

"That is loosely what 'numbers' is all about and you will be amazed how soon you get improved results for your efforts."

Both understood what Mac was saying and agreed to look at putting some sort of system in place. Mac suggested that they should leave the matter at that for this evening and, with their permission, he would take a look at their numbers as the days progressed.

Then, suddenly there was a knock on the back door and when Bob opened up he found Maggie who asked him if Linda was around and available for a chat.

"Certainly, come on in, she's in the sitting room with Mac - would you like a cup of tea?"

Linda had come partway to the door when she had heard Maggie's voice and welcomed her with the question, "Maggie, nice to see you, what brings you out on a Sunday evening?"

"I was out for a walk and thought that I would just pop in to see if you would be needing me at all during the coming week."

Linda replied that she thought it was very nice of her to ask, but she was lost more in the thought of whether or not she should tell Maggie about her own thoughts on the subject of Junior Burnett. Linda was sure that Maggie would certainly have memories of the American GI's names from the days of the village dances during the war.

Holding back her thoughts on the subject, Linda told Maggie to come through and meet Mac - her son from America!

Maggie was pleased to hear that Malcolm had arrived, but it brought back memories and conjured up thoughts of her own.

13. Mac Looks at the business

Early on Monday morning, over breakfast, Bob and Linda were keen to get Mac back on to the subject of 'numbers' and how it could improve their business at the pub.

"Well, as it is the start of a week, it would be a good time to commence some gathering of facts. We need a large sheet of paper with five columns headed, **Beer - Cider - Spirits - Soft Drinks - Food.** Then as each sale is made we enter the value of the respective item in the appropriate column."

"Blimey, that's going to create a lot of extra work," Bob worriedly pointed out.

"Yes it will to start with, but we can hire a more modern till within a few days that will process the details automatically, so bear with me."

Mac went on to explain that at the end of the week they would then be able to have some firm facts to start to make a judgement on their sales for the week.

"In the meantime, we also need to look at the costs involved for each of the five product ranges by having a similar sheet of paper with the same five columns and headings and recording every penny that is spent on getting them to the bar for sale," Mac firmly stated.

"Thirdly, we need to examine where the items are purchased from and to think if it is possible to buy them cheaper elsewhere."

Linda was quick to say, "I can tell you that straight away - we buy all the alcohol and soft drinks from the brewery and the food from the Co-op, the butcher and the pieman."

From that statement alone, Mac was able to spot two areas that needed immediate investigation. "Mom, I am amazed to learn that you purchase your food items from the Co-op. Although they do an excellent job for the general public, they are not the place that business people like you should be buying from. You need to set up an account with a wholesaler, whereby you get lower prices and also you do not have to pay for them until the end of the month. Also, eggs for example should be bought direct from a farmer."

Mac then turned to Bob and asked, "are you bound by any legal agreement that you must also purchase your cider and soft drinks from the brewery, in the same way that you have to with the beer and spirits?"

Bob was not sure about that, as he had always given an order to the brewery Rep for all liquid requirements, since the day that he had taken over the licence.

"Well we need to look into that straight away, for if you are not legally bound to do that, then you should purchase the cider direct from any cider processor and you will save money immediately.   It is called COST REDUCTION."

Although Bob and Linda were sceptical and nervous about changing their habits, Mac was delighted to see areas where he could help them improve their income, as it would help him to show the value of 'numbers' to a good advantage.

As Monday morning was very quiet in the bar as usual, it gave Mac and Bob the chance to set up the method of recording sales and it did not take long for two customers to arrive and for them to start the detailed recording process.

George and Billy came to play their usual game of crib and their order was one pint of beer, one pint of cider and two packets of crisps.

Bob went to put the whole price of the sale into the beer column, but Mac stopped him and explained that he had information on three different product groups, ie. Beer, Cider and Food.

Happily, Bob changed his thinking and it was not long before he got the hang of it and kept looking at the lists to see which product was 'leading in the race', as he put it.

Winnie and Madge arrived, which bumped up the amount in the beer sales column and then farmer Jim arrived with his brother, which shoved up the cider sales.

"So, what's ee doing there Landlord with that sheet of paper," Jim asked, as if he was being put under some sort of scrutiny.

"Numbers Jim, numbers that make any business a better business, don't you do it for your business?"

Mac stood back and smiled at the banter going on between the two of them, then Jim turned to Mac and asked. "So, who'm you then young man, sent down yer from the brewery to keep tags on the landlord to see that ee ain't on any fiddle?"

Bob interrupted by saying, "No he's our son who lives and works in America. He's here having a holiday."

"So you'm a Yank then?" Jim impolitely fired another question.

"No he's not American, he's British like you and me, but as he works in America, so he has to live there."

"So you'm not like my business friend Hank - ee's a true Yank and a good'n too."

Bob then introduced Mac in a proper manner to the two farmers and asked Jim who his colleague was.

"Well ee's my brother Stanley, Stan to everyone when our mother ain't listening. Ee farms over yonder with some cows and bullocks."

Stan stepped forward and said, "I hear that you've had my daughter Mary in yer with some others for a meal t'other night landlord."

Bob immediately remembered Mary and acknowledged it to Stan by saying, "Yes and a very nice girl to have as a daughter."

Mac was interested to know who Hank was and asked Jim a few questions about who and what is Hank and how did he meet him. This made Jim happy that he was being associated with Hank, even though he had only met him the once to have any sort of conversation.

"Well, ee was yer in the war with the army and ee's looking for a field that ee was living in a tent an ee asked me to find out more for im."

Stan then added, "Yes, and I think it could have been one of my fields, cause I'd had many Yanks sleeping in tents in my five acres down by the river. Nice chaps - they used to play baseball and give us cartons of orange juice."

Jim then chipped in, "Hank was one of them and he was an officer."

Mac then asked, "So have you told this Hank that you have found the field that he is looking for?"

Very artfully, Jim replied, "No I've lost his address and I wondered if your Dad, or Mum would be good enough to let me have it."

Bob explained that he didn't have it but would call Linda to see if she could oblige.

Linda, having been told of the request, came out of the kitchen and firmly told Jim, "Mr Burnett was a guest here and I am bound not to pass on personal facts about him to any third person, and in any case I do not have a forwarding address."

Linda's statement was partly professional ethics, but more to the point that now that she had an idea of who Hank was, she did not want anyone getting closer to him and enquiring about what might have happened in 1944.

Mac was sorry for Jim that his mother was unable to help and said, "Don't worry Jim, maybe he will turn up here again one day."

That reply sent Linda's head into a complete whirlwind as she wondered what may happen in the future, if matters were not properly explained before the gossipmongers stirred things up again. Was now the time to divulge to Mac who his true father was, she thought as she hurried back to the kitchen.

Bob continued to serve incoming customers, watched by Mac to ensure that he properly recorded the sales in their respective columns and during quiet periods they discussed the merits of purchasing the cider from another source.

Bob told Mac of H P Bulmer, who were the biggest manufacturer of cider in the UK and also mentioned a product called Scrumpy Jack made by a firm in Devon. Mac also added, "What about any local farmers who make the Scrumpy that most farm workers drink during harvest time?"

"OK," said Mac. "We have some ideas if your licence agreement will allow."

Immediately after closing the pub for the afternoon break, Bob got out the copy of the agreement that he had signed with the brewery just over two years previous.

It stated, *The Landlord of the Dog & Whistle, Mr Robert Charles Smart agrees to purchase and sell all alcohol products produced by this brewery.*

Mac said, "Good, it looks as though you are not precluded from selling other alcohol products that the brewery does not make, such as cider. I think that we should get some prices direct from the makers and then test it by not including cider on your next order.

Bob agreed with Mac, but was worried about what the brewery would say and how it would affect his relationship with them. "Business is business Bob, the brewery would not think twice about treading on your toes if it suited them," Mac reassured him.

Bob wrote out the order for beer and spirits ready for the brewery Rep to collect later in the afternoon, leaving off the usual cider order.

It was 3.00pm when the brewery Rep cheerily knocked on the backdoor as usual and Bob let him into the bar area to listen to whatever news or gossip that he had picked up on his rounds, before handing over the order.

The Rep glanced at it to mentally calculate what commission he would be receiving from the order. "You seem to have forgotten the cider landlord," the man from the brewery nonchalantly remarked.

Bob knew that this moment would arrive to test his resolve.

"No, I won't be buying my cider from you any more, I have established that I can get it cheaper by purchasing direct from a   local producer," Bob somewhat hesitantly explained.

"But I think that you are bound to buy it from us and I will have to inform my Area Manager about this."

"Fine," said Bob, with more confidence now that he had actually come out with it. Mac nodded his sign of approval and the man from the brewery quickly left the pub in not such a cheery mood as that which he had arrived with.

Mac was proud of the way that Bob had handled the situation and was pleased to see that his teaching was beginning to work.

Turning to Mac, Bob said, "So what happens now?"

Mac had been in this position several times when negotiating on behalf of the hotel where he worked.

"Just sit tight, I am sure that someone higher up in the brewery will come back to you with some sort of comments that we need to handle and be sure of our position before placing an order for the cider elsewhere."

Bob was concerned that by not ordering the cider, he may well run short when the weekend arrived.

"Don't worry Dad, for any order from a new customer, a new supplier will fall over backwards to get his product in here, just in case you change your mind."

Linda broke up the conversation when she called them to come to the kitchen for a meal that she had so carefully prepared for her two men.

Whilst enjoying the lamb chops, Linda asked how they had got on with the brewery Rep and had they taken action to get cider from elsewhere.

"Mom, this is the delicate time of any negotiation, just like making an offer on a house purchase, waiting to hear what the other party are going to say. However, I feel that we are on the right track."

Then, taking it easy in the sitting room after their lunch with a large pot of tea, Mac remarked how he thought that the pub had a very drab and weary look about it and that they should do something to attract more people to come.

"Also, you are relying on the same customers all the time."

"You are operating just like a post office, waiting for people to come in of their own accord. You need to attract people from beyond the boundary of the village if you are serious about wanting to improve your income," the young businessman with sound ideas continued to point out to his parents.

Just as they were about to talk about the details of what Mac was now calling SALES PROMOTION, the phone rang and a man announcing himself as the Area Manager from the brewery asked if he could pop in to have a chat, as he was in the area.

Mac knew this move - it was 'The fox among the chickens' scenario and nodded to Bob to let him come so that they could find out what he had to say.

At 4.45pm the Area Manager duly turned up and introduced himself as Robert Jeans and apologised for not having been to the Dog & Whistle during the two year period of Bob's tenure. Bob introduced him to Mac as his son who had an interest in the business and the three of them sat at a table in the bar.

Robert Jeans had some paperwork that told him the amount of each product that had been supplied by the brewery to the pub over the past year. He insincerely flattered Bob on the 'good work' that he had done on behalf of the brewery and soon came to the fact that his local Rep had informed him earlier that Bob was not going to purchase cider from the brewery in future.

Although he had been informed that the reason was price, he asked Bob the reason, as he needed to hear it from Bob himself.

The landlord repeated what he had told the local man earlier, to which he received an immediate offer of a price reduction of 10% if Bob continued to buy his cider from the brewery.

Bob looked at Mac for an answer, who then spoke for the first time.

"Thanks for your offer Mr Jeans, but that does not come anywhere near to the new lower cost incurred when purchasing direct and you should know that. Far too long we have been paying the wrong price for cider. You will need to come up with a better offer than that to keep our cider business. You see, in these times we are needing to look for real COST REDUCTION!"

Robert Jeans was surprised to hear such businesslike language coming from a person so young and detected that Mac had been well trained in negotiations elsewhere.

After more discussion, the reduction was increased to 15%, but Mac knew that would be the limit of discount that the brewery could afford to give and in any case it would probably get withdrawn sometime down the line under some scheme or another.

Reluctantly, the Area Manager had to accept the situation and sarcastically wished them good luck in their venture, when he bid them farewell.

"That went easier than I thought it would Mac," Bob said with relief. "I am surprised that he did not bring up something about us being tied tenants."

"That may well become an issue later Dad, as Robert Jeans's responsibility is only for the sale of products and not for legal matters. However, let's get on with placing that cider order so that you do not run out at the weekend."

Just before the evening opening time, another knock could be heard at the backdoor and when Linda opened it, she found Sarah Blunt, her next-door neighbour, who had come to say goodbye as she would be vacating the adjoining cottage the next day.

Linda welcomed her like a departing member of her own family. "Do come in Sarah and have a cup of tea with us before you go."

Sarah was reluctant to impose on them as she knew that Bob was about to open the pub for the evening session, but Linda insisted and in any case early Monday evenings did not usually see a rush of customers.

"Come and meet my son Mac, he will tell you all about America while I make the tea." Sarah accepted and eventually sat in the sitting room with all three of the pub residents.

Bob asked Sarah if the brewery had given her any idea of who was going to take over the cottage after her notice period was up.

It was then that she produced a letter from the property manager of the brewery, in which it said that now that they had honoured the agreement set up by her husband, they had no further use for the property and that it would be put up for sale.

Sarah's information came as a surprise to both Bob and Linda and their minds began to wonder who would be their new neighbours.

Bob had to excuse himself from the conversation so that he could open up for the Monday evening session that would see the arrival of the skittles team to play a home match against the 'Sturminster Stompers' who were near the top of the league.

First through the door after Bob opened was 'Old Tom' the thatcher, wanting to quench his thirst after a hard day on top of a cottage in Stourton Caundle. He ordered his usual pint of Mild & Bitter and Bob remembered to enter the value in the beer column on the record sheet. He was thankful that the order was not for a pint of Beer & Cider, otherwise he would not have known where to enter it.

Sarah said farewell to Linda and Mac politely let her out of the backdoor. As he returned, Linda had already set to work in the kitchen rolling pastry for the meat slices and pies that she knew would sell quickly before and during the break at the skittles later.

Mac offered to help and was given the job of washing the dishes that had been left since their earlier meal - not quite what the Assistant General Manager had in mind and laughingly told his mother.

"If you want to become somebody in this organisation my lad, you have to start at the bottom and spend time training in each department, just like you said you have done in America."

Mac accepted the comment, knowing that it was all in good fun and rolled up his sleeves to get on with the job.

While working together, Linda asked him if the order for the cider had been placed and Mac was pleased to tell her that a trial order for one barrel of Blackthorn and three dozen bottles of sweet cider had been placed with a company at Shepton Mallet. "We were also able to get the rough cider from a farm not far from here and all of it is promised for tomorrow."

The more she heard from Mac, the more proud she became of him and artfully told him, "If you do a good job of cleaning those dishes, I may promote you to a higher position in the organisation."

The first of the skittles group to arrive was Terry Smith, 'The Major', well before any of the others as he always did, to ensure that everything was properly in place. He explained to Bob that in addition to his team, some others are coming to watch and to learn.

"We really have got a good bunch of enthusiastic skittlers now and I want to make it interesting for them so that they do not drop out. The vicar has got a good group also, so what about us putting on an open evening later in the week, whereby everyone gets to play?" The Major suggested to Bob.

"Certainly, what about Wednesday evening?" Bob suggested.

"Fine, Wednesday it is then," confirmed Terry.

Just then Linda came through with a tray of freshly baked pies and meat slices to put on the hot plate and seeing The Major she confirmed with him that a break of 20 minutes would again take place at 8.30pm as they did before.

"Absolutely," said Terry, "and while you have those in your hand, I'll have a meat slice to go with my drink before they all go."

Linda was pleased to give him one without charge for the good work that he had done in bringing more people to the pub over the past couple of weeks. Bob also let him off paying for his drink, but was not sure whether he should enter it on the record sheet, or not.

Next to arrive was the Rev Timmy, keen as ever and with three of his team. "We have come to learn some more in the hope that we can form our own team," he enthusiastically told The Major.

"Good to hear it Reverend and by the way, we are arranging a get-together on Wednesday evening so that everyone can have a go," Terry informed him.

Timmy looked puzzled for a moment and then spoke aloud, "I'll have to arrange choir practice a little earlier than usual - can't miss the free-for-all." Both Bob and Linda welcomed that statement.

Mac then came into the bar and Linda introduced him all round as her 'Business Partner' son, an introduction which Mac happily took with a pleasing smile.

More people began to arrive for the skittles evening and among them was Tony and his father Henry Button.

Both were greeted by Bob. Linda went straight to Tony and put her arm around him with a very special welcome saying, "Tony, will you look after the food sales and take orders for the half time break, like you did before?"

"As I've said before Linda, anything for you," he happily answered and took up a position behind the counter alongside the hot plate.

Away from the crowd, Timmy struck up a conversation with Mac and asked him if he was happy in America.

"Certainly I am vicar, I have been well looked after by my employers and I give them my all for their business, which makes for a very happy life. One that I probably would not have been able to have if I had not taken up their offer in the first place."

Mac politely asked Timmy if he had ever been to America, for which he got a very surprised reply. "Yes, in my student days I was fortunate to have been able to spend a month with the Amish population in Pennsylvania."

Whilst Mac had heard the term Amish as something to do with the church, he was unaware of what it really meant and asked Timmy to improve his knowledge.

"Well Mac, The Amish are a group of people that follow strict traditionalist Christian rules. They are known for their simple living, plain dress and a willingness to maintain self sufficiency, while living by God's word."

Timmy's explanation rang a bell to Mac, as he remembered seeing a film about such people sometime in the past. "Don't they all live a rural life in the outback and drive around in horse and buggies?"

"You've got it, a hard working self-sufficiency existence that is not tainted by modern-day electronic gadgets, whilst maintaining a very close friendship to each other, through the workings of God."

"Sounds a good life, pity the whole world can't live like that," Mac wishfully answered.

14. Sales Promotion and Cost Reduction

Mac's conversation with Timmy came to an abrupt end when he saw that Bob was struggling serving drinks and trying to keep the record sheet in order. So, having excused himself from Timmy, Mac went behind the counter and to Bob's relief, took control of the paperwork. Tony was also asked to record his food sales following explanation.

In small groups, the visiting team began to arrive and a few of the locals pointed out the freshly made meat items on the hot plate, which one-by-one soon got purchased.

The Major welcomed the visiting team and pointed out that at 8.30pm there would be a break of twenty minutes for drinks replenishment and drew particular attention to the fact that Tony could now take orders for reasonably priced egg and chips suppers to be served at the break.

It was not long before Tony had a small queue forming to take up the offer and he ensured that all orders were paid for in advance.

Then, with everyone happy, The Major called time for the skittlers to go through into the backroom to commence the match.

Apart from the soft sound of some music on the radio, the bar went quiet, which enabled Bob, Tony, Linda and Mac to sit down with a drink and review what had happened so far.

Bob was the first to admit that he did not think that he had entered everything correctly on the record sheet and Tony was not sure if the meat slices and crisps that Bob had sold were entered at all.

"Never mind," came the voice of Mac. "I understand the reason and it makes it more important that we get a new till that will handle most of that recording automatically. The main thing is that we all now understand the reason for such recording."

As the time approached for the break in the skittles match, Linda asked Tony to come with her into the kitchen with the list of the egg and chips orders.

Tony jumped to it as he was always happy to be alone with Linda.

Linda warmed a pile of plates and as Tony called out the orders, she arranged the appropriate number of eggs ready to fry when the people came into the bar.

Mac was quick to see how well Tony worked with his mother and saw that they clearly had a good understanding of each other, one which was quite different from that which she had with Bob.

He also guessed that Bob would have the same hurried demand for drinks when the break came, so he prepared himself to again handle the recording of the sales and to learn more about what happens at a busy time in a pub of this nature.

First through the door came members of the home team eager to get at the bar before it became too crowded, followed by The Major talking happily with members of the visiting team. At the rear was the Rev Timmy who, with great politeness, waited until everyone else had been served.

Tony brought through some plates of eggs and chips, while Linda was frantically juggling with hot plates and frying pans to keep up with the demand.

With everyone tucking into their evening buffet, Mac took the opportunity to finish his conversation with Timmy and to learn how he had first taken up the thought of entering the church as a vocation.

"I guess Mac, that it was in the same way as you went off to America and found happiness, you could say that we both had a calling."

Mac was warmed by Timmy's explanation and considered him to be a man of exceptional understanding of life. He had obviously mixed with people at many different levels and although he condemned over indulgence in alcoholism, in the same way that John Wesley did, he was not too proud to come to the pub and join in a game of skittles.

Although the Dog & Whistle team lost again, it was not such an emphatic pounding as they had been getting of late. The Major was pleased that his team had at last 'pulled their socks up' and that he now had several other keen members who could take the place of any that did not come up to scratch.

Timmy reminded him that he would also soon have a team in place to challenge those who had taken things for granted so long.

The evening came to an end with all members of the pub staff happy with the evening, Bob with the beer and cider sales, Linda with the food outlet, Mac with the recording under the 'Numbers' scheme and Tony overjoyed that he had again spent the evening in the company of Linda.

Also, before retiring, Mac reiterated that there was work to be done the next day to keep up the revitalising of the pub and, not least, something to improve the appearance so it would attract new customers.

He summed it up as Cost Reduction and Promotion, then quickly changed it to Promotion and Cost Reduction, when he thought that no doubt some wag would use the initials of his first suggestion to spell out a very rude word.

Again, he reminded Bob and Linda that they may not have heard the last from the brewery, as no managers of any company liked losing business, or the commission that went with it.

Finally, they all went their separate ways, Tony off home, Mac to his room and Bob and Linda, after putting out the lights, up the stairs to bed.

Yet again, Linda was restless with the thought that Hank was one of the two Lieutenant GI's who she had known during 1944. She also continued to try to come to terms with the fact that she had never told anyone who Mac's father was - not even Mac and Bob.

15. Time for Action

Next morning Mac swung into action with a call to the local dealer of office machinery and arranged for a trial run of an NCR Point-of-sale Terminal, that would handle the till requirements of an expanding business as he put it, so that it would create their interest.

After that, Bob checked with the new cider suppliers if delivery would happen that day.

Mac also reminded them that something had to be done to open an account with a wholesaler - all before the pub was to open for the mid-day session.

Bob, with his gathering enthusiasm for success, put the sign back up in the bar that said,

Friday Evening is Steak & Ale Pie Night
Book now to avoid disappointment.

Linda was unaware that he had put the sign up and when she saw it playfully asked him, "So, who's making your pie this time landlord?"

Having forgotten to ask Linda if she thought that they should repeat the successful pie evening, he now had to grovel by giving her a loving hug and apologised for not conferring.

"Luckily my lad, there is still time to talk to Charlie the butcher, but I am not sure if the same cook is available for Friday," came her reply, whilst returning his hug.

Mac was pleased to witness the happy banter between the two of them and thought again how lucky his mother had been to link up with such a nice person as Bob, when she had been left with himself as a toddler.

Throughout their time together, the three of them had enjoyed such a happy relationship and it was mostly down to their love for each other and Bob's acceptance of Linda's situation.

Mac wondered how either of them would cope if a time ever came that they should became parted.

Just before Bob opened up for the Tuesday morning session, a lorry from the cider producers in Shepton Mallet arrived with the barrel of Blackthorn, for which Bob showed his relief to Mac.

"I told you they would deliver quickly; anyone would when it comes to picking up a new customer, now let's see if the farmer does the same."

As it was a quiet time in the pub, Mac told his mother that they should both go off and set up an account with a wholesaler, for what he called 'Dry Goods' and Linda agreed.

"You will need to bring some paperwork to prove that this is a proper business and I guess that you will also have to show them something to prove your own identity," Mac pointed out.

"Have you got any correspondence from the brewery with their heading, and have you a passport, or driving licence?"

Linda had all three and made sure that she took them with her.

Soon after they had left, the farmer turned up with the barrel of rough cider and told Bob that he had supplied the pub several years back, but stopped when the previous landlord did not keep up the payments. "So you see landlord, I need to have cash-in-hand these days from this establishment."

That was not a problem as Bob had intended to pay on delivery in any case.

"Well, thanks a lot, I hope you'm be satisfied and want some more soon," the farmer said, as he took off his hat and waved good-day.

Coming up from the cellar, Bob noticed a van draw into his carpark and out came a well dressed young lad who announced that he was from the Blackmore Vale Office Equipment Company to deliver a piece of machinery.

Bob guided the lad through the backdoor and let him place it on the counter, saying, "Is it possible that you could come back later to explain the workings to my son, who will be the first to operate it, - could we say three o'clock?" The young man agreed and off he went.

Sitting on his stool behind the bar, Bob could not help thinking that in little over a fortnight, the happenings in the pub had changed so rapidly.

First there was the arrival of Hank with his big red car and the extra trade that he had unwittingly generated virtually overnight.

The Major and the Vicar had livened up the skittles crowd.

Linda had re-engaged with her best friend Maggie, who in-turn introduced them to that polished waitress Jill.

Linda had encouraged Tony to get back to work.

The homecoming of Mac and what he had done to draw their attention to better business practices.

And looking at the shiny new piece of machinery sitting under wraps on his counter, he thought that life was running at a very fast rate for the Landlord and his wife of the small village pub.

When Mac returned with Linda, after opening a wholesale account in the name of The Dog & Whistle Public House, he was made aware of the new piece of office machinery sitting on the counter and was told that a man would be back at 3.00pm to set it up.

He eyed it with pleasure, as it was something that he had encountered in his own business a year or so ago. It made him pleased that, apart from a little reminder on certain things, he would be able to get started with the new till immediately the salesman had set it up.

Linda remarked to Bob how easy it had been to open the wholesale account and how much cheaper things would be from the store in Gillingham.

"So that's the end of the Co-op then?" Bob asked.

"Certainly, as far as the business is concerned, but I do like some Co-op items that we have occasionally for ourselves," Linda replied, reluctant to give up on her regular routine altogether.

Mac, listening to their conversation from the bar and called out, "Now for locally produced eggs Mom."

Three O'clock came and the lad from the office machinery company arrived to be welcomed by Bob, who took him through to meet Mac.

After discarding the protective wrapping, Bob was asked where the nearest electrical point was and after some rearranging of items under the counter, a suitable socket was found to plug in and start the demonstration.

The salesman explained that he had already set it up to handle three main headings of products called, *Alcohol, Food, and Miscellaneous*. Each of these could now be programmed with sub-headings such as, Beer, Cider, and Spirits, for the alcohol heading and other sub-headings for the other two groups. He also pointed out that the price of all the items to be sold through the till would need to be entered into the memory of the machine, a task that they did straight away.

More detailed information was then given about what the person entering the sale would have to do to ensure that sales would be properly recorded, but it was clear to Bob that it took the labour out of hand writing every amount on a sheet of paper.

"Then," said the salesman. "At the end of any given period, all you have to do is press this button and it will give you a print-out of what has happened, by numerical amounts and their financial values."

The workings of the machine all quickly came back to Mac and he was pleased that the salesman had got a good grasp of what was needed to get Bob on board.

Some paperwork was then signed allowing the pub to have the machine on trial for two weeks, afterwich it would need to be either purchased outright, or returned in good condition.

Both Mac and Bob thought that it was a very good offer and that they would do all they could to make it work for the benefit of improving the business of the pub.

"Before you go, young man," Bob said to the salesman, "what about a drink on the house and you can say that you had the first transaction through the new till of the Dog & Whistle?"

The salesman thankfully accepted a small beer shandy that confused them all, as they pondered as to which category it was to be entered, Beer or Soft Drinks.

"Oh just call it beer," said Mac. "We don't have to be that pedantic."

With all the prices finally entered into the memory, the salesman gone and the new till set up, Mac and Bob continued to make dummy entries to ensure that they would be completely confident with it when the time came to open for the evening.

Linda called out, "So who's going to teach me how to work it then?"

Mac, believing that Bob should be the master of his own pub, said, "The landlord is the one to give his staff tuition." To which Linda gave him a playful nudge in the ribs.

Mac then stood back and watched to make sure that Bob taught Linda the correct way of handling the new toy and was surprised to see how quickly his mother mastered the modern-day technology.

Happy with the way that things had progressed, Bob suggested that they should leave the till and all adjourn to the private quarters for a nice summer salad and relax from business matters until the evening opening time.

"O K, " echoed the two members of his 'staff'.

Tuesday evening in the bar was again very quiet, with only half a dozen people coming to the pub, so it gave Bob the chance to throw a few darts, while Linda and Mac sat in the kitchen talking about how things could be improved there.

Quite late on, Tony arrived to Bob's pleasure and was immediately greeted with a showing of the new till.

"Blimey Bob - this is modern technology, no more fiddling the books now," Tony said with a chuckle. "Big Brother will be watching you."

Bob had not thought of it in those terms, but was not worried as he had never been party to fiddling anything. He had been well brought up by his late parents to be honest or he would 'never go to heaven', as his mother told him many times.

Bob asked Tony how his job working at the cheese factory for his Brother-in-law, Georgie Bailey, was going along. With great enthusiasm, Tony explained to Bob and Mac that he was enjoying it, for as long as he completed the work to everyone's satisfaction, it meant that he could start and finish to suit himself - he was his own boss.

"Good," said Bob. "How about coming to help out tomorrow evening as The Major and I have arranged an 'Open Evening' of skittles and we are hoping that we will be over-run with takers?"

Tony readily agreed as it would give him a chance to use the new till and to see just what it is that Mac seems to think will increase business.

The rest of the evening was very quiet in the pub, except for the arrival of Constable Willis who had heard about the proposed 'Open Evening'.

"Now, I don't want any jamming up of the High Street with cars and tractors tomorrow, so I will have to put myself on duty throughout the evening," the policeman said to Bob.

"OK, but I guess that excludes you from joining in the free-for-all then Constable?" Bob replied in a joking manner. "You're right landlord, but be sure to save me a couple of those warm meat slices for when I have a break."

Tony and Mac who were playing a friendly game of darts, both looked at PC Willis and saw for once that he could also be human, like the the rest of the village people and have a need for Linda's home cooking.

Tony's father, returning home from a council meeting, also popped into the pub to confirm that he would be coming the next evening, for as he put it, "The Major has my arm twisted so far up my back that I just had to give in."

That caused laughter from everyone and Tony said, "Have you got Mum's permission?"

He replied, "She's coming as well, but she doesn't know it yet."

16. The Arrival of a Jukebox

Next morning was Wednesday and everyone was looking forward to the skittles Open Evening. Bob had cleaned the skittle alley and was back in the bar testing the pumps and making sure that the till still did what it should do. Linda busied herself preparing food for the evening and Mac took a good walk around the pub eyeing every corner as if he was a prospective buyer, but really looking to see if there was more that could be done to help the business to improve.

Then suddenly they were all made aware of a very large multi-coloured van that had pulled up outside of the main entrance of the pub. Out came a middle aged man and a youth who knocked on the window of the pub, asking if they could come in.

Bob opened the door to them and the elder man introduced himself as the proprietor of the 'Wessex Mechanical Music Company' and asked to speak to the owner of the pub.

Bob acknowledged him as the owner and courteously invited the man to step inside while he closed the door. The youth went back to the van. Bob recognised straight away that he was someone who was here to try and sell him something, but let the man to have his say.

"Well guvner, I have something on the van that will make you money at the click of a switch, or should I say at the insertion of a coin."

Bob smiled at the man's sales approach and asked just what was the quick money maker.

"A Jukebox - it's all the rage now and every coin that your punters put in, you and I will get a fair share."

Bob started to tell the man that he did not have a need for anything like that as he had a perfectly good radio, but Mac standing in the background, interrupted and asked the man what his terms were.

"A small rental charge of £25 a month and you get 30% of all the takings." What the man did not know, was that Mac had a lot of experience of placing Jukeboxes into his company's establishments throughout America, on terms that made good money for his employers.

Mac asked the man if the landlord and himself could have a private conversation whilst they gave his offer serious consideration.

So, sniffing the possibility of a deal in the offing, the man agreed to go out to his van and await their decision.

Bob asked Mac if he was serious about such a deal and called Linda in to listen to what was going on.

Mac explained that at the present time they were playing music to their customers from the radio free of charge and if they were to take out the radio and replace it with a Jukebox, then the customers would pay to hear whatever they liked, while putting cash into the takings of the pub.

Bob could see the sense in such a change, but Linda said to them, "If you remove the radio I will not be able to listen to my favourite tunes while I am working."

To which Mac replied, "Mother, with a Jukebox you can listen to your favourite tunes all day long." Adding cheekily, "Providing that you have enough coins in your purse."

Both of his parents, then made the point that the rental charge would be yet another expense, when they were supposed to be looking for COST REDUCTION.

"Just leave it to me to handle, as I know that we can get a better deal than the one he has placed on the table. Let's get him back in and if we do a deal then you can have the radio in the kitchen Mom."

The man was pleased to be invited back and Mac told him, "We are prepared to take up your offer, but not on your terms. We would expect the takings to be split 50/50 and we are not prepared to pay a rental charge."

The man somewhat agreed the first part, but was not prepared to drop the rental charge and told them so.

"So what if we were to take two machines?" Mac countered.

Bob looked at Mac as if he were mad and mumbled, "Why two?"

Mac whispered to Bob, "a second one in the skittle alley would make you even more money."

With the prospect of off-loading two machines, the man's eyes lit up and came back with a counter proposal.

"I'll drop the hire charge if you agree that we both take 45% and the other 10% goes to the upkeep of the machines."

Mac knew that a percentage should be allowed for the machines, even though the man would in effect get 55% and saw that as a deal very similar to some that he had worked well with in the past.

Bob then asked for a demonstration of a machine, to which the man readily agreed and went to his van to tell the youth to bring one in.

During his absence, Mac explained that his experience in the U S was that these machines made a lot of money without any outlay, except for the electricity used. "We may have to accept a three month minimum period of activity, but I promise you that it will be worth it and we can start straight away if he has them on the van today."

Back came the man with the youth pushing a hand truck with a new-looking Jukebox on board. "So where would you like it Guvner?" the youth asked, eyeing every corner of the bar area.

Linda asked that it should not be too close to the eating area and Bob said that he did not want it close to the counter where he spent most of his time.

"What about just outside the toilet doors?

We have found that whilst people are on their feet they will take a look at the playing list and in more cases than not, they will put a coin in," came the experience of the well practiced Proprietor of the Wessex Mechanical Music Company.

"Absolutely correct," said Mac laughing.
"You must have read my book entitled, *The Habits of People Outside Toilet Doors.*"

Detecting Mac's slight American accent and his negotiating skills, the man was prepared to believe him and found no reason to argue.

All connected up and the first dummy coin slotted into the machine, Linda was sold on it immediately, as it played a serenade of her favourite Mantovani music. Then into the skittle alley went the second machine with some Pop music that Mac knew would please the skittlers.

With Mac's assistance, Bob completed the agreement form and the man was happy for him to keep the two machines that he had off-loaded.

"I'll pop in to see you in about a week, just to make sure that everything is working all right. In the meantime, enjoy the music." Then off went the proprietor and the youth to seek out another prospective customer.

With the Mantovani music in the bar finished, Linda asked what she needed to do to get the Jukebox to play the same record again. Bob looked at Mac, who smiled with a cheeky grin and simultaneously they both replied, "Put some more money in!"

From that comment, Linda realised that as soon as they were to open up the pub, then there was a chance that the machine would start to earn money straight away. Bob was ahead of her and could not wait for the skittles crowd to arrive that evening, when both machines would be bringing in some extra cash that the brewery had no claim over.

After Bob opened up the pub for the lunchtime session, bang on time Winnie and Madge arrived and paid up for their usual bottles of stout. Then as Bob rang up the sale, Winnie was quick to notice the new till and asked Bob what the machine was for.

"It's modern technology Winnie, ensures that we are able to keep control of the numbers."

Numbers meant nothing to Winnie, but she offered a quip of her own when she said, "So that sends the money straight down the line to the brewery then?" "Yes something like that," replied Bob.

Not wanting to leave it there, Winnie came back with.

"Stops you'm fiddling the books then!"

Madge had listened to the volley of comments between Winnie and Bob and with a worried expression asked. "Do ee fiddle the books?"

Winnie explained that she did not know if he fiddled the books, but that her remark was only said as a bit of fun.

"It ain't no fun if ee's fiddling the books, is it?" Madge stated firmly.

Luckily, two young lads arrived and it broke up the silly conversation. "Two ciders please landlord", one of them said.

Bob enquired if they wanted sweet or rough, to which the second lad replied, "Sweet please, don't want any of that there Scrumpy while we're working, or we may drop off to sleep."

With drinks in hand, they both eyed the new Jukebox and went over to look at the list of records available. Straight away, in went the first coin and the start of some profit. There was a pause while the machine selected their choice and then came Bill Hayley playing Rock Around The Clock, to which they both joined in the singing and swayed together.

The music and the antics of the two lads startled both Winnie and Madge, who had not noticed the addition of the second bit of 'Modern Technology' to be added to the pub since their last visit. Bob hadn't considered what aggravation the Jukebox might cause to some of his existing customers and was suddenly concerned what harsh comments would be fired at him from the two ladies.

However, he was pleasantly surprised to see that both of them were swaying along to the music and he mumbled, "Thank God."

Hearing the music, Linda came through from the kitchen, where she had been preparing the food for the skittle evening and swung her upper body in time to the music.

Winnie, seeing her, got up from her seat and pretended to dance with Linda. Bob was even more surprised and could not believe his luck.

When the music stopped, Linda commented to Winnie that she had no idea that she could dance like that. To which Winnie replied, "You don't know what I got up to during the war when those American GI's were over here."

The music changed when one of the lads inserted a second coin and out came The Rolling Stones playing 'I Can't Get No Satisfaction'.

"Call that music?" Winnie said indignantly.

Madge didn't like it either and remarked, "what do you expect when they'm got dirty boots like that."

It was then that both Bob and Linda realised that the Jukebox did not always play the music that they liked and that they would be at the mercy of whoever put their money in.

"Don't worry, you will find that the sound of the money going into the Juke will drown out any music that you don't like," Mac, with his voice of experience gently informed them.

Farmer Jim was the next to arrive and before Bob could greet him, he bellowed out, "Where's that bloody noise coming from?"

"Over there mate, by the toilet," said one of the lads, pointing to the colourful new Jukebox standing outside the toilets.

"By the toilet, t'would be better off down the toilet," remarked Jim as he looked at Bob and further enquired, "Do you allow that then landlord?"

Bob explained that he had to allow whatever music the person paying the money had selected.

"So I could get'n to play what I like then if I coughed-up wi the cash?"

Mac nodded a greeting to Jim and said that if he wanted to, he could put many coins in and it would play his selections all day long.

"So this is som'thin that you've brought over from America then young Mac?"

Mac explained that he did not bring it over, but that this type of entertainment was available throughout most establishments of this kind in the US.

Jim nodded, ordered his usual glass of Scrumpy and thought things out about the Jukebox.

After a couple of sips of his cider, Jim remarked to Bob that it was excellent stuff and asked if he had done anything to change the taste.

Bob told him that he had changed to a more local supplier.

"So, who'm do ee get it from now then?"

"I'm trying out a barrel from a farmer called Tom Hayes over Milborne way."

Jim knew Tom from years ago and laughingly replied.

"Old Tom, is he still around? I thought that he would have fallen into one of his barrels by now - anyway, it's a good drop of stuff - tell im from me next time you see im."

Leaning back with an elbow on the counter, Jim suddenly saw that Bob had opened the new till to put his money in.

"Blimey landlord, is that another music machine that you've got there?"

Bob explained that it was a new type of till that now handled the business numbers automatically, to which Jim acknowledged Bob as someone who knew something about it.

Looking at the till and then to the Jukebox, Jim was not to be outdone in the conversation and remarked, "Looks like you've come into some money landlord."

Bob just had to trump him in the war of words and said, "Yes and there's another one out the back in the skittle alley."

The music suddenly changed to a more mellow sound, when Winnie went over and put a coin in. Out came Cliff Richard singing 'The Minute You're Gone', to which Jim showed his appreciation to Winnie and anyone else who he could engage in conversation.

The two lads drank up and left the pub with a cheery wave to Winnie and Madge before Jim was made aware of the delightful smell coming from some freshly cooked pies and meat slices that Linda was putting on the hot plate.

"Tell ee what Linda dear, I'll 'ave a couple of those pies right now."

17. A Mysterious Visitor

During the afternoon break, all three took it easy in the sitting room and reviewed the activities that they had achieved so far.

Bob remarked that it was mostly down to the knowledge that Mac had brought with him and had applied to their ailing business. The break away from the brewery with the cider procurement and opening of the the food account with a wholesaler showed immediate cost reduction.

Making them aware of the importance of the 'numbers' in the business was something that both he and Linda had accepted and the introduction of the new till appeared to be working well.

The installation of the two Jukeboxes is something that they would never have thought of, if it were not for the past experience of Mac.

Linda recalled the help that they had also received from Terry Smith, The Major, over the shakeup with the skittles that appeared would bring in several more people a couple of evenings a week.

Bob then praised Linda for the effort that she had applied to the food and in particular to the wonderful steak & ale pie that could become a regular feature.

Reference to the steak brought back thoughts about Hank and she added, "You could say that this all started with the chance visit of Hank and the mission that he was on to search out a satisfactory deal for his American client."

Mac asked his mother to tell him more about this American called Hank, but Linda was not happy to continue with that conversation in front of Bob.

"Old Jim said that Hank was here during the war and was based in a field that his brother owned, did you you know Hank in those days Mom?" asked Mac in an enquiring way.

For a moment Linda's mind went blank as she tried to think of how to reply to the question without giving anything away. "Well there were a lot of GI's here …….." Her reply was abruptly interrupted by a heavy tap on their sitting room window.

Bob went to look and saw a man trying to peer through the window. He beckoned him to go round to the back door, where they could have a conversation. The man introduced himself as Trevor Jones, Surveyor, of Wilkins, Mitchell and Jones and said that he had been requested to take a visual survey of the pub. "Nothing too technical at this stage Mr Smart, just a cursory glance at the state of the building and the cottage next door."

Bob asked him why the sudden unannounced visit and for what purpose.

"I've no idea landlord, my company has accepted a brief from the brewery and we have to file a report known as, 'Observation of Conformity'. This is to confirm that what is on the plans, is actually here and is usually requested before any client takes matters to the next stage - whatever that may be."

Although baffled as to why this sudden visit, Bob realised that the man had a job to do and he had no real option than to cooperate.

"I have looked at the outside of both buildings and if it is convenient with you, I would like to take a quick walk through the various rooms. No measuring or jumping up and down, just a look. If it is not convenient, then I would be happy to return by appointment."

Bob invited him in and asked Trevor to repeat his request so that both Linda and Mac could hear it directly from him.

All three agreed to let him do the viewing whilst he was here as it would save time for them all, sooner than have him come back again.

Trevor thanked them and suggested that two of them should accompany him to ensure that everything was above board. So Bob showed him around, with Mac walking behind watching every movement.

Linda stayed in the sitting room wondering what it was all about, but thankful that the man's arrival had saved her from answering Mac's question about Hank.

When Trevor noticed the bricked up doorway on the wall segregating the pub from the cottage, he remarked that he thought that the two buildings may well have been one in the past.

After Trevor had completed his walk through, he thanked them all and departed, whereupon Bob, Linda and Mac stood debating why the sudden survey without prior notice.

Bob was the first to offer an opinion that had any semblance of reasoning.

"This has probably been triggered by the fact that Sarah, our neighbour, has vacated the cottage next door and that the brewery are making sure that the place is in good condition before selling it."

Linda agreed with Bob, but was still worried in case it had anything to do with the fact that Bob had stopped buying the cider from the brewery.

With a little more business experience, Mac said, "I told you that I expected that something would rear its head from the brewery since the visit of Robert Jeans. It could be that the legal department of the brewery is revaluing their assets here, while assembling some sort of forward planning document."

What Mac feared was, that maybe the brewery was preparing to sell off the pub along with the cottage. However, he did not want to worry his parents with that thought as they had enough on their minds at the present time.

Linda, looking at her watch, suddenly expressed the thought that she should be getting on with the preparation of a meal for the three of them before evening opening time.

"Come on you two, I've work to be done," she said, playfully tapping Bob on the knee.

"Yes, me too," replied Bob.

Mac remained in the sitting room with his thoughts and made several written notes about the surveyor's visit, in case they may be needed at some future date. He also thought more about the American called Hank.

18. Sales Promotion

As the three of them sat around the kitchen table eating their meal before starting work for the evening, Mac took the opportunity to talk to them both about the the next phase of improving the business.

"Not only do we need to get more people coming in from the village, but we need to attract others from further afield; get folks to understand that the Dog & Whistle public house in Thimble Hardy is the place to be," Mac told Bob, looking him straight in the eye.

While he was doing that, Linda could not help but notice a strong resemblance between Mac to his true father, with handsome looks that rested under the slightly sandy hair, coupled with good manners and charm. It took her mind right back to those days in 1944 and how she had fallen for a man of similar character. A man whose name only she alone held the identity of, despite the speculation of many villagers over the years.

When Linda did bring her mind back to the conversation going on between her two men sitting at the table, she heard Mac say to Bob, "We can start with some simple advertising that does not cost too much. Take that sign about Friday night being Steak & Ale Pie Night for instance, you could put a similar sign in the pub window and another on the village notice board."

Bob agreed and Linda added that they could also put the same notice in the monthly Parish Magazine. "Then after that we could go 'world-wide' by placing an advert in the Blackmoor Vale Magazine." Bob smiled at the thought. "There you go," said Mac. "You have ideas already and you could add information about the Wednesday evening skittles free-for-all."

He then told them both that something ought to be done to improve the appearance of the pub. "The eating area should be screened off from the bar so to provide some privacy for the diners. Also, the seating in the bar could be rearranged to face the Jukebox, so that customers would feel more associated with it, and what about some coloured lights outside to draw attention?"

When the pub opened for what was expected to be a busy Wednesday evening, the first person to arrive was Tony, who explained that he had finished work early to come and help out.

Bob showed his appreciation of Tony's consideration by pulling him a free half, and to ensure that the till would tally at the end of the day, Bob duly put his hand in his pocket and paid for it himself.

Linda was pleased to hear Tony's voice and called him through to the kitchen, for which Tony didn't need to be asked a second time.

Entering the kitchen, Tony could see that Linda was more dressed-up than usual. She had a very attractive and colourful blouse peering out from underneath a brand new apron and as he got closer to her, his nostrils were filled with the aroma of an enticing perfume.

Tony lost himself in the belief that all this was for his benefit, but then realised that the skittlers this evening would also be attracted to her and that would be good for business.

Linda explained what food she had baked for this evening to be on the hot plate for the start of the evening and they both talked about how they were going to manage the orders that were expected to be placed for egg & chip suppers at half time. She also told him that if The Major wanted a mid-evening supper, he was to quietly let him have it free of charge for organising the evening.

"Oh, and by-the-way, will you reserve a couple of hot meat slices for Constable Willis for when he comes in later - but make sure that he pays for them," Linda notified Tony with a loving smile.

Well briefed by Linda, Tony went back into the bar to listen to Bob and Mac still talking about how they were planning to attract more people into the pub from further afield.

Tony then offered a thought of his own by saying, "What about putting adverts on the notice boards of other village halls within a ten mile radius from here?"

"Good idea Tony," Mac replied and Tony offered to undertake the task of delivering them whenever he had time.

As usual Old Tom, the Thatcher, came in to quench his thirst on the way home from another hard day on top of a cottage roof. Like Jim before him, he was surprised to see the new till and thought that the pub must be doing all right now.

As the evening moved on, people began to arrive and before long the pub was quite full with the Jukebox belting out acceptable music while earning extra money for the pub. Bob told everyone as they ordered drinks, that hot snacks were available now and that Tony was taking orders for egg & chips to be served during the interval.

All the usuals were there, The Major with the existing pub team, Reverend Timmy with the church group and probably about a dozen others who had turned up having been told about what was expected to be a good evening of skittles.

Outside, Constable Willis was in full police uniform ready to pounce on anyone who was about to park their vehicle in a manner that he did not like. Luckily though, most people had arrived without vehicles and PC Willis only had to have words with two youths who had arrived on a very large tractor straight from working in the fields all day and had parked with huge wheels on the small pavement.

Bob was doing what he did best, making sure that he did not leave anyone out from having a drink before going into the skittle alley.

Tony was working flat-out taking food orders and Linda was in complete control within the kitchen.

Mac stood back like a Customs Officer surveying the passengers passing through an airport, ready to handle anything that did not go according to plan, when he overheard two women talking together.

"That must be him, looks like he could be the son," one woman said.

The other replied, "But I only remember him as a little boy and he didn't look like that."

Mac found their speculation quite funny and went over to introduce himself so that there would not be any misunderstanding as to who he was. It surprised the women and left them quite embarrassed.

With absolute precision, The Major tapped on the counter and summoned all those who wanted to play skittles to move into the backroom, where he would give them more information on the format for the evening.

Surprisingly, the two women talking to Mac decided to stay in the bar and to carry on with their conversation. It did not take long for one of them to start enquiring about Mac's life in America.

"So you went over to America to live with your Dad then?"

"My Dad?" said Mac. "My Dad's not American and I live alone in a nice apartment in a swish hotel where I work."

The two women looked at each other and found it difficult to find words to respond with, as they clearly had fixed ideas in their own minds that Mac's father was American.

Bob innocently broke up the conversation when he asked the women if they intended to go and play skittles, to which they both decided that they would.

With some quietness returned to the bar, Tony totted up the supper orders along with Bob, who was thrilled with the amount of extra cash that the orders had brought in.

Tony, along with Mac went through to the kitchen to inform Linda of what she had to produce ready for the break.

When she looked at the paperwork she saw that several had ordered double eggs and chips, making an extra demand on her store of eggs.

The talk of eggs reminded Mac that they should, as he had said before, look for a new reliable local supply that would continue to help with the cost reduction programme, as he put it.

Hearing that, Tony told him that Stan Pearson, farmer Jim's brother, keeps hundreds of chickens and regularly sends eggs to a supermarket up-country which, according to Jim, paid him a 'paltry sum'.

"Well that's it Mom, let's speak to Stan and hope that we can both benefit," Mac said, as he tapped Tony on the shoulder in appreciation.

Mac and Tony then went back to join Bob in the bar to help him prepare for the onslaught that they knew would happen when The Major called a halt for halftime in the skittles.

Bob suggested that it would help to alleviate congestion at the bar if customers could be told to move away once they had received their food.

"Good idea Dad," Mac said. "Why don't we serve the food at the tables in the quiet part."

Tony then suggested that a place at each table could be reserved with the person's name and they could be told to go straight to it, at which Bob could also serve their drinks.

Mac agreed, "Let's give it a try, but make sure that Mom is aware of what we have decided."

"No Problem," Tony said, only too happy to have a reason to visit Linda and to take another whiff of that exciting perfume.

Hearing the plan from Tony, she remarked that it was not a problem for her and answered Tony with a smile and the comment, "You can tell the others Tony, that once the meals have left my kitchen door, you boys are responsible."

Tony returned to Bob and passed on Linda's comment, while Mac went to sit at a table deep in thought at what the two women had said to him earlier.

He had never found it necessary to enquire about who his true father was, as he had enjoyed such a happy time as a child with his Mom and Bob, even though he had put up with several taunts that his father was probably the obnoxious Tommy Chant.

Mac asked himself, why should they suggest that his father was American, just because he now lived and worked in America. Then he also wondered about the gossip that he had heard over the years concerning GI's stationed around the village, about the time that he was born. "Is there a connection?" he wondered and began to think that now could be the right time to ask his mother outright.

Bob poured a drink for the three of them while things were quiet and when Linda came through with food for the hot plate, she told Tony to help himself to something.

Thanking her and taking a freshly baked mini steak & ale pie, he happily tucked into it knowing that it had not been through any other hands, but Linda's.

With little time left before the break, Tony called out the customers names while Mac and Bob wrote them out on pieces of card and placed them around the tables.

By now, Linda had produced a huge pile of warm plates and had the chips simmering away in the deep fat-fryer. She asked Tony to help as soon as the skittlers started to arrive.

Mac went through to see how things were going in the skittle alley and quickly returned to tell the others that the time was about to begin for the break. So Linda put several eggs into the pan, with a whole lot more lined up ready to be cracked open as soon as there was a need.

As each person came through from the skittle alley, Bob and Mac politely directed them to the reserved tables and both thought that it was so different from the mad rush that had taken place during the previous gathering of skittlers on Monday evening.

Tony then brought through several plates, serving first those who had ordered double eggs. Mac took their drinks orders and Bob worked flat out to make sure that no one waited too long to be served.

While everyone was seated, Mac drew their attention to the notice referring to the fact that Friday Night is Steak & Ale Pie Night and took several bookings to add to some already taken during the day.

With everyone now satisfied, The Major asked them all to return to the alley for a final roll-up.

Then, with all the plates and glasses cleared, Bob and Mac tidied the bar area, while Tony helped Linda clear the mountain of dishes and plates in the kitchen. Bob thought about the evening, saying once again, **"In Walked Some Money."**

19. Mac Meets Mary

Over breakfast on Thursday morning, Mac pondered about whether or not he should ask his mother about his true father, but sensibly avoided the subject as he thought that it may embarrass Bob if he did. So he changed his thinking by saying to them, "well, how do we get hold of this Stan to ask him about the supply of eggs then?"

Bob replied that they could wait until Jim came into the pub and he could approach the subject with his brother, to which Mac replied, "Father that's just a chance and in good business we don't sit around waiting for a chance to happen - where does he live?"

Linda knew exactly where Stan lived as she had once given Stan's wife a lift home from the Co-op when she saw that she was having trouble with her car.

"Right," said Mac to his mother, "let's go right now and see if we can catch Stan before he gets too involved with other farming matters out in the fields."

On the way, Mac's thoughts again returned to the subject of his true father, sparked off by the comment made by the two women in the bar and as he was about to approach his mother on the matter, Linda suddenly said to him, "Malcolm, since you have been in America, we have not been able to celebrate any of your birthdays, so your Dad has booked a table for lunch at a very nice restaurant on Sunday as a treat before you return. It is on the coast quite near to Weymouth."

That pleased Mac, as he liked that area and it would probably give them a chance to visit Abbotsbury Swannery, where they had been to many times when he was a child.

"Oh that will be great Mom," Mac enthusiastically replied and for the time-being all thoughts of his real father faded from his mind.

As they approached the gate to Stan's farm, Linda saw Rita, his wife, walking across the yard carrying something in her upturned apron. Rita stopped to look at the unannounced car turning into their farm, from which Linda called out, "Hello Rita, it's Linda from the Dog & Whistle pub - remember me?"

"Oh Linda, of course, what's brought you to us then?"

Linda replied that it could be a bit of business for the farm.

"Come on in then," Rita replied. "Stan's here, he's had a late breakfast as we had a cow give birth soon after we got up this morning."

Linda parked up and introduced Mac as her son who is over here from America.

"Are you'm the little boy who used to play with other kids down in our pond years ago?" asked Rita of Mac.

Mac smiled and offered her some sort of recollection to the fact that he had once played about in a pond, but did not know at the time that it was Stan and Rita's pond, he only wanted some frogspawn and newts like the other kids did.

"Well you'm grown into a fine chap now, by the looks of it - mind your head on the doorpost as you come in."

Stan was still sitting at the kitchen table and as Rita started to introduce her visitors to Stan, both sides showed that they already knew each other.

"Hello Linda, what can we do for you then, so early in the morning?" Stan enquired, with a very surprised look at the two of them.

"Do I owe you some money and you've brought your big son to extract it?" Stan went on in a more jovial manner.

Linda replied with, "I wish that was true Stan, but seriously we need a new supplier of eggs on a regular basis - would you be interested?"

Stan looked at Rita in a pleasing way and both replied positively to Linda.

"Take a seat," Stan indicated to the two of them, while Rita asked if they would like a mug of coffee.

Both took a seat around the table and accepted Rita's offer of coffee. Then Linda told Stan that her Business Manager had informed her that she had to make a reduction in the purchasing costs of eggs.

Mac was armed with the details of the present costs and firmly had in his mind that nothing less that a 20% reduction would be worthwhile accepting, but before talking about prices, he had to be sure that eggs from Stan's farm met with any food regulations imposed by the government.

"Not a problem, we have that all in place in order to comply with the strict demands of several supermarkets."

Mac asked further, "So if you supplied to us, then the product would go through the same process?"

"Yes, cleaning, grading and date recording, just what we do with every shipment from this farm, there's no point of doing anything else," Stan said, pointing to a couple of framed certificates hanging on the kitchen wall.

With that settled, Stan asked Linda, with a secondary nod to Mac.

"What sort of price are you'm looking for Linda?"

Mac answered with a figure that would show a reduction well over the 20% that he was looking for.

"No can't make that figure young man, the cost of feed and the rates of the people that we employ have all increased lately."

Mac was not too worried and asked Stan at what price he thought that he could supply the Dog & Whistle.

Rita, speaking aloud, said to Stan, "don't forget we won't have the transport costs to deliver to Thimble Hardy as we do going up country."

Stan accepted Rita's comment and came up with a price that was acceptable to Mac, who worked out that it was about 18% lower than what his mother was paying through the Co-op.

Just as they started to talk about delivery dates, a very attractive young lady appeared from another room dressed in horse riding gear, who Stan proudly introduced as his daughter Mary.

"Hello Linda, remember me?" Mary asked, whilst eyeing up Mac.

"Mary, of course, sorry I didn't recognise you at first, how are you?" Linda went on to tell Mac of how Mary had brought a gathering of her friends to the Dog & Whistle one evening prior to his arrival.

Mac wasn't too concerned about how they had previously met, but was more delighted to see someone so attractive as Mary.

Resplendent in jodhpurs, yellow polo neck jumper, fawn coloured hacking jacket and jet-black hair swept back into a single plait, rounded off with ruby-red lipstick, made Mary a perfect picture in the eyes of Mac. Never before had a female raised feelings inside him as he suddenly experienced at seeing Mary.

Mac felt the need to engage her into conversation and asked if she was employed at a horse racing stable somewhere.

"No, not really Mac, I just hack out for a riding school a couple of times a week when time allows," Mary coyly replied. "I was trained as a music teacher but as I am just one year out of college, I could only find an afternoon part-time school teaching post, unless I am prepared to work away from here."

Hearing the explanation, Rita proudly added, "But she is also the brains on this farm. She looks after the books and is bringing us up-to-date with modern accounting methods."

Linda added, "Just like my little boy here." And then she brought Mac to heel by saying, "What else should we be talking about on this egg deal son?"

Mac at first found it difficult to concentrate on eggs whilst this lovely creature was close to him, but his professionalism returned when he told his mother that the rest was down to her delivery requirements and to show good faith, she should give Stan an order on the spot.

With thanks offered all round, Rita and Jim escorted Linda back to her car, whilst Mac, seeking the opportunity, walked with Mary and invited her to the pub when she could find time before he was to leave at the end of the following week. Mary took that as a compliment and was pleased to accept, saying, "I'll pop over tomorrow."

Without realising that tomorrow, Friday, was to be Steak Pie evening, Mac accepted that as a Date.

Driving back home, Mac suggested to his mother that the visit had been a profitable one as it showed a good reduction for her future cost of eggs.

Linda agreed and smugly added, "Looks like it may be profitable for you as well with that lovely Mary."

That made Mac very self conscious, who replied with, "I don't know what you mean mother."

With a sly glance towards him, Linda then said. "You do realise that tomorrow will be a busy time with Steak Pie evening."

That was an unwelcome blow to Mac as he had thought that he would be able to sit and have a chat with Mary all by himself, without the business matters of the pub interfering.

Linda could see that he was disappointed and let him flounder in his thoughts for a while, before adding a very welcome statement.

"Malcolm don't fret, you should take the evening off and treat her to a nice portion of my Steak & Ale Pie, just to show her what a gentleman you are - after all you are here on holiday."

Mac was so relieved to hear that come from his mother and if it were not for the fact that she was driving a car, he would have given her a big hug.

Back at the pub, Bob asked them how they had got on with the possibility of seeking out a new deal for the egg supply.

"I'm happy," she told Bob. "And I think that my Business Manager is also very happy with the way that negotiations went, as I think that he is going to add two more names to the Friday evening pie list."

After the pub was opened for the mid-day session, the usual four people arrived. George and Billy to play crib and Winnie with Madge to glean whatever they could pick up on the village gossip front.

They were joined by Len Scott from the paper shop, who seemed to be all hot and bothered about something.

"I need a drink Bob," he blurted out for all to hear.

"I was let down by the very late arrival of the papers this morning; the train from London was delayed, so late that I had to send my delivery boys away in order that they would not be late for school. So all the morning I have been trundling around the village pushing papers into letterboxes myself."

Bob sympathised with him and pulled him a pint of his newly acquired Scrumpy, as Len had requested.

"Oh, and by the way, thanks for sending that salesman with the glass cabinet to see me," Len mumbled between slurps of Scrumpy.

"I bought one and it has done wonders for my display of cigarettes and I'm going to buy another to show off some other nick-nicks."

It took Bob a few seconds to recall the cabinet salesman and just as he was about to take the credit, Winnie, who had not missed a word of the conversation, piped up. "Hey, 'twere I that told un to see you; the thanks are due over yer matey."

Redirecting his plaudits to Winnie and with half a nod to Madge, Len offered to buy them both another bottle of stout, which they both quickly accepted, before he could change his mind. Both thanked Len and as they happily lifted their glasses, Winnie then said, "I can't remember the last time that we had two bottles each."

Madge thought for a few seconds and came up with the answer. "Guess 'twas probably in the village hall on V-E Night when you got me to dance wee that Yankee GI sergeant, who tried to get me to go outside in the dark, just to look at the stars wee im," Madge indignantly remembered.

"So, did you go Madge?" asked Len,

"No, I gid un stars all right, I gid un a boot up the bum and ee went off we another woman." George and Billy laughed at the thought of anyone wanting to take Madge outside in the dark and Billy told her to be careful now that she was again drinking two bottles of stout at lunchtime.

20. A Letter From Hank

Postmistress Connie dropped in with the daily post and again pointed out that there was a letter from America.

"Can't be yer son this time, as ee's yer already," Connie loudly pointed out, just to make the two sitting by the door aware that she had something that they din't yet know.

Although it was addressed to the two of them, Bob took the letter into the kitchen for Linda to open and returned to the bar.

When Linda opened it, she quickly established that it was from Hank.

The letter contained Hank's thanks for their hospitality during his stay at the Dog & Whistle and also to confirm that the business he had done in the UK for his client had been accepted in full. He asked if they would be good enough to confirm that fact to Terry Smith and thank him again for his assistance.

The letter continued with some details of something that occurred on his flight back to New York, when another person claimed his baggage by mistake, but Linda seized on a surreptitious remark that confirmed in her mind that Hank was, in fact, the Junior Burnett that she had known back in 1944.

He said that his stay at the pub had recalled memories of his time in that area prior to embarkation to France in June 1944, when, sadly, GI's had to call a halt to friendships that they had made with local people.

However, he said that he had been pleased to leave behind some of the problems that GI's had with local boys and he remembered one boy called Chant being taken away by the police, after hitting a woman with a beer mug.

Linda grasped the letter to her chest with two hands as she remembered the incident well and if Hank was also there, then he must surely be the person who she knew as Junior Burnett back then.

Later, Bob read the letter, but did not pick up on the name Chant as it was quite a common surname in that part of the country.

However he was pleased to learn that Hanks's client was happy, which could lead to Hank coming back at some time to take matters further.

"So you'm got a letter from the President of the United States and ee wants to stay in this pub?" Winnie inquisitively enquired of Bob.

Taking Winnie's remark as a bit of fun, Bob replied.

"Yes and what's more he's bringing an old GI sergeant with him who's looking for a woman called Madge."

That comment caused everyone to laugh out loud, except Madge who was startled by Bob's remark and wondered if it was true.

Mac spent the rest of the morning and part of the afternoon, in his room thinking firstly about how he had managed to help his parents change their handling of the pub business. He then began to think about what he could do next to keep the ball rolling.

Promotion of the pub to acquire more feet coming over the threshold, he said under his breath.

Advertising beyond the village had already been accepted and Tony had been so good in offering to help on that score. More use of the skittle alley seems to be well underway.

Making the pub more attractive, both inside and out has definitely got to be the next thing, he spoke aloud, as if he was giving a presentation to a group of under managers back at the hotel in New York. Coloured lights has just got to be the thing to attract people's attention.

But overshadowing everything in his mind was the fact that only a few hours ago, he had been made aware that there was a person out there who he had suddenly taken a liking to. Apart from his mother, he had never before experienced the feeling of love for a woman and could not wait for Mary to fulfil her promise and come to the pub next day.

Reclining in an armchair during the afternoon break, Mac asked Bob if he had any coloured lights to hang outside on the wall to draw people's attention to the pub.

Bob told him that he had some stored away from the previous time that he hung them outside, however he was told to remove them by the Parish Council as he had not applied for planning permission.

Mac was pleased to know that some lights existed, but was not happy that they would have to submit a planning application.

Bob told him that it was a procedure that could take months to come up for consideration and in any case there was no guarantee that it would be passed, knowing that some village people were against it.

Linda added that she was very cross at the time. For some of the people that complained were the very same ones who raised objections when the brewery made noises about closing the pub a couple of years before they took on the licence.

"Talk about being two-faced," she stated with feeling.

Mac thought for a while and then asked Bob if there was anything in his agreement with the brewery that prevented him from hanging lights inside the pub.

Linda was quick to answer that last Christmas they did just that and were complimented by the brewery Rep on such a good display.

"That's it," said Mac. "Let's make a good coloured light display at the windows and around the inside of the main door, so that they can be seen from the outside and if the weather's OK leave the door open. That should not contravene any planning regulations."

Bob tentatively agreed, but suggested that they should play it softly by asking Tony's father, who is a parish Councillor, if he thought that it might cause any problems.

Mac replied "Baloney - that would put him on the spot and he would probably not want to be implicated. Let's just get on with it and let anyone raise their objections later." To which both parents agreed.

With that decision made, Bob settled back to have his customary ten minute snooze before starting work for the evening.

21. Disappointment for Jill

As Bob came round from his snooze, a rattle on the back door brought him to his senses while Linda went to investigate.

"Maggie - Jill, wonderful to see you both come on in."

She took them through to the bar so that Bob would not be disturbed in the sitting room and also so that Mac did not have to put up with woman-to-woman conversations.

"So what brings you?"

Maggie firstly explained that His Lordship from the Big House had informed the staff that he and his family would be staying on in their Spanish villa for another three weeks.

That pleased Linda, for she immediately reckoned that the two of them would be available to help out in the pub when required as they did before.

"So would you both be available tomorrow evening, as we have another Steak & Ale Pie evening and I could use your help?"

Maggie looked at Jill and they both nodded in agreement.

"So that's it then - 5.30 we open as you know."

Linda noticed that Jill was not quite her usual bubbly self and wondered if something was troubling her, but before Linda could enquire, Jill said that there was something else that they had come to tell her.

"I have broken off my engagement," she said holding back tears.

Jill went on to tell Linda that Keith, her fiancé, had been accepted for the navy before they met, but had turned it down when their relationship became serious.

However, it had been a decision that he regretted as he had always wanted to join the navy since he was a young boy and now it was a matter that continually played on his mind.

"You can guess that I did not want to be left alone and so we decided to end it," said Jill.

Linda was sympathetic and showed a motherly compassion towards Jill, asking if there was anything that she could do to help.

Jill explained that the whole matter had been done with complete understanding on both sides and it was very amicable. They had agreed to stay good friends and both families were supportive.

"You see Linda, I didn't want to stand in his way and he accepted that I could not put up with someone who would always be away from me."

Both Linda and Maggie nodded with cautious agreement and saw what a very logical person Jill was.

Linda offered to backtrack on her request for Jill's help the next day, but she would not hear of it and welcomed the chance to get out and do something different with her life.

As with all British women when there is the slightest suggestion of a trauma, Linda said, "Would you both like a cup of tea."

Both declined as they had to get back to the Big House and offer up food for the few staff that had been working in the grounds all day.

"Well I look forward to seeing you both tomorrow evening then, take care," Linda said as she waved goodbye.

When Linda went in to tell the news to Bob and Mac, both were very surprised, but Mac, remembering what the Reverend Timmy had said to him, he told his mother,

"Keith obviously had a calling."

With that, Bob and Linda went about their business to get ready for the opening of yet another evening in the bar.

Mac, in the meantime, returned to his thoughts of the lovely Mary and wondered if she had a boyfriend, after all she was at the age for romance and very attractive with it.

Then he consoled himself with the thought that maybe he was in the right place at the right time, as she could be waiting for the ideal person to come along.

Thursday evening in the pub was not known for a rush of customers eagerly wanting to spend their cash on alcohol, they were more prone to staying at home waiting for payday.

However, the word had got around the village that the Dog & Whistle now had a Jukebox and people could play their own choice of music any time that they liked.

This brought in a few younger people and Bob had to politely ask if they were all aged 18 or over, as he did not want to get in PC Willis's bad books and perhaps lose his licence.

There were three boys and a girl, who played a choice of music that was not to Bob's liking and Linda emer   ged from the kitchen to find out what was going on, as it was not to   her taste either.

Bob and Linda looked at each other with a delayed shrug of their shoulders and happily accepted, that apart from the coins going into the machine, all four had bought a drink.

As Linda turned to go to the sanctuary of the kitchen, Bob whispered to her, "Just think love, if it were not for that music now being played, we would not have taken the money that those four have spent."

Linda understood and smiling, said, "You can thank Mac for that."

Bob began to sway along with the music and accepted that as it was early evening and no other people were in the pub, 'The Rolling Stones' were not causing a problem.

Another boy and a girl joined the group, bought drinks and took a look at the musical play list in the machine. They then inserted a couple of coins to keep the music going.

Later, into the pub came Georgie Bailey with his wife Lucy and Bob greeted them with the question of why they were in the pub so early in the evening.

"Hi Bob, we were out for a walk on this lovely sunny evening and happened to hear the music," said Lucy.

Georgie added, "With that type of music, we thought that you had suddenly retraced your youthful years Bob."

Bob replied, "That sort of music was not around when I was a youth - we had Bing Crosby and the like."

Georgie recognising that Bob was having to put up with the modern stuff for the sake of business, thought that he would change the mood somewhat. So over to the Jukebox he went and fed in a couple of coins and made a selection that turned out to be Linda's favourite Mantovani string orchestra.

When their selection had run out and the Mantovani music started to play, the youths could see that their time of controlling the machine was up. So with a friendly thanks to Bob and a cheery wave to Lucy and Georgie, they left to seek further enjoyment elsewhere.

During conversation, Georgie told Bob how pleased he was that Tony had taken on doing work for his company and Lucy added that her parents were happy that he had again taken up the type of work that he had been trained to do.

"My Dad said that he thought that Tony had taken advice from someone at the pub," Lucy happily added.

Bob, wanting to take some credit for what had happened, but not wanting to seem boastful, laughingly said, "Well we do sometimes act as an employment agency if it helps to keep people off the streets."

Having listened to the Mantovani music come to a halt, Georgie drained his glass and told Lucy that they had better continue with their walk before sunset and left the pub.

Being all alone in the bar, Bob thought yet again, if it were not for the Jukebox, he wouldn't have had the financial input from the youths and also that which Georgie and Lucy contributed unexpectedly.

In the meantime, Linda had joined Mac in the sitting room and switched on the TV to watch some light entertainment.

Tommy Cooper was on with his magic tricks show, which always went wrong, causing hordes of laughter from the studio audience and viewers alike. Mac was doubled up and Linda was so pleased to see him relaxed and enjoying himself away from business matters.

22. Friday is Pie Evening

Friday morning saw the start of a very busy day and so immediately after breakfast, Bob busied himself in the cellar and Linda took a look at her pots and pans in the kitchen.

Mac continued his attention on the thought of making the pub more profitable and again took a good look at the rooms and their layout.

The bricked up entrance to the cottage next door figured much in his thoughts and he believed that if the brewery had any sense, they could reopen it so that the use of the cottage could be made to work for the profit of their brewery.

Mac's belief was that if his mother and Bob were to move into the cottage, the existing private part of the pub could be converted into a restaurant with additional guest rooms above. However that would cost money and according to his mother, the brewery had already made it clear that they were not intending to spend anything on the fabric of the pub.

Then, looking around in the car park, Mac could also see the obvious potential of extending the building, or even building some free-standing apartments away from the main building - just like the Motels that had sprung up all over America.

With further thought, the back garden of the cottage could also be developed into something that made money, sooner than letting it lie overgrown with weeds and brambles as it had done since the death of Sarah's husband.

Mac said to himself, so much potential exists in and around the premises of the pub and the adjoining cottage, that it is a crying shame that nobody has seen the opportunity and done something about it so far.

Linda, seeing Mac in the car park, tapped on the window and beckoned him to come in for a mid-morning cup of coffee. After which Mac took a long stroll around the village alone, to see what may have changed since his time away and also to estimate just what customer potential the village had for the pub.

While Mac was absent from the pub, a small van pulled into the car park and out got Mary, who came to the back door and told Linda that her father had asked her to deliver the first batch of eggs that had been ordered.

Linda was pleased on two accounts. Firstly that her eggs had arrived and secondly that she was delighted to see the lovely Mary again. She made coffee for Mary and settled the account that Stan had included.

Looking around her, Mary was aware that Mac did not seem to be about and politely told Linda that she had promised Mac that she would visit the pub today and enquired if he was in the bar.

"Oh Mary, he has gone for a walk and I am surprised that you did not see him on your way in."

Mary was disappointed to hear that and showed it by the sudden change in her body language, which Linda detected straight away. She went on to say that Mac should be back anytime now, but in any case she would be seeing him later that evening.

Mary frowned at the comment and asked Linda what she meant by 'this evening', conveying that there appeared to be some misunderstanding.

"Mary dear, aren't you aware that Mac has booked a table for the two of you at our Steak & Ale Pie Evening tonight?"

Clearly, this was news to Mary, who's face turned into pleasure as she realised that their arranged meeting was to be more than just a casual chat whilst delivering her father's eggs.

Just then, Bob came up from the cellar and seeing Mary jokingly said, "hello Mary, you are early, we don't serve the pie until 7.00 o'clock, but you are at least the first in the queue."

Mary accepted Bob's quip in the playful manner that it was intended and replied along the lines, that she had learned that she did not have to queue as a 'handsome prince' had made a reserved booking for them both.

That pleased both Bob and Linda, because it showed that Mary was no push-over and could hold her own in any conversation.

Having finished her coffee, Mary went out to her van and returned with the eggs that she had been asked to deliver and said goodbye to both Bob and Linda with a, "see you this evening."

As Mary was about to drive out of the car park, she saw that Mac had returned from his walk and winding down her window she called out, "hello stranger."

Mac was so surprised to see Mary and asked what she was doing at the pub so early in the day, to which she replied, "Business Mac - purely business."

Mac didn't care whatever her reason was, as he was exceptionally pleased to see Mary and blurted out, "but are you still coming this evening?"

Mary nodded in a very positive manner, but playing down her excitement at seeing Mac again, she told him that she had better be going for as she put it, "in business, time is money."

Although he was not pleased to see Mary go so quickly, he liked her statement about 'Time is Money', for it showed that she did at least understand what business is all about.

Both agreed that the time of their next meeting would be 7.00pm later and the van disappeared down the High Street.

As Mac went in through the backdoor, Linda said, "Oh, Mac, you have just missed Mary, she came to deliver the eggs."

"OK Mom, I saw her and we had a quick chat to confirm that she will be coming again this evening."

"Oh, I am so pleased that you have it sorted, as I think that there could have been a bit of a misunderstanding."

Bob, in the meantime, not involved with the purchase of eggs, or the sorting out of other people's meeting times, got on with opening the pub. He hoped that many folk would build up a thirst to go with their lunch on this nice sunny morning. He also began to apply his thoughts to the Steak & Ale Pie evening and wondered if Linda had arranged to secure the help of Maggie and Jill again for the event.

Linda confirmed that both of her willing helpers would again be available and asked Bob if he had made any arrangements with Tony for the same purpose.

"Crikey no!" said Bob, with a worrying intake of breath. "I'll just have to wait and see if he turns up, if not then Mac will have to help out in the bar."

"Sorry Bob," said Linda. "Mac already has another engagement this evening that he is unable to be released from."

Bob's mind was relieved from the problem when into the pub came Winnie and Madge as usual.

They were followed soon after by the two council workers, who announced that their work on the road had been completed. They ordered a couple of beers and told Bob that the road drainage at the far end of the High Street had now been improved, so there should not be any further complaints about water stagnating at the side of the road.

Bob was unaware of any such complaint, but Winnie knew about it and said to them, "I hope that you've done both sides of the road, 'cause it b'aint no good if you'm only done one side."

"All right Missus, we've done that and we've also done the middle of the road too", said the second man, sarcastically.

Madge questioned why they had done the middle of the road.   "Not much good putting a drain in the middle 'cause a tractor could damage it."

Winnie smiled at Madge's comment and said that she expected that the two men would put up a sign that said, "Tractors Keep Off".

"Oh that's OK then, don't want any broken pipes do we?" she replied

The two men laughed at the comments that they were hearing and ended the conversation by putting a coin in the Jukebox that released a song by Sammy Davis Jnr, called, "What Kind Of Fool Am I'.

This caused Bob to turn his back on the two women and suppress a deep snigger.

As Bob and Linda were clearing up and getting ready to close the pub on the mid-day session, Tony appeared to ask Bob if he was needed for the pie evening.

"Tony, just the man I wanted to see. Yes I do need you and thanks for your consideration," Bob answered.

Tony was happy to learn that he would be needed and agreed to help out later.

Hearing Tony's voice, Linda called him into the kitchen saying, "Hello my handsome, are you coming to handle my hot stuff this evening?"

Although Linda did not deliberately mean her question in any sexual way, Tony was happy to think that she did and was glad of the comment.

"Yes Linda, I'll be here for your services," he replied with an innuendo of his own.

Mac heard the banter and was again pleased to see how well the two of them worked together for the benefit of the pub.

Tony then left for home and the other three settled in the kitchen for a light meal before retiring to the sitting room for a rest.

Mac asked them what happens at this special pie evening and how many people would be attending.

Linda explained that she had 22 firm bookings all paid for in advance and that others may also turn up asking to take part.

"Gee Mom, that's a lot of meals to be catered for all at the same time, do you think that you can manage?"

His mother explained that she had the services of Maggie and Jill from the Big House and of course there is also Tony who knows the workings of both the bar and the kitchen.

"So can I help?" Mac enquired.

"No you are a customer with a special guest to entertain this evening, forget business and concentrate on pleasure for once."

Maggie and Jill arrived at 5.00pm and Bob made a pot of tea for them all while Linda ensured that Maggie and Jill were fully acquainted with Mac.

When they had finished their tea and chat, Linda jokingly told Mac to clear off to his room as the workers had work to do.

That he did and the three women set about their respective tasks, whilst Bob checked over the Jukeboxes in the bar and and skittle alley. He also brought in three large screens that he had stored at the back of the pub garage.

Linda told Maggie and Jill that in view of the large number of bookings she had decided to make five trays of pie, each containing six portions, but would have to bake them in two sessions.

Jill in her wisdom suggested that it could be handled in two sittings, say three quarters of an hour apart and she and Bob could handle the sittings on a 'first-come, first-served' basis, whilst keeping the late comers occupied at the bar.

"Jill, what a good idea," exclaimed Linda and Maggie nodded in agreement. "We will have to let Bob and Tony know the arrangement."

As Jill went into the bar, she saw Bob struggling with the screens and helped to arrange them so that they would give a degree of privacy to the customers in the eating area. Together, they arranged the tables for the seating of four and two people and Jill decorated each to provide a warm atmosphere for the customers.

When Linda saw what had been done, she was extremely satisfied and immediately reserved a table for two in a quiet corner for a couple of "Special Guests' who she knew would be coming later.

Bob was puzzled by the reservation and asked Linda who the occupants would be.

"It's a secret that is only entrusted to the Restaurant Manager," she laughingly goaded him. "You will have to wait and see like the rest of the staff."

Bob shrugged his shoulders and got on with his work.

Tony arrived in good time and was briefed by Bob and Jill about what was to take place at mealtime and then settled into a conversation with Jill about her work at the Big House.

In exchange, Jill was interested to learn something about Tony's engineering background, before Linda broke up their friendly chat by calling him into the kitchen to ask if he knew of any more names that needed to be added to her pie list.

Soon after Bob opened up for the expected Friday evening bonanza, 'Old Tom' called in for his usual drink on the way home from another warm day of thatching at a barn five miles away.

"Do I ever need that Landlord?" he told Bob, whilst downing half of his drink in one gulp. Then, walking over to the Jukebox, he put in a coin and out came Louis Armstrong singing 'What a Wonderful World'.

Tony's father and mother arrived at 6.45 and they were followed by Terry Smith, The Major, and his wife Joan who, after purchasing their drinks, talked freely about the excellent smell coming out of the kitchen.

To cause a bit of a laugh, Tony acknowledged his parents and asked, "Do you have a table booked Sir - Madam?"

To which his mother replied, "Who are you - are you new here?"

Among the laughter, Jill informed the kitchen that customers were beginning to arrive, which pleased Maggie as she had the starters ready to serve and needed the space that would be vacated.

Noticing that others were coming into the pub, Jill then politely invited the four to take a seat at whichever table they liked behind the screen.

Georgie and Lucy Bailey then arrived and entered into a banter with Tony along the lines that he would soon know enough about the hotel business to buy a pub of his own.

"Depends on how much welding work you can offer me, so that I can build up my bank balance," Tony replied to his brother-in-law.

23. A Friendship Develops

Realising that the time had arrived for the evening meals to be served, Mac came down from his room and entered the kitchen asking if there was anything he could do to help.

"I have told you Malcolm, it is your evening off and you should go and look out for the arrival of Mary," his mother told him. "Oh, and by-the-way, I have reserved a table just for the two of you in the corner. Don't tell your father as he is anxious to know who it is reserved for and I am keeping him guessing."

Mac laughed and went through to speak to Bob and Tony and as he was making sure that the till was still working to his satisfaction, he noticed Mary's parents, Stan and Rita, coming through the door. He assumed that Mary would be with them and anxiously looked for her.

Several others came into the pub and some wanted to talk to Mac, enquiring what life was like in America. Others asked when he was going back, but all the time Mac was scanning the room to see if Mary had arrived.

"Hello Mac, nice to see you again," came the voice of Mary's mother.

"Hi Rita," Mac replied. "Is Mary with you?"

Oh no, she has a life of her own and she told us that she had an appointment to keep with someone else."

Mac's face dropped to the floor and his body quivered from the knees up, at the thought that Mary had stood him up for someone else. The rest of the conversation with Mary's mother meant nothing to him and even when Stan came to enquire whether he and Linda were happy with the eggs that Mary had delivered, he did not really respond in the professional manner that he had always done to his suppliers.

As the bar was becoming quite crowded, Jill ushered a few more diners to take up their seats behind the screen. Among them was Farmer Jim, Mary's uncle and his wife Betty, who took seats at a table along with Mary's parents.

Mac, feeling somewhat dejected, consoled himself by opening the door to the skittle alley and let some youths through to play the Jukebox in there.

The first tune selected was The Rolling Stones with Mick Jagger singing 'I Can't Get No Satisfaction', which did not help Mac's feelings at all. So back to the bar he went and took up a conversation with Tony about the splendid way that Jill was working to the satisfaction of the diners.

Then suddenly, music to his ears as he heard Bob behind him say "Hello Mary my love, you are looking wonderful this evening."

Mac swung around and to his delight, he saw the lovely Mary looking like someone off the front cover of a fashion magazine.

"Hello Mary, I am so pleased that you have been able to make it," Mac excitedly announced.

Mary replied in a very positive manner and told him that she had been pleased to accept their arranged meeting and was looking forward to sampling his mother's steak and ale pie.

Bob poured a drink for the two of them and said that if they were intending to eat then unfortunately they would have to wait for the second sitting as all the tables had been taken.

"Don't worry landlord," Mac replied. "I have a table reserved for my guest and I in the corner there."

"Well blow me down," Bob chuckled. "So you are the important guests, you must be in the know around here to get a reservation like that on a busy night."

Both Tony and Jill had heard the conversation and realised the ploy that Linda had played on her husband and laughed along with Mac.

As Jill ushered the two of them to the reserved table in the corner, every eye in the dining area focused on the beauty of Mary with most men envying Mac. Georgie wondered how he had managed to secure the attention of Mary in such a short time.

Old Jim had an answer, saying aloud, "He's a good businessman."

Over dinner, Mac wondered why they had not met before, particularly when they were younger and he had floated around the villages with other boys.

Mary explained that she was educated at a private girls school in Sherbourne and didn't mix much with other local youngsters, particularly as her parent's farm was someway out of the village. She then went on to say that she then moved away to college in Bournemouth for three years and her social life centred around the college activities.

The next question that Mac wanted to know was did Mary have a boyfriend, or was she free of relationships with the opposite sex.

"Oh Mac, no I am not tied to anyone, I have been too busy studying to get qualified. Now that I help mother and father on the farm I have had no time to go looking for a husband."

Much of what Mac was hearing mirrored his own existence over the past few years and he was pleased to learn that no other person was involved in her life romantically. She had previously told him about her part-time music teaching and her mother had praised her worth in managing the farm accounts, so things were falling into place and he now had a good outline of who she was.

Mary, on the other hand, wanted to know about his life in America and asked why at such a young age he had decided to leave the village and cast his net overseas.

Mac explained how he had answered an advertisement for young British men to take up training in the US with all expenses paid, soon after he had left a trainee management position on the railway.

"So now you have a job in New York that is too good to leave and return back to the UK, or is it that you have romantic connections over there?"

Mac was hesitant in replying to the first part of the question, as he thought that his true answer may spoil his chances of developing this relationship any further. So he just smiled and firmly denied the second part, giving the same reason as she had done about her life.

Mac then very cleverly steered the conversation to the fact that she also rode horses and asked if she liked it.

"Oh yes, I have ridden since I was six years old, but keeping a horse just for pleasure these days is so expensive. Luckily I am able to keep up my riding by doing the stables a favour exercising their horses whenever they need me."

Again, Mac admired the clever way in which Mary had got round a problem that resulted in her favour.

"Mary, that is a very clever piece of thinking, you ought to be an adviser to the Government," he remarked.

That made Mary giggle with the thought that she could end up in Westminster one day.

Mary's mother and aunt could see how happy Mary was in the company of Mac. Jim remarked that he hoped that one day when Mac would be President of the United States of America, Mary could be First Lady, if she played her cards right.

As a few diners finished their meal, they left their tables and adjourned to the bar for further drinks and to play their selections on the Jukebox. That pleased Jill, who quickly cleared the tables and relaid them for the next sitting.

Very much to Mary's surprise, among the second-sitting diners were Patrick and Olivia O'Reilly, the owners of the riding stables, who immediately acknowledged Mary. She in turn, happily blew them a kiss as a greeting. Mary then explained to Mac who the couple were and said that she would introduce him to them when it was convenient.

In the meantime, the two in the corner who were exploring each other's background and present life, were so comfortable in each other's company, giggling at the least little thing that showed that they clearly had a liking for each other.

Jill cleared their meal plates and asked if they wanted the lemon cheesecake dessert made by Maggie especially for the this evening.

As both were satisfied with what they had consumed already they declined and settled for coffee.

Mary asked Mac when he would be leaving to go back to America.

"Well, I have one more week here in Thimble Hardy and then I plan on having a week sightseeing in London, after which, I need to be back to take charge of the hotel while my boss goes on leave."

Mac then asked Mary if she had ever been to America, to which she replied that she had not and really didn't have a reason to visit, when there were so many places in the UK that she would still like to visit.

The longer the conversation went on, Mac could see that he may have opportunities to tempt Mary away for a visit that would add to her knowledge of the world.

Mary on the other-hand, inwardly could see that she had made a friend in Mac and that might give her a reason to visit America one day and she told him so.

Mac was delighted to hear that coming unprompted from her and told her, "I will accept that as a promise."

Clearly they were both flirting with each other and each was enjoying the close liaison.

Settling back with a brandy each, after finishing their Steak and Ale Pie, Patrick and Olivia were curious to know who the handsome gent was that Mary was enjoying the evening with.

Olivia, 'Olly' to all, suggested to her husband that they could invite the two of them over for a drink, and so he beckoned Mary and Mac to join them.

Both willingly accepted the invitation and moved across to sit with them, whereupon Mary introduced Mac as her good friend from America.

Mac, ever the gentleman, politely shook hands with both of them and asked if he could get all four a nightcap.

Patrick turned the request around saying, "no, we invited you - I insist."

As Mac could see that Patrick's kind gesture would put more money through the till, he gladly accepted.

Jill took their order and passed it to Tony, who quickly came back with the drinks and gave Mac a wink that conveyed that he thought that Mac was doing all right.

Patrick thanked Tony and turned to Mary and then to Mac with a raised glass. Mac in return did the same to Olly and Patrick.

"So where in the US do you live Mac?" asked Patrick.

To which he answered New York and asked Patrick had he ever been there.

"Oh yes, many times, you see before we took on the stables, I was a Purser in the Merchant Navy and New York appeared a lot on my itinerary."

Mary didn't know that and asked if that is how the two of them met.

"Well, kind of, yes," answered Olly. "I was an Air Hostess and we rather bumped into each other in New York one day."

Mary saw both of their previous jobs as being something very exciting and wondered why they did not stick with that type of work.

Patrick replied that it was impossible to continue with that life once they had married, as they hardly ever saw each other.

"You see Mary, we valued our time together and you don't get that when you are travelling around the world separately as we were doing at the time."

Mac enquired as to whether or not they had any previous knowledge of horses before taking on the riding school, to which both replied with an emphatic yes.

"I was a farmer's son from Ireland and as luck would have it, Olivia was from a well-to-do family in Surrey and has had ponies and horses all her life," replied Patrick. At that point, Mary told Mac that both of them were excellent riders and that they had taught her a lot that had enabled her to improve since she joined the riding school.

"So you also ride Mac?" enquired Olly, assuming that he did.

Embarrassingly, Mac had to admit that the only thing that he had ever ridden was his bike, when he was a lot younger.

Patrick turned the tables on Mac and asked what he did for a living in New York and asked how he had met Mary.

"I am the Assistant General Manager of a very prestigious hotel", Mac replied to both Patrick and Olivia's surprise, which enabled him to avoid the second part of the question..

"Gee Mac, that's some heck of a responsibility that you have taken on," Patrick responded.

"Yes, but I have been well trained by my employers and in America one gets rewarded for ability and dedication," Mac quickly replied.

The more that Patrick heard of Mac's business ethos, the more his admiration grew for him and he began to think that Mary had landed a most intelligent and well mannered American friend.

As time was pressing for the two, Olly reminded her husband that they had better make a move, as there was still work to be done at the stables locking down for the night.

"Yes of course, but what a shame, as I was enjoying this conversation, " Patrick remarked to Olly and then with a nod to Mac.

"Tell you what," he came back. "Mary why don't you bring Mac to the stables one day next week and you can give him a basic lesson in horse riding at my expense?"

Olly agreed and came out with a statement that it would be like the old Chinese saying, 'Chip on House' - meaning that it would not cost him anything.

"Well that's nice of you Patrick, I am sure Mac would like that," Mary eagerly said, accepting on behalf of both, before Mac could utter a word of refusal.

Mac, for once was lost for words, but graciously accepted their offer with trepidation and escorted them to the door in his well trained manner.

When Mac returned to continue his most enjoyable conversation with the lovely Mary, he immediately noticed that her alcohol intake was having an effect on her, as she appeared quite sleepy. He realised that the end had come to any sensible conversation and that she was not in any fit state to drive herself home.

Luckily, Mary's parents were still in the pub and so Mac arranged for them to take Mary home and somehow he would see that her car was returned to the farm early next day.

Wisely, Mary accepted the situation and slurring her words, thanked Mac for a wonderful evening as she held onto her mother while she was escorted out of the pub.

As all the other diners had finished their meal and Linda was taking a breather from her work in the kitchen, she entered the bar and noticed Mary being escorted out of the pub.

"Mac, what has happened to Mary?" she gasped. "Is she ill?"

"No mother, she has just had a little too much to drink."

Believing that it was Mac's fault, Linda was about to rebuke him, but he said, "It was that brandy that her riding school Buddy bought her as a nightcap that caused the problem."

Linda was still worried that Mary's parents might think that Mac had deliberately caused Mary to get into that state and that they may not wish to accept Mac as an honourable friend for Mary.

As she went to tell Bob of the situation, he excitedly asked her how she had done in the kitchen and how many portions of pie might there be left over.

"I cooked 30 portions and sold 27, so that is good business in anybody's language," she replied.

That satisfied Bob, for his calculation deduced that Linda would give two of the remaining three potions to Maggie and Jill, as she had done before.

That meant that he was certain to have the remaining third portion later, when everyone had left the pub.

Jill cleared the dining area, while Tony rearranged the seating and cleared all the glasses in the bar, after which they both joined Linda and Maggie in the kitchen.

Mac, meanwhile, joined his father behind the counter and Bob began making mental calculations about what the evening had produced financially.

"Father, you don't have to do that, remember we can push a button on the till and it will give us a readout of exactly what has happened in every department," said Mac, using his experience over Bob's forgetfulness.

With that, Mac showed him again how it could be done and out came a piece of paper about six inches long, that contained all the facts of the sales for that day.

The two of them anxiously peered over the details and saw that 'Food' was the best seller, with 'Wine' and 'Beer' about equal. 'Cider' had sold well earlier in the day and Bob thought that it was because workers went for that type of drink as a real thirst quencher.

Bob was very pleased with the result, but Mac reminded him that the best sellers are not necessarily the most profitable and until they were lined up with costs, the amounts did not provide the full picture. "Remember the 'Numbers' game," he reminded Bob.

"Let's wait until we close tomorrow evening and then we will have the facts on the trading for a complete week."

Bob half accepted what Mac was saying, but really was more than happy that the total taken was well above what he had ever taken in one day before. Mac had to agree with him and did not wish to dampen his excitement, so he then finished talking about money and helped Bob lockup the pub for the night.

Bob's thoughts then turned to the final portion of pie that he knew Linda would have waiting for him in the kitchen.

So he then turned to Mac and he came out with his classic remark, **"In Walked Some Money."**

But, yet again WHAM! As he went into the kitchen he saw that his pie had been given to Tony.

Bob felt really cheated yet again, but was happy that Linda had rewarded her three workers with the remaining pieces of pie, after all what would she have done without their help at such a busy time?

Casting his eye around the dishes that Linda had used to cook the pies, he noticed that one still had some pastry and a lump of meat stuck to it, so he scooped it onto a plate and Maggie noticing what he had done, offered him some hot left-over gravy which he thankfully poured over his late night meal.

When Linda saw what he had done, she could not help but to laugh and commented that it really had come to something when the boss of the establishment had to go scrounging among the dirty dishes to get himself a free meal.

Bob was full of laughter and commented, "Waste not - want not."

Tony, happily sitting next to Jill, struck up a conversation with her about where she came from and enquired about where she now lived. He had heard about Jill splitting up from her fiancé and found that he was beginning to have a liking for her.

Jill replied positively to his questions and enquired about his work and eventually got round to asking Tony if he had a girlfriend.

"Not any more," he replied. "I did have a relationship once, but it ended when she decided to take a job on one of the ocean liners."

Jill sympathised with him and Linda showed surprise, as she had not heard that information from Tony before.

Bob added to the tittle-tattle by saying, "You know Jill, he would make a good catch for someone, because he's a jolly good worker."

With that remark, the gathering broke up, with Linda thanking them all for their contribution to a successful evening and they all went on their separate ways home.

Mac went to his room, feeling very much let down by what had happened to end his evening with Mary.

24. So What Next?

Next morning, Mac was anxious to renew his friendship with Mary and asked his mother that if he were to drive Mary's car to the farm would she follow him in her car to bring him back.

Linda agreed, as she was also anxious to learn if any harm had been done to her relationship with Mary's parents, over the situation that Mary had been led into last evening.

As they both parked up in Stan's farm, Stan emerged from one of the barns and acknowledged them as friends, saying, "Hello nice to see you, that was a jolly nice evening that you both put on last night."

What a relief that was for Linda, but Mac was still very much concerned that Mary may be thinking otherwise.

"Nice to see you also - how is Mary? I've brought her car back - Is she about?"

Words just tumbled uncontrollably out of Mac's mouth and he realised that what he was saying may be perceived as that coming from a guilty person, so he said no more and left the conversation for his mother to handle.

Stan did not seem too concerned about anything and took them to the door of the house and called out to Rita that she had some visitors.

"Well hello you two, what brings you out so early?"

Linda explained that Mac had driven Mary's car to the farm and that she had come too, so that he did not have to walk back home.

Rita thanked them both and said how she thought that Mary would appreciate their gesture.

"How is Mary?" Mac asked with concern.

"Oh you had better ask her yourself, she is in the other room - go on through - first door on the left along the passage."

Mac was not sure what to read into that, but summoning up all the experience that he had gained through his training, he put his head round the door and said, "Good Morning."

Mary, lifting her head from reading the morning paper, was surprised to see Mac and rather shyly invited him in.

"How are you Mary?" Mac enquired as though she had been ill.

"Still not quite myself, but more damaged inwardly as I am so embarrassed Mac, that I could not finish our enjoyable conversation last evening - I have never been like that before."

Mary's comment lifted a huge weight off Mac's mind, as it was clear that she was not cross with him for the way the evening had closed.

"Come and sit here beside me and I'll make it up to you," Mary boldly offered.

Mac willingly sat on the settee alongside her and as he could smell the delights of her morning perfume, she took his hand and kissed it.

"Thanks for everything," she said in a rather coy manner.

"That's OK Mary, I'm just glad that you are not angry with me."

Mary went on to ask why he had come to the farm so early and Mac told her that he had returned her car.

"My car? Of course I had forgotten about that, thanks a lot, so let me drive you back."

Mac explained that Linda had followed in her car for that purpose and was in the kitchen talking to her mother.

"So Linda is here now, when she has work to be done at the pub?"

Mac reaffirmed the fact that Linda was here and agreed that his mother ought to be getting back to her work in the Dog & Whistle.

"Mac, why don't we let your mother go now and I will run you back later when we have had a chance to continue our conversation for a while?"

A stream of excitement ran through Mac's body at that suggestion for it immediately told him that Mary wanted to be in his company and it echoed his own thoughts about her.

So, still holding his hand, she took him through to the kitchen to tell Linda of her suggestion.

When Linda heard what Mary had suggested, she readily agreed as she thought that it would do both of them good to be able to have some time together away from the pub.

Rita also believed that it would be a good idea and suggested to Mary that she should take Mac around the farm and show him some of the animals, particularly where the chickens are kept.

"OK that's settled then," Mary said as she smiled at Mac.

After seeing Linda safely back on the road to Thimble Hardy, Mary excused herself to finish a few things, while Rita was pleased to have Mac to herself so that she could enquire more about his life in America.

Both were getting on well together, when Mary reappeared saying,

"Right young man, let's see if we can make a farmer of you."

The thought of being a farmer was far from being in Mac's mind as his profession had very much made him a city dweller, however he would go along with anything at the present time just to be with lovely Mary.

When Linda arrived back without Mac, Bob enquired what had happened to him, to which Linda replied,

"I left him checking out the credentials of my new egg supplier and his staff."

Bob didn't quite understand why that was necessary, but when Linda whispered, "Mary," he fell into line with her thinking.

Mary first took Mac into a barn to see some cows that had young calves and where Stan was finishing feeding them some hay.

"Dad, Mum has suggested that I show Mac around the farm, after all he represents our new customer," Mary informed her father.

Stan was happy to oblige and told Mac, "Be careful where you'm treading with them posh shoes - cows ain't fussy what they'm doing around yer."

Mac had to laugh at Stan's comment and could see quite clearly what the difference is between working on a farm and working in an hotel.

After they had finished walking around the farm, the pair went back to the kitchen where Mary made coffee for the two of them, which they then took to sit at a table on the well kept lawn.

Mac thought that this was ideal, as it gave them the isolation to be entirely on their own and Mary thought likewise as it gave her the chance to quiz Mac further about his life in America.

"So what do you do with yourself away from work in New York?" Mary asked in an intelligent manner.

"As I frequently have to work until late in the evening and occasionally through the night, I have to catch up on my sleep through most of the day," Mac admitted in a semi-businesslike manner.

"But when I do have the opportunity to get out, I like to visit concerts, or go to Broadway shows - Oh, and then I go to the odd sporting affair, if I can get a ticket without having to pay an arm and leg," he laughingly put it.

"So do you do this alone, or do you have friends to go with?" Mary continued to probe.

"Mostly alone, because the nature of my work does not allow me to plan ahead with anyone," Mac sadly had to admit.

Then seizing the opportunity to flirt with her again, he added, "That could be different if I had you as friend in New York."

Those were nice words to Mary and so she came back with a flirt of her own when she replied, "You never know Mac - one day."

How well the two of them were able to converse and it was clear to both of them that they were very happy in each others company.

As the morning progressed they both felt that time was racing and Mac realised that he ought to be getting back to the pub to make sure that all was still going to plan there.

Before they went, both agreed that they should meet again before he had to leave for his return to America.

Mac explained that the next day was not possible as his parents had planned to take him out for a special lunch, but he was available on Monday.

"OK Monday afternoon it is, we will take up Patrick's offer and go riding at the stables," said Mary, waiting for a positive response. Mac nodded OK and then politely bade farewell to Rita and waved to Stan as they walked to Mary's car.

Arriving back at the pub, Mary again thanked Mac for returning her car and apologised for not accompanying him inside as she had many things to do as it was Saturday, but as he was about to get out of the car she lent over and gave him a quick kiss on the cheek, saying, "I'll collect you at two o'clock on Monday."

Mac waved her goodbye and walked in through the backdoor of the pub like a child who had just been given a whole chocolate bar.

Linda could see that he was full of pleasure and teased him by saying, "Well my lad, what happens next?"

To which he replied, "Horse-riding on Monday afternoon."

Linda was happy to learn that he was to have another meeting with Mary, as she thought that the two were very well matched, but thought that the horse-riding may not be what he would necessarily enjoy.

Bob closed the pub after the Saturday morning session and told Linda that he was going to spend the nice afternoon watching part of a cricket match in the recreation ground.

"OK Bob, that's a good idea," Linda said, pleased to learn that she would have the afternoon to perhaps talk to Mac about who his real father was.

But suddenly, Mac told Bob that he would also like to accompany him to watch the cricket, as he did not get that opportunity in the US.

Linda did not mind as she thought that the two should have some quality time together away from business, but then thought aloud, "Yet again, so near - but so far," referring to the subject of Mac's real father.

25. An Enjoyable Family Day Together

The three family members awoke to a nice sunny Sunday morning and Bob suggested that they should all get a move on for their drive to the coast, as no doubt many others would have the same idea.

So clearing away their breakfast dishes and gathering clothing to suit all occasions, Bob drove off in the direction of Dorchester, all happy that the three of them were able to have another day out together away from business matters.

As they drove closer to Dorchester, on the way to Weymouth, the traffic increased considerably due to holiday makers and day trippers all wanting to have a day at the seaside, so Bob decided to drive through Weymouth and onto the Isle of Portland where the traffic was less congested.

"We'll find a place that serves coffee and have a walk to take in the lovely refreshing sea air," Bob assured his passengers.

So having finished their coffee, they walked high up on the cliffs overlooking the English Channel watching many people out in boats enjoying the freedom of the calm sea.

Mac remarked on how much he was enjoying his vacation back home with the two of them and told them that he hoped that they could soon find time to come to New York, where he would arrange for the two of them to have a five-star suite in his hotel.

"Oh Mac that would be wonderful, but do you have that sort of authority and what would your boss say?" Linda doubtfully asked.

"Mother, I am the boss - well the assistant boss and I have the right to handle matters as I see fit on all occasions."

That made both Linda and Bob very proud that their little boy who played with frogspawn and newts some twelve years earlier had reached such a high level in the business world.

Mac, in turn, thanked them both for not standing in his way when he had decided to leave home and go off to America as he did.

With that said, Bob drove them to the restaurant for lunch.

After they had finished a wonderful lunch, the three of them adjourned to the restaurant lounge for coffee, whereupon Linda took out an 18 carat gold signet ring from her handbag and gave it to Mac as a present from Bob and herself, symbolising their strong love for him.

Holding the ring and lovingly looking at it, he noticed that it had been engraved with the initial letter 'M' boldly staring at him.

"Mom - Dad, what a lovely surprise, it is something that I will treasure for the rest of my life and certainly an indication of how bonded we are together."

He then slipped it onto his little finger and gave them both a huge hug and a kiss.

From those words, Linda was so happy to see how Mac had naturally included Bob and now believed that unless Mac raised the matter with her, she would have no further thoughts of telling him who his real father was.

Mac called for drinks all round to celebrate the affair, but Bob stuck to orange juice as he was the driver for the day. Then when it came to the time to return, Bob suggested that mother and son should sit in the back of the car, whilst their 'Chauffeur' would drive them home.

Both agreed and as they spent the journey huddled close to each other chattering about how the years had flown by, Linda brought up the subject of his friendly relationship with Mary.

"You know, Mac, Mary is a wonderful person and there is nothing more that I would like to see than for the two of you to become more than close friends."

Although Mac inwardly agreed with his mother's sentiments, he thought that after so long as a single person, a relationship of that manner may be something happening too quick in his life to be beneficial to both he and Mary.

"Hang on Mom, I have only known Mary for a few days and here you are wanting to marry me off like a 'Shotgun Wedding'," he embarrassingly laughed back at her.

Bob did not feel comfortable with all this talk about Mary and changed the subject by asking Mac what they should do about the loan of the new-style till.

Mac threw the question back at him by saying,

"How comfortable are you with the numbers game?"

"Fine, I can see the sense in it and I am happy to keep it going to see what comes out of it in the end," Bob replied.

Mac was pleased to hear that opinion coming so strong from Bob and so he asked, "So how will you compile the information if you have to give that till back at the end of the loan period?"

Bob flustered out a reply that made no sense and so Mac said to him, "Landlord, I think that you have answered your own question and I suggest that we call that office equipment company tomorrow and sort out a permanent deal."

Bob was happy that the short two-way conversation had provided a result that he wanted all the time, as he certainly would not want to revert to writing sales down on a sheet of paper.

"OK Mac, I agree now that we are making money that we can afford to spend on the business," Bob eagerly replied in a business manner.

Linda also added that she would not like to see them operating without that type of till in the future.

"Good, so we all agree that you will spend money on the purchase of a new-style till, exactly the same as the one that you are now operating on loan?" To which both parents agreed.

Happy with the result, Bob said to them both, "That's a fine way to make business decisions - having a day at the seaside."

Mac then turned their attention to another decision that could be made while they were having this 'Company Board Meeting' by asking what they thought about the Jukeboxes.

Again, Bob was all for retaining them, but Linda, who had no objection to the music being played that way, said that she thought that it depended on how much money had been placed in each.

Having returned to the pub early that Sunday evening, Linda made a few smoked salmon and cream cheese sandwiches, which they consumed with a nice glass of port wine whilst watching 'Sunday Night at The London Palladium' on TV.

All three loved that show, for not only did it contain some excellent supporting acts, but top of the bill this week was Andy Williams with a handful of melodious songs that were pleasing to anyone's ear.

When it had finished, Linda switched the TV off and Mac made the remark that he had had a wonderful day and thanked them both again for the ring, which he lovingly kissed.

Bob, ever eager to find his bed, remarked that it was time to retire as tomorrow was another day, with more challenges.

Lying in their beds, Bob was soon asleep, while Linda happily reminisced in her mind with the fact that her illegitimate child had risen against all the odds to become a senior manager in a prestigious hotel away from home and in a foreign country. He had done it without help from others and he had developed such a wonderful personality along the way.

Her mind then switched to Mary and from what she had seen of her in the past few days, she thought yet again what a perfect match the two of them would make together.

Although coming from rough farming stock, Mary, being an only child, had been blessed with a good private education and was very knowledgeable on many subjects. She had excelled at maths, geography and music, plus she had been good at gymnastics and played in the school hockey team. She had grown into a very sensible person, but most of all she was exceptionally good looking with a lovely natural smile for everyone she met.

Uppermost in Mac's mind as he struggled to sleep, was that Mary had talked him into going horse riding the next day. He had never ridden a horse, or indeed had anything to do with them, so he was very unsure of how he would take to it as a complete novice. Then again, he assured himself, he would do anything to please the lovely Mary.

26. A New Week

As Bob and Mac sat eating their breakfast at the start of a new week, they decided that the first thing to be done was to call the office equipment company and finalise the deal on the new till.

"Do we need to have a different one, why not keep the one we've got?" Bob asked Mac.

To which he replied, "You never know how many times that one has been in and out on demonstration to other people's businesses. Best we have one straight out of the box," Mac knowledgeably informed his father.

Mac agreed to handle it, but informed Bob that he would have to sign the papers to keep it in his name for warranty purposes. "And of course you will have to sign the cheque," he added with a laugh.

Bob agreed and moved his mind to the fact that there would be another skittles match later in the evening and he had to make sure that he had enough liquid supplies. He also called to Linda, reminding her that she would have to handle the requests for egg and chip suppers again.

"No problem my handsome," Linda called back in a confident manner. "Providing that I can have the services of Tony again."

Yet again, Mac saw how quickly his mother flew to acquire the help of Tony and began to wonder if there was anything shady in their relationship.

When Mac got through to the Blackmore Vale Office Equipment Company on the telephone, he was able to speak to the person who had delivered and set up the till in the pub. Mac explained that he wanted to move forward on the deal and if the salesman were to come with a completely new machine, then there was every chance that he would go away with a completed order. That was music to the ears of the enthusiastic young man and he promised to be at the pub later in the morning. Mac was happy and told Bob that they needed to press the button and get a statement showing all the transactions for the previous week before the till was removed.

Mac then explained to Bob that he now had a set of numbers that would form the basis to compare all future numbers against - sales up or down - best movers against slow turnover - profit or loss, all manner of comparisons to enable him to take action and be more commercially efficient.

He then added, "It will avoid being a Busy Beggar."

Bob liked that saying, as it described how he and Linda had felt many times in the past.

Then remembering what Linda had said about wanting to know what money the Jukeboxes were making, he suggested to Mac that it would be nice to know how much was in them at the start of the week, so that he could make the same numbers comparison on the two machines.

Mac thought how well Bob had latched onto the idea of comparisons and agreed that it would be wise to get the man from Wessex Mechanical Music Company to come and empty the machines for that purpose. So back to the phone he went to ask the man to come as soon as he was reasonably able to.

By mid-day, the man from Blackmore Vale had arrived as requested and Bob was happy that after signing the papers, he had a brand new till, which had a couple of extra features over the demonstration model. Linda was happy too and then turned her thoughts to the Jukeboxes, just as the man with the keys arrived.

Jovial as ever, he said to all three, "Now for the moment of truth."

Experience had told him to start with the machine that he knew would have the least amount of money in it, so into the skittle alley they went whereupon the machine produced £43. An amount that meant little to either Bob or Linda, but disappointed Mac.

Then to the machine in the bar which produced £105. "That's more like it," Mac exclaimed. "£148 over the first four days means that they could produce something in the region of about £200 in a full week. " The man agreed and to show his thanks gave Bob £75, which was a little over the agreed deal of 45%. Bob thanked him and off he went.

Bob thoughtfully handed the cash to Linda, saying, "There you are love, I knew you would agree to keeping those two machines once you got some cash in your hand."

Linda had to agree with his playful remark and gave him a happy tap on his cheek as she left to get Mac a light meal before he had to go off with Mary to take up horse riding.

Mary duly arrived on time and Linda gave her a loving welcome hug, while Mac was not sure how to greet her, other than to show his pleasure with a beaming smile that told Mary that they were still on the same wavelength.

After some small talk and a wave to Bob, Mary told Mac that they had better get going as Patrick would have the horses ready and waiting for them both.

On the way to the stables, Mac could not help to admire how lovely Mary looked and was so pleased that the two of them had met quite by chance.

As they drove through the gate of the stables, Patrick and Olivia were both waiting for them and greeted Mac like a long lost friend.

Olly said, "Well the first thing is to get you properly kitted out so come with me and I'll find some boots and a helmet to fit."

When he reappeared, Mary was already on her horse and Patrick gave Mac a leg-up, whilst Olly held the halter to steady the horse.

"Just walk slowly around until you feel that you are comfortable Mac," Patrick calmly assured him. "Then follow Mary as she will take you to the nursery track - you will be alright with her." Mac enjoyed that statement, but just wished that it did not relate to being on a horse.

After further walking, Mary gently eased Mac's horse into a trot and gave Mac instructions on how to handle things in a truly safe way and after a while he began to enjoy it. In fact, he was somewhat disappointed when Mary said, "Right that's it for today, or you will be very stiff tomorrow, follow me back to the yard and we will return the horses to Patrick."

As Mary drove Mac back to the Dog & Whistle, he thanked her for the tuition and said how much he had enjoyed the unexpected treat, then spontaneously he told Mary that being with her had raised feelings within himself that he had never experienced before.

With one hand securely on the wheel, she used her other hand to take his and firmly kissed it saying, "I know what you mean Mac, as I am beginning to get the same feeling about you."

Mac was so pleased to hear that come from Mary and asked if they could meet again the next day for some more horse riding.

"Oh I'm so sorry Mac, you see I have to take music classes every afternoon from Tuesday through to Friday."

Mac was so disappointed to hear that, but Mary went on to say that as she had Monday afternoons free, they could certainly do it again next week.

Mac agreed with that and took it as a firm date, then enquired, "Well what about an evening then, perhaps we could go to the theatre or the cinema together."

Mary agreed and suggested Wednesday evening as she was otherwise engaged the next evening.

Although Mac agreed, he thought that was a long way off and asked if she was free this evening.

Mary nodded.,"Yes that would be OK, but I must go home first to get out of these riding clothes." Her reply made him so happy that he could not wait to inform his mother, who he knew would be happy to hear the news.

So as Mary dropped him off at the pub, he almost skipped across the car park and through the back door, where Linda and Bob were waiting to hear if he had fallen off the horse which he had ridden for the first time. Seeing him alone, Linda wondered why Mary had left and not come into the pub as she expected.

"Don't worry Mom, she'll be back later-on, as we are going to find a movie somewhere this evening."

Linda was pleased to hear that, but Bob immediately thought that he would be a pair of hands short to handle the skittles evening, but then realised that when Mac had returned to New York, he would have to sort things out for himself then.

Hearing Bob mumbling about the situation, Linda reminded him that Mac was here on holiday and not to act as his assistant in the bar, in any case Tony would be along later - she hoped.

The evening started well for all, Bob had opened up and several young people came to buy drinks and to play the Jukebox. Then when Bob heard them squabbling about who's turn it was next, he opened the skittle alley and told some of them to go through and play on the other machine.

Although this produced a blast of opposing tunes, Bob was happy that it produced twice as much into the cash boxes than if only one machine was playing, so he closed the door to the skittle alley to deaden the sound a little.

Mary then arrived and took Mac off to find a movie and to enjoy each other's company for the second time that day.

The Major turned up well ahead of starting time for the skittles match. He eagerly told Bob that he had selected the Reverend Timmy into his team for the match as another player had dropped out due to family commitments.

Bob was pleased to hear that, for he knew that Timmy was a better player in any case.

Tony then arrived to the relief of Bob and he went straight into the kitchen to make Linda aware of his presence.

"Oh Tony, I am ever so pleased to see you."

Tony grinned with delight to hear Linda greet him in that manner, but then ended up deflated, when she told him that Mac was away for the evening and that Bob would have been on his own if he had not turned up to help. Tony soon returned to his normal self of helping out his friends and it allowed him to be in the presence of Linda after a hard day welding at the factory.

27. As the Week Dragged On

When the young couple returned to the pub, after watching a film at the cinema in Yeovil, they continued to stay in Mary's car and eagerly talked about each other's families.

Mary was unaware that Bob was not Mac's real father and Mac offered nothing in that direction, as he was not in possession of any facts to be able to expand on the subject.

Mary's interest was more about how she thought that both of his parents were well suited to each other and how hard they worked to make the pub a nice place for villagers to enjoy. She had particularly taken to Linda and told Mac that he was lucky to have had such a wonderful mother to bring him up in a manner that afforded him the chance to go to America and to rise up in the business world as he had done.

Mac enjoyed hearing about Mary's upbringing and also to learn about the struggle that farmers have in order to make a reasonable living. He too thought that Mary's mother was made of 'stern stuff', working as she does among the animals every day.

As the evening was coming to a close, Mac's thoughts then turned to when he could see Mary again.

"Well Mac, my time will be taken up for most of the rest of the week, but what about me coming to the pub on Friday evening and I will challenge you to a game of skittles, after which the loser pays for a nice meal of your Mum's pie?"

Mac was completely deflated on hearing the first part of Mary's response, but his mature mind reminded him that Mary was not on holiday and that she had a living to earn. So he accepted the Friday evening skittles challenge and relished the time that they would meet again.

Then realising that he had promised himself a week of sightseeing in London before he returned to the US, he thought that he would cancel it and continue to stay in Dorset so that he could liaise with Mary for a little while longer.

On telling Mary of his decision, she was so happy that she flung her arms around him and gave him a real nice kiss on the lips.

Mac was astounded that Mary had so much feeling for him that she actually took the lead in moving their relationship forward so quickly.

Then realising how late it had become, Mary playfully slapped him on the arm and said, "Out my boy, I'll see you on Friday, so get some practice in."

As he waved her goodnight and walked slowly across to the backdoor, he wondered what Mary had meant by "Get some practice in." Was that a sexual innuendo, or was she just referring to the skittles challenge?

Linda and Bob had both waited for his return and hoped that the evening together had been to their satisfaction.

Mac spoke first by enquiring how the skittles team had done in their match earlier in the evening, hoping that perhaps it would avoid questions about his date with Mary.

"Well, we have at last won a match, thanks to Timmy's performance," said Bob. "The Major certainly knew what he was doing when he drafted the Vicar into the team."

Linda was happy to tell Mac that the Jukeboxes played throughout the evening and no doubt took in a reasonable amount of cash.

"That's all good news then," answered Mac as he looked around the kitchen to see if his mother had any nibbles left to eat.

Linda asked him if he was hungry, but Mac replied that he just needed something 'to stop the worms from biting'. Linda offered to cook him something, but Mac said that he only needed a sandwich, which Linda was quick to make for him, then excitedly enquired,

"So how did you get on with Mary this evening and are you going to see her again?"

Mac told her that they had a wonderful evening, but he would not be seeing her again until Friday because of her work commitments, after which they were going horse riding again next Monday.

When Bob heard that, he reminded Mac that he had said that he was going to leave on Monday for a week of sightseeing in London before returning to New York.

"Well I'm sort of thinking that I might stay on here for the duration of my three weeks stay," Mac mumbled unconvincingly.

Linda was so pleased to hear that and suggested that maybe he could go up to London for a few days from tomorrow and still be back to meet Mary on Friday evening.

"Hey that's a good idea Mom, after all I only need a couple of days to see a few tourists spots and being alone, I can 'Hop on and Hop off' to suit myself, so to speak."

When Mary arrived back at the farm, her mother had similar questions about Mac and their evening together.

"You know Mum, out of all the friends that I have made at college and elsewhere, I have not met anyone that I have so much feeling for as I do for Mac."

"So are you going to see each other again?" enquired Rita.

Mary explained that she had challenged Mac to a game of skittles on Friday evening, followed by a meal at the pub. She then went on to tell her mother that Mac had enjoyed his first lesson at the stables and that she would give him another horse riding lesson next Monday.

"On Monday - so when does Mac go back to America?" asked Rita.

To which Mary replied with no degree of certainty, "I think it is at the end of next week."

From that information, Rita thought that with Mac leaving Thimble Hardy after such a short time, Mary's close friendship with him would probably fizzle out as quickly as it had started.

Her thoughts on the matter were suddenly put to one side when Stan appeared, having taken his last look at the animals in the barn, and Rita told him of how Mary had challenged Mac to a game of skittles.

Stan's response was precise, "in that case you'm had better get some practice in, my lady."

Early on Tuesday morning, Bob drove Mac to Sherborne station to catch the train to Waterloo, after which Mac spent the day sightseeing before setting about finding a hotel room for the night.

Linda and Bob spent an uneventful Tuesday at the pub, that reminded them of how things were before Mac had arrived.

Later in the day Mary phoned asking to speak to Mac and was disappointed to learn that Mac had gone off without telling her. She wondered if she had seen the last of him without saying a proper farewell, but was relieved when Linda explained exactly what Mac was doing so that he could stay another week at the pub.

"So he won't be here tomorrow when the skittles open evening is on?" Mary asked Linda.

When Linda explained that Mac would not be around, Mary jumped at the chance to take her father's advice and told Linda that she would come to the pub for some practice and advice from The Major on Wednesday evening, but also asked Linda not to let Mac know.

"OK Mary, I get your thinking, let's hope that you acquire the improvement to your skittles technique that you are hoping for, before my boy returns on Friday."

When Mac walked up to the desk at the Riverside Garden Hotel and enquired about a room for the night, he was asked by the receptionist for a form of identification. He produced his visiting card and the receptionist, after seeing Mac's title, immediately took it through to an adjoining office. Out came the Duty Manager, who introduced himself as Gordon Thomas, Assistant General Manager and as he had the same title as Mac, he immediately struck up a conversation about where Mac had come from and why he had chosen to call into the Riverside Garden Hotel.

Mac explained that he was on a quick sightseeing visit which had been undertaken at short notice and that he had called into the first hotel that had come into his view when he needed it.

"Well that is a welcome coincidence, as I plan to do the same thing in New York later in the year," explained Gordon.

He then invited Mac to a side room and ordered some coffee, whereupon the two had a very good conversation and compared notes on their two similar jobs. Then finally, Gordon offered Mac a very nice room, overlooking the River Thames, with complete free room service.

After settling into his room, Mac phoned his mother to let her know where he was and how he had had a stroke of luck in meeting Gordon. Linda was pleased to hear the news but told Mac that it would be wise to phone Mary and explain why he had left the pub so quickly and to let Mary know of his plans to return.

Mac then realised how thoughtless it was of him to have taken off in such quick time and understood that if he was to now have a close relationship with someone, then he could no longer act in the singular manner that he had always been used to doing. He was not sure in his own mind that he was ready to accept that way of life.

However, he phoned Mary's home and wondered just which way he was going to handle things, but when Rita answered and told him that Mary was not at home, he was somewhat relieved as it would give him time to think things out. "OK Rita, can you please ask her to phone me when she gets home?" Mac politely requested

When Mary returned, she was delighted to hear that Mac had phoned, for it indicated that he did have her in his mind and she immediately called him back.

When he heard Mary's voice on the phone, his mind quickly swung back into how much he loved being associated with her and he began to forget about his bachelor lifestyle.

For over half an hour they exchanged pleasant conversation about what each other had done that day and what their plans were for the rest of the week. Mary did not let Mac know that she intended to go to the skittles practice session before he returned home and joked that women do not really have the ability to compete with men at that game. Mac agreed and said that he would take it easy on her and the conversation closed with Mac telling her that he would phone her again on Thursday evening to let her know the timing of his return.

On Wednesday Mac watched the Changing of the Guard at Buckingham Palace and visited a couple of galleries, followed by a nice evening meal alone in Soho.

While matters at the pub were slow without much happening to enthuse either Bob or Linda during the morning, they opened up for the evening to a crowd of youngsters wanting to play the Jukeboxes. Novice skittlers eager to get started and regulars all wanting to enjoy a happy summer's evening out with a drink and a nibble of Linda's hot pies added to the unexpected throng.

Tony had arrived to help out as usual and Bob was pleased that he had another male in the bar to help with the enthusiastic rowdy crowd. Into the pub came PC Willis who, although off duty, was able to calm the noise down purely by his presence. "Hello landlord, seems that you've really got something going with this skittles open evening," he stated to Bob in a rather happy manner.

Bob gave him a 'thumbs up' in recognition of what the constable had said and at the same time saw that Mary had entered the pub dressed in slacks and a tee-shirt obviously ready for action. The Major also saw her and enquired, "so what brings a pretty girl like you to this unruly place?"

Mary told him of the challenge that she had made to Mac and in his absence she was hoping to get some help in bettering her skittles skills, so that she could give him a good 'run for his money' on Friday evening. "Then you have come to the right place Mary, everyone will get a chance to bowl, but listen to the advice that will be given to other people while you are just watching." Mary agreed, as she had been given the same advice many times during her student days and was well disciplined in such matters.

When it came to Mary's turn to bowl, The Major paired her with Georgie Bailey, who had many years experience and had become the Dog & Whistle's star player.

Although Georgie had known of Mary, he had not had the pleasure of her company before, but with his help, Mary greatly improved and felt ready to challenge Mac when he returned.

28. New Contacts

While Mac was having his breakfast in the dining room at the Riverside Garden Hotel on Thursday morning, he felt that although he was enjoying his sightseeing in London so far, the week was dragging and he began to think that maybe he would return to the Dog & Whistle later in the day, sooner than Friday as he had originally planned. Then suddenly he was approached by Gordon Thomas and another man who Gordon introduced as his boss, Angus McGregor, the general Manager of the Riverside Garden Hotel.

Angus, a man with many years experience in the hotel and hospitality industry, was pleased to meet Mac and to hear that he had come from New York. They compared a few notes on their respective hotels and was pleased that Mac had chosen to drop in as he had done. He told him that his stay was to be completely free of charge and that Gordon had some complimentary tickets for a West End Show that evening.

Gordon then asked Mac if he would like to join him, his wife and a friend that evening.

At first Mac was not keen as his mind was into returning home and to see Mary again, but when he heard that the name of the show was Cabaret, recently brought to London from the US, he gladly accepted Gordon's generosity.

"Right, we'll meet in the bar here at 6.30 this evening and I'll introduce you to my wife and friend over a drink beforehand," Gordon enthusiastically informed Mac, and off the two of them went saying, "Have a good day around London."

Now that he had a firm engagement for later in the day, Mac thought that he had better take it easy beforehand and so he took a leisurely cruise down the River Thames to Greenwich and back, where he had a nice lunch on the boat.

Back in his room late afternoon, Mac decided to telephone Mary as he had promised her with details of his intended return. He also thought that he had better phone his mother to arrange his collection from the train station in Sherborne on Friday.

When Mary's mother answered the telephone, she immediately recognised Mac's voice and asked him to hold while she went to fetch Mary, who was attending to some school paperwork in another room.

"Well hello my world traveller," Mary jokingly greeted him. "How are things at the other end of the line?"

To hear Mary's voice was pure heaven to Mac and he thought that he could not wait to see her again, but he now had an engagement to keep with Gordon.

When Mac told Mary about his chance meeting with Gordon and how he had been offered a ticket to the West End Show, she told him how lucky he was to have just popped into an hotel and met a man with a similar background to himself and who would appear to have the same outlook on life.

Mac agreed and then told Mary that he would be leaving London the next day on the 11.20am from Waterloo that would arrive in Sherborne at 1.32pm and that he was going to arrange for his mother to collect him from the station.

Mary was delighted to hear that news and said that with a little rearranging of her day, she could collect him and it would save his mother from having to leave Bob alone in the pub during opening hours. "Mary, how nice, I can't wait to see you again," Mac said with a loving reply. "I'll tell Mom of your thoughtful offer."

As Mac told his mother of the arrangement that he had made with Mary, she was pleased and thought how much she appreciated the thought that Mary had given to the situation.

When Mac was ready for his evening at the theatre, he went to the hotel bar as Gordon had requested.

There, he duly met Gordon's wife Sally and the friend, who turned out to be Sally's brother, Daniel Griffiths.

Daniel was an Architect and senior partner of a company called Griffiths, Johnstone and Lowe, that had its main office in Salisbury, Wiltshire. He shook hands with both and exchanged pleasantries about the weather and their day so far.

Mac liked Sally and Daniel and all three talked freely about their upbringing in the West Country. Like many others, Daniel was interested to know more about Mac's life in America and how someone so young had risen to the senior position that he had done.

Throughout the evening, all three made Mac very welcome and laughed at Mac's response when he had been asked where Thimble Hardy actually was.

Remembering how, when he was a young boy, a local farmer had described its location, he said, "Well it's between here and there." Then he added, "It's a long way from one place, but not so far from t'other."

Mac learned that Daniel was in London for meetings with clients and was also staying at Gordon's hotel, before returning to Salisbury on Friday. They got on well together during the evening and when it was discovered that they were both returning to the West Country the next day, they arranged to depart by the same train together.

The evening ended with all thinking how nice it was that they had met quite by chance and Mac offered them all the same hospitality whenever they thought about visiting New York. An offer that Gordon readily accepted as he had already planned a visit later.

Next morning when Mac was ready to leave and was in the foyer waiting for Daniel to arrive, Gordon and Angus McGregor appeared to wish him goodbye. Mac thanked them both for their wonderful hospitality that had made his visit to London so enjoyable and repeated his offer of an exchange.

After sharing a taxi to Waterloo station, Mac and Daniel boarded a train heading southwest and entered a compartment with only one other person in it. A man with his head in a newspaper, looked up and passed the time of the day to both, which they politely acknowledged and sat facing each other for the journey.

Daniel was interested to learn about Mac's upbringing in Dorset and returned to enquiring about this village called Thimble Hardy, just where it was, and how many people lived there.

Mac responded with a detailed description of the location of the village and told Daniel that his father is the landlord of the local pub called the Dog & Whistle. "If you are ever that way, drop in and introduce yourself."

An invitation to a country pub that he had not been to before interested Daniel, who told Mac that he often took his wife out for a pub lunch at the week-end and told him that he certainly would visit one day when he had time.

"If you can, I would suggest that you make it a Friday evening as it is my mother's speciality, Steak and Ale Pie evening, but do book as it has become very popular. And in any case they are closed on a Sunday," Mac informed him, wearing his 'Sales Hat'.

Mac gave Daniel details of how to get to the pub, together with the names of his parents, telling him that although he himself would not be there after the next week-end said, "Tell Bob or Linda of your association with me."

The two of them continued to exchange details of each others life and Mac gave Daniel the same invitation that he had given to the two hoteliers about whenever he visited New York and exchanged business cards.

After arriving at Salisbury railway station, Daniel gave Mac a really strong warm handshake, wished him the best for the rest of his stay in the UK and then left the train.

When the train departed from Salisbury, Mac was left alone with the man reading the newspaper.

Putting his newspaper down on the seat, the man apologised and said that he could not help overhearing what Mac had said and that a pub with a Pie Night interested him. He went on to say that he was the Chairman of a company social club and that he was always looking for new interesting venues to entertain his members.

"Thimble Hardy sounds like a quirky place to take a group of people who were always expecting me to find such places," the man said with a smile that showed his pleasure on the matter.

Mac was pleased that he may have found the start of what could be a very encouraging new aspect to the pie evenings and welcomed the man's interest with a question about how many people would be involved.

"Oh, usually it would be somewhere between 25 and 35 people depending on what else they may have on at the time."

Mac sniggered within himself, when he thought of how his mother would have to handle that amount of people, in addition to those locals who would also want to eat. He then said to the man, "Fine, but what about making an exclusive evening for your members, on another evening other than Friday? That way, we could also fix you up with a skittles evening."

That suggestion interested the man even more and Mac gave him further details of how he could make such an arrangement.

As Mac prepared to leave the train at Sherborne, the man gave him a card with his contact details that read, Geoffrey Hammond, Personnel Manager, Engineering Components & Systems Ltd. Yeovil, Somerset.

Mac thanked him and told Geoffrey Hammond that he would pass the card to his mother, who he was sure would be pleased to hear from him in due course. When the train braked to a halt, Mac left the man to continue his journey alone. Mac's thoughts then turned to the fact that he hoped that Mary would be waiting for him at the station.

On seeing Mac alight from the train, Mary stood firm with a most welcoming smile that told him how pleased she was to see him again and as he approached her she opened her arms to give him a loving hug, which he immediately returned with pleasure.

Walking hand-in-hand to Mary's parked car, she eagerly asked him how his trip had been and did it mean that he would now be staying in Thimble Hardy for the rest of his time in the UK.

Mac confirmed positively to Mary's question and added that although he would have to return to work at the end of the next week, he was already planning returning to the UK when he next had some leave. Then added, "It could be that I may have a meeting with a certain person."

Mary knew straight away what Mac was referring to and was pleased to hear that she figured in his future plans and gave his hand an affectionate squeeze.

Arriving at the Dog & Whistle, Mary confirmed that she would be back for her skittles challenge at six o'clock and gave him a peck on the cheek before driving off.

Mac thought that it would not take long to overcome her challenge and then he could enjoy the meal that Mary would buy for him.

"Hello son, how was London?" Bob enquired as Mac entered through the back door, but before he could answer, Linda appeared and asked the same question.

"Well I have had a very nice time and I have met some very interesting people," he happily informed them.

As Bob had just closed the pub after the morning session and Linda had not yet started her preparation for the pie evening, all three went into the sitting room, where Mac told them that he had invited the man on the train to bring a group of perhaps 35 people for a pie evening.

"Mac what have you done?" gasped Linda. "You know that I could not handle that amount of diners on top of the others that would be here."

Bob nodded in agreement and questioned how they could all be accommodated with seating on a busy Friday evening.

"Look you two - think outside the box," Mac said somewhat irritably. "It does not have to be a Friday, think of dealing with the visiting party exclusively on another night just for them, say Thursday when not much else is happening. That way you get two bites of the cherry in a more controllable manner."

Immediately Bob thought that another evening was a splendid idea, but Linda was more reserved as she was not sure if she could get Maggie and Jill two evenings in succession. Mac's reply was that they had time to think things over and to solve the logistics, but be positive.

Fifteen minutes before her appointed rendezvous with Mac, Mary arrived and happily chatted to Bob before he opened the skittle alley.

When Mac came down from his room, Mary laughingly taunted him with the comment, "Are you ready for this loverboy?"

Mac replied saying, "I hope that you have brought your money with you." Then giving her a hug, walked her through to the alley.

Bob could see how happy the two of them were together and was pleased that Mac had found something else to concentrate on whilst he was on holiday, sooner than always talking about business.

Maggie and Jill duly arrived and made their number with Linda who had already commenced preparations in the kitchen. Jill helped Bob arrange the tables, while Linda told Maggie about the invitation that Mac had given to the man on the train.

"Possibility of a group of about 35 people coming one evening?" Maggie questioned in disbelief. "Well that's marvellous news Linda."

Linda half-heartedly agreed, but told Maggie that it would have to be staged on another evening than Friday. Then she said, "But Maggie what am I going to do for help? I can't expect you and Jill to come two evenings in the same week."

Maggie understood Linda's predicament, but told her not to worry as she could no doubt recruit someone else from the Big House when the time comes.

Other customers began to arrive for the pie evening and Jill had everything under control in the screened off area of the bar. She placed reserved signs on each table and kept the special corner table for Mac and Mary as Bob had informed her.

As always, the reliable Tony turned up and immediately gave Jill a happy wink, before settling in with Bob to get organised for the expected rush for drinks as more customers arrived.

The Jukebox was soon brought into action by a young couple who appeared to be in the pub for the first time. "Good to see you both, are you here for the pie?" asked Bob.

To which the young girl replied, "Sure, we saw the advert in the church magazine."

That was good news to both Bob and Tony as their efforts to tempt people from a wider area had produced a result.

Tony remarked to Bob that as that had happened some others may also turn up, having read the same advert and that they may not have booked.

"You could be right Tony - better you go and tell Linda so that she is aware of the possible extra demand."

When Linda heard the news from Tony, she laughed aloud and remarked, "Could be that we will be the victim of our own success."

Jill was busy getting the early diners settled and Maggie was pleased that some dishes could now be served as she badly needed the space in the kitchen to prepare for the next phase of eager diners.

Mac and Mary emerged from the skittle alley with Mary beaming all smiles, as she had beaten Mac and was looking forward to the meal that he was now duty bound to pay for.

Mac was puzzled as to how Mary had played so well, when he had always thought of skittles as a man's game and asked where she had learnt to play like that.

Her reply came with a loving smile, "You never know what happens when you are not here." That made Mac even more puzzled, but he was prepared to let the matter drop in favour of a more pleasant conversation, even though he had lost the challenge.

Throughout the evening Linda and Maggie worked hard to keep up with the demand for the Steak & Ale pie, whilst Jill and Tony worked well together to support Bob in the bar.

At the end of the evening, Mac was well satisfied with his day. He had been made a good friend of Gordon and Angus at the Riverside Garden hotel and he believed that he had secured some future business for the pub by meeting Daniel the architect and Geoffrey Hammond, but most of all, he had fixed a another cinema date with the lovely Mary for the next evening.

During Saturday morning, Bob and Mac talked about the next action that ought to be taken to increase the fortunes of the pub. Mac thought that the capacity of the dining area needed to be increased and that it was too close to the open area of the pub where other people were hanging around just drinking, smoking and playing the Jukebox.

"Well there's not much we can do about that without help from the brewery and they don't want to know," Bob said, shrugging his shoulders. "There is you know - you could convert your sitting room into a proper restaurant area," Mac told his father.

Bob was aghast at the suggestion and thought that would mean giving up their restroom, something that he frequently needed. "So where do you think your mother and I will get any peace away from the bar then?" he asked Mac.

"Upstairs - the room that I am staying in at the present time."

Although Bob still did not accept the suggestion, he considered Mac was such a brilliant planner, as he always had answers to objections.

"You know Mac, although I don't like the idea, I can't think of any better suggestion," Bob grudgingly answered.

"Good, so that's it then?" Mac questioned him.

"No, hang on a minute, who's going to put that suggestion to your mother?" said Bob, backing off the idea.

"Why, you of course, you're the landlord and the one to make executive decisions around here," Mac laughingly replied.

Bob liked the suggestion that he was the one to make executive decisions in the pub, but did not really want to be associated with one that he knew his wife would surely be against. "I would like to ponder on that for a while, let's talk about the lights that we are going to hang up." Bob went on, saying that tomorrow would be a convenient time as the pub is always closed to customers on Sundays. He then turned his thoughts to opening up for the morning trade.

Linda told Mac that she needed to go to the wholesalers to replenish her stock and asked him to go with her.

Mac readily agreed as he thought yet again that it would give him the opportunity to ask his mother about the identity of his real father, before returning to New York.

Linda was of the same opinion, but when Mac raised the question on the way to Gillingham she backed off saying, "Mac this is not the place to answer that, wait until we return home." Mac could feel Linda's uneasiness and said, "Why not just give me his name?"

"Mac, if I do that without a proper explanation of the circumstances at the time, you will draw your own conclusions and that would discolour the whole matter. In any case, I would like Bob to be there when I tell you, so that he too would hear what is said." Mac, accepted that for the time being and Linda promised him faithfully that she would tell them both before he returned to America.

Into the bar, Winnie and Madge arrived as usual, with Winnie saying to Bob, "I understand that you made a lot of money with that pie evening last night."

Bob did not like that comment, but controlled his indignation by saying that it was events like that which kept the pub from closing altogether.

Winnie looked at her companion and said, "Don't want the pub to close , do we Madge?"

As usual, Madge got the wrong end of the stick and said, "So when's the pub going to close then?"

As trade was slack in the pub for the rest of the day, Bob and Linda took it in turns to serve at the bar, while each talked things over with Mac in the sitting room.

Mac followed it by enjoying a wonderful evening at the cinema with Mary, who chose to hold his hand throughout and returning to her car after the show, Mac told her that he had never been so happy.

"Mum and Dad appear to be very pleased with what I have done for them and now I have the friendship of you Mary love - all in the two weeks that I have been back in the UK," Mac said, summing up his change of fortunes in life.

Back in the pub car park late evening, Mary told Mac how much she admired his business knowledge and how he had enabled his parents to use it in such a short time. She also told him that she had lovingly taken to his parents and that she now felt very much part of his life.

"Mac I don't know what I am going to do when you return to the US next week." Mary trembled and hung onto him like she had nobody else to turn to.

"Don't worry love, we will work something out, for I feel the same," Mac replied, whilst returning her hug with a long awaited sensual kiss that meant a lot to them both.

While Bob was checking the back of the pub before locking up for the night, he noticed the two sitting in Mary's car and invited them both in for nightcap.

Linda was pleased that Bob had taken that action, as she was excited to see them both so happy together. She chatted away with Mary while Bob was itching to press the button on the till to get a readout of the trading for the week. Although Mac had other things on his mind, he was pleased to see the enthusiasm that his stepfather now had for the comparison of products being sold in his business.

"OK, let's have a quick look, as it will give us something to ponder over during the weekend," Mac said with the same desire. Then, when Bob came back with the readout, it was clear that FOOD had been the best seller, with Cider and Wine ahead of beer.

"My goodness, the brewery won't like that," exclaimed Bob.

Mac smiled in agreement, but turned his attention back to Mary, who was about to leave. Linda then invited Mary to have afternoon tea with her family next day. Mary accepted and suggested to Mac that perhaps he would like to join her beforehand to walk the dogs. Mac accepted and Mary then bade farewell to all and left for home.

29. Tragedy Strikes

Bob was up early on Sunday morning as he was eager to get on with Mac's suggestion of hanging coloured lights inside the pub windows and around the main door. Linda was not far behind as she wanted to get clear of all her duties before preparing a special afternoon tea for the arrival of Mary.

When Mac arrived, he was surprised to see the enthusiasm that his father was applying to the coloured lights project and was happy that things were going along as he had suggested.

From his store, Bob had produced a conglomerate of electrical wiring, fittings and coloured bulbs, which he laid out on a table in the bar and began to plan what-was-going-where. Mac accepted that he would only play a subordinate roll and no doubt be the dogsbody when things were needed to be collected from the garage workshop.

With the sun shining on a nice warm day, Bob opened the main door and waved to a few people who were late for the Sunday morning church service. A few others had earlier asked him why he had the door open when the pub was closed.

"Giving the old place a good modern uplift," was his stock answer.

Around the windows, inside the curtains, Bob fixed a chain of lights that met with the approval of Linda and Mac, but he was not sure how he was going to arrange those around the door without causing obstruction to people coming and going.

Linda told him that he ought to slow down and give it some proper thought before doing anything else. "Sit with Mac and I'll make coffee for you both - and make sure that you don't do anything that would cause the brewery to object."

Over coffee Bob worked out his plan and hurried out to the garage, whereupon he returned with a very tall set of steps so that he could get high enough to secure the lights at the highest point. He placed the steps in the open doorway with the feet resting on the quarry flagstones, that had been well worn down over the preceding years and asked Mac to collect some tools from the workshop.

Up the steps went exuberant Bob carrying an armful of wire and lights. Then, as people were coming out from the church, he joked with several who were making comments about 'getting on his high horse'.

Then suddenly, due to the unevenness of the floor below, the steps toppled over and he came crashing to the ground, hitting his head on the flagstones. Several people rushed to his aid, but he was out cold.

Among the helpers was nurse Lucy Bailey, who could see that Bob was in a very bad way and asked if someone could call Doctor Goddard who was among the people returning from the church.

In the meantime, hearing the commotion, Linda came through from the kitchen and Mac returned with the tools and on seeing the unexpected tragedy they rushed to Bob's aid.

Dr Goddard asked people to stand back and after checking him, he could clearly see that Bob's injuries were severe. So from the pub phone, he called the emergency ambulance and Bob was duly transported to the accident department of Yeovil hospital.

Luckily, Tony arrived and took control of the pub, while Mac drove his mother to the hospital, accompanied and comforted by nurse Bailey, who knew the procedure in the hospital.

For several hours, the three of them waited at the hospital for any news that could be obtained, but the Consultant explained that Bob was in a very serious state, with uncontrollable internal bleeding.

Meanwhile, Tony was sitting in the bar not knowing what was happening when Mary arrived in a confused state, as she had heard that there had been an accident at the pub earlier in the day.

She was followed by PC Willis, who had also heard the same story and told them that he was only there on a compassionate visit and to make sure that the pub was secure. "I will have to return in an official capacity to gather details of what has happened, but that can wait until Linda is able to tell me more," he added.

Tony told him that he could handle the security aspect and that he would stay until Linda or Mac returned. Mary also offered her help.

At the hospital, all was not well, the Consultant came again and told Linda that, although his team were working hard to revive Bob, he was not responding. He asked Linda if she would like to see him and suggested that nurse Lucy could accompany her for support. While Linda and Lucy went through to see Bob, Mac went to the hospital reception to phone the Dog & Whistle to enquire what had happened since he had left, as he was concerned about several things.

Tony answered and assured him that all was under control and that he would stay until their return. He told him also that the police had been, but not to worry as it was not an official visit. Mac then turned his thoughts to Mary and the arrangement that his mother had made for her to visit the pub for Sunday tea.

"Well Mary is here, have a word with her," Tony quietly replied.

Mary was full of sorrow for what had happened to Bob and offered her sympathy to Mac, who in turn was disappointed in not seeing her as arranged. They talked for a while and Mary was very understanding, saying that she would return home, but would be available if she would be needed for anything.

As Mary left, Georgie Bailey arrived to find out if there was any news of Bob and also to establish where his wife was, as Lucy had not contacted him since leaving for the hospital. Tony brought Georgie up-to-date with what news he had and told him that Lucy was still at the hospital with Linda and Mac.

Reassured that his wife was OK, Georgie told Tony that he was also available to stay at the pub if required. That gave Tony the opportunity to pop home and inform his parents of what was going on before returning and prepared to stay the night if needed.

When Mac returned to the hospital waiting room after making his phone call, he found his mother in a state of total collapse and was informed by nurse Lucy that Bob had died while they were with him.

Mac shook at the knees on hearing the dreadful news and hugged his mother in a form of comfort that he had not done before.

"Mac, what am I going to do without him?" Linda murmured.

Without delay, a member of the hospital welfare staff arrived and invited the three of them into a side room so that they could be alone and grieve in peace. From somewhere, a tray containing a large pot of tea, with milk and cups appeared, which was welcomed by them all.

A very compassionate lady doctor arrived and prescribed some medication to calm Linda and to help her sleep, if needed later on. The doctor explained to Mac what had happened medically to his father and Lucy was able to help him understand it in more simple terms when she had left the room.

Mac phoned the pub again in order to break the sad news to Tony, but was surprised to hear Georgie answer.

"Don't worry Mac, Tony will be back and in the meantime I am holding the fort. What is the situation with Lucy, does she want me to come to the hospital and collect her?"

Mac thought that it would be wise for himself to drive his mother and Lucy back to the pub, where further decisions could be made. Mac told Georgie that and thanked him for his help, asking him also to pass on his thanks to Tony when he returned.

When the three returned to the pub from the hospital well after midnight, they found both Tony and Georgie there to help with whatever was needed.

Together in the sitting room, Linda hung onto Mac amid a torrent of tears and with so many thoughts going through her mind now that she no longer had Bob at her side. Mac also had many thoughts about his immediate future and had already made the decision that he could not return to New York and leave his mother in this state.

Nurse Lucy stated that she would stay the night, as she was used to having to comfort people in distress, to which her husband readily agreed and he went home alone. Tony had already assured them all that he would stay throughout the night as long as they needed him.

So after taking the medicine prescribed at the hospital, Lucy helped Linda into bed where she dozed off in a complete daze wondering what had happened so unexpectedly to her husband.

Mac gave up his room to Lucy and settled in the sitting room with Tony for the remainder of the night.

Neither of the two boys could sleep immediately and Mac talked to Tony about how matters needed to be handled in the morning. Between them, they agreed that the pub should not be opened and Tony accepted that he would handle any questions from customers, firstly by putting a notice in the pub window. He also agreed to handle any trade callers and to speak to The Major about the intended skittles match, thus taking the pressure off the family.

Mac's thoughts were about the legal paperwork that would now be required to satisfy the commercial aspect of his father's death and he believed that the brewery should be notified without delay. He told Tony that he would have to phone his boss at the hotel in New York and ask for an extension to his stay in the UK.

Many things were turning over in both their minds when they dozed off to sleep, just as daybreak began to show through the curtains.

On Monday morning, Lucy was the first to awake and immediately went to check on Linda who was was still asleep. To the sitting room she then checked on Mac and Tony, who were beginning to rise from their makeshift beds.

Mac made coffee for them all and as they sat around the kitchen table reflecting on the events of the previous day, Linda appeared in a drowsy state looking for a coffee.

Surprisingly to the others, Linda, although very distressed, took a very strong approach to the situation which she now found herself having to cope with. She firstly thanked Lucy and Tony for their support and was concerned that their lack of sleep would hinder their normal work in the day ahead. To which, both informed her that as being self-employed they would not be working, but would remain available to help Linda and Mac with anything that was needed.

Like Mac, Linda believed that the brewery should be told before they received incorrect information from any third party and suggested that they start with Robert Jeans the Area Manager.

Robert Jeans was very sympathetic and told Mac that he would report it to the appropriate people within the brewery, but in the meantime not to worry about anything regarding the sales of beer.

PC Willis then arrived in uniform and offered his condolences to Linda. He then pointed out to Mac that he was obliged by law to take a statement of what had happened and asked to see the offending set of steps. Mac made the point that maybe some people who were passing at the time would be able to offer more precise details.

After making some notes, PC Willis told them both that he was available at all times if they needed his help, particularly with security of the pub. He then left with a reassuring wave to them both.

Linda felt the need to be busy in order to release her mind from some of the grief and, among uncontrollable tears, cooked Lucy, Mac and Tony breakfast, for which they were all grateful as they had not had a proper meal since breakfast on the preceding day.

As she sat down to join them, she asked Lucy what the doctor had said about returning to the hospital to complete formalities.

"Well, Linda you need to obtain paperwork from the hospital in order to register the death and to obtain a death certificate, for without that you cannot arrange a funeral or handle Bob's estate. "So when do I have to do that?" Linda asked.

"I think that you must do that within 5 days, but I suggest that if you feel up to it, then do it today."

Tony suggested that if she and Mac went later that morning, he would still be available to look after things while they were away.

"Tony, you are a love," Linda half smiled at him through her tears.

Consequently, Mac drove his mother to the hospital and then to the Register of Births, Deaths and Marriage office in Yeovil, where matters took several hours to complete.

Lucy, in the meantime went home to Georgie and Tony put up the sign in the pub window. **We apologise that due to bereavement, this hotel will be closed until further notice.**

While they were away, the man from the Blackmore Vale Mechanical Music company turned up ready to open the Jukeboxes and was surprised to see the notice in the window. Tony happened to see him and explained the situation, on which he said that he understood and would not call again until the end of the month.

Later the brewery dray arrived with the weekly supply of barrels of beer and Tony expertly handled the changeover with the empty ones in the cellar.

When Mac returned to the pub with his mother, he decided that he should phone his boss in New York to inform him of his predicament and explain that he certainly could not leave his mother to handle matters on her own.

Mac's boss, the General Manager, was absolutely shattered to hear the awful news and told Mac to take whatever time was needed to sort matters out to his satisfaction.

Mac thanked him and promised to keep him up-to-date on the subject and that he would call back in two or three days time anyway.

He was relieved by the generous offer that he had received from his boss, as for the time being, it took away some of the worry that was going around in his head.

With the pub closed and seeing that Linda and Mac were now able to handle things, Tony decided to leave for home, but not before Linda gave him a huge hug of thanks for all that he had done in the past 24 hours on her behalf. Mac shook Tony's hand and hugged him warmly for the same appreciation.

Mac and his mother took the opportunity to sit quietly in the sitting room and reminisce on times that they had both enjoyed together with Bob in the past. Linda told Mac that Bob had worked hard to ensure that he had been brought up in a manner that she could now see had paid off to Mac's advantage.

Just as Mac was about to recall memories of his own, a gentle tap on the window caused him to hesitate and to go and investigate. It was the Reverend Timmy and so Mac beckoned him to go to the backdoor.

When Mac let him in, he was full of sympathy and explained that he had only just heard the sad news as he had been away overnight and had attended a church meeting earlier in the day.

Mac took him through to the sitting room to meet his mother.

The priest was in full church dress, black suit and shirt with a gleaming white dog-collar and when Linda saw him she burst into tears, for his appearance immediately conveyed death to her.

Timmy sympathetically held her hand and spoke with a soft comforting voice, "My dear Linda, I am here to offer my sincere condolence and I am aware of how dreadful you must be feeling at this time." He then knelt on one knee and kissed the back of her hand, while offering a quiet prayer.

His gesture had a profound calming effect on Linda and she clasped his hand in acceptance of his presence.

She then asked Timmy if he would like to join her and Mac with a cup of tea, which he gladly accepted as he believed that by doing something together with her, it would further calm her into acceptance of the situation.

Mac liked the compassionate way that Timmy acted to soothe his mother and again regarded him highly as a priest and as a genuine person. He then went into the kitchen to make the tea and to leave them alone for a few minutes.

When Mac returned, Linda asked Timmy about making arrangements for the funeral, to which he replied that he would take care of that, once he had her wishes, but not to rush into anything until she and Mac had talked it through.

Timmy enquired if either Bob or Linda had any other relatives that needed his help, but Linda informed him that the current family consisted only of the three of them and now that was only two.

Again the Reverend had calming words on the subject when he told them both that they were not alone, as we are all part of God's family.

When Timmy left them, they both felt relaxed and comforted from his visit and knew that here was a man that they could turn to any time.

As the week progressed, Mac and Linda spent most of their time handling the official paperwork related to Bob's estate.

Banks, Insurance companies, pension funds, solicitor, funeral director, Tax Office, Probate Office all had paperwork to be completed. Then there was the brewery and the other alcohol suppliers to be notified.

Linda remarked that it was a good job that they did not have to open the pub to serve customers as well.

That remark set Mac thinking about what was going to happen when they did eventually open. How was his mother going to cope without Bob? After all, the brewery would not want the pub closed for too long - so would they provide help with a relief manager until Linda decided what she wanted for her future?

By the end of the week, many people had visited Linda to offer their condolences and Mary had been back to see Mac and Linda with offers of help from her parents, if needed.

Terry Smith was one, who along with Tony, offered to serve in the bar if they needed temporary staff to get the pub going again. Linda knew that she could call on Tony any time, but he had a job to do in the daytime and she accepted The Major as man of complete integrity, so she would trust him to help in the daytime if he could.

Maggie and Jill both offered their help on the food side, if Linda decided to start up again, but Linda thought that she would not be ready to do that until after the funeral.

On Saturday morning Timmy called to tell Linda that he had arranged with the funeral director to have the burial on Tuesday 23rd July 1968 at 11.30am. He then enquired if Linda was happy to have a preceding service of remembrance in the church at 11.00am.

Linda and Mac agreed to the arrangements and accepted that the Reverend 'Timmy' Smythe-Brown would handle the order of service.

30. The Funeral

After a light breakfast on the day of the funeral, Linda and Mac prepared themselves for the ordeal that lay ahead.

Tony and his sister, Nurse Lucy, arrived as they had agreed to attend as support to the family. Georgie also came prior to the cortege and agreed to stay at the pub as security while all others were away.

The church was packed with local people and many from outside the village. It seemed that the whole neighbourhood had ceased work to pay their homage to Bob and to everyone's surprise the brewery Managing Director arrived.

The Reverend Timmy led the service with great feeling, often referring to Bob as 'The Heart of the Village' and to Linda as the devoted partner who gave him enormous support.

Following the service, Bob was laid to rest in the village graveyard and all were invited to a light buffet lunch in the church hall supervised by Maggie and Jill.

At the gathering, the brewery Managing Director made it his business to speak to Linda and Mac, announcing himself as Sir Hugh Bright.

He offered condolences on behalf of the whole management of the brewery and said that his regional staff were available for any support that was needed to reopen the pub. He also asked if it would be convenient to take a look at the Dog & Whistle while he was in the village.

Linda thanked him and asked Mac to walk him over to the pub and to show him around the inside while it was closed to the public.

Inside the pub, Mac noticed that Sir Hugh was paying particular importance to the decorative state of the rooms and spent time studying the scene of the accident. Luckily, Tony had cleared away all evidence of the coloured lights project and the steps were removed.

Like many before him, Sir Hugh noticed the bricked up doorway to the cottage next door and asked Mac if he knew why it had been done.

Mac had no idea why it had been done, but overhearing the question, Georgie said that the cottage next door used to be another bar within the pub and believed that it was closed to reduce costs.

Sir Hugh then asked Mac several questions about the current state of trade and what he thought about the future prospects of the pub.

Mac smelt a rat. Here was a man who supposedly had come to offer his respect to the family and without remorse was seeking information about the business in a round-about way to suit his own ends. He was a very high powered person to come to the funeral of a person who he had never met. After-all, that function would normally have been undertaken by the Area Manager. Cleverly, Mac sidestepped the question by saying that he had no feel for the situation as he was only here on holiday from America.

With that, they both returned to the church hall and left Georgie to hold the fort until the family returned. Sir Hugh said his farewell to Linda and shook Mac's hand, then left Thimble Hardy.

Timmy also came to say farewell and Linda thanked him for the lovely service and for all the help that he had done behind the scenes. Mac also thanked him and said that he would see him later.

Mac then turned to Maggie and Jill, who were talking to Tony and Lucy, and he invited them them all to the pub for a drink.

While in the sitting room and still in a grieved state, Linda's thoughts turned to how she was ever going to manage to run the pub single handed when Mac returned to America. Maggie calmed her by saying that she would help and that for the time being she should not worry, after all she also had Tony who knew the routine.

Inwardly, Mac's thoughts were about Sir Hugh Bright's visit, as it came in addition to the earlier survey completed by surveyor Trevor Jones. He had met people like him before and wondered what would happen next.

Linda was happy to show the gathering several photographs of Bob, some taken recently and others from the early days when she first met him. She hugged one close to her after giving it a loving kiss.

31. Picking Up The Pieces

On Wednesday, the day after the funeral, all seemed so empty to Linda and Mac. As they sat at the breakfast table, Linda asked him what he thought should be done next.

"Well Mom," said Mac. "We have got to pick up the pieces and think how we are going to manage this situation."

He told her that they should take it in easy stages, by firstly concentrating on reopening the pub whenever she thought that she could handle it emotionally and without a demand on the kitchen.

"You have got to accept that you will need to hire paid help, you can't keep relying on the generosity of those around you." Mac said.

Linda had also been thinking that way since Bob's death and wondered how she could get someone reliable enough to take charge of the bar on a full-time basis and told Mac so.

Mac's reply was to question if it was the bar that needed a new person, or would someone in the kitchen be the answer, so that she herself could run the bar.

"Well, I had not thought of that," replied Linda. "Someone in the kitchen would only be needed for less hours and I could supervise that person in any case - Mac you always come up with an answer."

He was pleased that his mother was contributing to solving the problem and suggested that they should set a date for the reopening, to which Linda firmly stated. "Next Monday!"

"OK, that gives you four days to get used to the idea, it's nice to know that you are thinking positively Mom, because you are now the landlord."

Although missing Bob terribly, Linda liked the idea of being the landlord, but suddenly thought that the licence agreement needed to be changed into her name.

Mac agreed and during the morning wrote a letter to to the brewery requesting the change, which Linda signed and Mac posted later on when he went to the rectory to have a word with Timmy.

While Mac was away, Mary called and was welcomed by Linda as though she was her own child. Amid tears, Linda hugged her and Mary responded in a very sincere way.

When Mac returned, he was so pleased to see Mary and immediately gave her an embrace that ended with a warm kiss, something that now came easily to him and was warmly accepted by Mary.

All three talked about the lovely service that Timmy had presented at the funeral and Mac told his mother that he had been to see Timmy and thanked him for his tenderness on such a sensitive occasion.

When Mary mentioned that Mac's boss had been very magnanimous in allowing him to have an open-ended stay to help his mother, it reminded Mac that he had promised to keep Claude Leclerc informed of the situation and he told them both that he would phone his boss immediately.

On the telephone, Claude Leclerc was pleased to hear from his assistant and compassionately asked how his mother was handling the sudden change in her circumstances.

Mac explained that the pub had been closed since his father's death and that the funeral had only taken place the day before. However, his mother had now reluctantly accepted the situation and together with his help they hoped to reopen in four days time.

"And what about you?" Claude asked Mac.

"Well I am conscious of what I have to do here to make sure that matters return to some sort of normality, but at the same time I am aware that I can not stay here indefinitely as I have a need to get back to work."

It was a reply that Claude expected from Mac, as he knew how business like he could be. Claude then suggested that in order to help ease Mac's responsibilities in both situations, he could return to New York for a few days so that he could keep in touch, whilst still continuing to help his mother when needed.

A suggestion that Mac readily accepted and he agreed to return at the end of the next week, when the pub had been reopened for a week.

When Mac returned and told his mother and Mary of the arrangement that he had just agreed to with his boss, they both trembled inwardly at the thought of Mac going away and leaving them.

Linda was the first to speak as she believed that the suggestion of him returning to New York had to come at some time or another.

"Mac I understand what you are saying and I will miss you terribly, but you must repay the support your employers have given you."

Mary agreed completely with Linda's sentiments and added, "in any case it will give us something to look forward to when you return."

With such feeling coming from the two most important women in his life, Mac began to wonder how he would manage without them when he had to permanently return to America.

After a lot more conversation about the immediate future of the pub, Linda asked Mary if she would like to stay for a light lunch together with her and Mac.

Just as Mary had agreed to stay, Tony turned up to see how matters were with Linda and Mac.

"Oh Tony, what a welcome surprise," Linda expressed at seeing him at the backdoor. "Come on in, we are about to have a snack lunch, will you join us?" Seeing that Mary was also there, Tony was reluctant to stay, but Linda persuaded him.

Over lunch and after all conversation about Bob had subsided, Tony let it be known that he had been on a date with Jill and was looking forward to repeating it at the weekend.

All three raised their heads at the surprise news and Linda congratulated him on his new found interest. Mac was pleased also and Mary was delighted for Jill, as she thought that Jill was leading a somewhat sheltered life with her work at the Big House.

"Well that calls for a drink all round," said Mac, raising his glass.

For once, Tony was lost for words, but accepted their plaudits gracefully with a usual smile towards Linda.

Linda then told Tony that she had decided to reopen the pub in four days time and that she would handle the bar until she knew how things would work out.

Tony was pleased that the pub was going to open again, as several people in the village had asked him the question. However, he was cautious about asking too many questions, for fear of doubting Linda's ability to run the whole business single handed.

Fortunately, Mac gave Tony further details of the re-opening plan, when he told him that the pub would not offer food again until his mother could find someone suitable to be employed to handle the kitchen part.

Tony quickly picked up on the fact that Linda was prepared to employ someone in the kitchen, for Jill had told him that she was looking for alternative employment and it could be just what she was looking for.

Tony was not sure how to handle it, as he thought that he should not speak on Jill's behalf. On the other hand, he would not like to hear that Linda had employed someone else before Jill could even have the chance to consider it.

Then after giving it some thought, he asked them both if they had got anyone in mind for the job.

"Oh no, it's early days yet Tony," Linda answered with a forlorn sigh.

That pleased Tony, as it released his mind from having to speak out until he had informed Jill of the situation.

Mary then spoke, saying, "Tony have you anywhere in mind to take Jill on this intended date?"

"No, but she had mentioned going to a dance on Saturday evening at some place in Marnhull."

"Well that's wonderful. I like a nice dance, but I have not been to one since I left college."

Thinking that it would do them all good to have a night out together, Linda turned to Mac and said, "Why don't you take Mary?"

Mac thought that his mother had come up with a good idea, but was reluctant to gate-crash on Tony's date, after all it was only his second outing with Jill and he thought that Tony may have other ideas.

"Hey Linda, that's a good idea," Tony blurted out, thinking that it would perhaps help with his uneasiness in entertaining Jill alone.

Mary was delighted at the idea, but wondered what Jill may think about it without being in on the discussion.

"Well, I could give her a call, if you will let me use the phone," Tony said looking expectedly at Linda.

Linda had no objections and after a few minutes wait on the phone while someone at the other end went to fetch Jill, he happily told her of Linda's suggestion.

Jill was delighted to hear that Linda had considered her in such plans that involved Mac and Mary and readily agreed to meet them all at the pub early on Saturday evening.

"That's it then - job done," Linda said to all three.

Tony then told them that he would have to leave, as he still had some work to complete for Georgie and added that he would collect Jill from the Big House on Saturday and the two would arrive around seven o'clock.

Mary realised that she also needed to leave for a music tuition at a local school and told Mac that she would come to the pub in her own car on Saturday.

Mac thought that he could not wait until Saturday to see Mary again and so asked, "am I going to see you in the meantime?"

Playing him along, Mary smiled at Linda with a wink and said to Mac, "it all depends if your mother will let you out to play."

Mac came back quickly with a smile of his own and said, "if she doesn't, then I will play truant."

With that, Mary replied, "I'll come round tomorrow evening to give you a chance to get your own back at skittles - but not for a pie meal as we had before." She then left for her appointment.

Being on their own, Linda and Mac decided that they would take a walk over to the church cemetery and look at the flowers that were still on the grave. They read every message and concluded that the villagers thought more of Bob than they had realised.

To her surprise, Linda saw one that read, from Tommy Chant and Family, something that she believed would never happen.

Linda wondered, was he trying to win back her affection now that Bob was gone?

Then, as they were about to leave, Bert Mant the verger passed by and asked if there was any particular floral arrangement that they would like to take back to the pub.

Linda wanted her own wreath to stay on the grave with Bob, but thought that the one from Terry and Joan Smith would be nice to have, as The Major and Bob had a very close relationship within the pub over the past couple of years.

She told Bert that and he offered to deliver it to the pub later when he had sorted out the other wreaths in a more orderly arrangement.

After leaving the churchyard, Mac suggested that he would like to take his mother for a nice drive out into the Dorset countryside.

Linda readily agreed and replied, "Mac it will do us both good and will help to blow the cobwebs away." Meaning that they needed a break from all the happenings over the past couple of weeks.

After a cream tea at a wayside teashop and arriving back at the pub early evening, they found that the verger had delivered the flowers as promised. Also, inside the backdoor she found a note from Maggie and Jill, saying sorry that they had missed her but would look in again tomorrow afternoon.

Even though the pub was not open to the public, Linda placed the flowers in a vase on the bar, where Terry had leaned to have many a conversation with Bob. She then turned her attention to the intended visit of Maggie the next day and began to think that she would tell Maggie about wanting someone for the kitchen job, as she may know of a suitable person within her circle of friends.

Mac thought that was a very good idea and so when Maggie and Jill arrived the next day, Linda put the suggestion to Maggie, who immediately asked Linda to listen to Jill.

Jill then told Linda that she had decided to hand in her notice at the Big House as she was beginning to feel that she needed to widen her line of work, to advance her career.

Linda showed surprise at the news and asked Jill what sort of work she was considering taking to satisfy this advancement.

"Well, anything connected with the catering or hospitality trade," she replied.

Linda soon picked up on the thought that Jill could well be just the person to fit in with her plan to employ someone in the kitchen. After all, she knew what a good worker Jill was with her knowledge of serving meals at the pub.

She kept her thoughts to herself while she considered all the implications of offering the position to Jill and signalled Mac to the kitchen so that she could seek his advice.

Mac was all for it, but told his mother that working hours and salary would need to be carefully considered, so that the outlay did not upset the finances of the pub. He also pointed out that it was time that she considered paying Tony something for his efforts in future.

"Let's just float it in to Jill and get her reaction, that way you will be able to take the next step," Mac suggested.

After Linda put the suggestion to Jill in the presence of Maggie, she showed excited interest in the position, adding, "although I get free board and meals at the Big House, the wages are poor, so if I were to go back home to live with my parents and I could have meals here at the pub, all I need to know is if the wages are acceptable."

Maggie also liked the suggestion and told Jill that she would be learning the kitchen side of the trade from Linda, who was an exceptionally good cook with years of experience. After settling the working hours and the wages, Jill happily accepted the position and told Linda that she couldn't wait to start.

32.   A New Era

The next day, Friday at the Big House was quiet and so Jill went to see Mrs Evans the housekeeper to hand in a month's notice, whereupon she asked Jill with whom she had accepted another position.

When Mrs Evans heard that it was to be at the Dog & Whistle, she was pleased, for she was aware of the tragedy of Bob's death and realised that Linda would need to employ someone with experience to help rebuild her business. She also believed that it would do Jill good to get knowledge of the wider side of the hotel business.

With kindness, Mrs Evans allowed Jill to leave her employment immediately with one month's salary, so that she could start working for Linda without worrying too much about her income. She also told Jill that she could continue to live in her apartment at the Big House during that month until she sorted out alternative accommodation.

Jill was so thankful for the generosity afforded to her by Mrs Evans, that she gave her a big hug and assured her that she would always receive a warm welcome if she ever came to the pub.

When Linda and Mac heard the news later from Jill, they were delighted and began to work out how best to employ her so that both she and the pub would benefit.

Mac suggested that on Monday morning as soon as they reopen the pub and before it would get busy, that Jill should be showed how to pull a few pints of beer and how to work the new till, in case of any emergency that may crop up. After that she could be taught the fundamentals of the kitchen to at least cook a few meat slices and small pies for the bar. Long term cooking tuition could wait until the pub was up and running properly again. Linda accepted Mac's suggestion and was pleased that despite his impending return to America, that she would at least have him around to supervise things during the first week of reopening.

Early in the evening, Mary turned up as promised to challenge Mac at skittles and he lost to her for the second time.

After breakfast on Saturday morning, Mac and Linda busied themselves with getting the pub ready for the reopening on Monday, when Tony arrived and jokingly asked Mac if he was ready to go to the dance.

From that remark, Mac could see that Tony was just as excited about the coming foursome that they had arranged for the evening, but Linda played along with his amusing witticism by asking, "What time does this afternoon tea dance start Tony?" That caused laughter all round, before Tony offered to sort out the barrels in the cellar.

A little later, Tony's sister, nurse Lucy Bailey arrived at the back door enquiring how Linda was and said that Doctor Goddard had asked her to call to see if she needed any form of medical assistance.

"Oh no, thanks all the same Lucy, I am OK since the hospital gave me something to help me sleep. Please thank Doctor Goddard for me."

Linda told Lucy that her brother was down in the cellar, to which she replied, "Best place for him - I hope you've locked the door."

With more laughter, Linda realised that she was easing back to some form of normality and although she was missing Bob terribly, she knew that life must go on and that Lucy was helping.

After a light evening meal, Linda told Mac that he had better start to get ready for his evening out with Mary, Jill and Tony.

When the others arrived at the pub, Linda could see that all four were very happy to be having an evening out together and she was pleased that she could be alone to reflect on the happenings of previous years, not only with Bob, but about the times that she had so enjoyed with Mac's father.

At the dance, it was clear that Mary was the only one with any previous knowledge of ballroom dancing and so it was to her that they all turned to learn some basic steps of the waltz and the quickstep. At first, Mac was all of a muddle, but once he got hold of the rhythm he was at least able to get around the floor holding Mary close without looking a fool. Jill mastered the waltz and Tony enjoyed a version of the quickstep that he had invented to keep in time with the faster beat.

Mary had driven all four to the dance and on the way home they were full of laughter and hummed to several of the tunes that they had heard during the evening.

Arriving back at the Dog & Whistle, Mac invited them all in for a late night coffee and found Linda waiting for them. Anxious to know how they had all got on together, she soon learnt that they were so pleased with the way that the evening had gone that they were planning to do it again soon.

During their conversation, Linda made it known that Jill had accepted a position at the pub and that she could start straight away on Monday ready for the reopening.

Tony was so relieved to hear that from Linda, for he had been pondering all evening as to whether or not he should tell Jill of the opportunity that Linda had at the pub. So with a great big smile of delight, he turned to Jill and gently tapped her on the back with a great deal of affection saying, "Well done."

Mac then lifted his coffee mug towards her and said, "Welcome to the family Jill." The others all followed suit.

Tony and Jill were the first to leave for home and then Mac escorted Mary to her car, where she invited him into the passenger seat for a late night cuddle, before also leaving and saying, "I'll call you tomorrow morning lover."

On Sunday morning after Mac and Linda returned from church, Mary phoned and told them that her parents would like to invite them to afternoon tea later in the day. Both Mac and Linda willingly accepted, as they thought that Mary and her family were now close friends.

With a ham, egg and cheese salad, all freshly produced locally and taking place on the farm lawn during a sunny afternoon, Stan and Rita asked Linda how she was going to handle the opening of the pub the following day and Linda was keen to learn more about their lives as farmers. Although the end products were completely different, both families had the same distinctive spirit about work, whatever happened in their lives they had to get up and get on with it.

Mac thought that there was no better place to be. He could not take his eyes off Mary as he now believed that he was well and truly in love with her. Both Rita and Linda could see that too and later in the evening when they were driving home, Mac told his mother just that.

Linda was happy to hear of her son's feeling for Mary, as she thought that now that Mac had an understanding of love he would be more acceptable to her situation when the time came to explain how he was conceived out of wedlock.

Reclining in their sitting room, watching TV, both were deep in their thoughts about the coming week.

Linda was exceptionally concerned about how she would feel when meeting the public again and being at the counter where Bob had spent so much time working to provide a living for them both.

Mac on the other hand, was deep in thought about his relationship with Mary and how it would work out when the time came for him to return to America permanently. He was aware that long range courtships frequently faltered and fizzled out and he did not want that to happen to their relationship.

He thought about resigning from his employment and returning to live in Thimble Hardy, but that meant giving up all what he had studied and worked for and in any case he enjoyed living in America.

He considered asking Mary to come and live with him in New York, but that meant Mary leaving her parents to be alone to run the farm. In any case what if she did agree and ended up missing her parents and then wanting to return home.

Marriage?

It seemed far too early to consider that.

Although it felt to him that he had known Mary all his life, the reality was that he had only known her for just over four weeks and he didn't know what her parents would think about that idea.

Turning to his mother to seek her views on the subject, he noticed that she had quietly drifted off to sleep and he avoided waking her as he believed that she needed the rest.

33.   Reopening The Pub

When Linda awoke to the sound of a cockerel offering its services from a nearby farm early on Monday morning, she felt refreshed after the first good night's sleep that she had experienced since the death of her husband. She felt ready for the challenge ahead and was encouraged by the thought that she had the support of her ever loving son. She also accepted that she had to show strength in order to train the willing Jill into the next stage of her career.

After getting dressed, Linda wandered alone around the bar, making sure that all was ready, then she straightened the sign in the window that Tony had placed, telling the world that the pub would reopen today at 11.00am.

Mac arrived later and Linda cooked a good 'Full English' for both of them, whereupon their thoughts turned to the subject of the brewery.

Linda thought that it was odd that nobody from the brewery had shown any interest in coming to witness the reopening of their pub. After all it had been closed for two weeks and she thought that would have triggered off something in the minds of those who mattered.

Mac had thoughts about the brewery not wanting to further the interests of the pub and still believed that some sort of 'Jiggery-pokery' was going on behind the scenes, but still kept his thoughts to himself for not wanting to worry his mother at this time.

Jill then arrived saying that she brought the good wishes of Maggie for the reopening and asked Linda what she wanted her to do.

"Well Jill, while I sort out a few things in the kitchen for you, let Mac show you how to handle things behind the counter," Linda replied.

Mac explained the difference between the pump handles that served beer and those that dispensed cider and showed Jill how each should be recorded through the till. At first, Jill found the pumps difficult to handle, but with encouragement from Mac, she got the hang of it. Ringing up the cash on the till was no problem to the intelligent Jill and she enjoyed the new experience to be of her liking.

Linda then called her to the kitchen to start training to be a cook.

With some sandwiches made and a few meat slices in the oven, Linda left Jill to try her hand at some more pastry items, purely for practice.

Mac took down the sign in the window and opened the main door of the pub, while Linda took up her position behind the bar.

First to arrive were the crib players, George and Billy, who both offered their respects to Linda and were delighted at the idea, when Linda told them that they were the first to drink in the 'Re-born Dog & Whistle'.

Len Scott, from the paper shop was next to show his delight that the pub was open again and wished Linda success in her new roll as official landlady, or was it landlord?

Inevitably, Winnie and Madge turned up for their usual bottle of stout and took their seats by the door.

Other than expressing their sympathy, most people avoided talking about Bob until farmer Jim arrived.

"Hello my dear, I was so sorry to hear about Bob's tragedy, it won't be the same as without im," he said, not realising quite how that remark affected Linda.

He meant well, but Jim didn't have a good way of handling words.

"But 'ow you'm getting on my dear?" he continued, offering sincere concern in a continuing awkward way.

"Oh I'm OK Jim, I have Mac for support and several others are around if I need them," Linda replied in a soft voice.

Jim went on to offer any help that he could and Linda thanked him whilst pulling his pint of scrumpy.

As he turned around, he could see the two old ladies eyeing him up and down and so he interrupted their glare by saying, "Well how'm you two getting on since you'm not been able to have your usual?" Both looked at him in amazement and were lost for words to reply to such a personal question. With that, Jim carried on with his glass of cider and a hot meat pie.

With the Jukeboxes still disconnected, all was quiet in the pub and when the Reverend Timmy came in dressed in his dog collar, all could hear him say to Linda that he was not stopping but had just popped in to wish her well on the first day of reopening. Jim looked at Timmy and jokingly said, "Well Vicar, I guess that you'm off down to the beach then, seeing as you'm only work one day a week."

Madge, only getting half of the conversation, said to Winnie, "Was he'm going to the beach for, dressed like that."

To which Winnie replied, "he didn't say he was going to the beach, that there farmer said that."

"So what's the farmer going to the beach for?" Madge questioned again. "And in any case he's still got dirty boots."

"Forget it Madge, no one's going to the beach from yer."

Completely perplexed, Madge took a good sip of her stout and looked around the pub for something else to talk about.

Terry Smith came in to tell Linda that the skittles team were playing away this evening, but all were meeting in the bar before departing. That was good news, for she could get Jill learning how to bake some meat pies.

Mac had watched the proceedings of the morning trade and was pleased to see that Linda was more than capable of handling the bar alone and that Jill was very eager to learn whatever she could on the kitchen side.

More people than usual came in, mostly to offer Linda their condolences and to wish her well in continuing to keep the pub open. Even Sam James, the landlord from the Five Bells pub, came to relay the sympathy of many of his customers.

Sam also took Mac to one side and quietly told him to watch out for anyone from the brewery coming, as his experience of their handling of such matters was not always above board. Mac thanked him for his advice and asked him not to suggest that to his mother as she already had a lot on her mind. Sam agreed and shook Mac's hand.

At the end of the morning session, Linda closed the main door, while Jill and Mac helped her by collecting the empty glasses and straightening the chairs and tables.

Linda thanked Jill and told her to take the afternoon off before returning at 5.00pm ready for the evening shift.

Jill was pleased with her morning at the pub and went back to her apartment at the Big House for a rest.

Linda and Mac went into the kitchen for a light snack and then relaxed in the sitting room to reflect on the first session of the reopened pub. Mac then decided that he should phone his boss in New York to bring him up-to-date and also to confirm that he would be back at his hotel to start work next Monday.

Claude Leclerc was delighted to hear from Mac and sympathetically asked him how his mother was coping with the loss of her husband. He also asked Mac if he needed more time to ensure that his mother could handle matters when she would be left on her own.

Mac told him that the pub reopened this very morning and that she now had a permanently hired hand with Jill and that Tony had agreed to help in the evenings. Also, that several friends had offered to help if required. Mac said that he believed that with that help, it would be wise to let his mother handle things and that he certainly would return to New York in a week's time.

"Sounds like you have got things well under control Mac, so if you are happy, let's meet at 10.00am next Monday in my office." Claude then wished him success with the rest of the week and a safe journey.

After Mac had told his mother of Claude's conversation, Mary popped in on her way to a music teaching session at a school in one of the villages just to explain that she and her parents were planning to come to the pub during the evening.

Mac was delighted to see her and to hear that she would be back again later on and held her hand with an affectionate squeeze. Mary then teased him by saying, "Don't worry lover boy, I won't challenge you to skittles again this evening, just a nice family gathering to help with the pub finances."

The reliable Jill arrived as agreed at five o'clock and immediately Linda got her to make some small meat pies and showed her how to work the ovens. She also made some sandwiches when Linda left to open the pub for the evening session.

It wasn't long before Old Tom, the Thatcher, arrived on his way home from work and a couple of lads from the quarry came to quench their thirst. Mac explained to them that for today only, the Jukebox was not connected and apologised that they could not play their choice of music for once.

Unusually, Connie the postmistress arrived to have half a glass and to wish Linda well. She was followed by The Major, who offered any help before his skittle team would arrive with their supporters

"Well thank you Terry, at the moment I am able to cope and I am expecting Tony soon," Linda replied in a grateful manner.

"Fine, then I'll have a pint and anything that you have hot to eat."

With that, Linda went to see how Jill was managing in the kitchen and to her surprise found sandwiches and hot meat pies all nicely laid out on trays, ready to serve to the bar.

Linda gave Jill thankful words of encouragement and took some pies into the bar, ready to serve to The Major. Jill followed with more, which she put onto the hot plate as she had seen Linda do before.

"There you are Terry, freshly baked by Jill my new trainee cook, who has come from the Big House to work full time at the Dog & Whistle."

Terry was surprised to hear that Linda had found someone of Jill's caliber so quick and took his first mouthful of the very first meat pie to be made alone by the new cook. In her enthusiasm Jill had rather overfilled each with gravy that ran down The Major's chin, causing him to act quickly to avoid it from reaching his clean white shirt.

Then, through the door came PC Willis still dressed in his uniform.

"Don't worry I'm not here to complain about anything, just to wish you well with the reopening," he told Linda, and gave Mac an affirmative nod of approval.

Georgie then arrived and was soon followed by the rest of the skittles team, with several wives and girlfriends, who all pushed and shoved to get a drink before The Major called for them to leave for the away match.

In amongst the mêlée, Linda was relieved to see that Tony had arrived and called him to come and help satisfy the sudden demand for drinks and snacks.

Seeing Tony at the bar, Jill gave him an affectionate smile and in return, he wished her well in her new appointment.

More people arrived, generally pleased to see that the pub had reopened, although Mac guessed that some nosy parkers had only come to gawp at Linda, to see how she was managing after being left without Bob. Whatever the reason, it was good for trade and the new till was red-hot for a while.

After the skittles team had departed for their game at Buckhorn Weston, things became a little quieter and Tony asked Linda if the brewery dray had arrived earlier in the day. When she confirmed that it had, Tony went to the cellar to change over the the empty barrels with the freshly delivered ones.

When he returned, he saw Linda giving Jill a further lesson in how to pull a pint or two in quick succession. "So, my lady, you're after my job as well," Tony playfully teased her. To which Jill remarked, "watch out boy, women are going to take over this world!"

Although Tony was a man's-man, he had always succumbed to the cheeky remarks thrown at him by Linda, the one woman that he had always respected and now he had a second woman to contend with.

Gradually, the 'one-glass' drinkers began to leave the pub, having seen how Linda was managing, albeit with the help of Tony.

To Mac's delight, Mary and her parents arrived and Linda suggested that he should take them through to the sitting room for a private drink and conversation away from the gossipers of the village. This he did and Linda joined them when more people left, leaving Tony to handle the bar alone.

Stan and Rita felt privileged to have been invited into Linda's private accommodation and Stan willingly bought drinks all round.

Mary, having been there before, made her parents feel comfortable and showed her mother some of the photographs of Bob that Linda had recently placed in frames on the sideboard.

Stan was interested to learn more about Mac's job in the USA and wondered what his long term prospects were in this 'hotel game', as he put it.

Mac answered Stan's questions with confidence and apart from actually asking Mac what his salary was, he then had a much better understanding of the person who his only daughter seemed to have taken a loving liking to.

Rita asked Linda how she was managing and if she thought that she would still be staying on at the pub now that she was alone.

"Well, apart from having to take on a lot more responsibility now that I don't have Bob, I am fine," Linda answered to the first part of the question. Then to the second part she most firmly stated that this was her life and that she had no intentions of leaving the Dog & Whistle.

From his mother's confidence, Stan could see where Mac had obtained his determined objective in life and thought that he was certainly a right person for his daughter to be looking to the future with.

Rita, although liking Mac very much, kept her thoughts to herself about how unhappy she would be if Mary ever went off to   live in America with Mac.

Mary moved closer to Mac and lovingly held his hand as if to show her parents that their relationship was a serious affair and that she sought their approval in front of Linda, who had stated several times that she approved of their relationship.

Mac then confirmed to them all that he would be leaving for America on Saturday and if all went well that he would probably be away for a week, depending on how his boss saw things.

"Quite the international traveller," Mary said, playfully teasing him.

Back in the bar, Jill who had finished her work in the kitchen , stood talking to Tony as she questioned him about his involvement in the pub. As he was always around and was willing to turn his hand to anything, she wondered if he had a financial interest in the business.

"Oh no, I am just a good friend of Bob and Linda's and I have always been happy to help them whenever they have needed it," Tony said with a shrug of his shoulders.

Then, before Jill could ask any more questions, Linda appeared and told them that as most customers had left she could manage and that they could both leave if they wanted to.

Seizing the opportunity to walk Jill back to the Big House, Tony readily agreed and off they both went together.

Soon after, Mary and her parents left, but not before Mac had arranged to meet Mary the following evening at the farm.

Then, with the last customer gone, Linda locked the pub door and Mac pushed the button on the till to see just how well things had gone on the first day of reopening.

With a late night coffee, Mac and his mother sat in the kitchen and scrutinised the tab from the till in detail and found that they had sold more beer during the evening than at any time since they started with the numbers analysis.

"That should please the brewery," Linda said and Mac pointed out that it was without some regulars who were away with the skittles team.

He then asked his mother what she thought of Jill's effort, to which Linda answered that she was pleased to have someone who was so eager to learn for her own advancement and not a person who just treated it as any old job.

So, with both mother and son happy with the day, they retired to their beds for a well earned rest.

Mac applied his mind to how the rest of his week should be spent before he had to leave for the US on Saturday, but he could only think of Mary, Mary and Mary!

34.   Learning Part of the Truth

With trade in the pub being relatively quiet over next few days, Mac took the opportunity to help his mother with the continuing amount of paperwork that needed to be attended to.

Notification of the change of name from Bob to Linda with such organisations as the electric company, water board, insurance documents, solicitors, pension authorities and so it went on.

However, on Thursday afternoon after closing for the break, Linda thought that the time was right for her to talk to Mac about his real father, as she had promised that she would before he had to leave for New York. So she asked him to come with her to the sitting room, where she began with words of explanation that connected his mind with that which he was now feeling for Mary - LOVE.

"Mac, you need to understand that throughout the early part of 1944 southern England was swimming with American troops prior to the D-Day invasion of France and they brought a different way of life to the people of the villages around here. It opened up the minds of many of us."

With the scene beginning to unfold, Mac was eager to learn how his mother, a girl of just 18 years, was affected by this 'new life' as she was putting it.

"Well, the soldiers attended dances in the villages and they were keen to learn more about our way of life too. Many people invited them into their homes. In return, we girls were often invited to functions at theirs camps and it was at one such event in the officer's mess that I met a very handsome young lieutenant."

Linda went on to explain how they both fell deeply in love and enjoyed a wonderful time together over the next three months. Then one day came the awful news that the regiment was to move on from the area and that their time together would be very uncertain. "As it turned out, we only had two more evenings together, during which time our love knew no boundaries."

"So you fell pregnant with me?" "Yes, you are his son," Linda replied.

Mac needed to know more, but found it embarrassing to talk to his mother about her sex life and so he asked, "So what happened to this guy, did you hear from him again, or did he just ditch you?"

"Mac, although I lived in hope for many years after, I eventually had to accept that he had probably returned to the States after the war was over and no doubt he was respectably married to someone else."

Anger built up inside him at the thought that anyone should treat his mother in such a thoughtless and inconsiderate manner and asked what her parents thought about him.

"Oh they never knew the true person and if my father had known, he would have killed him."

Wanting to be sure of things, Mac swallowed his embarrassment and asked his mother how certain could she be that this GI was his father.

"Mac, I promise you that despite what many people in the village said at the time, he was the only one. So I am absolutely certain and I have never told a soul about this before."

Linda was now crying with relief that she had at last told her only son who his true father was and asked him if he wanted to know his father's name.

"No Mom, I am completely confused and full of sorrow for you and I do not want to know his name; I am Malcolm Tanner and I do not want that changed due to some scoundrel who left you in the lurch."

Linda tried to calm Mac down and told him that that may not be the end of the story as she had recently obtained information that might turn out to be useful, but at the moment it could not be confirmed.

"So what's that then, has he turned up and wants to claim the pub as his legal rights?"

"No Mac, it's nothing like that, but please bear with me for a few weeks longer, then, if my facts are correct, I will know more for certain."

Mac sighed and then suddenly said, "Christ mother, this means that I am half American and that now changes a lot in my life!"

Linda hugged and kissed him with tears still running down her face.

"You know Mom, before coming home like I have, I was about to apply for American citizenship, which takes a long time to achieve, but what you have revealed to me this afternoon will make things a lot easier."

Mac was even more confused now that he realised that he was of dual nationality. Still angry with the way that his mother, as a young girl, had been treated by the American, but also somewhat happy to know that at least he was not a product of that scoundrel Tommy Chant, as he had boasted on many occasions.

"Mom I want to thank you for being so honest with me so far and I guess that this calls for a nice pot of tea to calm our nerves, before you need to open up the pub again for this evening."

The ever reliable Jill arrived, eager to learn more from Linda and when Linda took up her place behind the bar to serve the first customers of the evening, Jill busied herself in the kitchen preparing food for later on.

Mac concentrated his mind on his new found dual nationality and was pleased that his application for American citizenship would become a lot easier. Then, suddenly, he thought that if he had been registered in the name of Tanner in England and that his mother did not have any paperwork to prove that his father was American, then his application would not be as easy as he had first thought.

Later on, Tony arrived to offer a hand to either of the two women, who both got him doing a few minor jobs.

As he thought that the pub had enough staff to cater for the Thursday slow trade, Mac decided to phone Mary, who gladly invited him to her place for a cool drink on the lawn during a nice sunset.

It was just what Mac needed to help clear his head of the sudden surprising information that he had experienced. He toyed with the idea of telling Mary his news, but decided that it would betray his mother's confidence and so decided not to. Instead, he focused on the beauty of Mary and the fact that she was now offering to drive him to the railway station on Saturday.

Over breakfast on Friday morning, Mac asked his mother if she had any documented proof of who his real father was, as he would certainly need it if he were to continue in his desire for dual citizenship.

Linda replied that she had nothing like that, but she did have some old photographs stored away somewhere that showed the two of them together.

"Do you have any letters that may contain details of who he was, his service number for instance, or the name of his regiment?" Mac continued to probe.

"I don't think so, as I probably destroyed them so that my father could not find out his name at the time."

Mac felt sure that there was a way of tracing this lieutenant through US Army Records, but he needed a starting point and at the moment his mother could not, or would not, willingly provide it for him.

Their conversation was interrupted by a knock on the back door and when Linda opened it, she found the Reverend Timmy, who said that he had just popped in to wish Mac bon voyage on his trip back to New York and to assure him that his mother would be in safe hands whilst he was away.

"Oh Timmy, do come in and tell it to Mac yourself, and would you like a cup of coffee?" Linda happily asked him.

While drinking their coffee together, Mac wondered if it would be wise to tell Timmy what he had suddenly been told about his real father, as maybe there was something in the church records that would have a bearing on the matter.

Timmy could see that Mac was troubled about something and asked him if he had anything on his mind that he, as a trusted 'man of the cloth', could help him with. Linda was quick to answer and politely said to the vicar, "Timmy, we both have something that we would like your help on, but with Mac being away for the next week, I would like to leave it until his return." Mac looked at his mother with surprise and then nodded in agreement.

35.   Mac Leaves for New York

Awake early on Saturday morning, Mac prepared himself to leave Thimble Hardy and Linda braced herself for his departure.

After breakfast, Mac looked his mother in the eyes and praised her with words of encouragement. "Mom, you have been brave throughout this terrible time and during the past week you have shown how you can manage to continue to run the pub, albeit with the help of Jill and Tony."

Linda put her hand on his arm and stopped him from saying any more, for fear of bursting into tears at the kind remarks.

Soon there was a tap on the back door and a very welcome face appeared at the kitchen window.

"Come on in Mary," Linda called out to her. "Your travelling man is nearly ready."

Mary made straight for Mac and gave him a huge hug, followed by a kiss on the cheek, adding a throw-away remark, "have you got all that you need for the journey?"

It was a time that none of the three wanted, but Mac knew that his business life was very important to him and whatever else was happening in his life, he had to be honourable towards his employers and return without question.

With Mac and Mary well on the way to the station, Tony arrived and found Linda in a very sorrowful state with tears running down her face. Tony tried to comfort her and she hung on to him saying, "Tony, the two most important men in my life have now left me alone."

Jill then arrived and Linda knew that she should not let her emotions be seen to her new member of staff.

"Hello Jill, Mac has gone, but Tony is in the bar and so it is left to the three of us to make a real good go of keeping this pub open to the satisfaction of our customers."

Jill was pleased that she was openly included in the management of the pub and told Linda that she had some ideas of her own.

At the railway station, Mary clung to Mac as they waited for the train to arrive and without any hesitation told him that she LOVED him. Mac responded with similar affectionate remarks but both had to separate when the London bound train pulled in alongside them.

With one more kiss, Mac hopped aboard and with a wave left Mary to walk back to her car very much down in the dumps.

Mac felt the same way when the train left Sherborne station, but was soon engaged in conversation with a man sitting opposite.

They discussed the fact that the train was quite full and the man suggested that many people were travelling to London on a Saturday to attend some sporting event. A woman sitting next to Mac, overhearing the conversation, said that most people were returning from holidays in Devon and Cornwall.

The man looked at her with a frown that indicated that he was thinking, "who asked you to speak?"

He then changed the subject in his continued conversation with Mac and established that Mac was on his way to New York.

Again the women chose to involve herself in their conversation and told them that she didn't like New York, London, or Paris. This time the man took her up on her statement and asked why.

"Well, they tell me that the weather's always rotten there, not like Spain where they've got lots of sunshine."

"So where do you come from then?" He asked

"Brighton, in the south where it's always sunny, if fact we've got a nudists beach where you don't have to wear any clothes if you don't want to," was her answer.

Another woman sitting in the corner said, "When I went to Brighton, it poured with rain all day."

"Well we do have rain occasionally, but it's usually because it comes from New York and is on its way to London, or Paris."

The man smiled at Mac and edged his way out of the conversation, which left the two women arguing about the weather in Brighton.

High in the sky off the southern coast of Ireland, Mac settled back in his seat on the aircraft to try and sort things out in his mind whilst being away from the various people involved.

His mother and the pub; his future with Mary; his position and loyalty to his employers; his new found information about his real father; but most of all the position that he had since found himself in now that he was half American. He found it difficult to dissociate any one from the other and soon dozed off to sleep.

After leaving the station, Mary decided to drive back to the Dog & Whistle to tell Linda that Mac had safely caught the train and that he would now be well on his way to the airport. In essence, she needed to be with someone who would appreciate how she was feeling, as her parents would not really understand how much she was already missing Mac.

When she arrived through the back door, she found Linda teaching Jill how to crimp pastry around various pies. Both were pleased to see the attractive Mary, although she was not quite so vivacious as usual.

"Come on in and let's all mope together," said Linda to Mary.

That caused a laugh to all three and soon they all concentrated on what they had to do next.

Mary told the others that she would be riding two horses from the riding school at a gymkhana in Wincanton during the afternoon and needed to be off to prepare for the event.

After she had gone, Jill remarked to Linda how socially confident Mary was and so talented with her music, horse riding and ability to run the business side of her parents' farm. To which Linda replied, "that's what a private school education does for you."

Linda went on to say to Jill, "but don't you worry my love, you have many talents in other directions and I intend to make you the envy of the village with your future cooking skills."

That made Jill laugh, but at the same time she was inwardly proud that someone of Linda's calibre would recognise that she also had talent, albeit not with the same subjects as Mary.

Saturday morning saw a slow trickle of people come to the pub and Linda gave Jill the opportunity to leave early, which she was pleased to take so that she could walk back through the lovely gardens of the Big House, where the roses were out in full bloom.

Throughout the afternoon, Linda felt lost without the presence of Mac and Bob and so she took a walk around the village. She went into the recreation ground and watched the men playing cricket, where Bob had so often spent time doing the same thing.

Saturday evening in the pub saw many people come and go and Linda admired how well Tony and Jill worked together keeping customers satisfied with drinks and food. Clearly they both enjoyed what they were doing.

Many customers asked when the Pie Night would be reinstated and one or two from the skittles team enquired about egg and chips.

Linda was pleased to hear such comments and asked Jill if she was ready to handle another Pie Night, but this time she would be doing the cooking.

Jill was delighted with the idea and was pleased to learn that Linda was going to put her in the driving seat for the next Pie Night.

In the mean time, Jill suggested to Linda that they could be making more use of serving hot food at lunch times.

"We could even put a couple of tables outside the front door and serve pie and chips, or something similar, that way passers by would see people eating and that could make them want to do the same thing."

Linda thought that to be a very good idea and gave Jill a pat on the back, before returning to work alongside Tony serving more customers who had arrived late.

At the end of the evening, Linda sat with Jill and Tony discussing the idea that Jill had put forward and Tony offered to come in on Sunday morning to root out some tables from Bob's store room, ready for the ladies to put outside on Monday when he would be at work.

"Thanks Tony, you are such a helpful person," Linda said to him.

36.   Mac Receives a Generous Offer

On Monday morning in the US, Mac kept the appointment with his boss, who was so sympathetic to the traumatic events that Mac had experienced. After all, it was intended to have been a lovely two weeks vacation at home with his parents.

Claude Leclerc was particularly concerned about how the demands on Mac had affected him mentally and said that he had arranged for the Group Personnel Director to come and have a talk with him about his immediate and long term future with the company.

Mac wondered why Claude had taken that step without consulting him first and, although he had no reason to believe that Claude was doing anything underhanded, it did add another matter for him to worry about.

Claude suggested that they should both take a stroll around the hotel together, as it would help to make sure that Mac was up-to-date with anything that may have changed whilst he had been away.

As they passed various members of staff, they all welcomed Mac's return and several who had heard about the death of his father offered their sympathy.

When they returned to Claude's office, they found Irving Bloomenfeld, the Group Personnel Director waiting for them. Mac had met Irving several times previously, when he was progressing through his training period.

Like all others, Irving expressed his condolence to Mac and at first was particularly interested to know how the accident had happened to his father and how it had affected his mother.

Mac told him the bare details of the accident and went on to say that his mother was determined to carry on with the business.

"She has all the skills to run the pub and has now employed a very capable girl to help with the kitchen side. However, as my father had always handled the commercial side of the business, she now needs my guidance on most financial things until she is able to pick up the reins, particularly the added legal matters," Mac stated clearly.

Irving asked Mac how he intended to cope with these commercial matters at long range.

"Well, apart from telephone calls, I would like to visit her more frequently, probably when I have a few days off from my work here."

Irving looked at Claude, who nodded back at him, as if to agree with something that had already been planned.

Irving then addressed Mac in a semi-formal manner, but still offering compassion to his employee.

"Mac, this company has invested a lot of time and money in your development and you have responded in an excellent way. We see you with great promise and we would not want to lose you."

Claude then added his endorsement to the statement, before Irving went on to say more.

"I have discussed the situation with Claude and now having listened to you, I have, with the blessing of the Group Managing Director, a plan that we would like you to consider."

Mac could feel that something was about to be said that he may not like and shuffled his feet uneasily beneath his seat.

"So that we all know where we stand on this matter, we would like to offer you three months compassionate leave on half pay. You may continue to occupy your apartment here and be free to use it whenever you want to visit during this period."

Irving's offer continued. "If you accept this, it will give us the chance to put a trainee in to work with Claude during your absence, but I guarantee that you will be offered your existing job back when the three months are up."

Mac could hardly believe what a generous offer the company was putting to him. Many things flashed through his mind; it would mean that he could continue to support his mother at close range; he could handle any correspondence and visits from the brewery personnel and, of course, it would give him more time with Mary.

"Just think about it Mac," Irving said and Claude nodded to him.

Mac did not want to jump in too quickly and accept on the spot, just in case he had missed anything.

Irving went on to say that this offer had been based on the good recommendation that he had received from Claude, his immediate boss, and several other of his previous bosses from the past.

Mac, smiled to Claude and thanked the two of them, asking if he could have a little time to consider the offer.

Irving responded favourably and asked him to work the week out with Claude as usual, but that he would like to know his decision by Friday morning.

Mac was very happy with the arrangement and assured Irving that he would have his reply by Friday.

Irving then left the hotel and Claude suggested to Mac that it would be wise for him to go to his apartment to think things over, before coming back to take over from himself at 6.00pm this evening, as he had done on many previous occasions.

With seven hours still available in the day before Mac had to relieve Claude, he changed into casual clothes and took a walk through the streets of New York and into a park, where he sat on a seat and contemplated the offer that had been presented to him.

The first thing on his mind was how much he liked life in America and particularly the job that he had in new York. He was concerned about being away from his work for three months, after all, many things could change in that time and he could find himself without employment. However, he dismissed that thought as he trusted Irving Bloomenfeld to honour his word of a guaranteed position.

He then thought about his new found status in life, now being half American, and how he needed to obtain documentation as proof.

His mother and her business was certainly something that he could handle to her satisfaction if he were to be with her for three months. Then there was Mary. Maybe he could bring her to New York for a short holiday, during which time it would give her a taste of what American life was like.

As he walked back to the hotel, it became clear in his mind that three months back home would be ideal on all counts and that he would accept the offer gladly.

Throughout the week, he kept his decision to himself and did not even mention it to his mother, or to Mary when he phoned home a few days later.

Then on Friday morning, as agreed, he gave his decision to Claude, who in turn, passed the message to Irving.

Both were delighted to learn of his decision and Claude informed him that his last duty would be on Saturday evening and so he would be free to make arrangements to leave New York after that.

Claude then told Mac that he could not leave without the two of them having a nice farewell dinner together later, away from the hotel. Mac thought that Claude was an exceptionally good boss and a nice person with it and gladly accepted the invitation.

At the restaurant that evening, both agreed how nice it was to sit back and watch others working unsocial hours to please the public. Mac was particularly interested to watch the Maitre d' skilfully guiding his customers to their tables and ensuring their comfort, while at the same time having complete control of his staff.

Claude was interested in learning a little more from Mac about life in an English pub back in the Dorset village. He asked if the customers were mainly tourists and how many bedrooms did it have for these tourists.

Mac explained to him that it was nothing like that, as the pub had always relied on regular local customers from the village, but it was his intention to get his mother to a position where she could attract people from beyond the village of Thimble Hardy.

Claude could hear Mac's hospitality training coming out and suggested that the name Thimble Hardy would be an attraction in itself to many American tourists.

Mac agreed, but said that the pub needed extra bedrooms and a proper restaurant added, before it could be advertised for tourists.

37.   Shocking News

Meanwhile, back in the pub at the start of a new week, Linda continued to teach Jill new skills in the kitchen and as they were alone, she asked Jill how her relationship with Tony was going.

"Oh great, it's becoming quite serious now and he has introduced me to his parents and openly talks about family matters with me," Jill excitingly replied.

"And your parents?" Linda questioned.

"Yes they have met Tony and appear to approve of our relationship."

Linda was so pleased to hear that, as she liked a good romance and with Mac and Mary well intrenched, she now had two romances to lovingly follow.

Throughout the week, Linda was well supported by Jill, Tony and occasionally by Terry Smith. Maggie also came in on a couple of occasions to boost her morale and to enquire how Jill was progressing. Trade was picking up to where it was prior to Bob's death and when Linda went to bed on Friday evening, she was very pleased to think that she had managed the business for a week without the aid of Mac and she slept soundly for the first night in a long time.

On Saturday, Linda opened the pub on a bright sunny morning and with the aid of Tony, who had called in on his way to help at his brother-in-law at the iron works, they set up the tables outside the main door. A couple of lads soon turned up and took their drinks and some sandwiches out to sit at the tables.

Just as Jill had thought, people eating outside caused a passing car to stop and the occupants came in for refreshment. Linda told Jill and they both thought that Mac would be proud of what they had done to entice business from outside the village.

There were three tables outside and with two of them now occupied, it gave a good impression to all passers-by that the Dog & Whistle was open for food. Three men on motorbikes travelling to the coast also stopped and bought food with drinks, after seeing the tables.

There was no doubt that Jill's idea of placing some tables outside had attracted people who would not normally have come to the pub and so when Linda closed at the end of the morning session, she thanked Jill before she left for her break and Linda was a happy person.

While Linda was having a snack lunch, the post arrived and among the pile was a letter from the brewery that read along the lines that it was in answer to her letter to them.

It started with a few lines of sympathy over Bob's death, but soon entered into a very official businesslike manner.

"As you will be aware from the terms of the licence allocated to the running of our establishment known as the Dog & Whistle public house, the licence was issued to your late husband Robert Smart. Furthermore, it is the the policy of this company that all licences will only be issued to male landlords.

With this as a ruling and considering the decline in beer sales at the said premises over the past two years, the board of directors have decided not to issue a new licence, so the premises will be closed and put up for sale along with the adjoining vacant cottage.

We therefore give issue that the business is to be closed after final trading on the 31st October 1968.

As sitting tenant that means that you are to vacate the building and remove all of your personal possessions within one week of the closure date."

The letter went on with more legal jargon, but Linda's mind could not take it in, as she was in complete shock at receiving this devastating news in such an inconsiderate way.

Her first thoughts were to ring Mac in America, but decided not to as he would be back in a few days time and in any case she did not want him worrying during his flight home.

For a while she just sat with head in her hands, thinking, I have lost my husband and now I am about to lose my home and my livelihood, so she called out aloud, to nobody in particular.

"What am I going to do?'

After a while, Linda pulled herself together and tried to control her feelings, for she did not want to convey the bad news to anyone, particularly to Jill and Tony, or let it get around the village.

When Jill arrived for her evening shift, she was accompanied by Maggie who had an evening off from her Big House duties. Jill set about her tasks in the kitchen, but Maggie could sense that Linda was not her usual self.

She asked Linda if she was all right and if there was anything that she could do for her.

"It's OK Maggie, I'm just a bit off after all that has been going on these past few weeks," Linda said, intelligently sidestepping the real problem.

"Why don't you take the evening off and just put your feet up for once?" Maggie asked.

Linda reminded her that she had customers to attend to and that she had never taken time off before.

Maggie then offered to help out in the kitchen and so let Jill handle the bar until Tony would arrive later.

Although Linda had not thought of Jill running the bar alone, she now believed that she was versatile enough to hold the fort until Tony would arrive latter.

So, she reluctantly accepted Maggie's idea as she did not really want to face customers at the moment. Also it would give her some more time alone with her thoughts and to think about what she may have to do in the future.

When Maggie told Jill that Linda was not feeling well and that it would help if she could rest for while, Jill was pleased to help out in any way that she could and willingly took on the responsibility of the bar, as Maggie suggested.

Luckily, the first hour in the bar was quiet and Jill did not have much to do, while Maggie busied herself in the kitchen making a few tasty items. This allowed Linda to drop off to sleep for a well needed rest to both her body and mind.

38. The Return of a Friend

When Linda awoke, she felt much better and in control of her thoughts and actions. She thanked Maggie and went into the bar to thank Jill, where she found her and Tony happily serving a number of customers who were looking for a good Saturday evening out.

Among the gathering was The Major and his wife, who were pleased to help open up the skittle alley for a small group of people who wanted to pit their skills against each other. Some others ordered food, which kept Maggie busy, while Linda got lost in supervising the whole ball game, helping her to take her mind off her real problem.

Then suddenly into the pub came a very welcome face, that made Linda gasp with surprise and then with excitement.

"HANK!" Linda called out and moved quickly to greet him.

"Hello lovely Linda." He returned her greeting, giving her a hug.

"How's Bob?" He politely enquired.

Linda told Hank that she had some sad news to tell him and then asked him to accompany her to the sitting room.

Sitting close together, Linda informed Hank of the tragic death of Bob and also the consequential letter that she had received from the brewery.

"Hank, I have not told anyone of the brewery letter as I am waiting for my son to return from America in a few days time, so please keep it to yourself for the time being."

Hank felt so sorry for Linda that he just wanted to take her in his arms and hug her forever, but he needed to establish one thing for certain before he let out his true feelings.

"Linda, I think that you and I should have a very honest talk and if my thoughts are correct, your life may not be such a bitch as you are believing it to be," the likeable American said directly to her face.

He then enquired. "Were you once called Linda Tanner?"

To which she replied, "Yes, and were you once called Junior Burnett?"

With both now having clearly established that they were two people who knew each other back in 1944, Hank needed to know if Linda's son was the product of a liaison from that time.

However, he thought that this evening, with Linda in a distressed state, was not the time to delve further into her past and suggested that as she had had enough shocks for one day that he would return another time for a further conversation.

Linda asked Hank what he was doing back in north Dorset, to which he happily replied,

"I arrived in London on Thursday with my client Ivan Framburg, where we had a meeting with his UK solicitors to conclude the official takeover of the Sherborne factory. Ivan has now gone to Paris for the weekend and I took the opportunity to settle into our hotel in Yeovil, prior to work that we have to do during the coming week."

Linda was pleased to hear that Hank would be in the area during the week, as she now believed that he should meet Mac after he would arrive home on Monday. So she told that to Hank, who was all for it.

"Linda, I have other things that I would like to discuss with you alone, so why don't we meet up tomorrow somewhere?" Hank enquired.

"Tell you what Hank, if you come here tomorrow morning, say about 12.00 noon and as the pub is closed for the day, I will cook us both a nice Sunday roast, after which we can talk more."

Hank was keen on that and after giving her another affectionate hug, he went through to the bar to have a chat with Tony and Terry Smith. He then left the pub so that Linda could get on with her work.

Maggie could see that Linda was now much happier than when she first arrived and thought that something must of happened during her meeting with Hank, that had cheered her up.

With Maggie, Jill and Tony having held the fort for her, she realised what good friends they really were. She also thanked Terry Smith for his contribution to the evening before he left.

When Hank arrived on Sunday morning carrying a large bunch of flowers, Linda greeted him like a long lost friend, which of course he was. Lunch was ready and over a glass of wine, they both enjoyed a friendly conversation about the times that they remembered from earlier years.

Relaxing cosily in the sitting room after lunch, Hank decided that it was time for some serious conversation.

"Linda, there is no other way of putting this," he said bluntly.

"Is your son Mac the product of a liaison with my good buddy Joe MacKenzie back in 1944?"

Linda was waiting for this question and had already worked out her answer to tell Hank.

"Hank I must honestly answer YES, and you are the only one that I have ever admitted that to, so please keep that to yourself. Although my son knows that his father was a GI, he has not been told his name as I am not sure where Joe is now."

Hank gave her his word on that delicate matter and then listened more to Linda.

"Hank do you know the whereabouts of Joe MacKenzie now?"

Hank then explained that together, the two young Lieutenants, as they were then, stormed the beach of France along with thousands of other American and British troops on D-day. After a day and night of fierce battle, Joe was tragically killed when he stepped on a mine.

Linda went stiff with shock at hearing such news, but was somewhat relieved to know that Joe had not offered his love to another woman since the birth of Mac. Then looking at Hank, she said, "Hank I must tell you that I was so in love with Joe and I know he felt the same."

Hank smiled at Linda and told her that he had proof of Joe's sincere feelings for her and produced a note in Joe's handwriting.

As she unfolded it with trembling hands and saw the fading handwriting, she read it with loving memories of Joe and those last days together, that it made tears run down her face.

It read,

Dearest Linda,

Our last few evenings together will remain in my heart forever and should a child be born from that relationship I give you my word that I will support you and it without question. I look forward to loving you again when I return and hope that we will have a very happy life together.

However, should anything happen to me in this dreadful war, then I hope that my buddy Junior Burnett will somehow be able to contribute to your welfare by passing on any money that may be due to me.

I, and he, can be traced through military records by our consecutive service numbers, but whatever happens, please remember me to my child.

My love is yours forever.

Joe MacKenzie

5385721 Lieutenant, US Army.

Linda held the note to her chest and sobbed aloud, while asking Hank how he had come by it.

"Linda it is somewhat complicated to explain, but to cut a long story short, Joe and I made each other executors to our wills and because of this note written by Joe, I was able to claim it and some money for you through the courts on the sworn promise that I would pass it on whenever I could trace you."

Linda listened to what Hank was saying with mixed feelings and asked what money he was he talking about.

"Well, as Intelligence Officers going to war, the US military deposited a $1,000 into two banks for each of us in case we ever found ourselves on the run from the enemy, so to speak. Our knowledge was something that they did not want to fall into enemy hands."

He explained that the money was credited as non-refundable and was theirs to keep at the end of the war.

Hank went on to explain that Joe's apportionment had been sitting with $1,000 in a Swiss bank and another $1,000 in a London bank untouched for 25 years and a rough estimate indicates that both amounts will have doubled in that time, making some £4,000 available to you after administration costs.

Linda was taken aback by the amount of money involved, but thought the return of Malcolm's father would have meant much more to her than money.

Hank wanted to know more about Mac now that he understood that there existed a direct descendant of his buddy Joe and Linda told him that he should come back again when Mac had returned, so that he could hear details about his father from a person who knew him well.

Hank was only too pleased to oblige, but pointed out that time may not be his to determine when Ivan returned and they get started on the redevelopment of the factory to Ivan's requirement. There would be designers and building contractors to negotiate with, before organising some of Ivan's own staff to arrive from the US.

That Linda understood and in any case she would have so much to talk to Mac about when he arrived, plus he would want to be with Mary. There was so much going around in her head that she just wished for Mac to hurry up and arrive and she told Hank that.

"Linda why don't you put it all to one side for a few hours and let me take you out for a nice drive in the countryside and we can stop off at a quaint pub for a celebratory drink."

Hank's offer was accepted and they took a drive around south Somerset that ended with them stopping at the Henstridge Ash pub, where it is alleged that Sir Walter Raleigh had a bucket of water thrown over him, when a servant saw him smoking a cigarette and thought that he was on fire. Hank thought that the fable was hilarious and one that he would take back home to tell his friends and staff in the office.

39.   Mac Hears The Truth

When Mary met Mac at Sherborne station as arranged late on Monday morning, they were both delighted to be reunited and she was even happier to learn that Mac would be home for three months.

As they arrived at the pub, Linda saw them enter the car park and opened the back door to greet them and wondered why Mac had so much luggage with him.

"Well Mom, the company has given me three months compassionate leave to help you out and so I've brought a lot more of my clothing and possessions back with me."

"Three months?" Linda gasped. "Why do you need three months?"

Both Linda and Mary wondered why three months. Was there anything sinister in the company's motives they both thought, while at the same time they were both happy that they would have the companionship of their man for such a long period.

After more conversation over a pot of tea, Mary told them that she had to leave as she had a music lesson to supervise at a school in Sherborne.

"I'll call you later, after you have had time to shake off your jet-lag," she said and blew them both a kiss as she left by the back door.

Now that they were alone, Linda could not contain the bad news any longer and showed Mac the letter from the brewery.

"I knew it!" Mac explained angrily. "I suspected it from the very day that the surveyor came and said he was doing some sort of conformity survey. Then there was that rat of a man who came to Dad's funeral. He was more interested in the building and its potential, than he was of any grief that you and I were suffering."

Linda quivered with worry as she had not seen Mac so angry ever before.

"What are we going to do Mac?" she asked, half hoping that he had some sort of immediate fix. "Do nothing Mom, for now."

After Mac had taken his luggage to his room and freshened up, he returned to the sitting-room where Linda was fidgeting with the note that Hank had given to her.

"Mac, sit down, for I have some other news for you, that hopefully you will be pleased to receive."

Mac looked at her in anticipation and wondered what the good news may be, for he certainly needed some good news after reading the devastating letter from the brewery.

"Mac, I told you that your true father was an American GI and that you chose not to want to know his name, well I have now had some facts that contribute to the truth about him."

Remembering how he felt about the American guy who he thought ran off and left his mother pregnant, Mac was not really interested to listen to anymore about him. However, out of politeness to his mother, he asked her to go on and tell him her news.

Linda told him that she had had a further visit from Hank and together they had confirmed that they had known each other back in 1944 and that Hank had given her the note that Joe MacKenzie had written. She then handed it to Mac who read it with a somewhat doubtful curiosity.

When he got to the name at the end, his eyes lit up with a new found interest.

"Mom this could be just what I need to establish my birthright in order to claim dual nationality."

Mac then read it again, and seeing how much Joe had cared for his mother at the time, he realised that he had not ditched her, as he had first thought, so he changed his opinion of the person and gradually warmed to him as a war hero.

He suddenly had many questions that he would like to put to Hank and asked his mother, "So where is this Hank now?"

Linda told him that Hank was staying in Yeovil on business, but aimed to revisit her later in the week when time allowed.

With the news that his mother had given him, first bad then good, he was pleased that he had accepted the generous offer of three months off work as he could handle the brewery problem for her and he could not wait to meet Hank.

Time came for Linda to open the pub for the Monday evening, that would see the skittles team and their opponents arrive for a challenge match. Jill arrived on time and between the two of them, they started to produce food that they knew would sell later on.

Dependable Tony arrived and was pleased to see that Mac had returned. The two of them chatted about life in America and Tony was beginning to envy Mac's life there.

As usual, The Major arrived well before the appointed time of the skittles match and ensured that all was in order for the challenge.

Others arrived until the pub was quite full. Tony took orders for eggs and chips for the halftime break and Jill was busy in the kitchen.

After The Major had called his teams to start the match, all became quiet in the bar. Mary then arrived and Mac openly kissed her with delight at being back together.

Linda suggested that the two of them should go to the sitting room, where they could talk privately about anything that they did not want to be broadcast around the village by earwigging customers.

After lots of compliments to each other, Mac decided to tell Mary about the news of his real father and how he was pleased to be able to establish himself as American English, or was it English American, he joked with her.

Mary was concerned about what this would mean to their relationship, as she did not want to lose the love of Mac in his quest for international opportunities.

He recognised the change in Mary and asked what she was worried about. When she told him of her concerns, he replied,

"Mary, this is good news for you also, for when we are married, you will be able to claim American citizenship and work there if needed."

Mary was taken aback by the words, "When we are married" as they had not spoken about that, but at the same time she was delighted to learn that Mac was already thinking in that direction.

With the news about his real father's name being MacKenzie, Mac put two and two together and realised why his mother had always called him Mac. It was a name that he had always been happy with and now he was very proud of it and exceptionally pleased to have been secretly associated with his father for the past twenty-four years.

When Mary left for home, Tony and Jill also left and Linda locked the pub for the night. Mac then told his mother that he now understood why she had always called him Mac.

"Malcolm, there was a time in my past when all I had to cling to was you and my memories of the love that I had for your father. The name Mac was a way that I felt that I was at least in control of something in my life that others did not know about."

Mac was proud to hear of his mother's determination at a time when the whole world would have appeared to be against her.

"Good for you Mom, Mac is what I am and Mac is what I want to be."

As he laid awake in his bed, he recalled to himself, what a varied day he had just witnessed.

Having started out in America; flown to England; learned about the horrible letter from the brewery; found out the name of his father; talked about marriage to Mary; but most of all he had discovered who he really is, Malcolm MacKenzie, half British and half American.

Finally jet-lag took over his body and he drifted off to sleep.

Linda though, could not let her mind settle. She was very pleased that at last she had released the secret that she had held to herself for the past twenty four years and that Mac had accepted everything relating to his father. However, she could not stop thinking about the brewery letter and that she only had three months to decide her future. Then there was the problem of where to live when the time is up. She thought to herself, 'I will be back on my own again.'

40. Hank May Have An Idea

Late afternoon the next day, Hank arrived and Linda was pleased to allow him and Mac to have an open conversation about the time when Hank and Joe were in the army together. Hank then informed him about the money which had been sitting in the two banks for so many years and that, with his help, his mother could rightfully claim as hers.

"Gee Hank that's wonderful news as it will help my mother through a crisis," Mac said with relief.

Hank immediately knew that Mac was referring to the time ahead when his mother had to vacate the pub, but did not betray Linda's confidence in allowing Mac to know that he had already been made aware of the brewery letter.

However, when Linda came back to join them, she immediately told Mac that she had already told Hank about her plight in having to leave the Dog & Whistle and now all three were able to talk openly about the Brewery company's intention of selling the pub and the cottage next door.

Hank listened to Linda and Mac contemplating their future and could hear that Linda was so very disheartened to have to leave her home and the business which she so enjoyed. He asked a few questions about the business and what they thought they would miss the most.

Before his mother could answer the question, Mac replied that this had happened just as there was about to be a good upturn in trade, following some of the American business methods that he had introduced prior to Bob's death.

"Yes, Bob and I were so very keen to take on what Mac was teaching us and we could both see the immediate rewards that customers were also liking," Linda announced.

Hank nodded in agreement and asked them what they thought would really make the business progress profitably, to which Mac told him that the building and its surrounds lend itself to being developed into a good restaurant with accommodation rooms above.

"You mean a good old roadhouse, like we have back in the States."

"You've got it Hank," Mac replied.

He went on to tell Hank that if the doorway into the cottage next-door could be reopened, it would add so much more to the facilities.

"If only the brewery had the same foresight as Mac, then we wouldn't be in this situation," Linda added.

Having listened to their points of view, Hank then asked. "So where are the customers going to come from to provide this extra trade?"

Mac was clear on that score, as he believed that with his mother's culinary reputation and proper promotion, people would come from miles around, particularly during the summer months and other evenings at weekends during the closed season.

"Then, as we are in the centre of a well known tourist area, it would not take long to tap into the lucrative tourist trade, with its demand for overnight accommodation."

Hank was impressed with Mac's enthusiasm and drive and could see that he had been well trained in the hospitality business.

All went quiet for a few minutes with the three deep in thought.

The silence was broken by Linda. "Well that all costs money and the brewery has told us that it isn't going to happen."

Hank kept his silence on the matter, but inwardly began to see an opportunity emerging, as he thought that Ivan may well be interested in such a deal.

While flying over from America last week, Ivan had told Hank that he would soon be having several of his staff needing to stay in the area whilst they were getting his UK business up and running. He also said that he thought that there would be a constant demand for good class local accommodation for his prospective business clients.

Hank knew that Ivan was a person to seize on any good business opportunity and that he was not against taking a risk if it helped him in other ways. Ivan also had the money, so could he be interested?

All three could hear a noise in the kitchen and Linda realised that Jill had arrived, indicating that it was time to start preparations for the evening.

Hank excused himself as he had arranged dinner with Ivan later on, but as Linda showed him to the back door, he put his arm around her shoulder and said, "Linda don't let it worry you, something will turn up." Linda, with a smile, squeezed his hand and said, "I wish that I had your confidence - Junior Burnett!"

With it being a nice sunny summer evening and with the tables outside being an attraction, it did not take long for a few people to drop in for a glass - or two. Places at the outside tables were soon occupied and with Linda taking food out to them, Jill was pleased to see that her idea was paying rewards.

Mac noticed that most people were placing orders for cider and he put it down to the fact that cider was more refreshing in warm weather. Requests for beer seemed to be restricted to a few old faithfuls who had been swigging the same drink since 'Pontius was a Pilot', as the saying goes.

If only the brewery were to come out and check what customers require, instead of just relying on repeat orders for the same old stuff that they have been supplying for years, they would have a better idea of why they had declining sales, Mac mumbled to himself.

As Linda came from behind the bar to collect some empty glasses, into the pub walked farmer Jim and his wife Betty.

"Hello landlord," he said, looking directly at Linda and unable to break himself of a lifetime habit.

"I hear that your'm son is doing all right we my brother's daughter." He crudely referred to the loving relationship that Mary was enjoying with Mac. "So when's theck wedding gunner be?"

Linda smiled without comment, for right behind him stood Mary who had entered without him noticing.

"Hello, Uncle Jim," Mary said while tapping him on the shoulder.

41.   Hank Acquaints Ivan

Over dinner and after they had completed their conversation about matters concerning the engineering business, Hank loosely informed Ivan about the plight of his friends at the Dog & Whistle pub in Thimble Hardy.

Ivan was full of sympathy over the death of Bob and even more astounded to hear of the dreadful way that the brewery had taken in wanting to eject Linda from her home and business.

"What did you say this place is called Hank?" Ivan curiously asked.

"Dog & Whistle at Thimble Hardy."

Ivan laughed spontaneously and tried to repeat what Hank had said.

"Dog & Thimble at Whistle Hardy, gee that's quaint, I'd like to see it sometime."

Hank thought that Ivan may have risen to the occasion and dropped in the idea that as the pub and adjoining cottage would soon be up for sale, there could be the chance of a business venture which may interest him.

"Well you never know Hank, as I told you coming over, my staff will need accommodation and also my clients will in the longer term. Can you set up a visit?"

Hank was delighted that the germ of an idea that he had was beginning to interest his valuable client.

"OK, but I suggest that we try and make it when the pub is closed for the afternoon break, as there will not be any customers around."

"Fine, as soon as you like, we'll make some time," Ivan said.

So next morning, Hank spoke to Mac and told him that his very important client would like to take a look inside a quaint old English pub before returning to the US on Friday.

Mac understood Hank's business ethics in keeping his client happy with any request put upon him and saw it as a returned favour for what Hank had done for his mother and himself and readily agreed.

So, soon after closing for the morning session on Thursday, Hank brought Ivan to the Dog & Whistle and introduced him to Linda and her half American/half English son Mac.

Linda soon offered what many British housewives do in all situations with strangers, "Would you like a cup of tea Mr Framburg - and you Hank?" she enquired politely.

Ivan willingly accepted the offer and noticed the beauty in Linda's face, which immediately gave him a liking to her. He was also impressed with the suave personality of Mac and told them both that Hank had told him of their sad plight.

Linda was quite unwilling to discuss her personal situation with a complete stranger, but Mac had an inkling of what Hank and Ivan might be thinking.

So when they had finished their tea, Mac offered to show Ivan around the pub and explained some of the workings behind the bar. He also showed him the skittle alley and the impression on the wall where there once was a door leading into another part of the pub that had since been turned into a separate dwelling.

"So what about the outside?" Ivan asked.

Mac took him down into the cellar to see how the barrels are stored and then out through a small door and up some steps to the large car park and rear gardens of the two adjoining properties.

"Gee Mac this is some property," Ivan exclaimed with surprise.

Mac told him that his parents had not been able to exploit the potential of the place because of the negative attitude of the brewery. He also said that he had begun to help them improve things when the sudden death of his father, and now that the brewery want to get rid of the place, meant that his mother could not continue with it.

Ivan took a walk around the car park and suggested to Mac that if the huge pile of debris was removed, several Motel type dwellings could be erected to make the place more attractive to potential customers. Mac agreed, as he had been thinking on the same lines and he also showed Ivan the huge back garden of the adjoining cottage.

When they returned through the back door of the pub, Ivan asked about the cottage next door.

"So who lives in this cottage now?" He asked.

When Mac told him that it was empty, he immediately enquired about the size of the place.

Linda told him that there is a very large lounge on the ground floor, that used to be another bar room before the two places had been segregated. She went on to tell him that there was also a separate dining room and a fitted kitchen adjacent to it.

"And what about upstairs?" Ivan asked.

"Oh, there are three quite large double bedrooms, but my previous neighbour Sarah had only used one since her husband died."

Ivan now had the picture, but being the businessman that he was, he chose to play his cards close to his chest by generally showing no further interest. He changed the subject by asking about the name of the village and wondered about how the pub got its enchanting name. He also saw the beauty in Linda's face again, as Hank had done on many occasions before.

As all four walked through to the bar area, Linda cheerily offered Ivan the choice of an alcoholic drink, saying, "You can't leave here without a drink on the house."

"Oh Linda that would be lovely and then I will forever be able to say that I once drank in the Dog & Whistle at Thimble Hardy - that will be a conversational piece at all future social gatherings." He then lingered with a pleasant conversation with Linda.

Hank, who had been quiet throughout the visit, thanked Mac for showing Ivan around and the two of them eyed each other up with a wry smile that indicated that they both thought that this meeting may produce some 'good pickings' later.

When time came to go, Ivan shook hands with Mac and then held Linda's hand with a lingering soft grasp in a very flirtatious way.

42. Hank Gets a New Assignment

Sitting in the lounge of their hotel with a drink after dinner that evening, Ivan thanked Hank for taking him to the Dog & Whistle and told him how he had enjoyed the visit. He then asked Hank for his opinion of the place.

"Well, quite by accident, I stumbled across it and I have since stayed there overnight a couple of times. It's nothing to write home about, but Linda's cooking is superb and it is what keeps the place going. It seems to me that the brewery have not grasped the potential of the place and have decided to take an easy option."

The word 'Potential' is what Ivan seized on.

"So you think that there is potential there - in what way?" Ivan asked.

Hank propounded the theory that Mac had put to him earlier in the week, about opening up the doorway into cottage and making the whole place bigger, with a proper restaurant and more accommodation for travellers.

Ivan smiled and declared, "You know Hank, that's exactly what I was thinking - and then there's that huge wasted space at the back of the pub that is just waiting to be developed for a separate accommodation block."

Hank nodded with the same recognition and added that there was also the nice back yard of the cottage, that is also ripe for expansion.

"You know buddy, I think that we could be onto something here that would fit nicely into my future plans," Ivan offered to Hank.

He went on to ask how they would explain that they knew about the impending sale of the pub and how could they start to register an interest without the brewery taking advantage of their early enquiry.

"Well, if you want to employ my services for that purpose, I would soon find a way - that's my expertise," Hank replied.

"OK Hank, you've got an assignment," Ivan said, offering his hand out in a Gentleman's Agreement. "Let's take it to the first stage."

Early next morning and before they left for the airport Hank, who knew the name of the brewery, phoned them to register an interest.

He was put through to several departments and eventually to the Property Director, who asked him how he had become aware that his company were considering selling the Dog a & Whistle.

Hank politely told him, that like any good journalist, he would not disclose his lead to anyone, but if he was serious about selling the pub then he had better take his interest as genuine, adding that it would need to also include the adjoining cottage.

With that, the Director showed interest in Hank's question and asked him for more details about himself and when he heard that Hank was operating on behalf of a major US business developer, the Director became extremely interested and gave Hank his name as Brian Drake.

Having exchanged their contact details, Hank informed Brian that as he was leaving for New York later that morning, they would need to curtail the conversation.

Brian told him that he would need to raise the matter at the next board meeting and promised to let Hank know more details within a few days.

"I would need to know by Wednesday next week!" Hank said with the firmness of a man who was not used to accepting people dragging their heels.

"OK Mr Burnett, I will write to you in due course," came the reply.

"Nope - I need a phone call by Wednesday," Hank insisted.

Brian Drake could feel that here was a person not to be messed with and gave him his promise to do what Hank had requested.

With that, Hank had to rush in order to drive Ivan and himself to the airport in time to catch the late morning flight to New York.

On the way, he told Ivan of what he had already done to start the ball rolling on the prospective roadhouse project. Ivan was delighted, as the idea of owning an English pub had rather excited him, he told Hank.

Sitting together on the plane back to the US, Ivan told Hank that he believed Linda was a central player in any future development of the pub and if the deal progressed as he wanted it to, then somehow Linda should be tied into the deal.

"I'd like to make sure that she had a cut in the rewards according to how successful it became."

"You would need to put her on some sort of profit sharing scheme in order to achieve that," Hank remarked.

"No, I'd like to see her as a shareholder, but I'm not a believer in just dealing out those positions without that person committing financially. That way, they have something to lose if all goes wrong," Ivan added as a head with experience.

Hank, thinking of the cash that Joe MacKenzie had left for Linda, asked him what financial level would he expect that person to contribute.

"Oh, in the case of a manager like Linda, probably only around £10,000, enough to ensure that she kept her eye on the ball and she had something to lose if she didn't."

Hank quietly thought to himself, that no doubt with the help of Mac adding something to his mother's inheritance from Joe, she could easily meet Ivan's demand financially. The question would be, what if Linda didn't agree to tying herself to such an arrangement.

On the other hand, it could be just what she wanted to ensure her future and for the time being he acted positively to Ivan's idea.

Ivan then turned his thinking back to the acquisition process of the deal and spoke quite firmly about a few points that he wanted Hank to concentrate on.

"Don't under any circumstances let them talk you into paying anything for the 'Goodwill' of their business. It can be seen that there ain't any Goodwill. The only Goodwill is that I could possibly be prepared to take a lame-duck off their hands."

Hank smiled at that remark, when after all they were both thinking that here was a good investment.

When they arrived back in America, Ivan took off to his home and family in Boston, while Hank went to his office in New York to update his number two and his secretary that the file on the Sherborne engineering company could now be closed and his company charges presented to Ivan's financial department.

He then informed them of the new assignment that Ivan had given him and like others before, they wondered if their boss was serious when he gave them the names, Dog & Whistle at Thimble Hardy.

"Sure, I kid you not," Hank smiled back at them. "It's a whole different ballgame from anything that we have done before - we are going to buy an English country pub for Mr Framburg."

After their few moments of fun, both updated Hank with what had happened on other projects that they were handling and he welcomed the news that two other assignments had been successfully concluded while he had be away in England. Hank was exceptionally happy to hear that and thought that life was wonderful right now.

Meanwhile, back at the pub, Linda remarked to Mac that she thought Ivan was a thorough gentleman and hoped that he would come again whenever he visited England.

Mac thought that he was a wily character, but a very smooth business operator who would no doubt always get what he wanted out of life because of his wealth. He also thought that Hank may well be thinking more about his mother's business, now that Ivan had seen the potential of the pub. So, the sum of it all was that the two of them could well be capable of providing help of some kind.

The mood of the evening was suddenly changed when a couple came into the bar who Linda did not know. After purchasing a drink for his wife and himself, he asked Linda if Jill was available, then before she could enquire who they were, a voice from the kitchen suddenly called out above all the other noise - Mum - Dad.

Jill was so pleased to see that her parents had arrived from Templecombe and that she could now introduce them to Linda and Mac. She also introduced her parents to Tony's mother and father who were sitting at a table in the pub that evening.

43.   What Next For The Pub

Throughout the weekend, Mac continued to enjoy his close relationship with Mary and he was beginning to act as though he was married to her. Apart from his mother's requests, he did not do anything without first talking to Mary and making sure that she had no objection. Mary loved that, as there was nothing more that she wanted than to be totally connected with her 'Half and Half British American' boyfriend.

Jill was also delighted by the fact that Tony was showing a more tender feeling towards her and now that her parents had met his, she firmly believed that he would be hers one day.

On Monday when trade was quiet, Linda leaned on the bar tapping on an empty glass, as she had done thousands of times before, very happy to know that both relationships were blossoming. However, overshadowing her delight was the fearful thought that one day ahead, unbeknown to her customers, the pub would be closed and sold off, probably to some property developer. Just what the village did not want.

As the day went on, customers came and went without any idea of what may lay ahead and of the anguish that Linda was going through while keeping the knowledge to herself and Mac.

Then on Wednesday, as Hank had requested, Brian Drake phoned him with the good news that his fellow directors had given him permission to open a discussion with him about his client's interest in the Dog & Whistle public house in Dorset.

Secretly, Hank was delighted, but in his usual way wanted the opposition to make the first move.

"Fine Brian, you don't mind me calling you Brian?   I'm Hank by the way."

Brian did not object and Hank thought that the first objective had been achieved and so he asked Brian to kick off so that he could get a feeling of his thoughts on the matter. He could hear that Brian was a bit uncomfortable with that request and listened for his next move.

"Well Hank, although we don't see the pub fitting in with our future business plans, it is never-the-less a very worthwhile piece of real estate and sits on our books as a valuable asset."

Hank had heard it all before and countered with the comment that his information was that the place was run-down and situated in a 'Customer Blind-hole'.

Inwardly, Brian thought the same, but according to the brief that he had from his board of directors, it was his job to to offload the place at the best possible price and with the minimum of fuss.

He hesitated at hearing Hank's remark and said, "So we have different views on the place and we need to find a middle point."

Hank replied, "There's only one middle point - the price, let's see where we are on price and by the way, it is to include the cottage and yard next door."

Again Brian hesitated for a while and then said, "Why don't you make me a bid?"

Experience told Hank not to fall for that one and he reminded Brian that he was the one doing the selling, so he needed to put a tag on it to get the ball rolling.

"Well, with goodwill …."

Remembering what Ivan had told him, Hank stopped Brian right there by saying, "Brian there is no goodwill, my client is an engineer, not a darn publican."

That surprised Brian as he had naturally thought that Hank's customer would want to carry on with the business as it was.

"OK, so that means that the premises would be developed for other reasons, making it even more valuable," Brian struck back at Hank.

Again Hank countered with a statement.

"I am not privileged to know what my client wants it for, so let's just stick to the freehold price of the two buildings and their surroundings as they stand today," Hank stated firmly.

Brian heard what Hank was saying and thought that there was no point of dressing things up any more and so he gave him a figure of £300,000 to get the show on the road.

Hank did not express comment either way and, with that price in mind, he asked Brian if there were any claims on the properties and if there had been any planning applications turned down in the past.

Brian was able to confirm that neither had been made during the time that his company had owned the property, which was more than a hundred years.

That gave Hank enough detail for Ivan to think about and so he told Brian that he would now need to talk to his client and promised to come back to him by Friday.

Both men then thanked each other for their input on the subject and hoped that matters could be concluded to the satisfaction of both sides.

Hank immediately phoned Ivan and gave him Brian's price.

"So what's that in dollars Hank?" Ivan asked, knowing that he would have already worked it out.

"Very roughly, at today's exchange rate, it is $345,000 give or take a few bucks."

Ivan dwelled on that figure for a few seconds and then told Hank that he had already thought that the deal would cost him about $300,000.

"So it looks like we are in the right area, to knock them down a few thousand bucks," Ivan confidently replied.

Hank agreed and as he knew that Ivan was a man never to accept any first offer, he asked Ivan what price he wanted him to go back with.

"Well, I guess that we throw in 300,000 dollars and see where it gets us," Ivan said, knowing that there would be an acceptable agreement somewhere between the two figures.

Ivan then asked Hank if the brewery's price included all the fittings, furniture and existing stocks, to which he replied that those details were still to be talked about. "OK, over to you," Ivan told Hank.

As the days passed, Mac told his mother to carry on with the business as though nothing had happened, that way it would ensure that business did not drop off through customers going elsewhere.

Linda found the outward appearance hard to handle at first, particularly while keeping it from Jill, but with Mac's guidance and while business held up, she put the thoughts of leaving the pub to the back of her mind.

Mary was also a help in maintaining the pretence and gave delightful friendship to many people with her vivacious appearance and encouraging smile.

While Hank was in his office on Friday morning getting ready to call Brian Drake with a prepared statement that included Ivan's offer of 300,000 dollars, he had a further call from Ivan.

"Hank, while you are on this case can you please explore the suggestion of tying Linda into the deal on the terms that we spoke of last week?"

Hank accepted Ivan's request, but pointed out that as it was a very personal subject, it would be better done at a face-to-face meeting with Linda later on.

Although Ivan agreed on that score, he told Hank that the whole deal depended on getting Linda locked in.

"Alright Ivan, if I can get today's discussion with the brewery to a satisfactory level, then I'll get back over to England as soon as other commitments allow and put your proposal to her and to her son."

Ivan was happy with that and again thought how lucky he was to have someone of Hank's ability at his finger tips.

Hank phoned Brian Drake as promised and told him that his client had accepted an outline proposal to make an offer for the two buildings, but the price needed to come down to 300,000 dollars, not pounds.

Brian quickly did a rough conversion and arrived at 300,000 dollars would be around 260,000 English pounds, some 40,000 pounds down on the figure that he had asked for.

Both men knew that there was room for negotiation on their prices and Brian came back saying that if they could split the difference, then there was a good chance of a deal.

Hank was happy with that and was surprised how quickly Brian had come to a sensible acceptance. However, he wanted to hear Brian state the actual figure before giving him his word.

"OK Brian, so what's your actual figure?"

Brian then made it absolutely clear that the price was to be fixed in English pounds and not dollars and said, "Two hundred and eighty thousand ponds sterling!"

Hank knew that Ivan would be delighted to be able to get the two buildings at such a reasonable price and told Brian in a business-like manner that he would accept his price on behalf of his client. Then, thinking about what Ivan had said about Linda's possible involvement, he told Brian that he would be travelling to the UK some time during the following week.

Brian was surprised at that, as he knew that Hank had only just returned from a similar trip. Nevertheless, he welcomed the news and said that he would get the basic paperwork arranged for the signatures of both sides.

When Hank went back to Ivan with the news that he was on the way to buying an English pub for about $325,000, he was pleased and found it quite amusing. "Right Hank, so what's the next move?"

"I'll go over towards the end of next week to settle the preliminaries with the brewery and I'll stay on for the week-end to talk to Linda and Mac about your suggestion."

"That's my boy," Ivan called out, "I look forward to hearing from you on your return." Then he rang off to concentrate on his engineering.

Hank then realised that he suddenly had a lot to do and must make some unexpected travel arrangements. He also thought it would be wise to see if Linda could accommodate him in her guest room, thus making conversation easier with her and Mac.

Arriving in the UK on the following Thursday morning, Hank went straight away to keep a prearranged appointment with the manager of the London bank where Joe's money had been held for 25 years.

When Hank told him the story, the manager was amazed to hear of the reason why the money was deposited in the first place by the US military and even more surprised to learn that Hank had been successful in finding Linda after all these years.

He told Hank that providing he could produce genuine paperwork to support his Power of Attorney claim, together with a copy of the note that was found on Joe when he died, he saw no reason why the money should not be released to Linda in due course.

The manager went on to say that he would have to write to the US military to ensure that they would not be making any claim on the money and that may cause a delay. He also said that he would liaise with the Swiss bank in order to get that part of the deposit transferred to his bank, prior to a full release.

All that was good news to Hank as he had anticipated the paperwork requirement and had brought copies with him, therefore matters could get started right away.

In checking the documents, the manager informed Hank that there would of course be a charge for his bank's services. Hank had already assumed that, as no business could afford to take on such work without reimbursement of their costs and he had already decided that he would foot that bill through his own company, as a favour to both Joe and Linda.

At the end of the meeting, Hank thanked the manager for his helpful assistance and gave him his business card saying, "If I can ever be of use to you in New York, just give me a call - business or pleasure."

With that, the two shook hands and Hank went on his way to an appointment with Ivan's solicitors, to inform them of maybe another transatlantic arrangement for which Ivan would need their services.

David Lincoln was pleased to see Hank again and when he heard the details he wondered what Ivan was up to, in wanting to buy a pub.

Hank replied, that knowing Ivan as he did, the pub would soon be turned into something grand by the time that he had finished with it.

From there, Hank went to an hotel in London that his secretary had booked for him and he was able to call Linda and confirm that he wished to stay at the Dog & Whistle for the next two nights.

Linda was so surprised to learn that Hank was back in the UK so soon after leaving the previous week, but readily agreed to take him in as it would add a few more welcome pounds to her takings.

Next morning Hank drove to the London office of the brewery and duly met up with Brian Drake, who welcomed him with the same reception that he gave to all his VIP visitors - a glass of the company's best ale.

They then moved to the boardroom, where the brewery Managing Director, Sir Hugh Bright was waiting to meet Hank and to find out more about why his client was eager to purchase a run-down pub, as some people were calling it.

In his usual businesslike manner, Hank was polite and helpful, but gave no indication of Ivan's reasons on the proposed deal.

Sir Hugh told Hank that he was familiar with the pub and that it was a very valuable piece of property in a nice area.

Hank, countered with the knowledge of a card player holding all the aces and informed Sir Hugh that he had stayed at the pub several times in the past and was familiar with the poor state of the building and that he could see that trade was not what it probably had been in the past.

That remark hurt Sir Hugh and he wondered how a foreign visitor could equal the knowledge that he had of something within his own business.

Then, also because he could see that Hank was not forthcoming on other matters, he excused himself and left the rest of the meeting for Brian to handle, saying sarcastically, "Good Luck, Mr Burnett, I hope your client will be happy with the purchase."

Brian Drake was much more cooperative with Hank and talked about the fixings and fittings, stock-in-trade, and a possible completion date, as he was keen to get the sale moving without more fuss.

Then apart from a few financial adjustments with fringe items, they both signed a letter of intent which Brian had prepared beforehand.

Hank wondered why Sir Hugh had intervened as he had tried to do and Brian told him that although a sensible business decision had been made by the brewery's directors, Sir Hugh may be a little sorry to see a good old English pub fall into the hands of an overseas company.

Then, as he had done with the bank manager, Hank gave Brian his business card and said, whenever you come to New York, buddy, give me a call and I'll buy you lunch.

That pleased Brian, who said, "Thanks, I'll take you up on that one day Hank."

Hank then asked if he could make a phone call to his secretary so that she could inform his client that the letter of intent had been signed and that the matter should now be handled by his London solicitor.

Hank's secretary knew the drill and and gave him a couple of other messages that involved other projects that their company were handling in the US.

Brian Drake offered Hank another glass of beer, but he declined, telling him that he had a long drive to do in order to get to another important client in the UK and did not want to be pulled over by the police for drink-driving.

Brian understood and so with a departing handshake, Hank left to make the drive out to the A30 road and on to the quaint Dorset village of Thimble Hardy that he had come to like.

While heading west in his hired car, Hank reminisced on how a chance meeting with Linda, who stood in the doorway of the Dog & Whistle, had led to such unexpected business happenings for him and now he was on the way to give her some news that he hoped would please her and secure her future at the Dog & Whistle.

44.   Linda and Mac Hear The News

When Hank arrived at the Dog & Whistle it was mid-evening on Friday and thinking that he now had a vested interest in the place, he let himself in via the backdoor and went through to the bar. A few people were seated and being served by Jill, who had finished her first attempt at cooking the large version of the pie. Linda and Tony were busy serving the drinks and it was noticeable that Mac was not there.

When Linda saw Hank, she was so pleased to see that he had returned so quickly and ushered him through to her sitting room, where he gave her a hug, followed by his usual remark, "Hello lovely Linda."

She immediately asked him why he had returned so quickly and with a jovial remark he teased her by saying that he had mis-laid his spectacles somewhere and thought that they could be here in the pub. That brought a hint of laughter from Linda, but did not really satisfy her curiosity.

With a more serious explanation, Hank told her that he was on another assignment for Ivan that had happened very quickly and in any case he always enjoyed the chance to have a week-end in Dorset.

He went on to ask where Mac was and Linda told him that he had gone to the cinema with Mary, but he was expected back soon, as Mary was not a 'late-bird'.

Hank was itching to tell Linda the good news, but thought that it should only be given to her in the presence of Mac, who would understand the various implications that come with the disclosure.

Linda told him that his usual room was available and if he could settle himself in, she would rustle up a nice homecoming hot meal for him in the bar when he was ready.

Tony was pleased to hear that Hank was back and asked Linda what sort of car did Hank have this time.

"I don't know, maybe it's a Mercedes, or a Bentley," Linda laughed. To which, he replied, "are you sure it's not a big red Rolls Royce?"

When Linda was closing the pub for the evening, Tony and Jill went off happily holding hands and Mac came in through the backdoor alone and greeted Hank with a, "Nice to see you buddy."

When both were settled, it seemed to Hank that it was the right time to let out the news as he could not hold it any longer.

He firstly explained how much Ivan had been surprised to learn of the rotten way that the brewery had given them notice to quit and then reiterated what Mac had said about the potential that the brewery had chosen to ignore. He told them that although his client was a hard-headed businessman, he also had a kindhearted supportive manner when needed and felt that he wanted to do something to help Linda out of her unfortunate predicament.

Both Linda and Mac looked at each other in absolute amazement and then turned open-eyed towards Hank to listen at what more he had to say on the subject.

Hank told them that Ivan was now well on the way to becoming the owner of the Dog & Whistle and the cottage next door, but as it was early days, they should tell absolutely no one.

"So what does that mean for Mom?" Mac enquired with caution.

"Well it is Ivan's intention that your mother should remain as the proprietor of a revamped 'Free House' and with some early reorganisation, the cottage next door would be brought back as part of the pub very quickly."

Hank went on to explain that the longer-term aim was to seek planning permission to build Motel style apartments in the backyard and that Linda would supervise several full-time employees in the bar, the kitchen and eventually the Motel. In fact she was central to the success of the idea.

While Mac asked Hank a few other questions, Linda turned over the benefits in her mind and then looked for any snags. "So, I would become one of Ivan's employees?" Linda smugly smiled at Hank.

"No, it is Ivan's intention that you would become a joint share-owner with him of the new Thimble Hardy Roadhouse."

Mac was quick to ask the question, "So where's the catch in this and why is your client so keen to drag my mother into such an arrangement?"

Hank again explained that Ivan saw his mother as a central player in his ambitious plan and by investing, she would have security of home and income for years to come.

"Investing - do you mean putting money into his scheme?" Linda asked.

"Yes, but only a token amount to ensure that you felt a belonging to the whole project - Ivan would be the main financier."

Mac immediately asked what amount 'Token' meant and when Hank informed him that Ivan had about £10,000 in mind, Linda gasped and said, "Where am I going to get that sort of money?"

Hank then informed the two of them about his visit to the London bank and gave them an idea of what they could expect from that direction.

"My guess is that you would only need to find about £4,000 to top up what I can get released for you in order to meet Ivan's suggestion."

Mac knew that his mother had received money from an insurance policy after Bob's death and then thought that he could no doubt put some of his own savings in to meet the balance. In fact, the more he thought about it, the more he became excited about something that would provide security for his mother in a job that she so liked doing and she would own about three and a half percent of the business.

When Hank had finished explaining the whole synergy, Mac explained to his mother that he was very taken by the philanthropic approach that Ivan was showing towards her and that it would be a certain way of getting out of the plight that she had been so unexpectedly exposed to.

Hank suggested that they should not jump into anything too quickly and that they ought to sleep on it to ensure that they did not have any reservations. With that, they agreed to talk again in the morning and all three retired to their rooms.

After breakfast next morning, both Linda and Mac were keen to quiz Hank with various questions that they had thought of. The main one being, how certain could they be that Ivan was trustworthy?

Hank informed them that he had dealt with Ivan over a period of twelve years and that he had always found him to be a man of his word. He had a successful engineering company in the US and was now expanding into the factory that he had purchased in Sherborne.

"Like all successful businessmen, Ivan wants his pound of flesh from the business, but is also very quick to ensure that his colleagues also get a fair share of the spoils," Hank explained.

Mac was happy to hear that, as he had been educated with the same ethos while coming through his training in the US.

Linda was still not clear on how she would be paid and also wondered about her living quarters.

Hank pointed out that she would have to take those details up with Ivan direct, as it was not in his brief to handle personal matters.

Mac accepted that explanation and asked when was it likely that they could meet Ivan to settle those matters, as they were clearly important to his mother's future.

Hank told them both that if he could inform Ivan of their general acceptance of the idea and now that he had things moving with the brewery, that Ivan was likely to come over to the UK very soon to take matters forward on both counts.

Linda was very happy to learn of the unexpected offer from Ivan, but wondered what would happen to her money if the project did not succeed, to which Mac replied, "Mom, don't worry, you have nothing to lose as it was not your money in the first place - I will be the one who has something to lose, as my investment is hard earned cash."

With that explanation, Linda felt more assured and told them both that she would be happy to proceed and to help with the development of the Dog & Whistle into a highly regarded roadhouse.

Mac also gave Hank his acceptance and all were willing to advance.

45.   Ivan Moves Quickly

Before Hank departed the next day, he promised to get Ivan to speak to Linda about her personal side of the deal and that she and Mac should draw up a list of questions that they would want answered.

Mac was so happy with what had happened and recognised the wonderful way that Hank had sought out his mother and looked after her interests, after all the years that had passed.

He was also so pleased that Hank had played such a big part in identifying him as the child of his wartime buddy Joe MacKenzie and how it had enabled him to learn the truth about his real father.

"Hank, it seems that 'Thank You' is not enough to say to you for all the help that you have given us, but there is no other way," Mac told him, while warmly shaking his hand.

Linda also knew no other way than to hug him affectionately and to give him the kiss that he had waited so long for. That made Hank tremble with delight.

When he reported to Ivan that the brewery had played ball and were happy to proceed quickly with the sale of the Dog & Whistle and also that Linda had accepted his generous offer to take her in as a shareholder, he was delighted.

Ivan told Hank that it was his intention to return to the Sherborne factory with his Engineering and Personnel Directors before the end of the month, in order to employ some local staff. Also he needed to get things moving so that he could fulfil an order for the Westland Aircraft Company.

On hearing that, Hank suggested that he should take the opportunity to meet again with Linda and so settle her personal details about investing her money in the Roadhouse Project.

"Sure will buddy, that was my intention anyway, as the two businesses are situated in close proximity, it will always make sense to hold such meetings on a single visit," Ivan replied, with an air of excitement. With that, Hank left Ivan's office and returned to New York to concentrate on other assignments.

Not being one to let the grass grow under his feet, Ivan phoned Linda immediately and thanked her for her decision and welcomed her as a fellow shareholder. He also spoke to Mac and allayed any fears that he and his mother had about taking on such a new experience.

When they had finished talking, Linda was so excited that she hugged Mac and at the same time quietly gave thanks to her departed lover - GI Joe MacKenzie.

Two weeks then passed before any further contact between Ivan and Linda, but through the post came a letter from Ivan's London solicitor, David Lincoln. It outlined the fact that his client had made a bid for the pub and that she should be aware that her licence agreement with the brewery was to end. He went on to add that he was aware of the fact that his client, Ivan Framburg, had offered her the opportunity to take out a share in the future of the two buildings and that she should now acquaint him with the name of her own solicitor so that they could work together to achieve a conclusion to the satisfaction of both sides.

Mac was happy that things were moving without delay, as he hoped that all could be finalised before he had to return to America.

The next contact was a phone call from Hank informing them that Ivan and his co-directors would be at the Sherborne factory the following week and that Ivan had informed him that it was his intention to meet up with both of them as soon as possible during that time. He also told Linda that he had heard from the London bank and that they had stated that all was in order for the money to be handed over to her account whenever it was needed.

With the good news, mother and son had difficulty keeping the secret to themselves and both thought that they should tell Mary, Jill and Tony, so that they would understand any peculiar actions going on.

All three were sworn to secrecy and told that as the handover was not yet finally settled, it could scuttle the deal if any information about the future intention of the place got back to the brewery.

Linda assured Jill and Tony that their services were part of the plan and that it may well be the future that they would want together.

When Ivan arrived on the Monday afternoon, he brought his Personnel Director, Samual 'Sandy' Lawton with him and told Linda and Mac that Sandy would handle all matters pertaining to staff and asked them to tell Sandy what they thought the future requirements would be.

All four then put their ideas on the table and a very ambitious, but likeable plan emerged.

Ivan stated that as soon as the deal was completed, Mac's suggestion of rejoining the next door cottage to the pub was to take priority. The living quarters on the ground floor were to be fitted out and redecorated to a good modern standard for Linda to live in, with a small room made available for use as an office.

One of the rooms upstairs in the cottage was to be Linda's bedroom and another for family members, while the third was to remain empty for the time being, but would eventually be made available for VIP guests. The remaining ground floor rooms in the cottage would eventually become an extension to the bar facilities, but that must wait until Linda was settled in with secure accommodation.

The existing sitting room in the pub was to be fitted out as a quality restaurant, as it is close to the kitchen and away from the bar area.

Linda was pleased that she would have new modern living quarters and asked about the rooms on the first floor of the pub.

Ivan then stated that his idea was that all three, would eventually be available for paying guests, but that would be phase two of the plan.

Phase three, would be the development of the carpark area where planning permission would be sought to build six Motel-style apartments.

Mac was delighted to hear all this, as it generally followed what he had proposed to Hank and Ivan earlier. He then suggested to Ivan that the backyard of the cottage could be levelled and made into an outside drinking area for people with children and with dogs, also in any case it would make for a nice place on summer evenings.

Ivan liked that idea and said that it was to be included in phase one.

With the broad outline now acceptable to the four of them, Ivan said that he had to leave in order to get back to the engineering matters in Sherborne, but Sandy would stay on to talk about the details of Linda's personal side of the deal.

During the discussion, Mac said that he thought that although his mother now had the services of Jill in the kitchen, she relied heavily on the part-time help from Tony in the bar, which was a hit-and-miss arrangement that needed to be put on a more formal arrangement.

Sandy wanted to know more about Tony and was surprised to hear that he just popped in whenever he thought he would and did not receive a regular wage from the business.

"So what does this Tony do to earn a living that allows him to pick and chose when he comes to help you?" Sandy enquired.

Between them Linda and Mac described that Tony was a skilled stainless steel welder, who had been made redundant when the Sherborne factory closed and that he now worked freelance for his brother-in-law, from time-to-time.

With that revelation Sandy gasped, "a skilled stainless steel welder!"

Linda confirmed it and Mac nodded in confirmation.

"Jesus, that's just the type of person I am looking for to get our engineering work started, do you think that I could meet him?"

Linda said that Tony would probably be around this evening, but for now she must go and help Jill in the kitchen before opening the pub for the evening session.

Mac thought that Sandy was a valuable person to have on his side for the future and so offered to drive him back to his hotel in Yeovil and said that he could also talk to Tony on Sandy's behalf, if and when he did turn up that evening.

Sandy was pleased to accept Mac's suggestion and gave him his business card, asking if he could somehow get Tony to contact him, if he was interested to talk about a position at Ivan's Sherborne factory.

46.   Does Tony Want The Job?

Before they left the pub, Linda offered Sandy a 'drink on the house'.

"Sandy, you can't leave without having a good old pint of Dog & Whistle best beer, or would you prefer Somerset Scrumpy?"

Sandy laughed at the word 'Scrumpy', but thanked Linda, saying that he would stick to Dog & Whistle beer as it sounded that it was the very heart of the pub.

Mac joined him with a soft drink and while sitting at the table, Jill came into the bar with some hot snacks and offered them to both.

"So you are Jill, who Linda speaks so highly of?" Sandy said to her with a smile, while accepting one of her freshly cooked meat slices.

Jill was a little embarrassed at that statement and while thinking of what to say, she saw Mac wink at her with an expression that invited her to reply positively to Sandy's remark.

"Yes Sir, I'm the only Jill around here and I'm pleased to meet you," she confidently replied, while backing off to return to the kitchen.

"She seems like a nice confident person," Sandy said to Mac.

"Oh, she's great and has been well trained on the hospitality side of the business, and when mother is finished with her, she will also be an excellent cook."

"Good to hear that Mac, we certainly need to hang onto people like that if the new Roadhouse is to succeed." Both finished the hot nibbles that Jill had made and were about to leave when in walked Tony.

Mac explained who he was and Sandy was immediately happy that he could perhaps get the chance to speak to Tony, and maybe offer to meet him on a more formal basis, if he would be interested in the job that Sandy had to offer.

Mac allowed Tony to settle in and then went over to him and explained who the guy sitting at the table was and asked him to come over and meet Sandy.

After introductions, Mac backed off and went over to help his mother, leaving the two of them to talk privately.

Tony was so surprised to learn that Sandy's boss had bought the remnants of the factory where he had worked prior to being made redundant. Equally, Sandy was surprised to hear that Tony had played such a valuable part in the previous business.

When Sandy explained that he was looking for someone with Tony's skills to work in the new business being opened in the factory, Tony at first thought that it was a setup arranged by Linda and Mac to get him back to full-time employment. However, when Sandy explained that the whole idea was his, Tony showed more interest and asked what sort of work would he be needed for.

Sandy told him that it was stainless steel welding to Air Ministry standard and as a lot of the work was classified he could not give more details at this stage.

Tony told him that although he was not certified for Air Ministry work, he did have qualifications that allowed him to work for the Admiralty on seagoing vessels.

"In that case, it seems to me that it would not be too difficult to get you qualified to our requirements," Sandy eagerly informed him.

That interested Tony and when he showed enthusiasm, Sandy suggested that he should meet with Ivan's Engineering Director, Klaus Nielsen, who would be at the Sherborne factory all week.

Tony was happy to do that and together they agreed to meet at the factory the following morning, whereupon Sandy would introduce him to Klaus and he could learn more about the company's product range. With that, Sandy excused himself and accepted Mac's offer of driving him back to his hotel.

On the way, Sandy asked Mac more about Tony as a person and about his personal life. Mac was discreet about such matters, but gave Tony a very good character reference, explaining that he was a person who was always willing to 'think outside the box' and do whatever was thrown at him. In other words, a Team Player!

That was just what Sandy needed to hear and thanked Mac, first for the introduction to Tony, and then for the additional information.

Sandy then asked Mac a little about his own situation, both with the pub and also something about his work in America and suggested that they should meet socially in New York when he returned to his position at the hotel. Mac agreed and they swopped contact details when they arrived at Yeovil.

When Mac got back to the pub, he found Tony in quite an excited mood and his mother was was all-aglow about her side of things, suggesting that he should go to the kitchen where Jill would cook him a nice steak dinner.

Jill could see that Tony was happy about something and wondered if it was anything to do with the conversation that she saw him having with the American man who spoke to her earlier.

Now that he had a special relationship with Jill, he told her that he thought that he was on the way to being offered a job back at his old factory, but with a new employer. Jill was pleased to hear that, as she was not really happy to see him doing part-time work for his sister's husband.

Linda though, was concerned that if Tony settled into a full-time job then he may not always be available to help her in the pub.

While Mac was eating the meal that Jill had prepared for him, Mary arrived from an evening with her friends and was eager to learn from Mac what had happened during Ivan's visit.

Mac brought her up-to-date with the proposed alterations to the pub, if all went through without any problems. Whilst Mary was happy to learn that Linda's future looked safe, she asked where all the money was to come from to finance the project.

Mac explained that Ivan had stated that he, or his company, would provide the cash throughout and that he wanted to get started as soon as possible following the completion of the purchase. Mary then asked the question of who was going to supervise these works, particularly after he, Mac, returned to America.

Mac assumed that Ivan, would employ an Architect, who would then choose the contractor to get on with the job.

When Mary heard the word Architect, she told Mac that one of her friends was married to an Architect and if it helped she could put Mac in touch with him.

Mac, thought that it was early days for that, but that he would pass the details to Ivan, or Sandy when he next spoke to one of them.

Then all aglow with the sight of seeing his lovely Mary again, he changed the subject to something more in keeping with their romance and fixed another date for some horse riding with her.

When Tony met Sandy the next morning as arranged, he was taken to a newly decorated office where he was introduced to Klaus Nielsen, who did not take long to dig into Tony's background and engineering qualifications. He then outlined the type of work that his company provided for the aircraft industry in America and how that was going to expand into the UK and perhaps Europe in due course.

Then as Klaus walked Tony around the new facilities at the factory, they met Ivan who was watching a new crane being installed and when he saw Tony, he remarked, "Gee, ain't you the guy from the Dog & Whistle?"

When Tony confirmed that he often helped Linda in the pub, Ivan remembered that Mac had said how valuable Tony was to his mother's business, thus it made Ivan think that he did not want to attract him away from the pub because of his need there in future. So he just shook Tony's hand and wished him good luck.

At the end of the interview, Klaus was very impressed with Tony and his knowledge of the type of work that was to be undertaken at the new factory. So he offered Tony a job with an exceptional salary, hoping that he would accept and commence work without delay.

Tony though, wondered what his brother-in-law, Georgie would think if he could no longer help him with his various projects. He wanted to be fair with him, as Georgie had given him an income, albeit nothing like what Klaus had just offered him.

Tony explained that to Klaus, who understood his predicament and suggested that he should speak to Georgie as he was not out make an enemy of any local engineering company. Tony agreed and told Klaus that he would give him an answer the next day.

Later in the day, Tony met up with Georgie and the two of them talked openly about the offer that Klaus had made to Tony.

At first, Georgie thought that losing the expert services of his wife's brother would be a problem to him, but then thought that if Tony was to get his feet under the table with the new factory, it could offer some opportunities for his own business, while ensuring that Tony got back to a full-time job - something that he was not able to offer Tony.

So Georgie advised Tony to take the opportunity and pointed out that he needed to look to the future, for one day he would have a family to support.

Tony was thankful for the way that Georgie had taken his news and then felt that he needed to talk it over with Linda, and of corse, with Jill to ensure that there were no hidden hard feelings from either.

When Tony arrived at the pub it was closed for the afternoon break and the two women were resting in the sitting room with a snack.

Both were very happy to hear that Tony had been offered a full-time job at the new business in the factory where he had worked prior to his redundancy. Tony also explained that he thought that it would not prevent him still helping out in the bar on busy occasions, which delighted both of them.

With the encouragement from the two women and also the advice from Georgie, plus the very good salary offered, Tony soon came to the conclusion that he would accept the position and that he would inform Klaus the next day and immediately offer his services.

"That calls for another pot of tea," Linda excitedly proclaimed as she went off to the kitchen. That gave Jill the opportunity to snuggle up to Tony and give him a real good kiss of appreciation.

"Tea up!" Linda's voice called out as she came back into the room.

When Tony went to the factory next morning to tell Klaus of his decision, he was met by an old friend, Gordon Tuck, who had been his previous Works Manager.

"Hello Tony, Klaus has asked me to meet you as he is engaged for a short while."

Tony was baffled, as it was like old times, seeing Gordon again in the factory where they had both worked before it closed.

"Gordon, so what are you doing here?" he enquired with surprise.

"Well, I was contacted by Sandy Lawton as someone had put in a good word for me and then Klaus offered me my old job back as Works Manager in the new business."

Tony was pleased to hear that, as he had worked well with Gordon in the past and it seemed a good way to start off his new career with a person whom he knew and could trust.

They talked about old times and of the various people that they had worked with over the years. Gordon then told Tony that he knew that Klaus had offered him a position, but told him that he should keep his answer to himself until he was able to tell him in the presence of Klaus.

Tony liked that, as it showed that Gordon was still a person to handle matters in an impeccable manner and just as he was about to say more to Gordon, Klaus arrived and beckoned both through to an office that he was using for interviews.

Opening the conversation, Klaus needed confirmation that the two knew each other and that they both understood what their relationship would be if Tony accepted the offer of being Foreman of the welding section.

After both acknowledged the fact, Klaus asked Tony for his answer and when he was told by Tony that he would accept and was able to start immediately, he stood up and gave a 'high-fives' towards both of his new employees. "This calls for a good old English drink," Klaus imparted with joy, as he called to the lady in the canteen to make a large pot of tea.

47.   Mac thinks about returning to Work

With his mother's future hopefully becoming secure and all of the legal matters that were brought about because of Bob's death now cleared, Mac began thinking about getting back to work. His three months companionate leave would soon be up and he should return to his employment in the US.

Whilst he thoroughly enjoyed that work and was very well paid, he would have liked to be able to stay in the UK and contribute to the proposed modification of the pub, which, after all, would be mainly what he had suggested in the first place.

He also dreaded the thought that he would have to leave Mary, a person whom he had met quite by chance and who now featured so much in his life and hopefully for the future.

At times, he thought that as his devotion to his mother and to Mary were the strongest of his convictions he would do the honourable thing and resign from his position and return to the UK permanently.

However, he could not shake off the feeling that through the US company he had achieved the success that he now enjoyed in life and he certainly did not want to give up the superb lifestyle that he had come to accept in America.

Throughout the day, he contemplated one and then the other, but never came to a definite decision. Then all of a sudden he thought the best place to make up his mind would be to get out of Thimble Hardy for a while and to evaluate matters on neutral ground, so to speak. So, on the pretext that he needed to do some research on an hotel in Weymouth for his boss, he told his mother and Mary that he would have to stay away overnight, which they both readily accepted.

After arriving in Weymouth, Mac checked into an hotel, changed into shorts and casual shirt and went for a walk along the seashore while the tide was out. He kicked several small pebbles and flotsam while he was lost in the peaceful swirl of the receding water, giving himself the chance to think more clearly about his dilemma.

Seeing people happily enjoying themselves on the sands and in the water, a voice within him was saying, "What is going to make you happy in the future?" But it was this very question that he could not answer right now. Then walking along the promenade, he noticed that most of the happy people were generally couples with children, which made him think beyond his present situation and to a time when he may well be one of a couple, but he had yet to get there.

So, after dinner in his hotel, Mac sat in the lounge with a drink and focused on his future, which he decided definitely needed to include the lovely Mary.

Then it hit him, although he needed to get back to the work and lifestyle that he so enjoyed he also needed to make sure that he was able to tie Mary into it. So why not propose to her now and hopefully they would become engaged before his return in a month and maybe she would agree to accompany him for a stay at his hotel and then agree to live with him in New York after they were married.

Although it would appear to be rushing things, at least he could see something that would embrace most of his concerns to his liking and he could not wait to put the idea to Mary.

Having had a very restless night, he arose early and immediately after breakfast returned to the Dog & Whistle, where his mother was surprised to see him back so soon.

"Mac what has gone wrong?" Linda asked with concern.

"Nothing's wrong Mom, I have solved the problem that I went away for in double quick time and I need to move on."

Following the closure of the pub after the morning session when Jill had left for her break, Linda prepared a meal in the kitchen for the two of them, whereupon Mac told his mother of his decision to ask Mary to marry him.

Linda was so surprised to hear his news, and as Mac had already thought, she wondered if it was a bit too soon to take such a major step in life and also enquired as to where he intended to live if she accepted his proposal.

After hearing the rest of his plan, Linda was so excited to think that her son had found a perfect match and so hoped that Mary would accept and that her parents would have no objection.

Linda then suggested to him that if he was absolutely certain, then he should do the proper thing and speak to Mary's parents, but first of all he should sleep on it for another day before jumping the gun.

Mac accepted that and as Mary was not aware of his early return, he spent the rest of the day in his room at the pub without any contact with Mary. It also gave him the chance to contact his boss, Claude Leclerc, who was so pleased to hear from Mac and asked how things were going with his mother and her problems at the pub.

When Mac told him about Ivan's wonderful offer and how it had been brought about by the chance meeting that his mother had with Hank several months back, Claude could not believe it and remarked, "Mac you know, those things only happen in the movies."

Finally they got around to talking about Mac's intended return to work, which delighted both Mac and Claude as it confirmed that he would be welcome back in his rightful place, as Claude put it.

When Mac phoned Mary next day, he told her that he needed to talk to her about a very important matter and that it needed to be somewhere away from the pub, to which Mary readily agreed as she thought that it was something about the dealings at the pub that he did not want his mother to hear.

"OK lover, what about a nice drink on the lawn at my parent's farm late afternoon- say 4.30 ?" Mary eagerly suggested.

That suited Mac, as he needed to get things off his chest and if she agreed, then maybe they could talk to her parents together when they had finished on the farm for the day.

Mary then asked him how he had got on during his business trip to Weymouth and if it was successful.

Mac informed her that he hoped that the information that he had acquired during his stay there would eventually lead to a satisfactory conclusion and that he would tell her more about it in due course.

Mac thought the visit should be semi-formal, so he dressed himself in a smart pair of light coloured slacks with brown suede shoes, together with a freshly ironed white short-sleeved shirt and a yellow cravat around his neck.

When he arrived at the farm he saw Mary looking at him with an element of concern, for she on the other hand was just the opposite, as she was dressed casually in white shorts, red top and was wearing white sandals.

After hugging him with delight for not seeing him over the last couple of days, she stood back and looking at his smart attire said, "Mac are you sure that it is me that you have come to see?"

Although that remark made him even more embarrassed about handling the task that he had come to deliver, he nevertheless proceeded towards a seat on the lawn whilst pleasurably gripping Mary's hand.

Sitting side-by-side, Mac uncomfortably twiddled with his signet ring, while Mary wondered what was troubling her man. She then stroked his forehead while asking him about his concern.

Then without any preamble, he turned to look her straight in the eyes and said, "Mary, I don't know any other way to say this, but will you marry me - soon?"

The question rocked Mary and although she was delighted to hear it, she thought that the word 'soon' suggested some sort of panic and enquired why he had said that.

Relieved with having got the proposal off his chest, Mac was now able to talk coherently again and explained his reasons, adding the attraction of an early visit to the States for her if she agreed.

Mary now understood the reason why he was dressed so elegantly and without hesitation said, "Yes, of course buddy!"

After more hugging and kissing, they both agreed that they should talk to her parents about their decision, particularly as it would eventually lead to them losing their only daughter who managed the accounts of their business so professionally.

When Mary saw that her father had finished for the day and had gone into the house, she told Mac that now was the time to go in and speak to her parents.

Both welcomed Mac, and Stan pulled his leg about him looking so smart, "I can see that you b'ant no farmer my lad," to which Mac laughed and replied, "No, I can't afford to buy a tractor."

Mary then told her father that together, she and Mac had some good news to tell him. "So what's that, 'ave ee decided you'm gone'r get married?"

Hearing the friendly way that Stan had made that remark helped Mac to steady his nerves and Mary helped further by saying, "Dad how did you know - you must be psychic."

Mary's mother had also guessed that something of that nature was in the air, as she had watched them enjoying such happy times together.

"Well my dear, your mother and I have talked about it several times and we have had a plan in place for when that day would come."

By now, Rita was holding back tears of joy and before Mac could say anything, she went across and gave him a big hug, that filled him with confidence for what he was about to say and hoped that it would be accepted by both of Mary's parents.

"Stan, er Mr Pearson, may I have your daughter's hand in marriage?"

Before replying to the question, Stan looked at Rita and then they both answered with a resounding 'Yes!"

This led to Mac and Mary explaining that they, of course, would have to live in America, but that would not be until they married.

With the happy four all congratulating each other, Mary asked her father what the plan was that he seemed to convey would soon come into being.

"Well, my dear, for some time now, we've had a very good offer from the managers of the Billington estate, who want to buy this farm and to integrate it into that of the Big House. I've told em that not until my daughter gets set up in marriage wee a bloke that we like."

That surprised Mary, as she did not know of the offer and so she asked her father what they intended to do, if they sold the farm.

"Nothin!" Stan answered.

"We'll buy a cottage somewhere around yer where I can potter about in a workshop, while your mother makes jam and chutney wee the fruit from the garden. Then we'll 'ave plenty left over to come and see you two for an 'oliday in New York."

Rita then told them that they had drawn up this plan for their retirement several years back and now that Stan had passed 55, it was a very convenient time for Mary to be leaving home.

Mac could not believe how easy this whole conversation had gone and how much he enjoyed the company of Mary's parents, so he shook her father's hand warmly and hugged her mother again, then without any embarrassment he gave Mary a whacking big kiss. Rita suggested that they should now get off to tell the news to Mac's mother and so they drove to the pub in a very happy mood.

Linda was naturally very pleased to hear the news and hugged Mary to show her so. She then turned to Mac and asked him if he had bought Mary an engagement ring.

Mac had not given that a thought, but realising his blunder he suddenly tried to wriggle out of it by saying, "Mother, how could I when the shops are now closed for the day."

Then turning to Mary, he told her that he would take her to a jewellers in Yeovil as soon as she could find some free time.

Mary could not wait to be able to show off her fiancé's ring to her friends and said, "OK darling, what about first thing tomorrow morning?"

Mac rocked back with surprise at Mary's eagerness, but without hesitation happily agreed to her timing.

With both being so happy with the fact that they were now engaged, Mac asked his mother if he could purchase a bottle of fine champagne.

48.   News Travels Fast

Soon after Mac had left to meet Mary next morning, Connie came with the post. It contained a copy of a letter that Ivan's UK solicitor, David Lincoln, had written to Ivan saying that the paperwork was ready for him and Linda to sign in preparation for the exchange of contracts for the sale of the Dog & Whistle pub, together with the adjoining cottage. Linda was overjoyed to learn that things were moving so quickly, but wondered what she needed to do next as the legal matters were very much above her head. However, the problem was soon out of her thoughts when a few customers started to arrive in the pub and conversations on other subjects occupied her mind.

Terry Smith, The Major, came with a new skittles fixture list that he had received for the next winter session, the dates of which he wanted to discuss with Linda. Len Scott from the paper shop popped in to tell her that he had now taken delivery of another glass cabinet and how pleased he was that the salesman was originally referred to him by Bob. Then PC Willis came in and told her that the police file on Bob's accident had now been closed and that there would be no further police interest in the case. That was quite a surprise, as Linda was not aware that there was such a police file.

Soon one of the jukeboxes came into action when a lad from the quarry, who was off work with a broken arm, put in some coins to set off some swing tunes.

All-in-all, it was a very varied morning that Linda handled completely by herself and she realised that this is what life would be like when Mac finally retuned to America and she would be left in complete control to handle everything that cropped up in the business.

Winnie and Madge had sat quietly throughout the morning as there did not seem anything worthwhile to gossip about, and Billy and George were happily playing their usual game of crib. Then suddenly the peace was shattered when a tractor pulled up outside the door.

Out jumped farmer Jim who blurted out to Linda how pleased he was to hear that her American son had got engaged to his niece.

Winnie was the first to react. "Engaged! No-one told me that they were going to get engaged," she said, as though all future activities in the village should be channeled through her. Madge added, "Does that mean that they'm gonna get married?"

Linda was also surprised that Jim should know of the engagement so soon, but he explained that Mary's mother was so excited that she had phoned his wife earlier in the day to give her the happy news.

When Jim ordered his usual pint of cider, he asked where the happy couple were now and Linda told him that they were away in Yeovil to buy the engagement ring.

"So that means that we'm gonna 'ave a bit of ding-dong in the pub tonight to celebrate, do it Linda?"

Linda told him that it was too soon to be thinking about that, but no doubt Mac and Mary would organise something for the family and friends in due course.

"Family and friends?" Jim questioned. Then artfully added, "That means that I and Betty would get two invitations each as we'm both family and friend."

Linda laughed at his cunning joke and told him that after the marriage she and he would become some sort of distant relatives.

Jim continued with the banter by adding, "That could mean that I could 'ave some sort of share in the pub." Linda closed the fun by saying that if that happened she would claim her share of his farm.

Whilst Winnie kept up with the conversation and was pleased to have gleaned some information to pass on, Madge was totally confused and thought that there was going to be a ding-dong in the pub because Linda owned a farm.

The two card players had listened to the silly talk and sniggered to each other. Then Billy said to George, "We must watch out for this ding-dong and make sure that we arrive early to get a good seat in the front row." With that, Winnie and Madge got up and left the pub, hoping that they would find Connie to tell her something that she didn't know.

With it being Jill's day off, Linda closed the pub and relaxed alone in the sitting room to reflect yet again on what had happened to her in such a short period of time. She had tears of sorrow for the loss of her wonderful husband and companion Bob. Then there were joyful tears as she thought about how Hank had arrived and started a chain of events which now safeguarded her future.

Before long, her peace was broken when Mac and Mary excitingly burst through the back door full of the joys of spring and ready to show the engagement ring that Mac had bought for his future bride.

Linda was so pleased to see how happy they were together and also to realise that her son was now on the way to marriage with a person who she so admired, that she opened a bottle of wine to celebrate.

After the excitement calmed down, Linda told them both about the letter that she had received from Ivan's solicitor and gave it to Mac to read.

"Mom this is such good news for you," he happily told her, then added, "this looks like 'one in the eye' for the brewery, but still keep it under your hat until completion."

With Mac's blessing on the subject, Linda then felt confident about the whole affair and hoped that Ivan would soon come to discuss matters with her, before Mac departed back to work.

Mary was also happy for Linda and offered her help with the accounting, if she ever needed it in the future, a matter that pleased her future mother-in-law.

The whole meeting ended with a laugh, when Linda told them what Jim had said about being entitled to a share in the pub when the two of them are married and he becomes a relative.

Mary, commented that it was just what she expected to come from her uncle, who had played jokes for as long as she could remember. She then added, "But Linda, you would not want a share in his pig farm, it's a smelly old place."

Linda shuddered at the thought of having to work among pigs and swiftly got on with opening the pub for the evening session.

Next day, Linda did not have to wait long before Ivan phoned to enquire if she had received the letter from his solicitor and to confirm that David Lincoln would also act on her behalf, thus avoiding her having to entail any legal costs. That was welcome news to her and she thanked Ivan for his consideration.

Ivan then went on to tell her that his men had now got the Sherborne factory working well and that he would be coming back to England for negotiations on a new engineering contract and it would be a good time to tie up the signing of the pub documents whilst he would be here.

"So Linda, we should meet in London to sign together, so what about meeting me in three days time at the offices of Lincoln, Jones & Lewis in Brook Street, West One, after which we can have a nice lunch together to celebrate?" Linda was startled by such a request, but knew that something like this would need to be done in order to keep matters moving, so without any hesitation she agreed and asked what time she should be there. To which, Ivan stated that his secretary would make all the arrangements and that she would contact her very soon and so, with that agreed, Ivan rang off.

With the excitement of the news, Linda ran upstairs to tell Mac, who was busying himself with other matters. When he had listened to what she had to say, he pulled her leg by saying, "Mom you will need to go out to buy yourself some city-type clothes so that you will look the part, as you can't go to Mayfair in that old apron."

Linda had not given a thought to the dress code. She was more concerned about travelling to the big city alone, for she had only been to London on a few occasions when she was much younger. Then what about the pub, should she close it for the day?

As usual, Mac came back with all the answers. "Mom, Jill and I will look after the pub and I'll get Mary to take you to the train station."

"But what about the other end?" She enquired with trepidation.

"When you get to Waterloo, you take a taxi to 44 Brook Street and walk in with confidence. You then say to the receptionist, I am here with an appointment to meet Mr Lincoln and they will do the rest."

So when she did arrive in London during the latter part of Thursday morning, Linda did exactly what Mac had told her to do and the receptionist put her at ease by welcoming her before taking her to a nice conference room to await the arrival of Ivan. Then another young girl brought her a pot of tea served on a silver tray.

David Lincoln soon arrived and after introducing himself, put her further at ease by asking her a bit about the pub and the village, questions that she could easily answer with confidence. He also explained that when Ivan did arrive the matter would not take long to conclude. Linda found David to be a very charming person, with a manner that portrayed confidence with everything he did and so she was very happy to be looked after by a man with this expertise.

When Ivan arrived, he shook David's hand warmly and turned to Linda with an over-exaggerated smile and clasped her hand with both of his to show how pleased he was that events had now reached this stage.

Around the conference table, Ivan asked a few questions of David to ensure that certain points had been covered in the documents, to which David assured him that they had and that it was a perfectly straightforward contract, which he had handled many times before.

David's secretary then arrived and in her presence, he asked Linda if she had any questions, or concerns, to which she told him that she had not. So with that assurance, Ivan signed and David asked Linda to sign and then added his own signature, followed by that of his secretary as witness to all the signatures.

"Well thank you folks, I will get that to exchange status very quickly and providing that the brewery play ball, matters should reach completion within 14 days," David told them with a firm guess.

Before leaving the room with the paperwork, David's secretary confirmed to her boss that she had booked a table for the three of them across the road at Claridge's Hotel for lunch. She also offered Linda the opportunity to freshen-up in the rest room, a gesture that Linda welcomed, whilst it also gave Ivan the chance to talk to David about a couple of other matters that were unrelated to the Roadhouse.

As they stepped inside the entrance door of Claridge's, Linda was astounded with the grandeur of the place and realised that if it were not for the fact that she had been invited, she would never have dared to set foot inside the place. She also wondered if Mac's hotel in New York was anything like this.

Over lunch David asked what they intended to do with their purchase of the village pub and Ivan informed him of the plans to extend the facility and to build it into an American-style roadhouse, with motel rooms eventually added at the back.

David thought that it was a very ambitious project, but admired Ivan's determination and could see that he needed to get the contract exchanged without delay. He then returned to his office, leaving Ivan and Linda to discuss details of what would happen as soon as the deal was completed.

Ivan told Linda that the first thing to take place would be for the builders to sort out the cottage to her liking, whilst leaving the adjoining doorway still bricked up. Then when the work was completed and she was happy with it, they would open up the doorway so that she could then move into her new dwelling.

Linda asked how long that would take, to which Ivan said he had been told that it should be completed within three months of the work being started. "You see Linda, you now need to start thinking about the move to make sure that you'll be happy with everything, for it will be your home and office for a long time to come."

When they had finished discussing the matter, Ivan told her that he had other business to handle in London, but would be back in Dorset in a couple of days. That left Linda to take a taxi back to Waterloo station, from where she phoned Mac to tell him the time of the train back to Sherborne and to arrange for Mary to collect her.

49. Linda's New Confidence

Sitting in the first class compartment waiting for the train to pull out, Linda again thought how lucky she had become since the arrival of Hank and how she was now a shareholder in a company, albeit with a minor shareholding, that gave her a seat at a board meeting.

She was also thinking about how she had taken lunch at the world famous Claridge's hotel, something she could never have dreamed of before, when a very smartly dressed man entered the compartment and took up a seat diagonally opposite her. He was wearing a smart suit and carried a bowler hat, rolled umbrella, briefcase and a copy of the Evening Standard.

Immediately, Linda thought how suave he looked and thought that if he was not some financial wizard from the City, then he was probably a country landowner who would not look out of place as a judge at a horse show.

He smiled at Linda and she exchanged it with a welcome glance of her own, thinking yet again how suave he looked. He was followed into the compartment by an elderly lady who sat opposite Linda and who immediately struck up a conversation with her. Then, by the time that the train had reached the short distance to Clapham Junction, she had asked Linda how far she was going. When Linda told her Sherbourne, she remarked how lucky she was to be living in the delightful county of Dorset.

Whilst this was going on, Linda noticed that 'Mr Suave' was occasionally peering over the top of his newspaper and showing an interest in the conversation between the two women. His eyes were fixed only on Linda, who was becoming somewhat uncomfortable with the attention.

When the train reached Basingstoke, the friendly lady bade farewell to Linda and left the train, leaving Linda alone with 'Mr Suave'. This gave him the opportunity to start a conversation with Linda himself. He commenced with an apology for overhearing that she was travelling to Sherbourne, where he himself was due to alight and asked if she actually lived there.

Being somewhat guarded, Linda replied with a vague answer indicating that she lived generally in that area and reversed the question to him.

"Well, yes so to speak," came the reply. "You see I actually live in Buckinghamshire, but my occupation gives me a comfortable residence on a large estate south of Sherbourne."

Linda was intrigued to know more about 'Mr Suave' and asked him why the double residence and then wished that she had not done so, as a long semi-boastful explanation poured from his lips.

From the long spiel, Linda learnt that his name was Jeremy Finch, he was 50 years of age, was employed as an Estates Manager for a Lord of the Realm and was frequently asked by the Kennel Club to be a judge of the Gun-dog section at Crufts Annual Dog Show.

Linda thought that that just about summed him up and when he enquired what line of business she was in, she rose herself above his level by saying, "I am a director of a hospitality company and I am returning from a board meeting and luncheon at Claridge's!"

'Mr Suave' was taken aback by that statement as he believed that a women's role was to have her hands in the sink and look after the children.

Linda could see that he was surprised at her remark and pressed him more about his occupation, as she did not want him probing her any more about her whereabouts and status in life.

"Well, I set the policy of how His Lordship's land and animals are to be profitably worked and I engage the staff to enable targets to be achieved," came the reply. "I also handle all negotiations with contractors and settle invoices for payment." He went on about other aspects of his wonderful appointment.

Their conversation was suddenly halted when the train arrived at Salisbury and another man and a young woman entered the compartment. Both smiled at Jeremy and then to Linda and they took their seats facing each other in the centre of the compartment.

It was clear that they were together and started a conversation that now took 'Mr Suave's' attention away from Linda as he listened to their excitable chat about dogs - a subject that he considered himself to be an expert on. So as the train sped through the towns and villages of Wilton, Tisbury, Gillingham and Templecombe, Linda aimlessly looked out of the window and allowed her mind to focus on what Jeremy Finch had said to her.

She thought that if he was being truthful and not just saying these things to impress her, then he may well be a useful contact for her future business activities when Mac had returned to America, for no doubt he would know some people in the right places.

When the train slowly pulled into Sherbourne station, both Linda and Jeremy collected their belongings and walked out into the corridor with 'Mr Suave' showing his manners by allowing Linda to make her way to the entrance first.

Just as the porter opened the train door to allow them to alight, Jeremy gave Linda his business card, adding, "Thanks for your company, maybe we could meet again?"

Linda had already seen Mary waiting for her and to avoid passing any of her details over to him, she took the card, politely thanked him and said, "Sorry, I must rush as one of my staff is waiting to collect me and time is money as you may well know."

Jeremy was left completely bewildered at her sudden departure as he had hoped to develop the conversation into something more meaningful and now had no idea how to contact her again.

As she sat alongside Mary in the car, Linda chuckled to herself thinking that she had acted well and truly in the manner of a Manager - Director - Shareholder, where she held her cards to her chest, as Mac had taught her.

When they arrived back at the pub, Mac was delighted to hear that all went well with the signing of the paperwork in London and that Ivan would be back to meet with them again in a few days time to talk about the next action needed to convert the old Dog & Whistle pub into a trendy Roadhouse in Thimble Hardy.

50.   Completion

It was three days after the two weeks predicted by David Lincoln, that completion of the sale actually occurred and the Estate Agent acting on behalf of the brewery erected a SOLD notice on the outside of the building.

Ivan had phoned Linda with the good news and told her to close the pub for three weeks so that the brewery could take an inventory of their belongings and that she could make a complete record of her stock. He also said that during that time his Works Manager would organise some changes to the bar and give it a good lick of paint to get rid of the many years worth of cigarette stains on the interior walls. He suggested to Linda that she and her staff may like to take a few days off to relax, as he forecasted a busy time ahead for them all.

Most of all, Ivan told Linda to refrain from telling anyone beyond the chosen few of her involvement in the sale. He thought that the silence would create much intrigue and excitement for when they did reopen. "If anyone asks, just say that an American company had purchased it."

When Mac heard of Ivan's plan, he too agreed that the course of action was a good one and told his mother to rigidly stick to Ivan's instructions.

It was not long before customers, having seen the SOLD notice, started to ask questions, but Linda stuck to her guns by saying that after the end of this week, the pub would close. This information soon wizzed around the village and a lot more people came to try and find out what was going on. This was good for trade and takings went through the roof for the remaining few days trading.

Even the evil Tommy Chant came in to goad Linda about being evicted from her house by some Yanks, as he put it. "I told you at the time, all those years ago, that going off with Yanks would do you no good; you should have stuck with me Linda," he retorted. That made Linda chuckle to herself for little did he know that 'Those Yanks', together with her half American son, had in fact come to her rescue in a time of need.

During the next week and with the pub closed, Mac informed his mother that he had arranged to get back to work in America and that Mary had agreed to accompany him.

Linda and both of Mary's parents, were delighted with the news and Stan, Mary's father, agreed to give the happy couple a farewell dinner at an hotel in Yeovil prior to them leaving. He also arranged that the five of them would stay overnight at the hotel so that they would not be restricted from having alcohol during the evening.

So, two days before Mac and Mary were due to leave, Stan, Rita, and Linda, together with the departing couple, arrived at the hotel and were shown to their table by the head waiter.

As they made themselves comfortable, Linda remarked that the table had been set for six places and was speaking to Stan about it when, just as he struggled for an explanation, in walked a tall, slender, well dressed man by the name of Harold Burnett, Junior. When Linda looked up at him, she went weak at the knees and called out with a loud expression of delight - HANK!

It would appear that all knew about the forthcoming arrival of Hank, except Linda, from whom they had kept his visit as a surprise. He walked directly to Linda and gave her a hug and a kiss on both cheeks before sitting down right next to her. Linda was so happy to see the man who had started the journey of improving her fortunes that she lovingly held his hand under the table with an affectionate squeeze.

At the dinner, Linda and Mac gave Mary's parents the full story of what was to happen with the Dog & Whistle and asked them to keep the secret until an official announcement would be made some time in the future.

Both Stan and Rita gave their assurance that they would keep the secret and then told Linda of their own plans now that their farm had been sold at a handsome price. They said that they had found a private cottage locally that suited them both now that Mary had decided to leave home and seek her fortune in America with Mac.

Hank listened to all of their excitable plans and ordered champagne to add to the already consumed dinner drinks, then raised his glass to celebrate what had come out of a chance meeting earlier in the year when he stopped at the Dog & Whistle for some refreshment.

More and more stories were exchanged about the intended roadhouse business and after further glasses were raised in honour of the absent Ivan, the intended marriage of Mac and Mary and a toast to Her Majesty The Queen, all were more than a little tipsy.

Mac was the only one in complete control of his senses as he had been trained to take part in many official dinner functions without losing his wits. He understood how the hotel staff had to control well-oiled customers without being offensive and therefore did not drink like the others. He recognised when it was time to leave the dining room and so took the initiative to rise from the table.

As they all walked along the hotel corridor and back to their rooms, Rita held Stan's arm to steady herself, while Mac and Mary lovingly held hands. Bringing up the rear were Linda and Hank embraced in a cuddle that was not usual between a landlady and a customer and when those in front of them bade each other goodnight, Hank whispered to Linda, "What about a nightcap in my room before you retire?" which she happily accepted.

Two days later, Stan and Rita brought Mary to the Dog & Whistle where, together with Linda and Jill, they waved the young couple off on their way to Heathrow airport in a car driven by Tony - and to a new life together.

As the tears flowed down the cheeks of the two mothers, Linda did what all sensible British women do during times of anxiety; she asked Jill to put the kettle on for a good cup of 'Old English Tea'.

Next day was Sunday and in the peace and quiet of the closed pub and before the workmen were due to start the following day, Linda trawled through her photographs and memories. She kept coming back to Joe MacKenzie during 1944 and to the fact that by sheer chance Hank had arrived in 1968, and in the words of Bob -

- **IN WALKED SOME MONEY.**

Characters in this book.

Characters in this book, 'In Walked Some Money'.

Name	Known As	Occupation	Age at June 1968	Age on D-Day, June 6th 1944
Bailey	Benny	Iron Works	50	26
Bailey	Georgie	Iron Works	26	2
Bailey	Lucy Ann	District Nurse	28	4
Bailey	Stanley	Iron Works	80	56
Bennett	Fred	Dairy Farmer	54	30
Bloomenfeld	Irving	Group Personnel	56	32
Blunt	Sarah	Neighbour	84	60
Bond	Maggie	Linda's Friend, a cook	41	17
Bright	Sir Hugh	Brewery Man. Director	62	38
Brown	Winnie	Widowed	70	46
Burnett	Harold /Hank	Real Estate Business	45	21
Burt	Charlie	Butcher	57	33
Burt	Connie	Postmistress	47	23
Button	Henry	Mike's father	51	27
Button	Tony	Unemployed Engineer	24	0
Chant	Elizabeth	Gardener	46	22
Chant	Tommy	Dumper Truck Driver	43	19
Drake	Brian	Brewery Property	46	22
Evans	Mrs	Housekeeper Big	60	38
Farthing	James	Salesman	32	8
Finch	Jeremy	Estates Manager	50	26
Framburg	Ivan	CEO Aviation	52	28
Goldberg	Arnold	Solicitor	46	22
Griffiths	Daniel	Architect	42	18
Hammond	Geoffrey	Personnel Manager	54	30
James	Sam	Landlord, Five Bells	44	24
Jeans	Robert	Brewery Area	40	16
Jones	Trevor	Surveyor	35	11
Lawton	Sandy	Personnel Director	52	28
Leclerc	Claude	General Manager USA	55	31

Characters in this book, 'In Walked Some Money'.

Name	Known As	Occupation	Age at June 1968	Age on D-Day, June 6th 1944
Lincoln	David	Solicitor	46	22
Mant	Bert	Verger	52	28
McGregor	Angus	General Manager	58	34
Nielsen	Klaus	Engineering Director	41	17
O'Reilly	Olivia	Riding School Owner	42	18
O'Reilly	Patrick	Riding School Owner	46	22
Pearson	Betty	Jim's Wife	50	26
Pearson	Jim	Farmer	56	32
Pearson	Mary	Stan's Daughter	22	2
Pearson	Rita	Stan's Wife	51	27
Pearson	Stan	Farmer (Jim's Brother)	53	29
Pullman	George	Retired	77	53
Roberts	Esme	Accountant	43	19
Scott	Len	Paper shop owner	50	26
Smart	Bob	Landlord	52	28
Smart, (Tanner)	Linda	Landlady	42	18
Smith	Terry (Major)	Retired Estate Agent	66	42
Smith	Joan	The Major's Wife	64	40
Smythe-Brown	Gerry	Vicar	33	9
Smythe-Brown	Timmy	Vicar	37	13
Tanner	Mac	Asst Gen Manager	23	0
Thomas	Gordon	Asst Gen Manager UK	36	8
Thomas	Sally	Gordon's Wife	37	9
Tuck	Gordon	Works Manager	53	29
Watkins	Billy	Retired	76	52
Williams	Old Tom	Thatcher	60	36
Williams	Young Tom	Thatcher	34	10
Willis	Gordon	Policeman	48	24
Wilson	Jill	Waitress	21	3
Wilson	Madge	Widowed	68	44

Printed in Great Britain
by Amazon

32815261R00165